Readers love the BJ Vinson Mysteries by DON TRAVIS

The Zozobra Incident

"I loved this book. I loved the setting and feel of being in Albuquerque. I loved our protagonist. I loved the pacing and suspense. This was a complete win for me."

—The Novel Approach

"There are many likable secondary characters who play significant roles in the story. Combine that with the setting, beautifully detailed writing and a solid mystery makes this novel a must read for any mystery lover."

—Gay Book Reviews

The Bisti Business

"BJ Vinson is one of my new favorite sleuths…."

—B. A. Brock Books

The City of Rocks

"It's yet another wild ride as we follow BJ as he solves his latest big case."

—Michael Joseph Book Reviews

By Don Travis

BJ VINSON MYSTERIES
The Zozobra Incident
The Bisti Business
The City of Rocks
The Lovely Pines
Abaddon's Locusts

Published by DSP PUBLICATIONS
www.dsppublications.com

ABADDON'S LOCUSTS

DON TRAVIS

DSP PUBLICATIONS

Published by

DSP Publications

5032 Capital Circle SW, Suite 2, PMB# 279, Tallahassee, FL 32305-7886 USA
www.dsppublications.com

Abaddon's Locusts
© 2019 Don Travis.

Cover Art
© 2019 Maria Fanning.
Cover content is for illustrative purposes only and any person depicted on the cover is a model.

Trade Paperback ISBN: 978-1-64108-119-1
Digital ISBN: 978-1-64080-718-1
Library of Congress Control Number: 2018938536
Trade Paperback published January 2019
v. 1.0

Printed in the United States of America
∞
This paper meets the requirements of
ANSI/NISO Z39.48-1992 (Permanence of Paper).

And there came out of the smoke locusts upon the earth: and unto them was given power, as the scorpions of the earth have power.

....

And they had a king over them, which is the angel of the bottomless pit

whose name in the Hebrew tongue is Abaddon, but in the Greek tongue hath

his name Apollyon.

Book of Revelation 9:3 and 9:11

Thanks to members of the Bernalillo County and Rio Rancho Police
SVU departments for their help… you know who you are.

Author's Note

DUE TO local headlines, I wanted to do a book on human trafficking. Given the reaction of readers to Jazz Penrod, a character in my second book—*The Bisti Business*—I knew it had to be about him.

ABADDON'S LOCUSTS

DON TRAVIS

Prologue

TWO MEN gazed down at the sleeping youth sprawled across the mattress. The older, his pleasant features blemished by a glint of cruelty in his dark eyes, smoothed silver wings of luxuriant hair at his temples before handing over a number of $100 bills to a young Hispanic almost as handsome as the boy on the bed.

Now fully clothed, Silver Wings exuded the authority of a player, of someone who counted. "Fucking beautiful. How old did you say he is?"

"Eighteen. Barely. Know that's older'n you usually like. But he's a rare one, no? As *linda* as a woman and as macho as a man. He took care of you, huh?"

Silver Wings rubbed his eyes as if remembering the last hour. "Fantastic. Must have worn himself out. Does he usually go comatose?"

"Ah, that is the drug. He claims he gets a bigger bang by charging up. But you benefit as well, no?" He eyed his companion. "He is yours for $25,000."

Interest flickered and died. "Tempting. But my household isn't set up for that kind of arrangement. I prefer to call when I feel the need. Even if that means sharing him."

"You don't take him, then we move him south."

"South? To Mexico, you mean? Juárez?" That wouldn't be too bad. El Paso was a short hop, and Juárez lay just across the border.

"At first, but then we gonna trade him up."

Silver Wings understood the human trafficking language of *trading up*, but it was unusual to move members of the "family" out of country these days. "In Juárez? Sounds more like trading him down."

"*¡Órale!* There's some big money in Juárez. But a bigwig in the Middle East went apeshit over the kid's pics. He wants him. And for a lot more than twenty-five. I only give you that price to let you know how much we 'preciate your help."

"Middle East, huh?" Silver Wings licked his lips. "Put off that transfer while I see if I can work something out."

"Two days. Then I gotta move him. You know, easier to ship him overseas from Mexico than from the States."

Silver Wings' voice hardened. "You can do better than that. Give me a week to reorder my life. I'd like to visit him a couple of times. Usual fee, of course. That gives you reason enough to hold him here."

"Okay, but not no more'n a week. I got people to answer to, you know."

"I'd like him again tomorrow night, but it will have to be late. I have a dinner meeting."

Hispano lowered his head. "As you wish. All you gotta do is call me."

Silver Wings left the motel reluctantly. What would take place in that room now that they were alone? Just thinking about it raised a bead of sweat on his upper lip.

His mind returned to the offer he had received. The boy was expensive, and the economy was still struggling to recover from the Great Recession of 2008… but it was only money.

Chapter 1

I PARKED the Impala in front of my detached single-car garage and sat for a moment trying to figure out the cacophony on the radio. I'd failed to reset the station after Paul and I went for a rare game of weekend golf at the North Valley Country Club. Paul Barton was the sun in my sky, but I still struggled to understand my companion's taste in music. Now something called "Alejandro" by a gal proclaiming herself to be Lady Gaga committed assault on my classical-music-loving ears. As I switched off the noise and stepped from the car, a high, uncertain voice snagged my attention.

"Yoo-hoo, Mr. Vinson. BJ!"

Mrs. Gertrude Wardlow, the late-afternoon sun catching in wayward strands of her white hair, waved at me from the foot of her driveway. She had lived in the white brick across the street for as long as I could remember. Mrs. W. and her husband, Herb, had been with the Drug Enforcement Administration from the time it was formed in 1973 until their retirement. Some ten years ago, Herb passed on to his reward—an urn on his widow's mantelpiece. I walked out to meet her in the middle of Post Oak Drive.

"I'm so glad I caught you." She fiddled with frilly lace at the neck of her lavender blouse. "A man on a Harley has been driving up and down the street. He stopped at your place twice. Rang the bell and then rode off."

No doubt she was recalling the time when two thugs on another motorcycle attempted to gun me down. When she'd yelled to distract their murderous attention, they shot up the front of her house, scattering her husband all over the carpet.

I touched her shoulder. "Don't worry, I'm not involved in any gang disputes at the moment. Not that I know of, anyway."

Her smile turned impish. "That was an interesting day, wasn't it? I just thought you should be aware someone was trying to contact you."

"Thank you, Mrs. W. I'll be on the lookout."

After exchanging pleasantries, we parted. I mounted the steps to my front porch and paused to enjoy the welcoming aroma of tea roses my late mother planted. No evidence of a note on the door or in the mailbox. That meant the mysterious biker would probably return. I went inside and forgot the matter as I removed one of Paul's casseroles from the fridge and got out a pan of rolls. I enjoyed their yeasty aroma almost as much as I liked their yeasty taste. Our household mantra was Paul Barton, freelance journalist, whips up gourmet meals; B. J. Vinson, former Marine and ex-cop turned confidential investigator, burns toast.

We planned to stay home tonight and watch an episode of a new gumshoe program on the tube called *The Glades*. Matt Passmore, the guy who played the detective, was a way-cool customer who Paul claimed should be my role model. I'd no sooner set the dishes to heating than a rumble on the street caught my attention. A moment later the doorbell rang.

I turned off the stove and opened the door to reveal a tall raven-haired Navajo with high cheekbones. It took a moment to recognize the good-looking guy. "Henry Secatero, as I live and breathe."

His deep voice came up out of his nether regions. "Wasn't sure you'd remember me."

"How could I forget the guys who helped me solve a case. Is Jazz with you?" His quick frown told me he was about to deliver bad news. "Come on in."

We settled in the den with a couple of jiggers of Scotch. He laid what appeared to be a sleeve for a laptop computer on the floor beside his chair and took a sip before speaking. "Jazz is gone."

"Gone?" My hand tightened on the rocks glass halfway to my mouth. That free spirit was too young and lively to be... gone. "You mean—"

"Naw, not bit the dust. Just disappeared. Poof. And that ain't like Jazz."

Jasper Penrod, who'd dubbed himself Jazz as soon as he was old enough, was Henry's mixed-blood half brother. The two helped me solve a case I mentally called the Bisti Business up in the Four Corners area three years ago.

I rubbed my chin, trying to recall what I knew of Jazz's situation. "Are you sure? Way I understand it, he spends some of his time on the Navajo Reservation and some in Farmington. Hard to keep track of him."

"Yeah, he bounces around, but he don't go outa touch for long. He calls me regular-like. If he can't reach me on my cell, he leaves a message at the chapter house. I didn't get worried until I saw his uncle

Riley in Farmington and found out Jazz hadn't called him or his mother either. Been three… four weeks since anybody heard from him."

"Do you have any idea why?"

"Not sure, but this might have something to do with it." Henry leaned over and picked up the canvas case. He hesitated after pulling out an Acer laptop computer. "Man, I sure hate to show you this."

My raised eyebrows probably expressed my surprise better than my spoken "Why?"

"You'll see a Jazz you ain't seen before. Hell, *I* ain't seen before. You gotta understand. Jazz being like he is—you know, gay and all—it's not easy for him up in Farmington. When he was growing up, he didn't mind casual… affairs, I guess you'd say. Until he saw what you and Paul had together, he didn't believe nobody was out there for him. Permanent, I mean." Sweat formed on Henry's upper lip, attesting to how hard it was to talk about his brother's homosexuality.

I called to mind an image of the uncommonly handsome, unabashedly gay, and friendly-as-a-puppy kid I'd come to admire. All his life he maneuvered successfully in an environment of miners and oil field workers normally hostile to his lifestyle, thanks in large part to the aggressive protection provided by Henry; their Navajo father, Louie; and Jazz's Anglo uncle, Riley.

Henry drew a deep breath and let it out. "Anyway, he started looking for a steady. Someone he could build something with. And there wasn't nobody in Farmington. Nobody he could attach to, at any rate. Not on the rez neither. He'd try with this guy or that but didn't find what he was looking for." Henry gave an insincere laugh. "Jazz looking like he does, lotsa guys you wouldn't even expect would go with him for a while. Some might even have stuck, but they wasn't what he was looking for." Henry's face twisted in perplexity. "You want the truth? I think he was looking for another you. He really dug you."

"There was never anything between—"

He waved a hand. "I know. He told me he offered, and you said you already had somebody. That really impressed him. That's what he was looking for. A guy who'd turn down an offer because they belonged to him." Henry ran an agitated hand through thick black hair. "Aw, I'm screwing this up. All I'm saying is he was looking for love. Just like I do, but on the other side of the bed."

"You're doing fine. Tell me something. What do you really think about your brother being gay? I know you won't stand for people picking on him, but how do you feel about it down deep?"

"I don't understand it. I look at a guy—hell, I look at *you*—and ask myself what would Jazz see?" Henry shrugged. "He'd see mutton stew while I see cactus. Sometimes I sorta understand when I remember that it's the same as me looking at a woman. At least to him, it is."

Despite just being called a cactus, I nodded. "Now show me what you came to show me."

He fired up the laptop and stared at the blank screen as the device went through its booting-up process. "How'd you get his password?" I asked as we waited.

"It's taped on the back of the computer. Jazz was private… but not secretive, I guess you'd say. I felt like shit going through his stuff," he added in a low voice. "But I'm glad I did. I found these."

He handed over the machine. Jazz used aol.com for his email, and Henry went to the Sent section to select a message. "That's the first one I found. After you read it, scroll up to the next one. Jeez, I need to go for a walk or something while you do that. Okay?"

"Leave the door unlocked. Just come in when you work it off."

Henry had selected the first email message where his brother responded to a contact from someone named Juan. They apparently connected through a site called nm.lonelyguys.com. Unwilling to switch back and forth between Jazz's Sent and Trash containers, I searched his My Folders until I spotted one labeled Juan. Upon opening that file, I found messages between the two stretching back about four months and ending five weeks ago, right after they exchanged Skype addresses. The pair started off using Aesopian language, but as time went on, they became more direct.

The first photograph in the email file was a bust shot of Juan showing an attractive, smiling Hispanic on the shy side of thirty with a white blaze in his dark hair. He wore a bright yellow polo shirt. Jazz responded with a photo of himself standing beside the old '91 Jeep Wrangler ragtop I'd helped him buy during the Bisti case. He wore a pair of walking shorts and a blue sleeveless pullover that clearly showed his six-pack.

Juan responded with a request for a headshot, a close-up to see if he was as "beautiful as he seemed to be." Jazz's next photo was a *wowser*, as I used to say when I was a kid. Jazz qualified as stunningly handsome, and the camera wallowed in it. The half-dozen messages led me right where I feared this was going. Juan's second photo was shirtless; Jazz matched it. Long before I reached the modest naked and the stark-naked shots, I knew what happened to Jazz Penrod. The internet had swept him into a sex ring. Grateful his brother was out walking off his frustration, I considered my conclusion for a minute before acceptance came. The Jazz I knew was open and honest, and if you couldn't take him the way he was, he'd write you off. He wasn't venal. Money had its place, but it wasn't that important to him.

When Henry returned, I set aside the laptop.

He balked at my conclusion. "No way! Jazz ain't... whata you call it? Promiscuous. He had sex with guys, but he didn't spread it all over the place. He wouldn't go to bed with nobody he didn't like."

"Which is why this Juan—probably not his real name—took his time. He reeled Jazz in like a deep-diving trout... playing him and teasing him until he landed him. As soon as Jazz sent his first picture, Juan knew he had a winner. So he played him, feeding him more and more. That's what the pictures were all about. Getting Jazz to commit deeper and deeper to what he thought was a kindred soul."

Henry poked a finger at the Acer. "Some of them emails *do* tell me Jazz was getting to like the guy. When you get to the end of them, you can see where they talked about meeting here in Albuquerque. At someplace called Robinson Park."

"Then they went to Skype, and we don't know what they said after that because they were talking face-to-face with cameras and mikes," I said.

"Where's Robinson Park?"

"It's a city park in the southeast section. Lots of big trees. They could sit and talk without being bothered. It looks like he might have come to Albuquerque to meet the guy."

"That don't hold water. He wouldn't go this long without getting in touch with none of us. I'm worried, man."

I studied Henry. "You know what puzzles me? Jazz once said he wasn't usually attracted to people who looked like him. You know, black hair, brown eyes."

"This Juan guy has a big white streak in his hair. Maybe that's enough to make him different."

"Maybe. But it's more likely the butterfly effect."

"Huh?"

"Small things leading to big changes. Juan devoted the time necessary to snag Jazz's attention. In some of those messages, they talked about what they liked and disliked. But if you noticed, Juan asked, and Jazz answered. And then, of course, Juan liked everything Jazz did. One small step led to another until Jazz finally took the bait and came to Albuquerque."

Henry bounced out of the chair and stalked the den stiff-legged. "But if it's what you say, if he's been tricked into a sex ring, why does he stay? He don't look all muscled up, but that boy can fight when he wants to. How come he don't just take to the road?"

He wasn't going to like my answer, but before I could deliver it, Paul came through the back door and yelled a greeting.

Chapter 2

"WHOSE BIKE is parked out there?" Upon entering the den, Paul stopped dead still. "Henry? Is that you?"

The Navajo had made an impression. They'd only met briefly once about three years ago. Of course, both Henry and Jazz were impressive guys—as was Paul.

"'Fraid so. Hope you don't mind me coming over without no warning."

I cut straight to the issue. "He's got a problem. Or at least, Jazz has."

The love of my life took a seat as I explained the situation. I wasn't certain how he would react. The green-eyed monster had showed up briefly when I introduced Paul to the sexy teenager I'd been working with up in Farmington while searching for a wine mogul's missing son. Paul was as secure as any man I knew, but Jazz Penrod was such a package of raw sex that he made most men—gay or straight—feel threatened. But once again, my lover fooled me. He was pretty good at that, even though I knew him better than I had ever known another man.

"Vince, you gotta find him." The world called me BJ, but two men referred to me as Vince: Paul and my ex, an attorney named Del Dahlman. "Check this Juan guy's username through that fraud service you use."

"I can almost guarantee it's going to be a dead end."

The two of them followed me into my home office so I could use my own computer to conduct the search. The NoFraud.com service I used wouldn't lead us to a URL address unless one was exposed as a fraud. Then these guys published the internet address. Juan's wasn't listed, which was no comfort at all. He simply hadn't been exposed yet.

"Well, crap," Paul said.

Henry blew air through his nose. "I thought these things was easy to run down. You hear about guys getting hacked all the time."

"You've just said the magic word. Hacked. Hackers do it anytime they have the time and equipment necessary. Law enforcement has to get a warrant, hand it to the server, and wait for a response." I took Jazz's computer from Henry. "Don't know if you caught it, but there were a couple of messages where Jazz and this Juan guy exchanged personal information."

I searched until I found the email I wanted. "Here it is. Juan Gonzales with an address of 111½ 59th NW in Albuquerque. And there's a phone number." I asked the two of them to be quiet while I dialed. The telephone proved to be disconnected.

"Well, we have his name and address anyway," Henry said with a dangerous look in his eye.

"They're both probably phony," I said.

Paul put in his two cents. "And Juan Gonzales is like John Smith. There are a million of them."

"Let me get my office manager, Hazel, on this," I suggested. "She's better than I am at locating people over the internet. Give me Jazz's cell phone number so Charlie can start trying to trace it." Charlie Weeks, Hazel's husband, was a retired APD cop and my partner in Vinson and Weeks, Confidential Investigations.

The number Henry supplied matched the number already in my records for Jazz. He also handed over the license plate number for his brother's Jeep, after which I phoned Hazel at home. She agreed to get right on it. That done, I called my old APD riding partner, Lt. Gene Enriquez, and explained the situation. He was still at the downtown police headquarters.

"You know this Jazz kid pretty well?" Gene asked after I explained things.

"He was one of the local assets I told you about on the Alfano case up in the Bisti Wilderness. He's a good kid."

"If I remember, you said he was pretty open about being gay."

"Honest and open. Why?"

"How do you know he didn't just go off and meet this other guy for a fling?"

"Because he's got his head screwed on right. He's more responsible than that. He would have contacted his mother at the very least. No one's heard from him for a month. At least put out a BOLO on his vehicle."

"Okay. Give me the details. But this means I gotta open a case. Have the brother come in and file a request."

"We'll do that first thing in the morning. In the meantime, will you put out the order?"

"Yeah. Be here at nine, okay?"

When I hung up, Henry asked what a BOLO was.

"Be on the lookout," Paul answered. "But tell me something. You say that's Jazz's computer. If he was going outa town to meet someone, wouldn't he take it along?"

"He's got a smartphone and a tablet, whatever that is. He claims that gives him access to anything he needs. He usually leaves the laptop at home when he travels around."

"With photos like that on it?" Paul asked. "What if his mother saw them?"

"Nobody walks on Jazz's privacy. Only reason I did was I'm worried about him. If he turns out to be all right, he'll give me hell for peeking at his photos." Henry scowled, showing his uncertainty. "And I hope that's the way it goes. BJ, you sure we gotta involve the Albuquerque cops in this?"

"We need their help. And somebody, Jazz's mother or uncle Riley, needs to go to the Farmington PD and file a missing person's report."

"Riley promised to go in this morning. Gonna ask for that Sgt. Dix Lee we met back when we was working together."

"Good. Henry, you've got to get over your aversion to authority. If this is what I think it is, the feds will be involved."

"Which ones?"

"I don't know much about it, but when the victim is a US citizen, the FBI is called in. I think they have a Domestic Sex Trafficking Program. If it's over-the-border stuff, ICE will be involved. That's US Immigration and Customs Enforcement. They're both a part of Homeland Security, so it's apt to be an interagency thing. A task force, maybe."

"Crap. What if he just went to meet a guy, and they got wrapped up in each other?"

I leveled a look at the hunky Navajo. "Do you believe that?"

He blinked. "Naw. Something's wrong. So let's get the big bad Feebees involved. Whadda we do now? Set around and bullshit one another till the sun comes up?"

"Nope. We're going to check out 111½ 59th NW—even if it is a fool's errand."

As I suspected, there was no 111½ 59th NW, but there was a 111. The short, frazzled woman who answered my knock seemed startled to confront three strange men on her doorstep. Even so, she stood her ground and answered my questions. She didn't know the man in the photo I'd made from the

picture on Jazz's laptop and didn't recognize the name Juan Gonzales...
except for a cousin in Brownsville, Texas, who didn't look anything like
that. She did, however, remember a small, vacant apartment in the building
behind her house that was in such bad shape, she and her husband converted
it into a storage area when they bought the property five years back. She
thought that might have been the "half" added to their address.

She was patient enough to search through her cigar box of records
and come up with the name of the prior owner of the property, a man
named Alberto Suarez. Something else Hazel would have to check out
for me tomorrow.

After that, we returned to the house and talked Henry into sharing
Paul's savory, reheated cheddar potato casserole and spending the night
in our guest bedroom. After I called Charlie and brought him up to date
so he and Hazel could kick off their searches while we were at Gene's
office, we retired.

I seriously doubted Henry would get much sleep. He was wound
up over his brother's disappearance. Nor did I rest well, despite being
worn out from watching the small black dragon on Paul's left pec prowl
as he performed his bedroom gymnastics. Very well too. Even Pedro—
that was the name Paul gave his tattoo—seemed a little weary after that
performance.

Chapter 3

HENRY COULDN'T quite hide his discomfort at shaking hands with a policeman—even a friendly one—the next morning when the two of us met Gene in the downtown stationhouse. I could see that my ex-partner was aware of the Navajo's attitude, and no doubt he would run Henry's ID through the system the moment we left. I was wrong; he'd already done it.

"You always get in fights when you go to the Blue Spruce?" Gene asked.

"Mostly."

"It's a good place to find them. Bad place for staying out of them."

"You got that right."

The Blue Spruce was an Indian bar out on East Central near the fairgrounds. The place was notorious for its police calls. On the other side of the coin, it was a good spot for cops short on traffic tickets to make quota.

"Your brother like to fight too? Or is he all sizzle and no steak?"

Henry's face clouded for a moment. "He's better at starting them and standing around watching ever'body scrap, but he's good backup when it's needed."

After that, Gene settled down and guided Henry through filling out a request to search for his brother's car. There hadn't been any results overnight, but none were expected, unless Jazz was moving around. Or someone was using his Jeep. There were a couple of Juan Gonzaleses in the system, but when I hauled out the photo of Jazz's email contact, none of them matched.

Henry tapped his finger on the photograph. "Don't you guys have some kinda gizmo where you can compare photos and make an ID?"

"A facial recognition program, you mean?" Gene asked. "Scuttlebutt says it's on its way, but we don't have a system yet. The state boys have something, but I'd have to have probable cause for an arrest before I could even ask them to run a search."

"My brother's missing, and he was talking to this guy. Ain't that enough?"

"No evidence this guy's the cause of your brother's disappearance. Hell, for all we know, he and his new friend are just out having a good time. But I think BJ's right on this, Mr. Secatero. Your brother's caught in the sex trade racket."

"Call me Henry, and just because my brother's gay don't mean he goes around selling his body. Never has. Never will."

"Look, fella—" Gene pointed a stubby finger at Henry and nodded at me. "—don't get your back up. I rode with this guy for three years, and we never had trouble over him being gay. But the human trafficking racket is getting to be big business. Some people figure there are more people in slavery today than before the Civil War. And I made some calls this morning and found out more kids than we'd like to admit disappear from Indian reservations. I grant you it's mostly women and girls that get caught up in the sex part of it, but some boys and men do too."

"Jazz wouldn't stand still for that. He'd just walk out the door and go home."

"Unless they're holding something over him," Gene said. "I'll admit he doesn't fit the pattern. He's older than the norm, and he's male. Most are female somewhere around the ages of thirteen to fifteen or sixteen. Usually, the traffickers claim a debt's gotta be paid or threaten somebody—maybe a family member—with bodily harm or death. They've got lotsa ways of making victims toe the line."

"Not Jazz. He'd go postal."

"Some of them do, but they're overpowered or done away with. So maybe he did fight them."

Either the implications of that remark went over Henry's head or he chose to ignore them. "I can't think of a damned thing they could threaten my brother with. He knows his dad and me can take care of ourselves. His uncle Riley will make sure his mother's okay. There ain't nobody else."

Gene held up the photo of Juan I'd given him. I hadn't shared the naked ones. "What about this guy? Maybe they're threatening to take him out."

"Jazz doesn't even know him. Not really. Few months on the internet is all. Why would he prostitute hisself for a stranger?"

"I can think of one scenario," I said. "Drugs."

Henry came out of his chair with a face like thunder. I tensed. "My brother don't do drugs. Never has. Got in fights as a kid because he wouldn't even try weed with some guys."

"What if something like this happened?" I asked. "He's intrigued by this Juan Gonzales fellow and agrees to meet him in Albuquerque. We know that much from the laptop."

"Yeah. Robinson Park."

"Juan turns out to be everything Jazz is looking for. A decent guy seeking affection... maybe even love. But that's not who he really is. When he takes Jazz home or to a motel, there's someone waiting for them there. They overpower Jazz and start feeding him drugs. Hooking him."

"Makes him dependent on them," Gene put in. "Once he's hooked, he'll do anything for a fix."

"Why go to all that trouble?" Henry demanded. "They can get plenty of guys off the street to whore for them. I get propositioned ever' time I walk up East Central. Bet you do too, BJ."

"Why go to the trouble, you ask?" Gene held up Jazz's photo. "Look at that. That's prime beef on the hoof to slave traders. What could be better? A kid from the reservation. Probably nobody will put up much of a fuss if he disappears. Like I say, he's older than usual. He's a fish, not a minnow. But Christ, this kid doesn't even look eighteen. He'd have to prove to me he was twenty-one if I caught him in a bar." Gene shook his head. "You have any idea how much he's worth to a slave trader? Stateside, twenty to thirty thousand dollars. Overseas? Who knows?"

"How would they get him out of the country?" Henry asked.

Gene spread his hands. "There are different circuits to different places. I'd guess Albuquerque to El Paso and then across the border to Juárez. How? Put him beside them in a car or truck with fake papers and just drive across. After that, take any of a dozen established routes overseas."

"Oh God!" Henry said. "He might be out of the country by now."

"Possible," Gene replied. "But I understand they don't move victims around as much as they used to. He could be in Albuquerque or across the border. No way of knowing."

After Gene finished putting the fear of God into Henry, the two of us piled into my Impala parked on the street outside the station and drove to the parking lot behind the historic building at Fifth and Tijeras NW where I maintained a suite of offices. We entered by the rear entrance and walked up three stories. Henry showed some curiosity at the hollowed-out core of the building, which left the offices hugging the outer perimeter of each floor and accessible by a balcony open to the atrium.

"How's Paul?" were the first words out of Hazel's mouth as we came through the door. From the way she eyed the big handsome guy at my side, I gathered she was worried.

"Great. He went to the country club for some aquatic meet he's in charge of. As soon as that's over, he's coming here. He'll be with us on this one. He senses a story, I think."

I rushed through introductions before we gathered around the small conference table in the corner of my private office. Hazel determined that Jazz's cell phone was not on the grid anywhere. Someone probably removed the battery. Charlie used a contact at the phone's carrier to kick off a search for Jazz's call history, but it was too soon for a report.

Hazel gave us one piece of information we might be able to sink our teeth into. She had located Alberto Suarez, the former owner of 111 59th NW, and he agreed to talk to us. Henry and I raced downstairs for the Impala and headed south to Barelas.

ALBERTO SUAREZ turned out to be a widower who lived in a small home that looked a great deal like 111 59th. His complexion was as dark as the adobe bricks of his home and his skin about as flaky. He greeted us with old-world courtesy and invited us inside. Within minutes I realized his willingness to talk to us was because we were someone to talk *to*. Henry's teeth were on edge by the time I managed to pry the conversation away from the inadequacy of his social security checks and the joy his Meals on Wheels lady brought him.

Mr. Suarez scratched his balding pate and nodded when I asked about the renters in the "one-half" part of his former street address.

"I remember them. Wasn't no family named Gonzales, though. Best I can recollect, they was called Flores. The man worked in construction when he could find work, and the woman stayed at home with their daughter, who was around seventeen at the time. They had a son too. Don't recall his name, but he was grown-up and already left home. Come to think on it, the youngster mighta lived over on the other side of the border and just stayed with his folks when he was visiting from Mexico. I don't recall if his name was Juan."

Suarez ran a hand across his bald scalp again. "Coulda been. Lotsa Juans around, you know. That's the same as John to an Anglo."

I took out Juan Gonzales's picture and held it up. "Do you recognize this man?"

Suarez accepted the photo and fumbled around on a lamp table beside his worn overstuffed recliner for a pair of glasses. He moved the photo back and forth until it was in focus.

"This fella's older, but it could be the Flores boy. I recall him as being a good-looking kid, but kinda soft. Still, he was one the girls made a fuss over." He pursed his lips. "Still looks good, but life showed up in his face, didn't it? Looks rougher now. His eyes, I guess."

"Try to remember his first name," I said.

"Coulda been Juan. But I think it was Jose."

Mr. Suarez could add little to what he'd given us. He lost contact with the family once they moved out of his little apartment. Then he sold the house and moved to the Barelas area.

On our way back to the office, I used my hands-free cell to phone Gene Enriquez and provide him with the name of Juan or Jose Flores to search for a mug shot matching the photo I'd provided.

PAUL HAD completed his swim meet and greeted us with questions when we arrived back at the office. He was ready to pitch in and help with the search for Jazz. He readily admitted that a story about a man, not much different from himself, being caught up in the human trafficking industry was something he could probably sell to his magazine and publisher contacts.

Gene's call interrupted us. "Found him. Juan Jose Flores-Gurule. Twenty-nine. Native of Ranchos de Albuquerque. Single. Several arrests, mostly for drunk and disorderly, but the last one is interesting. On June 21, 2001, he and a companion, a Dominican named Florio Gaspard, were arrested on a complaint of kidnapping a nineteen-year-old man. They apparently held him in a motel room on the west side until he managed to escape. After filing the original complaint, the vic recanted, and the two were released. After that, Flores went off the grid."

"Probably across the border. Suarez said he thought the boy lived there for a while."

Gene cited the 59th Street address and a few other details. It looked as if we'd identified Jazz's contact and confirmed our worst fears. By virtue of his last arrest, Flores appeared to be involved in human trafficking... specifically in sex trafficking.

Armed with this new information, we all went to work checking databases for Flores and Gaspard. We searched Social Security, utilities, credit reports, criminal jurisdictions elsewhere in the state and in El Paso. Nothing.

At wit's end, I decided to bell the cat and message Flores's—or rather Gonzalez's—email address. But what to say? I was unwilling to alert the man we were on his trail, so it had to be a subtle approach. After discussing the idea, we decided to throw out some bait. Henry offered himself. He was sexy enough to capture attention, but Charlie rightly pointed out that at thirty-one, he was obviously older than the slavers wanted. Then he said the words I didn't want to hear.

"Paul's the likeliest candidate. He's midtwenties, but like Jazz Penrod, he doesn't look his age."

I balked, but Paul jumped right into the middle of the pool, loudly declaring he would do it. He'd send a message right now with a photo, clothed or unclothed. It didn't matter. After they convinced me this plan of attack presented little risk for Paul, I acquiesced. Gene, however, when I called him, figured it had disaster written all over it.

"For crying out loud, BJ. We got detectives for that. Or uniforms. I got guys who look fifteen. Use one of them. They're trained for it."

I couldn't object, but Paul could. And did. I'd made the call on the speakerphone, and he spoke right up. "I know Jazz. More importantly, he knows me. I can tell this Juan or Jose that I got his email address from Jazz. Jazz sent me a photo. I was intrigued. Blah, blah, blah."

"And what if the guy checks with Jazz?" Gene asked.

"That's the advantage of him knowing me. He'll recognize my name and associate it with Vince and know we're looking for him. He'll support my story."

"Yeah, right. If Penrod's stoned on drugs, he'll catch on right away. Besides, any of my detectives can make the same claim, and this Juan wouldn't know any better."

I ignored his sarcasm and warmed to the idea. "Jazz is a sharp kid, Gene. Unless they keep him completely zonked, he might catch on. And if the contact's successful, we can always substitute one of your detectives at that point."

"If you can find one that looks like me," Paul said. "If not, I'll make the meet with your guys backing me up."

"Keep me posted." Gene's voice held a note of fatalism.

I PULLED a couple of photos of Paul off my phone that were taken shortly after I met him in the summer of '06. He looked impossibly young and handsome, making him ideal bait for a trafficker. At the time Paul had been a UNM undergrad, a senior majoring in journalism. I was in the middle of a long dry spell at the end of a protracted recovery from a gunshot wound to the thigh received while I was an Albuquerque police detective. Paul, the lifeguard at the country club pool where I swam as therapy, casually asked about the puckered scar, showing no aversion to what I considered its ugliness. I lost my heart to him at that moment— and never recovered it. He still held it in his gentle hands.

"These ought to do the job," I said, holding them out to Charlie.

He examined them briefly. "Never been inclined that way, but if anyone could bend me, it would be Paul."

"Stop that!" Hazel snapped. "He's a human being, not an object. A perfectly nice human being." She loved us both fiercely, but she still hadn't figured out this man-on-man thing.

"So how we gonna do this?"

Before I could answer, Paul and Henry returned from the Courthouse Café where they went to fetch sandwiches for us. I waited until everything was sorted out, and we sat around the small conference table in the corner of my private office before addressing Charlie's question.

"The way I see it, we work with Gene at APD for Paul to make contact with this Juan fellow, so they can try to trace the location of his computer."

"Can they really do that, or is that just something you see on TV?" Henry asked.

"They can trace locations, but it's not as easy as the tube shows make it. Nor as precise."

"But what if we get it all set up, and the guy doesn't answer back right away?"

"You're right," I said. "Not only possible but probable. Paul will have to contact him and try to get the guy to agree to a time certain for a follow-up contact."

"I can ask for a Skype sit-down. I noticed Jazz's laptop has the app. As does mine."

"So you talk *and* see one another, huh?" Henry looked as if he had discovered something that might be of use to him in other circumstances. According to Jazz, his half brother sowed wild oats all over the Four Corners area.

"Why not just make initial contact and ask for a meet?" Henry asked after polishing off a corned beef on rye with german potato salad and kosher dill pickle.

"He'll be more cautious than that," I said. "Push hard, and you'll scare him off. Paul needs to send an email saying he's a friend of Jazz's. Maybe he saw Juan's picture on Jazz's computer during a visit. Paul, tell him you're trying to get in touch with Jazz and know he was considering coming to Albuquerque to meet Juan. If he did, it would be neat if you could all get together. Something like that."

"Do I have to coordinate it with Gene?"

"We'll take the initial step on our own and see how it goes."

While Paul composed his email, I got Gene on the telephone and told him of our plan. As usual, he told me why this was all wrong and then pledged to help however he could. Initially, there wasn't anything for him to do. Paul needed to cast his net and snare his prey and progress to the point where they were going to do a scheduled Skype before Gene could be of any value to us.

After hanging up, I turned and saw Henry sitting at my conference table amid the ruins of our lunch, looking as though he was about to explode. I needed to find something for him to do. Or send him home to the rez. I sat down beside him.

"Why don't you head back to the Four Corners and check on Riley? See if he's come up with any leads."

"I can do that by phone. I'm gonna stay right here until we find my brother." He took such a deep breath his impressive chest expanded as if it would burst. "There's gotta be something I can do to help."

I asked a question Gene had already asked before putting out the BOLO. "You're sure Jazz doesn't have a GPS locator on the Jeep?"

"Naw. I got one for my bike 'cause I go all over the rez. But Jazz stays pretty close to the towns or the chapter house. Didn't feel like he needed one." He ran an impatient hand through his hair. "Look, why don't I take one of those photos and head out to East Central. I'll walk the street, and when somebody tries to pick me up, I'll ask if he knows this guy."

"Not a good idea."

"Why the hell not?"

"In the first place, the odds are against you finding someone connected with this particular man. Jazz isn't the kind they put out on the street to hustle, so chances are that's not the way he works."

"Then how do they make money off him?"

"Have you ever been to Las Vegas?" Henry shook his head. "You can find streetwalkers there, but for marks with money, the hotels will set you up with an escort service. They're usually fine-looking ladies with some class. Someone a man wouldn't be ashamed to be seen with. And they charge lots of dollars. Sometimes thousands."

"Shit!"

"But if you go asking around about this guy, chances are someone will report it to his pimp, and that pimp might know Juan. Then all you've accomplished is to alert Juan we're on to him. Let Paul make his pitch. If that fails, maybe we'll all walk East Central."

Henry's disappointment showed in the slope of his broad shoulders.

"But it would help us if we could locate Jazz's Jeep. If I give you a few places to look, could you do that for us?"

"Ain't Lieutenant Enriquez already doing that?"

"A BOLO's a general request. The cops will keep an eye out for the Jeep, but they're not actively searching for it. You will be."

"Yeah, sure. Take me back to the house to pick up my bike, and I'll head out."

"Use my car. If I need to go anywhere, Charlie or Paul can take me."

I wrote down a few neighborhoods where stolen vehicles occasionally showed up and the specific addresses of a couple of suspected chop shops and handed the information along with my keys to Henry. He asked a couple of questions to orient himself and headed out the door.

After he was gone, the rest of us huddled over Paul's email to the mysterious Juan and made a couple of small changes before he sent the message, including a fetching close-up of my lover as bait. That thought soured my stomach.

Rather than just sit and wait, we needed to reach out to our respective contacts in search of a clue. Any clue as to the whereabouts of Jazz Penrod. And the email Paul was working on was the first such effort.

Chapter 4

THAT EVENING, Paul and Henry moped around our den at home while I tried to convince them any sex trafficker worth the name would be cautious about responding to an unsolicited email asking about a guy he'd just kidnapped. But I had faith my partner's sexy picture would be something Juan couldn't resist. Henry struck out in his search for Jazz's Jeep, but I hadn't expected positive results. That was just to keep him busy.

Later that night while we were all staring at an episode of *Breaking Bad* without hearing or seeing much of it, Paul's laptop beeped, signaling an email. As he led an active social media life, that wasn't meaningful—he'd received a dozen messages that day, none of them from Juan. This time, it was. Henry and I hovered over Paul's shoulder as he opened the message.

Hey, man. How come you looking for Jazz? Ain't seen him. But you a hunky-looking dude. Don't need nobody else. You and me can get it smoking all by ourselves. Tell me more. Hell, show me more.
Juanito

After settling down from the excitement of a contact, I analyzed the message. Despite the street grammar, I had the feeling this Juan was reasonably well educated. *All by ourselves* was a giveaway for me. And while the email implied he knew Jazz, this Juanito denied seeing the missing man. Did it mean anything that he failed to send a photo of himself in return? Probably not. Paul's original message acknowledged seeing a picture of him on Jazz's machine.

Henry was impatient for action. "Come on, man. What we waiting for? Send a message back and tell him let's get it on."

I shook my head. "No. That's pushing it. But we need something to speed up the process without spooking the guy. Paul, how far are you willing to go on this thing?" Bad question. Paul was always willing to help a lame dog.

"Whatever it takes. Jazz is one of the good ones. And he needs help."

"Let me call Gene and see if he can cover what I have in mind. I'll be back in a minute."

I left the two of them in the den and reached Gene at home. After a long conversation, I returned to the den.

"Okay, I want you to send a message along the lines of what I've written on this page. But put it in your own words."

Paul studied the paper I'd handed him for a minute and then typed out his message on the laptop, pausing before hitting the Send button so Henry and I could review it.

Juanito,

Lucky you caught me at home. I usually go to the C&W for a little line dancing on Tuesdays and Wednesdays but got lazy tonight. Probably make it tomorrow. Have a phony card that lets me slide in. Maybe I'll see you there sometime, but in the meantime, here's a selfie that shows a little more skin. Expect the same in return, okay? Keep in touch. And if you hear from Jazz, tell him I'm trying to get in touch with him. Going to Farmington at the end of the week and would like to see him. He's pretty cool in addition to being prime beef.

Paul

The selfie he referred to was a shirtless shot he took of himself a few minutes earlier. The reference to the C&W, a big nightclub out on East Central that attracts cowboys and wannabees, would allow Juan or one of his associates to see the prospect in the flesh. The bit about a phony card to get in the bar hinted at an underage minnow. Gene was confident he could provide protection in such a public venue. Even so, I hesitated before telling him to send the message. This was the man I loved above all others offering himself as bait to human traffickers… sex traffickers.

After the message went out, Paul came up with an idea. "We've got his Skype address. Why don't we see if he's online?"

"What are the risks?" I asked. "Can he see you're online as well?"

"Yes."

I dry-washed my face with a palm. "Don't push it. We've got him on the line. We'll reel him in slowly."

"Jazz might not have time for us to pussyfoot around," Henry said. "He might be outa the country by now."

"If he is, there's nothing we can do about that. But we need to penetrate the pipeline in order to follow him and bring him back. To do that, we have to be careful and let things take their course."

Paul's laptop pinged. It was a message from Juan.

Hey, dude, the C&W's the wrong place for what you want. There's a club on Jefferson that more your style. Nice pic. Hell, nice pecs. And everthing else for that matter. You and Jazz ever get it on? Like to see that.
Juanito

Paul looked up from the message and caught my eyes. "I heard of the club he's talking about. Maybe I oughta agree to go there."

"I know it too," I said. "And there's no way Gene can provide protection there. Too many strange faces would spook the whole place. The gay community is still cop-averse. Decline the invitation."

Paul worked at the keyboard and came up with a new message.

Juanito,
Don't know how to say this without just putting it out there. I'm not out of the closet, so I wouldn't be comfortable in a place like you're suggesting. Surprised I screwed up the courage to email you, and wouldn't have except I know how careful Jazz is. Like I say, I'm shy—which means I'm hungry. But I just can't see myself in a place like that. No, I'll stick to the C&W where I can dance with girls and look at boys.
To answer your question, Jazz and I never got together like you mean. Friends only. Might not always stay that way, but that's the way it is right now.
Your friend, Paul

We heard nothing further from Juan and went to bed at the usual time. Around 2:00 a.m., I heard Henry moving around and went out to find him in the kitchen pouring a glass of milk.

"Can't sleep, huh?" I asked.

"Naw. Every time I manage it, I dream about Jazz calling for help."

"Would it be better to go back home and be around people you're comfortable with?"

He shook his head. "I'm comfortable with you guys. At least here I can *try* to help, even if you send me off on wild goose chases."

"I'll admit there is an element of that in chasing after Jazz's vehicle. It's likely parted out or down in Mexico by now. Just remember, 60 percent of what I do is boiling the ocean."

"Huh?"

"A waste of time. But that has to be done to reach the 40 percent that matters. We'd all feel pretty dumb if we didn't look and later discovered Jazz's Jeep was parked out on West Central for the whole time."

"I guess so."

"What about your work? Are you still employed at the coal mine?"

He pinched the bridge of his nose between a thumb and forefinger. "Got a leave of absence for a family emergency."

"You okay for money?"

"Yeah. I'm good. Appreciate you letting me stay at the house. Saves on motel bills."

"Tell me something. Why didn't you come straight to my office instead of waiting until I got home?"

He shrugged. "Feeling my way. Some people get bent outa shape when they find out my brother's gay. Knew you wouldn't, but I don't know the people in your office."

"They'd be okay with it. You want something to help you sleep?"

"The milk oughta take care of it."

"Good, because we're going to need to be on our toes tomorrow. You ever been to the C&W?"

"Couple of times."

"Then you know how big it is. We're gonna need all the eyes we can get to watch out for Paul. He's putting it all on the line for Jazz, you know."

"Yeah. He's aces."

After we both returned to our respective rooms, I had trouble taking my own advice. I lay beside a peacefully slumbering Paul for a long time before sleep stole in to claim me.

THE NEXT day was a quiet one, devoted to searching databases and trying to find connections, a process that about drove Henry wild. He took off on his motorcycle on another search for Jazz's Jeep even though he knew it was nothing more than "make-work."

I hated to see the daylight hours pass. Come night, my lover would put himself at risk by showing up at the C&W. Nonetheless, they did pass; they always did. I arrived home as Paul stepped out of the bathroom, freshly showered and barbered. It was all I could do to keep from grabbing him and locking him in the basement. We might have all the protection we needed from Gene and his crew this evening, but what if they traced Paul back to the house? If so, then all bets were off. The traffickers could take him at their leisure.

With all the invincibility of the young, Paul shrugged aside my concern. Even so, he allowed me to rent a car for him to drive this evening. His black Charger was very distinctive. The middle-aged brown Ford I had delivered to the house brought a curl to his lip, but he got in and headed for the nightclub nonetheless. Henry and I trailed him by half a block in my Impala.

Wednesdays were one of the lighter nights at the C&W. Paul managed to park near the front entrance. I found a spot a row behind and slightly to the west of him. We allowed him to enter the club before us. As soon as Henry pulled open the heavy front door to the C&W, a blast of raucous music assaulted my ears, underlain by the subdued roar of conversation and alcoholic-laden laughter. The club didn't charge an admission fee except on weekends, so we walked straight into the big joint and paused at the bar to collect a drink.

Paul was nowhere to be seen. He'd apparently gone straight into the crowd. I panicked until Henry touched my arm and nodded. My love was talking to three college-age girls seated at a table near the big dance floor. Paul loved to dance, and the gals loved to dance with him. Some of them never tired of trying to get him into bed. But that was a privilege he accorded only to me.

There was no live band tonight, but the sound system struck up a lively tune as the deejay announced a line dance. Before I could suggest Henry join in, he handed me his glass and dashed off to find a partner. I settled at a table on the edge of the dance floor and saw that Paul and Henry danced side by side with two attractive females lined up opposite them. Neither acknowledged the other. Gene took a chair beside me and nodded wordlessly.

That pretty well described the night until around eleven. Paul walked up to the table where Gene and I sat and shook hands as if meeting acquaintances.

"Anything?" he asked in a quiet voice.

"Nada," Gene answered. "Haven't seen hide nor hair of this Juan fellow." He glanced around casually. "But there's some possibles. Guy over there looks like him, but he didn't have dreadlocks in that picture you showed me."

He was right. The man he indicated could have been Juan absent the snaky coils of hair. "A wig?" I suggested.

"Could be. I'd hate to spend my time weaving all those damned things. But I can hardly go over and ask him, can I?"

"Has he taken any interest in Paul?"

"Most guys watch Paul when he dances," Gene said. "You got good moves, man."

"Thanks."

"Not much of a crowd tonight," I noted. "At least not compared to the weekend."

A pleasant contralto interrupted us. "Cowboy, are you gonna save one dance for me tonight?" A tall woman with a complexion too dark for her long ash-blonde hair moved to Paul's side and clasped his arm.

He swept off his black Stetson and held it over his heart. "Why sure, ma'am. Yours is coming up next, as a matter of fact. My name's Paul, and these other fellas don't matter."

She slapped his arm lightly. "Course they do. I'm Ellen. And you are?" She pointed at Gene.

"I'm Gene, and my feet hurt, so don't look to me to do any dancing."

She transferred her gaze to me.

"My name's Burleigh," I said, one of the few times this year I've revealed my true name.

"No"—she pouted prettily—"I meant your Christian name."

"That *is* my Christian name. See what a burden I carry? Too heavy to waltz around on the dance floor. I guess you'll have to rely on this Paul fellow here to carry that stick."

The deejay obligingly put on a polka at that moment, drawing the two of them to the dance floor.

"What do you think?" Gene asked.

"Damned if I know. I was expecting Juan, but maybe they sent Ellen."

Henry joined us from a nearby table where he had been keeping three Native American women giggling between turns on the dance floor.

"Any sign of that Juan fellow yet?" he asked.

"No Juan or Jose or whatever his name is, but Paul just met a gal trying to get in his pants," Gene said, leaning back in his chair and watching the couple sweep around the floor. He sat up abruptly and put a finger to his left ear. "Hold on, I can't hear you." He stood and looked at us. "Too much noise in here to hear my bug. Gotta go someplace where it's quieter. Be back in a minute."

Henry watched Gene's retreating back before transferring his attention to Paul as the couple swept past our table. "Not a bad looker. If Paul doesn't want her, maybe I'll give her a try."

The music came to a stop with the couple on the far side of the floor. We watched as they spoke briefly. Then Paul took her hand and lifted it to his lips before turning and walking away. Although I was dying to hear what went on, I understood when Paul joined a table of mixed couples. Probably some UNM kids he knew. I caught a flash of movement at my side and turned to find Henry striding across the now vacant dance area toward where he last saw the blonde. Gene rejoined me at that moment.

"What's up?" I asked.

"Somebody bugged Paul's car. My man in the parking lot watched the maneuver and got a shot of the guy. Not a good pic, but it's enough to see it wasn't Juan. He look familiar to you?"

I glanced at the photo he handed me, but it was indistinct, especially in the low lighting of the nightclub. Unwilling to look at it by the small light on my keychain, I handed it back. "Can't make it out. Anyone you know?"

"If I had to guess, I'd say it's the Dominican arrested with Juan for kidnapping that kid a few years back."

"Gaspard?"

"That's the one."

"Where is he now?"

"My man said he got in a car and drove away."

"He get a plate?"

"No, too far away. But it was a late model Buick LeSabre. Gold, he thought, but it's hard to tell under these parking lot lights. Do we remove the bug?"

"Crap. I hadn't counted on this. If we do that, they'll know we're on to them."

"We can always drop it in the parking lot. Maybe he'll think he didn't fasten it securely."

"Maybe. Why don't we just have Paul leave the car at some motel tonight?"

Gene nodded. "That's the thing to do. Let's wrap this up. Tell Paul to leave the car in the parking lot at the Holiday Inn Express on Hotel Circle. I'll go on over there now and wait to bring him home."

"Okay. Did you notice our guy with dreadlocks has vacated the premises?"

Gene looked around. "Lots of people have vacated the premises. It's getting late. Past my bedtime."

Henry arrived back at the table. "Did you catch blondie?" I asked.

"Nope. Looked everywhere. But she disappeared. Went home, probably. Alone."

I filled him in on our plan before heading for the men's room, catching Paul's eye as I passed the table where he was sitting. After a minute or so, he joined me in the vacant toilet, where I gave him his instructions.

HENRY AND I sat in the car until Paul pulled out of the C&W's big parking lot. We allowed him some distance before pulling out after him. No one seemed to be following his rental, but they wouldn't have to stay close, not with the locator bug they'd planted on his car. We followed him up Eubank until he turned off the main drag, heading for the motel. Resisting the urge to stay on his tail, I drove north to pick up Montgomery Boulevard before turning west toward my North Valley home.

Then Henry and I sat and stewed for another hour before we heard a car pull into our driveway. A moment later, Paul let himself in the back door. I hadn't realized how concerned I was until I saw his smiling face. My muscles relaxed so totally that I felt lethargic.

"I thought tonight was a bust until Gene told me my car was bugged," he said. "Guess I got a good looking-over." He frowned. "But it must have been from a distance."

"How was that blonde?" Henry asked. "I tried to find her after you two split up, but she must have left."

"Persistent." Paul laughed. "She sure wanted me to go home with her. Almost wouldn't take no for an answer." He sobered. "The strange thing was, I was kinda attracted to her."

Bolting straight up in my chair, I exclaimed, "Son of a bitch!"

Paul caught on immediately. "Be damned. That was Juan in drag, wasn't it?"

Henry flushed. "No way. That was one fine-looking woman."

I laughed at his obvious embarrassment. After all, he had been sniffing around after her in a pretty serious way.

"Paul, you held Juanito in your arms and let him get away."

Chapter 5

"HEY, WAKE up. Need to ask you something."

Jazz roused from a dream as Juan shook him roughly. "Lemme alone," he mumbled, seeking to recapture the reverie. *Water Sprinkler and some other Navajo Yé'ii were in it.* He grew surly when he realized the details escaped him. Wouldn't have mattered much even if he could recall. He wasn't raised on the old legends like most guys his age and didn't understand a damned thing about that side of his blood. Water Sprinkler was the rain god—that much he knew. So likely that meant his parade was going to get rained on. Big-time.

"Man, that crack shit's taking you over," Juan complained. "All you do's fuck and bitch. Come on, man. Wake up."

Jazz pushed himself against the headboard and tried to focus. The sheet fell away to reveal his naked torso. Seemed like he was always naked nowadays. Juan reached out and stroked his pecs. Jazz had liked and encouraged his touch... once. Now not so much. He shrugged the hand away. "Lemme alone. I finally got to sleep and you wake me up. I need a pipe, okay?"

"A shower's what you need. Silver Wings wants to meet you tonight."

Jazz's stomach did a flip-flop. "I don't like him."

"Well, he digs you. Think he's gonna want you to move in with him."

The idea was a crowbar jammed into the gears of Jazz's mind. His thinking came to a halt. He needed a pipe. That was the only good thing about Silver Wings. Jazz always got good crack before the man arrived. "Smoke," he mumbled.

Juan shoved two photos at him. "Later. Right now, I need you to look at these pics."

Jazz struggled to focus as he scanned the photos. They were the same handsome man, one with a shirt, the other without. His stomach cramped, and he felt itchy. "Who's this?"

"You tell me. He says he knows you. Says you told him about me?"

"I did?"

"You know him?"

Jazz blinked a couple of times and moved one picture back and forth until it became clearer. Struggling to get his mind to work, he rubbed his eyes before taking another look. The guy seemed familiar. But Jazz associated him with someone else. Someone he liked. Admired.

"Dude lives here in Albuquerque," he said at length. "Don't remember his name."

"Does the name Paul mean anything to you?"

"Yeah. That's it. Paul." Jazz had no idea if that was correct, but it was easier to agree with Juan.

"Paul what?"

"I dunno. Just Paul."

"You tell him about me? Send him my photo?"

"He says I did, I guess I did," Jazz mumbled, sliding back beneath the thin covers. His eyes were closed as Juan left the room with a warning they'd have to leave for the meeting with Silver Wings in an hour.

But Jazz was struggling to think. Make connections. Paul. *Barton!* That was the guy's last name. And they'd never exchanged emails or pictures. He'd only seen the good-looking dude once. In Farmington. In some motel room. Had they got it on? Could be. He wrinkled his nose. Had he gotten with so many men he couldn't remember them all? He shook his head emphatically. No, he wasn't like that. He only went with guys he....

Jazz came upright in the bed as a shadowy figure flitted just out of reach in his head. *BJ!* BJ's Paul was talking to Juan? Was the fucker two-timing BJ? His skin crawled as he shook his head again. No. No, Paul got in touch with Juan because... because *BJ was looking for him*! But how did he know about Juan?

Jazz lay back and battled his emotions. Henry musta given BJ his laptop. A flush enveloped his whole body as he imagined BJ reading his mail and looking at the photos. His blood pressure rose, sending beads of sweat down his sides. "Fuckers!" he muttered aloud. Shouldn't be looking at his private stuff.

He let out his breath, and the pressure eased. He had ventured out of his comfort zone for the promise of a steady connection. A loving, intelligent, exciting man of his own. Looking for what BJ had with Paul. It was all right at first. Practically everything he'd dreamed of. But it all turned to ashes. Pipe ashes.

Why had he let Juanito talk him into smoking crack? His new life was good without that crap. But Juanito promised him the pipes would make things even better. And they were—for a bit. Then it changed. He changed. The world changed. Now he pleasured men in exchange for the pipes. Men? Well, Juanito and Silver Wings. But he knew there would be more men one day. Probably when they took that trip to Mexico Juan talked about.

His frazzled mind called up the image of BJ. BJ was a detective. He'd find him and drag his ass out of this tangled mess. His heart soared until it nearly burst before abruptly slowing, leaving him woozy. Did he want out? Yeah, it would be good to go home. See his mom and uncle Riley. Henry. His father. But if BJ got him out, the man he idolized would see what he'd become. He musta already seen the things he'd written to Juan. And the pictures. The last one was bad. Showed him manipulating himself as he smiled at the camera. His stomach plummeted as something drove him to bury his head beneath the bedcovers. Probably shame.

Jazz sobbed and willed his heart to stop. To cease. To spare him anything that lay beyond this moment, this room, this bed. *But Coyote refused to throw a rock into Black Water Lake to summon death*, so his heart ignored his wishes and thudded against his ribs in a stubborn, determined beat.

Chapter 6

I HADN'T decided on our next move by the time Henry dragged into the office around eleven the next day from scouting for Jazz's Jeep. He told of spying a dark-headed guy with a white spot on the crown of his head standing on the sidewalk near Louisiana and East Central.

Thinking he might have found Juan right out on Central trolling for tricks, he parked his bike around the corner and walked back to sit down at the bus stop near where the guy was drumming up business. Sure enough, the dude came ambling over and sat down beside him.

Henry's a damned good-looking fellow, but he can be intimidating too. So nothing happened until he asked about the white mark on the kid's pate. According to the spiky guy, he and some friends dyed places on the middle of his head on a dare. Now he was stuck with it until it grew out.

Feeling low to the ground because his hopes were dashed, Henry groused aloud. "It was a total bust. It wasn't the Juan guy. Way too young, and the skinny kid with the white stain wasn't interested in nothing but hustling me."

"How'd you get away from him?" Paul asked, a tease hiding in his voice.

"Wasn't easy. Had to tell him three times I don't go for that shit. Finally said if he didn't go away and leave me alone, I'd do something about it."

I did some thinking while Paul tried to bring Henry off his low. "Maybe it wasn't a bust after all. From all I've heard and read, some of these traffickers brand their victims. Maybe dyed hair is this gang's brand. Do you think you can find that kid again?"

"Dunno. All I can do is try. I'll head out on my bike again."

"No, let's take my car."

"He might not go for a twosome. Might scare him off."

"If you see him, I'll let you out, and you can bring him to me."

"To us," Paul said. "I'm going too."

Despite my reservation about three men being too intimidating, I nodded, and we took off up Central in my Impala on the lookout for a kid with a white patch in his hair.

WE ARRIVED at the east end of the Expo New Mexico grounds—which we old-timers still refer to as the state fairgrounds—in time to see the kid get out of a gold LeSabre. It took a long second to snap to the situation.

"Henry," I yelled, "Get out and grab that kid. Don't let him get away, no matter what. Paul, call Charlie and have him come pick up Henry. Take that kid back to the office and hold him there."

"What's going on?" Henry asked.

"That car he got out of matches the description of the LeSabre belonging to Florio Gaspard, the kid's pimp. I want to follow him."

Without a word Henry bailed, and I did an illegal U-turn at Louisiana Boulevard, heading back down Central in pursuit of the rapidly disappearing Buick. Paul pulled out his cell and reached Charlie.

We would have lost Gaspard had he not stopped near the University of New Mexico Bookstore to pick up another of his minnows. Even so, the car disappeared by the time I turned left on Yale, as Gaspard had done a minute before.

"Dammit! He's pulled off into an alleyway somewhere to collect the money his kid made."

"He took the other guy back to where he picked him up. Maybe he'll do the same this time."

We found a parking spot on Central near the bookstore, but after fifteen minutes we concluded he had not repeated his pattern. This was confirmed when we spotted a girl with a white streak in her hair strolling down the other side of Central.

Paul got out of the car and crossed the street. The girl brightened appreciably at the handsome man but lost her smile when he spoke for a few seconds before taking her arm and leading the way to the car.

"What is this?" she protested in a childish voice when he pushed her into the back seat and shoved in beside her. "I don't do twosomes."

"Not asking you to," I said. "We just need to talk to you a few minutes. I'm going to drive downtown to my office. After we talk, I'll bring you back here and give you your price for a trick. How's that?"

"You fuzz? Show me your shields."

"No, we're private. Talk and then pay, okay?"

She settled down on the drive back to my office parking lot. Paul held her arm in a firm grip on the way into the building.

Hazel's eyes widened when we entered my door on the third floor. Then she inclined her head toward my private office. "In there."

The girl stopped dead still when she spotted the thin teen sitting at the table with Charlie and Henry.

"Streak," he said, his Adam's apple bobbing.

"Spot. What're you doing here?"

"Kidnapped like you was, I guess."

"Not kidnapped," I said in a rough voice. "But if you want to be certain of that, I can call APD and ask for a detective to join us. Would that make you feel better?"

"Uh-uh," the kid said.

"No way," the girl agreed.

"Then sit down, and let's start."

I got my digital voice recorder from my desk, plopped it in the middle of the table, and identified the date, place, and participants, identifying the two victims by their street names. After finally getting the two teens to audibly agree to being taped, I started with the interview.

"First off, let me reassure you we mean you no harm. We are looking for a specific ring of sex traffickers who brand their victims with white spots in their hair. We know one of the pimps controlling some of them is a Dominican by the name of Florio Gaspard, the man who just picked up both of you and relieved you of your earnings. We want to hear your stories and learn whatever you know of their network."

The girl broke first, but out of fear of her pimp, not intimidation by us. "Flo will kill me when he finds out!" she moaned. "He'll beat me and lock me in a box. He makes me sleep there when I act up. And when I don't make enough money."

The girl called Streak turned out to be a fifteen-year-old orphan named Barbra Swan who ran away from a bad foster home and lived on the streets until Gaspard picked her up, bought her a good meal, and described how much better life would be if she let him become her "daddy." She agreed and found herself sharing a room with five others—both boys and girls—at a dump called My Other Home Motel off West Central somewhere on Nine Mile Hill. Whenever she rebelled, Gaspard locked her in a perforated four-by-four pine box in a small building behind the isolated motel. Every time she ran away, he tracked her down and beat her before locking her away.

The boy's story was similar. Spot's real name was Clancy Truscott. His father beat him before throwing him out of the house after catching him naked beneath a rampant older boy in their detached garage. An immediate outcast in his little Oklahoma Bible Belt town, he thumbed his way west, headed for golden California. Broke and hungry in Albuquerque, he stole a purse from the front seat of a car parked at a busy shopping center. Gaspard, who apparently had been watching him troll the streets, confronted him and threatened to take him to the police.

Spot hadn't proved to be much of a problem. After he serviced Gaspard, he was introduced into the life and controlled by regular doses of heroin. Nonetheless, he came in for his share of beatings, although he wasn't taken to the "pines," as the kids referred to Streak's pine box. I was shocked to learn he was only seventeen. He looked to be at least two years older.

The two teens knew of at least a dozen other kids housed in the motel. Not all of them wore dyed hair, the identification mark of the White Spot family. Some carried actual tattoos or intentionally inflicted scars to brand them for other pimps. Hunger, fear, disease, beatings, and worry about the law haunted the minnows every day of their lives. The two knew of a couple of their group who suddenly disappeared after becoming obstreperous or threatening to go to the law. They assumed the recalcitrants were murdered. If they were to be believed, at least fourteen kids were collected, trained, controlled, and turned loose by trafficking thugs upon the city.

I thought of passages in the Book of Revelations speaking of Abaddon the Destroyer releasing locusts from the underworld upon the land. I'd once sat through an impressive series of lectures on the End Times and recalled that when the fifth—or maybe it was the sixth—angel sounds his trumpet, the Abyss opens, and a horde of demonic "locusts" rise out of it to torture anyone who does not bear God's seal. The pain they inflict will be so intense the sufferer will crave death, but that relief will be denied him.

Our lecturer was careful to point out these were not actual insects but rather a demonic army inflicted by God as a scourge upon mankind for five months. Why five months? The answer given was "Perhaps because that is the lifespan of the actual insect."

And now this horde of children was being trained and turned loose on the world. How many houses or motels such as this were spread over the state and beyond? Over the entire nation. Over the world. Like the lord of the underworld's locusts, these victims were not designed to kill or destroy—although they might inadvertently result in such damage—but to wreak mayhem. But these locusts—our locusts—were victims as well as perpetrators. A new world—one hidden from me all my life—opened up before my eyes. And it had claimed someone I held dear.

Despite the teens' fear, I phoned Gene and told him what we'd uncovered. He and a female officer came over immediately, almost undoing what we'd accomplished.

Barbra let out a cry and broke for the door when she spotted the woman's uniform. The officer, who wore a name tag reading Glenann Hastings, caught her and hugged her tight.

"It's all right, child. We won't harm you," she cooed.

But the street urchin fought to free herself from the embrace. "You're gonna put me in jail! Please don't."

"Hush now, nobody's going to put you in jail."

"Yes, you will! Flo told me so. And… and he'll beat me when he hears. Lock me in the box."

"Why would he do that?" Officer Hastings asked.

"Because I let myself get caught."

I transferred my gaze to the boy. He seemed to have shrunk. He huddled in his chair, pale and shaking. Slobber dribbled from his lips onto his ragged shirt. He flinched when Gene moved to his side and dropped a hand on his shoulder.

"It's okay, son. We're going to take you somewhere that fella Flo won't be able to find you."

Streak turned hollow eyes on Gene and blurted, "But you won't give me my fix. Flo'll give me my fix. I need my fix, man."

The rest of us withdrew as the police officers sat the two juveniles side by side at my conference table and spent some time convincing the two runaways they intended them no harm but rather offered a way out. New Mexico, Gene explained, had laws to assist underage victims in these exact circumstances.

Gene paused long enough to call headquarters and arrange a raid on the motel on the west side before taking the two children away. The timing needed to be right. If Gaspard discovered two of his minions were missing, he might suspect they'd been picked up and move the rest of his people. On the other hand, the raid had to be planned for a time when at least some of the kids were in the motel.

After he left, Henry shook his head. "Something about this don't make sense to me. This Juan dude spends all that time baiting and hooking Jazz just to put him out on the street? You said they wouldn't use him like that."

"We haven't found Jazz's kidnapper. That gang goes for quality. Gaspard's goes for quantity. But remember two things. Juan, or rather Juan Jose Flores-Gurule, and Florio Gaspard, were arrested together for a crime similar to this, so Gaspard knows Juan. And secondly, Juan has the brand. The white spot in the hair that marks one of Gaspard's people."

"Which means," Paul said, "they're both part of the same gang."

"Gaspard doesn't have a white streak. At least, I didn't see one when he passed us in the car. Of course if he's the boss, maybe he doesn't need one."

"There's another possibility," Paul said. "I've been reading up on sex trafficking, and I understand sometimes pimps sell their victims to other pimps. Maybe this Juan was bought by someone else and his hair hasn't grown out enough to get rid of the white brand."

"Possible. But if we can run down Gaspard, he might know where and how to contact Juan. Cross your fingers and hope Gene's raid snares the Dominican."

"I wanna be there when it goes down," Henry said.

I shook my head. "Gene won't permit civilians on such a raid. There might be violence."

"I'll sign a waiver or whatever you call it. I wanna be there, BJ."

"The best thing we can do is be at headquarters when whoever they snare is brought back. Gene might let me sit in on the interviews."

WAITING WASN'T going to do it for Henry, so to forestall a potential explosion, I suggested that Paul email Juan and express disappointment they hadn't met last night at the C&W. After huddling in my office, Paul sent a message from his laptop.

> *Juanito, disappointed you didn't show up at the C&W last night. Hoped we'd get a chance to meet. You know, see if we're compatible. Don't want to sound desperate or anything but… damned if I don't think I am.*
> *Paul*

After that message was sent, I phoned Susie Garcia, a supervisor at the Motor Vehicle Department who was once sweet on me before I knew who I really was. She usually helped me out in the information department so long as I was willing to put up with her occasional needles.

"You must want something. I never hear from you unless you do."

"We went to lunch just the other day."

"Yeah, just the other day... three months ago."

"Can't be that long."

"It was, but what do you want?"

I fed her the information on Florio Gaspard and his LeSabre, and she went to work. In a few minutes, she was back. "You still a licensed private investigator?" she asked.

"Uh...yeah."

"So why didn't you look this up yourself? Or have Hazel do it?"

"I'm not at the office where I have access to my program," I fibbed. "And I can talk to Hazel anytime."

"If you weren't a three-dollar bill, I'd think you were hitting on me. You haven't switched sides, have you?"

"Afraid not."

"Thought not. Anyway, here's what I have on Florio Gaspard." She provided a year and make on the automobile and an address 145 Ocotillo SW, which I recognized as the My Other Home Motel.

I thanked Susie, hung up, and asked Hazel to give the license number and address to Gene. He likely already had them, but better safe than sorry.

From the table in the corner of my office, I heard Paul's laptop ping. "It's him," he announced. "Juanito himself."

We all crowded around. He paused with his finger over the email notice. "Whoa now, guys. This might be highly personal. Maybe—"

"Open the damned thing," Henry said.

Paul, baby. I was there and my heart reached out to you. You looked good enough to eat, but dude, you were having too much fun dancing with the ladies (and looking good swinging your thing, too). Not sure you're looking for what I'm interested in.

Juanito

"You're losing him," Henry said.

Without bothering to reply, Paul placed his long fingers on the keyboard and pounded out a response.

Juanito—that means "little John," doesn't it? Sure hope that's not an accurate description. We started this off with me looking for Jazz, right? Let

me put it this way, if I could find him, I'd tear off his clothes, throw him on the bed, and not think about a damned thing except what I was doing to him for the next hour. Have you heard from him, by the way? But since Jazz isn't available, I'm hot and hungry. We both know I can go on campus or walk up Indian alley and find plenty. But I'm looking for quality. I'm looking for a lot more than just a one-night stand. Now what do we do about it?
Paul

"My stars!" Hazel exclaimed. "Have you done this before?"

"Well, maybe practiced on BJ when he was out of town a couple of times. But other than that, no."

The laptop pinged, startling us all. Paul opened the message.

Paul. Why don't you give me a look at what you're carrying. Then maybe I give you a peak at Juanito's Juan.
Juanito

Paul didn't hesitate.

Uh-uh, I don't send photos when I don't know where they're going to end up. Wouldn't want to meet myself on some weird website one of these days. And if I don't send you one that shows my face, as well, it could be anybody. Jazz's brother Henry, for example. Paul

Henry started to protest, but it was too late. The message was already winging its way to Juan.

Ping.

This Henry dude, was he that good-looking Indian you talked to at the C&W? S-E-X-Y. But what is it you wanna do? Meet somewhere?

Henry turned two shades darker but kept his mouth firmly closed.

Don't see how we can get our needs taken care of if we don't. Any suggestions? Paul shot back at him.

"Wait a minute," I said. "That was quick. How did he put a casual reference to Jazz's brother together with the man you talked to at the

C&W? Henry, I didn't see any photos attached to the emails except for those of Jazz. Did you?"

Henry shook his head. "Nope."

"Of course, we don't know what went on after they switched to Skype," Paul said. "Maybe Jazz showed him one in their face-to-face."

"Uh-uh. Jazz don't mix me up in his business. Knows better."

"Then it doesn't make any sense. Unless...." I let my voice trail off as I thought. "Henry, does Jazz have any family pictures in his wallet? One of you, specifically?"

Henry pulled out his billfold and extracted a snapshot. It captured the two brothers standing with arms around one another's shoulders as they smiled into the camera. It would be hard to pick out the more attractive man from that photograph. "He carries one just like this on him."

We didn't wait for Juan's response. Paul typed as I dictated.

Juanito, you're fast on the uptake. How'd you know that was *Jazz's brother at the C&W? He moved down here to take a landscaping job a month ago and got in touch with me. That's what got me to thinking about Jazz. Course, Henry could take care of my needs, but suggesting that would earn me a black eye. He doesn't swing that way. But Jazz sure does. Have you heard from him?*

After the message was sent, Charlie asked if I shouldn't have included a place and a time to meet. I shook my head, explaining we needed to let Juan do that.

Ping, again.

Bet that hunky Indian could take care of us both… at the same time. But I hear you, man. Not everbody feeds outa the same trough, right? Nothing from Jazz. But okay, maybe we oughta sit down and size one another up. Be at the C&W tonight at 8:30 p.m. If you can't make it, then that's the way it was meant to be.

"Bingo, we got him." Paul gave a thumbs-up sign.

I held up a hand. "Wait a minute. Let's think this thing through. The last time we went to the C&W, they bugged your car. It went to a motel parking lot, where it stayed until the car rental people picked it up the next day. How does Paul explain that?"

"He crashed there that night and turned in the car the next day."

"Why?" I asked.

"That's easy," Paul said. "I'm as careful as Juan is. I wasn't about to drive my own car into a situation I wasn't sure of."

I smiled. "Defending paranoia with paranoia. It might work. Someone as secretive as Juan will understand caution on the other side. Okay, let's go for it."

Chapter 7

GENE'S RAID on the My Other Home Motel went down at 5:00 p.m. that afternoon and was a total bust. He sounded tired when he gave me the results by phone.

"Not a kid in sight. Matter of fact, there was a sign the place was closed for renovations. Searched every one of the twenty-five rooms anyway. Nothing. Nobody. Zilch."

"They were warned," I said.

"Yeah, we got hung out to dry." He hesitated. "Or there was nothing to find. Those two kids made up the whole thing."

"How'd they know about a motel way out on the west side of town?"

"How do kids know anything these days? Heard about it. Snuck in to sleep in a vacant room a night or two. Some trick took them there. Who knows?"

"Okay, then explain to me why Florio Gaspard's address on his New Mexico driver's license lists the hotel as his home address?"

"You got me there. Can't be coincidence."

"Hell of a big one if it is. And we know Gaspard is connected to those two. Paul, Henry, and I saw him with the Truscott boy, and Paul and I saw him with the Swan girl. So let's talk about the other possibility. They were warned."

"How? Nobody knew about it except those involved. And you people, of course. How about this Henry Secatero guy? He seems about one step short of a hood to me."

"Henry's okay. Grew up rough is all. He's the one who kicked this off by looking for his brother, remember? Who else in your department knew?"

"Plenty of people involved in arranging, planning, and executing the raid. But I don't believe it was any of them. Course, there's lots of money involved in human trafficking, and more'n one cop's been turned by money. Not many, but a few."

"I have trouble believing it as well. Anyone outside of the department know about the raid?"

"Somebody probably let the Citizen's Commission Against Human Trafficking know about it. It's protocol."

"That's Roscoe Haldemain's outfit, isn't it?"

"He's chairman of it. Bishop Justin Gregory's vice chair. But a gal named Betsy Brockmire pretty well runs it."

I called up a mental image of Roscoe P. Haldemain, an attorney I'd done business with a few times. A partner in a successful private practice specializing in both civil and criminal defense work, he was about ten years my senior, which would put him around forty-eight. My height— six feet—but carried about ten pounds more than my 170. Tanning salon complexion and gym-buffed frame. Brown hair heavy with gray, but in a suave, sophisticated way. I'd never particularly associated Ross—as he preferred to be called—with good works, but I had heard him give a speech or two about the horrors of human trafficking.

The good bishop I'd met only socially. I knew nothing of his life before he moved to Albuquerque from wherever and started building an unaffiliated, nondenominational church. He'd apparently done a good job of it since he went from pastor to bishop in about five years. Bishop Gregory was also a sophisticated-looking man, somewhat shorter and carrying more weight than his chairman. But he also had sleek hair— black—shot through with streaks of gray.

Betsy Brockmire, a nodding acquaintance, was dumpy but not unattractive, with brown hair carrying auburn highlights. She was a ball of energy who tended to wear me out in a hurry whenever I heard her address a luncheon or something.

"Is the Citizen's Council a state commission?" I asked.

"It's what they call an NGO, a nongovernmental agency. NGOs carry a lot of the water in fighting human trafficking. They may get some state money, but Haldemain and Gregory are elected by the organization, not appointed by the governor."

"Could there be a leak there?"

I could almost hear Gene shrug on the other end of the phone. "I guess. But they're all about fighting trafficking. Why would they tip off anyone about a raid?"

"Let's see," I said. "What did we say some cop's motivation might be?"

Gene let out a sigh. "Money. From all I hear, neither Haldemain nor Gregory need any."

"You ever hear of a churchman who wasn't scrambling for money? What about Brockmire?"

"She's a wealthy widow from back east somewhere who's a civil rights activist. But point taken. The whole kit and caboodle's loaded. What do you want to do?"

"Let's go see them anyway. Test the waters, so to speak," I said.

"All that'll get us is a legal dissertation, a sermon, and a lecture. But I'll see if I can set it up."

Then I told him about Juan's request for a meeting with Paul this evening. Gene bitched about the short notice before agreeing to have his people on hand. In fact, he set me up with a date with Officer Glenann Hastings, who, it turned out, was in APD's Special Victims Unit.

PAUL AND Henry were both disappointed when I told him of the failure of the raid, but I faced a potentially violent revolt when I told Henry he couldn't go to the C&W tonight.

"Be reasonable," I pled. "You're on Juan's radar. He sees you, he'll likely take a powder."

"I don't have to be with Paul. Hell, I'll get my own date and just go dancing."

"Henry, you're a free warrior of the Navajo persuasion. If you decide you want to go, there's nothing I can do to stop you. I just hope Jazz doesn't pay the penalty."

"What penalty?" His black eyes lost some of their stubbornness.

"If we scare him off, Juan isn't going to come back for another bite of the apple. Or a nip at Paul either. We'll lose the best lead on the whereabouts of your brother we have."

I could see Henry didn't like my line of reasoning but couldn't escape the logic of it. "All right, but you keep me posted, okay?"

Officer Glenann Hastings stopped by the house at seven thirty looking very fetching in gray slacks and white blouse with a vaguely western-looking vest in deference to the cowboy ambiance we were heading into. We wanted to arrive well before Paul. Henry took off for the Blue Spruce, which wasn't far from the C&W in case something broke. That assumed he didn't start a fight and get hauled downtown by Albuquerque's finest—a distinct possibility given his foul mood.

The Thursday night crowd at the C&W was heavier and the activity on the dance floor brisker. Real cowboys shuffled around the floor with wannabe cowgirls—and vice versa. The sound system was cranked up to full volume, and when music didn't roil the eardrums, the deejay's patter did. Glenann and I got in a couple of dances when the music was appropriate to my abilities.

So far as I could tell, Juan wasn't among the frequent dancers, but he might have been seated at one of the back tables. Of course, if he was in his distaff dress tonight, I'm not sure I would recognize him. We needed some of that facial recognition equipment everyone kept talking about. Software that would match a live face to photographs more or less absolutely and beyond denial. Yeah, right. That would happen about the same time we got Dick Tracy wristwatch radios. Of course, I'd heard those were practically here.

Paul came through the door looking like a million dollars, followed a minute later by a tall blond APD detective named Don Carson. He'd followed Paul's newly rented car from the house to the nightclub. Paul immediately joined some UNM friends at a table. Not a good move. He needed to be solitary in order for Juan to approach him.

After a few minutes, he ambled over to another table to greet other friends and acquaintances, but he didn't stay long. He broke away after five minutes and moved into the bar, where he produced his ID and bought himself a mug of beer. Then he stood near the dance floor and sipped his drink.

Eight thirty came and went, but my heartthrob played it cool. He danced a few dances with cowgirls but spent most of his time watching the dancers from the sideline. Glenann spotted our quarry quicker than I. She poked me in the ribs.

"There the suspect is. Coming from the bar. Approaching Paul from behind." She patted my hand resting on our small table as if we were lovers. "What do you want to do?"

"Keep an eye on them. Paul knows he's not to leave with the guy unless he knows he's covered. And not to get into Juan's car whatever the circumstances."

As we watched, Juan took a place near Paul and stood sipping his own drink, a highball of some sort. He watched Paul with half an eye for a couple of minutes before tapping him on the shoulder.

Paul looked surprised before he smiled and shook hands with the man. They talked for a minute, but we were too far away to hear what was said. We'd considered wiring Paul, but Gene argued the place was so noisy the mikes wouldn't be effective. Gene elected not to come tonight because he'd been made by "Ellen" last night, and to have the same players on display might frighten our mark away.

I grew antsy when the couple started roaming the big room looking for a vacant table. I lost them in the crowd, but before I panicked, Carson walked up and shook hands as if meeting a friend.

"They're at a table at the back near the restrooms. A female undercover snagged a table nearby. I'm going to get us a couple of drinks and join her. We'll keep a close eye on the situation, BJ."

"Thanks. Any movement, let us know."

Half an hour went by before a man dragged an empty chair from the table next to us and sat down at ours. He leaned over and gave Glenann a hug.

"BJ, this is Shelby Horne."

"Hiya, Mr. Vinson. Needed to let you know that Florio Gaspard just arrived in the parking lot. There's an arrest warrant out for him in connection with the raid on the motel this afternoon, so I gotta take him. Hope that doesn't screw things up for you."

"Everyone knows about the raid by now, as well as the two minnows who disappeared. Don't think there'll be any damage done. Might crimp Juan's style but not ours."

"That's the way I figure it too. Glenann, looking good. Wanna quick dance before I go?"

She declined with an admonition to keep his mind on business. The undercover cop grinned and drifted away.

A few minutes later, Paul and Juan walked in our direction. When they got close enough, I saw both had us on their radar. Then Paul did exactly the right thing. He stopped and said hello. I introduced Glenann as he shook my hand. He named his companion only as Juan. Paul asked about a game of tennis at some unspecified date in the future, and I agreed before they moved on toward the front door.

"Why did he spotlight us?" Glenann asked after they left, closely trailed by Carson and his escort.

"Juan knows we're acquainted. Last night when Juan was posing as Ellen, he saw us all together and managed to get us introduced. That's why Lieutenant Enriquez isn't here tonight. Guess Paul thought it would look strange if he didn't acknowledge us."

Glenann nodded. "He thinks fast on his feet."

"I don't like them leaving the club, but I can't follow them."

"Don will keep an eye on them. But I can go outside if you want me to provide backup."

"No, we don't want anyone we haven't spotted getting suspicious. How about another dance before we head out?"

"You're a pretty cool customer. I know you're dying to know what's happening, but here you want another dance with little old me. Lead on, cowboy."

"First, let me text Henry and let him know people are on the move."

I DIDN'T spot any familiar cars as we recovered my Impala and headed out onto Central for the long drop into the valley. We hadn't covered a block before Glenann's cell phone rang. She listened a minute before hanging up.

"Don says Juan and Paul split up, and Paul seems to be heading back to the house. Shel—that's the officer keeping watch on the parking lot—is going to follow Juan."

"Not too closely, I hope. We don't want to spook the guy—if we haven't already. I thought Juan would try to lure Paul to a motel."

"Maybe he did, but Paul wouldn't bite."

Just as we reached the corner where the Blue Spruce squatted, Henry pulled out on his motorcycle and roared down East Central. He looked steady enough on the machine, but he showed little regard for the speed limit. He soon left us behind.

By the time we reached 5229 Post Oak Drive NW, the house looked as if it hosted a party. I parked on the street in front of Mrs. Wardlow's white brick. An anonymous brown Ford taking up my spot in the driveway indicated Gene had joined us. He'd been offered a new car when he made lieutenant but declined. It looked as if Charlie was here, which probably meant Hazel was too… fretting over Paul's safety.

Everyone was seated in my den except for Paul, who was in the bedroom changing into more comfortable clothes. Henry stood leaning on the small wet bar in the corner of the room.

When Paul walked in from the bedroom area, Gene spoke up. "We're all here now, so let's get started. Before we hear Paul's story, let me tell you Florio Gaspard was apprehended in the parking lot of the C&W. We took him without incident. Doubt if anyone even knew he was arrested unless they were watching closely."

That was significant, because a distinguished, silver-haired gentleman by the name of Brookings Ingles would show up as soon as the arrest was discovered. Brookie seemed to represent most of the people involved in the prostitution trade, pimps and whores as well.

"Where is Gaspard now?" Charlie asked.

"In an interrogation room at headquarters. We're questioning him about the two kids we picked up this afternoon. Not sure if we can hold him, but the interrogators have been told not to mention the other end of the operation."

"You've got two witnesses who connect him to the trade," Paul said. "Why wouldn't you be able to hold him?"

"The girl's shaky. When she faces a defense lawyer in court, she'll dry up and blow away. The boy's on heroin, so who knows how he'll handle himself. I wouldn't count on anything unless Gaspard trips himself up."

"Which isn't likely," I said. "Paul, tell us about your hot date."

My lover looked me full in the eye. "It could have been a hot date. That Juan guy is a born seducer. If I'd been free and didn't know anything about him, it's likely I would have gone along. Except—" He paused. "—he didn't ask me to. We just agreed to meet for lunch tomorrow."

"Where?" I asked.

"Flying Star on Juan Tabo. Eleven thirty. His treat."

I thought for a moment. "Makes sense. He probably wants to question Jazz about you, learn all he can before making his move."

"But Jazz doesn't know anything about me," Paul said.

"Maybe enough to make this work." I sighed in exasperation. "I can't be there tomorrow. He's seen me twice at the C&W. My presence at the Flying Star would be too much of a coincidence. Henry can't be there either. But Charlie can. Along with some of Gene's cops. But we're getting ahead of ourselves. Officer Horne's trailing Juan from the C&W. Have you heard from him, Gene?"

I didn't like the sour look on my ex-partner's face. "Called just before you got here. Juan gave him the slip down in the barrio."

"Shit!" Henry exclaimed. "How did that happen?"

"He couldn't make himself obvious, so he hung back. Wasn't hard for Juan to turn into an alley and sneak away."

"Well, at least we know what kind of car he's driving."

"Yep. A 2009 dark blue Ford Fusion."

"Did Horne get the plates?"

"Uh-huh."

"Good. That'll give us an address."

Gene grimaced again. "Sure did. The My Other Home Motel at 145 Ocotillo SW."

This time, *I* uttered the profanity.

Chapter 8

JAZZ HUDDLED against the wall in a corner of the room. Only one lamp relieved the darkness, but he liked it that way. He didn't know what time it was, but then he didn't give a crap either. One minute was as good as the next.

This was a nice room. White walls and airy. Big television in the living area. Gold drapes with some kind of figure woven into them. It was a woman, repeated over and over in the curtains. Was it Spider Woman? White Shell Woman? The more he stared, the more he became convinced it was *Estsanatlehi* or Woman Who Changes. It pissed him that Henry could pronounce her name better than he could, but he'd never heard of her until a few years ago, while his half brother sat at their grandmother's knee as a child and learned all about the Navajo pantheon. But Jazz knew she was called Changing Woman because she went from youth to maturity to old age. And so, year after year, this earth goddess ushered in the seasons.

The beige carpet against his butt proved more comfortable than some of the chairs at home. But soon, his nerves rankled and pulled him to his feet. He paced the room, his hands fidgeting, touching this and that. This little bungalow behind a fancy redbrick house was new to him. Somewhere on the west side of Albuquerque, he guessed, although he wasn't familiar enough with the city to be sure.

Juan brought him here two nights ago after telling him he owed Silver Wings a lot of money and had to stay with the older man until it was repaid. That was news to Jazz. He didn't owe anyone a damned dime. Something about the pipes he smoked, Juan said. Jazz couldn't decide how he felt about seeing the Mexican go. He liked Juan okay, even though the guy hadn't turned out to be the loving companion he originally seemed. During that first week with Juan, Jazz thought he'd found what he was looking for. A steady. A companion for life—through thick and thin.

Then Juan introduced him to the pipe, and the second week was even better. Nirvana, or what Jazz thought nirvana would be. The sex was powerful, all-consuming, overwhelming. But it wasn't long before the pipes became more important than the sex. He craved a smoke more than a tumble with his lover. When he asked what he was smoking, Juan told him plain tobacco with an herb in it that gave him a little high. Jazz knew better, of course, but by this time, he didn't care.

Then Juan introduced him to Silver Wings in a motel room. Jazz refused to have anything to do with the man at first. The crack in his armor came when he understood that if he didn't service Silver Wings, there'd be no more pipes. No more nirvana. The first time, Juan lay beside him in bed, kissing and fondling him until he got so charged up, he didn't realize Silver Wings joined them until Juan slipped out of the bed and let the older man take over. After that, Jazz permitted his hormones and the crack cocaine to dictate what to do.

He didn't really like Silver Wings, but at least the man was clean and less obnoxious than some people who'd tried to get with him in the past. And Silver Wings kept the pipes coming. Sometimes when Jazz craved a smoke, his senses went dull, but sometimes—like now—they got super sensitive. He knew the moment someone entered the backyard and walked toward the apartment. The step wasn't heavy like Silver Wings'. Lighter. Like Juan's. Jazz's spirits climbed, jolting him into action. He stood in the middle of the room, waiting expectantly. But before the door opened, he was drained of energy. Exhausted, he sank onto the thick plush cushions of the sofa. Juan greeted him with a smile. Jazz responded with a wave of the hand.

"Hey, man. How'ya doing?"

"You bring a pipe?"

"You're going apeshit over that crap. Mr. Silver Wings says you getting expensive."

"Good. If he doesn't like me, I can come back to you."

"Oh, he says you as good in bed as you ever was. But he hoped you'd spend some time with him at the pool. Be sociable, you know."

"Why? All he wants is for me to fuck him."

"Sure, he wants that, okay. But he'd like to show you off now and then. Make his friends jealous. Maybe share you with them now'n then."

Jazz's stomach turned. For a moment he thought he was going to lose it. Some deep slow breaths dealt with the weird feeling crawling around in his blood vessels. His cheeks burned. Aware that Juan was watching him closely, he changed the subject. "How come Silver Wings thinks I'm eighteen?" he asked.

"'Cause I told him you was. He likes them young. You tell him any different?"

Jazz shook his head. "What's the man's real name? Calling him Silver Wings is stupid."

"That's what he likes to be called. And the man who brings the pipes gets called what he wants, no?" Jazz nodded, and the man relaxed before casually saying, "Met a friend of yours yesterday."

"Who's that?"

"That Paul fellow. He's damned good-looking. I dig that blond hair and blue eyes."

Jazz struggled to focus. That didn't sound right.

"Why you frowning, man?"

"He's not blond," Jazz said.

"Did I say blond? Black hair, right? He's so sexy I don't blame you for getting it on with him. Who gets to be top in that arrangement?"

Jazz shook his head. "I never made it with Paul."

"Why not?"

Alarm bells went off in his head. Something wasn't right. Something he needed to remember. BJ! He glanced at Juan and found himself under scrutiny.

"What's wrong?" Juan asked.

"Nothing." He struggled to pick up the threads of the conversation. Man, he needed a pipe. "I wouldn't have minded, but Paul was with somebody else last time I saw him. That's a couple of years ago."

"You ain't seen him since then?"

"Naw. He lives in Albuquerque. I'm up in Farmington... well, before."

Juan's scowl worried him. Had he screwed something up? He worked to keep from shaking his head to clear his thoughts. BJ. Good-looking, sexy BJ. That's who was searching for him. Why? That part of his life was past. Why the hell would B. J. Vinson be looking for him? Then he remembered again. BJ was a detective. He looked for people. For lost people.

Jazz couldn't contain his frown. Was he lost?

Chapter 9

I BACKED the Impala into a parking space right in front of the Flying Star. Henry and I had a view of part of the outdoor sitting area, although it was below the level of the parking lot, which meant the restraining wall blocked a number of tables from our sight. I use my car for surveillance on occasion, so the windows were tinted a little darker than was legal. I know confidential investigators who won't use tinted windows, saying they attract attention, but in Albuquerque, the windows on half the cars are opaque.

"I didn't see Juan's Fusion," Henry said.

"There's excess parking in back. Here's Paul," I said as a red Focus passed slowly between us and the restaurant. I checked my watch. Eleven twenty-five. "Right on time. Put the bug in your ear."

This time we had elected to wire Paul for sound. The Flying Star wasn't the quietest place around, but neither was it the noisiest. Gene felt we had a good shot at overhearing the conversation between the two of them.

"Where's his cop tail?"

"Probably already inside with Charlie. It's Detective Carson. He'll be sitting along the rail in the upper area where the power outlets are. He can hook up, look like a computer geek, and talk away without anyone thinking anything about it."

A moment later Paul apparently activated his mike, as we heard sounds from inside the restaurant. I imagined I heard his heart pounding from excitement. Mine was racing from fear.

Five minutes later, a figure entered the restaurant by the lower-level door off the patio area.

"Was that him?" Henry asked.

"Yep. The party's on."

Then we heard a rustle as if Paul got to his feet. "Hi, Juan. Glad you could make it."

"Looking good, man. You been waiting long?"

"Nah. Just got here myself."

We heard some meaningless, getting reacquainted, sizing-one-another-up stuff. The Flying Star is a self-order place, but neither man went to order a meal. That was partially explained when Paul said he hoped Juan liked espresso, because that's what he'd bought.

Silence, and then: "You want something to eat, man?"

"No," Paul said. "Just want to meet and talk."

"Cool." A pause. "That dude you asked me about, you ever catch up with him?"

"Jazz? Uh-uh. And I'm getting a little worried about him. Nobody's heard from him in a month or so."

"How you know?"

"You remember his brother, Henry? I saw him the other day, and he said Jazz is still missing."

"His brother still in town?"

"Yeah. So far as I know. Think he took a job somewhere."

"C&W?"

"Don't think so. Believe he's a landscaper. Didn't ask for particulars."

"Why not? He looks like a handful. They grow them good in that family."

"Don't think he swings that way, and I'm not about to find out. He'd probably wring my neck if I tried anything."

"We can only dream, no?"

I glanced at Henry's flushed face. I don't think he imagined ever being discussed like a piece of meat by a couple of guys. If he only knew. It probably happened at least once a day.

"How about Jazz?" Juan asked. "He looks like a wet dream, but is he any good?"

"You tell me. Is he?"

"You never made it with him? Why not, man?"

"Only met him once up in Farmington. It was sorta a business trip, and I was with other people. We just never managed to get any time together."

"Where'd you meet him?"

"Place called the Sidewinder Inn on the south side of Farmington."

"Gay place?"

"As far as I know there isn't a gay place in Farmington. But Jazz hung out there. I guess word got around that if you mess with Jazz, you've got Henry to deal with." Paul cleared his throat. "What happens now? With us, I mean?"

Juan's chuckle came across the wire. "You getting anxious?"

"I'm getting hungry."

"Man, you oughta have boyfriends hanging all over you. Just crook your finger, and they'll come running."

"Look. I'm careful, and I'm cautious. I don't want every man I see. But when I see one I want, well...." Paul left the thought unfinished.

"You steaming me up, man. I ain't gonna be able to get up and look decent."

"And if you know where Jazz is, well, let's just say that while I'm not usually into threesomes, I'd make an exception for him."

"Wish I did, dude. Last time I heard, he was all wrapped up in Mr. Silver Wings."

"Mr. Silver Wings? Who's that?"

Juan paused a beat. "Dunno. That's all I ever heard him called. You see him on the scene from time to time."

"Scene?"

"You know, parties."

"Parties? How do I get invited to that kind of party?"

"Might be able to get you an invite. But right now, it's just you'n me. And we come to the crunch, no? It's different strokes for different folks. How you go, man?"

"I'm a top."

"Like Jazz, huh?" Perhaps as if realizing his mistake, Juan rushed on. "Meet me at the Anasazi Motel at eight tonight. Room 110, and I'll make you forget about parties. Hell, we'll have a party of our own."

"So we're compatible?" Paul asked.

"Don't you worry, guy. Juan will make sure we fit like a glove."

In seconds, Juan appeared at the patio door and vanished around the corner. I expected to see Carson on his tail, but instead I heard a commotion inside the café. The voices were muted, indicating the trouble wasn't in Paul's immediate vicinity. Then I heard my lover's worried call.

"BJ, inside!"

I tossed the keys to Henry, yelled for him to follow Juan, and bailed to run for the restaurant. By the time I maneuvered the steps down to the patio level and reached the door, a man burst through, knocking me on my butt. I managed to snag his arm as I went down, dislodging the laptop he was carrying. It clattered to the concrete. Charlie was on his heels but tripped over my legs and almost went down. The fleeing man didn't pause to pick up the laptop.

Paul appeared and helped me up while disturbed and excited patrons took their seats again after witnessing an event neither they nor I understood. I began to fit things together when a disheveled Don Carson appeared in the doorway.

"Fucker stole my laptop!" he exclaimed.

"It's there on the deck. Fell out of his hand when he barreled into me."

The detective lunged for the machine and picked it up gingerly. "Damn, hope this didn't break. It's my personal computer."

"What happened?" I asked as we walked around the corner to the rear parking lot to get away from curious ears.

"I was sitting at the row of tables with power plugs for computers, watching Paul and recording their conversation. I have this Dragon program that translates speech to the computer. But I have to edit it to—"

"And?" I prompted.

"And this guy kept walking back and forth," Don explained. "I didn't catch on at first because he wore a hat, but I think it was Gaspard."

"I thought he was in custody," Paul said.

"I did too."

Charlie walked back from where he'd disappeared down the alley. "Gaspard got away. Yeah, it was him. Heard he bonded out this morning."

Carson picked up his tale again. "Anyway, all of a sudden, he shoves me off the stool and grabs my computer. Think he caught on to who I was."

"I'd say so," I agreed.

When we returned to the restaurant, I saw my Impala turn in off Juan Tabo and knew that Henry hadn't been able to follow Juan. Our only links to the people holding Jazz had vanished. And they wouldn't be easy to find again.

Chapter 10

NAUSEA AND a slight cramping in his gut pulled Jazz from a restless sleep. Surprised to find it was morning, he hugged his belly as he kicked off the light sheet covering him. The gagging eased, allowing him to stand. He drew on a pair of walking shorts and shrugged into a white T-shirt. At least they kept him clean. *They.* Who were they? Silver Wings, he supposed. He slipped his feet into thongs and prepared to face another endless, boring day. The big television set—the thing must have measured fifty inches—played only porn. Probably on a tape, since the films seemed to repeat themselves no matter what channel he tried, and there were only four of them. He disdained raw films that once would have titillated him but now were simply offensive.

Kim the houseboy usually brought his breakfast before now. Half the time he didn't want it. He was off his feed. Seldom got hungry... except for the pipes.

The shy Asian servant must have been part of the "family," because he sported a small white spot in his coal black hair. Jazz figured that was a brand. His own was located on the back of his head and required the aid of a mirror to see.

He glanced toward the door and was surprised to find it ajar. He approached cautiously and swung it wide. A covered tray sat on the threshold. Had Kim brought it and left the door unlocked so he could escape?

Jazz stepped over the tray and out onto the walkway, pausing to allow a wave of dizziness to pass. Should he eat something before he escaped? Nah. What afflicted him wasn't hunger but his craving for a pipe. The thought of food turned his stomach. The pipe or the snow-white rows of powder would settle his stomach. Only the cocaine provided relief.

The hacienda-style house blocking the far end of a broad, manicured lawn was the biggest home he'd ever seen. A castle without turrets or ramparts. A swimming pool lay close to the rear of the big house, glistening green and sparkly in the morning light. No one was in sight.

Increasingly jumpy, Jazz inspected the tall wall that surrounded the place. Light brown stucco with no hand or toeholds. He was pretty sure a running jump would allow him to lay hands on the top, but it was rounded and smooth. Nothing to get a grip on. He scratched his arms to free his skin of tiny creatures that were not there as he wandered the yard, looking for something to give him an advantage. Nothing... until he spotted a light fixture near where the wall adjoined the bungalow blocking this end of the property.

It took him three running tries to grasp the stubby fixture. Shocked that he lacked the strength to simply pull himself over the wall, he fell back to the grass. What was the matter with him? Why was he so weak?

He tried again. By shedding his sandals, he was able to grasp the light fixture, walk up the wall, and eventually pull himself atop it. Exhausted and seized by sweats and tremors, he sat for a moment. No one stirred from the house. Jesus, he needed a pipe!

Once he collected himself, Jazz got to his feet atop the wall with the strong scent of sage assaulting his nostrils as he searched for a good place to drop on the other side. A vast field of spiky cacti and other desert plants stretched to a distant line of green trees. That must be the Bosque he'd always heard about, groves of cottonwoods lining either side of the Rio Grande. He'd been right; he was on the west side of town.

As he decided on a likely landing place, nausea struck him again, this time so sharply he almost doubled over. He paused to gather his strength before escaping.

Escape to where? To what? He had no ID, no money, no telephone. Hell, he didn't even have shoes. They were in the grass on the other side of the wall. Ahead lay a terrain guaranteed to cut his feet to pieces. Behind, lay comfort... and a pipe.

He wasn't certain if it was by design or if the mischievous Coyote nudged him, but he toppled backward. He hoped he broke his neck in the fall. But the jolt as he hit the ground merely knocked the breath out of him. As he lay stunned on the grass, movement caught his eye.

Ants. A column of ants marched across the leafy grass not a foot from his nose. Ants. Silver Wings' castle wasn't perfect. He had ants. Like everybody else, the man had insects. Jazz giggled.

A shadow covered him, causing him to glance up. Silver Wings loomed over him, a smirk on his broad mouth. "Going somewhere?"

Jazz didn't bother to answer. He just smiled and pointed. "You have ants."

"So I do. It's good to see you smile, Jazz. It's a great smile. Makes you more handsome than ever. Would you like your pipe now? Think we'll try a bong instead of the glass pipe this time with a little cannabis mixed in. Makes things higher and the comedown mellower."

"Cool."

Chapter 11

HENRY WAS almost to the point of needing a straitjacket. The failure of his first investigative case made Paul morose. But I didn't have time to flail or brood. I needed to find another way into the traffickers' family—and quickly. After our Flying Star fiasco, they'd ship Jazz out of the country, if they hadn't already. Another thought chilled me. Or kill him if he presented a risk to them.

I left Paul trying to reach Juan by email and walked the two blocks from my office building to police headquarters on Marquette. Gene, Don Carson, and I sat in his office and listened to a tape of Paul's meeting this morning and read the automatic transcript Dragon made of the conversation. The laptop wasn't damaged, and we sat analyzing the exchange between the two men.

"Paul made a mistake right there," Gene said when my lover asked if Juan knew where Jazz was.

"Possibly, but it didn't seem to bother Juan any. And Juan made his share of them, especially when he acknowledged that Jazz is a top."

"Is he?" Gene asked with a laugh lurking in his eyes.

"I wouldn't know."

"Yeah, right. This Juan's not gonna show up at the Anasazi tonight. I hope you know that."

"I do. What happened between Don and Gaspard took care of that."

"But we'll be there, just in case. Room 110, right?" Gene said.

"I hope that damned Gaspard shows up," Don put in. "I owe him for a scraped elbow and a skinned shin."

NOT SURPRISINGLY, Paul failed to receive a response to any of his email messages. Without much hope, Paul, Henry, and I set out for the Anasazi Motel on East Central not far from downtown around seven thirty. Don Carson and a backup detective left before we did to get into place—just in case. At the same time Paul knocked on the door to 110—with Henry and me hovering just out of sight—Don and his partner entered the motel office and demanded to know who was registered in that unit. No one answered Paul's knock, and the manager, an untidy man with a scraggly beard, insisted the room wasn't rented and readily handed over keys to the two detectives. That, of course, ensured that the place was scrubbed down and would give us nothing. Even so, Don called in a crime scene unit to see if they could raise any fingerprints that might prove useful.

Gene joined us in the parking lot while the forensics people worked on the room. The mood was sour even though the results were not unexpected. As Gene and I leaned against the fender of the Impala, I gave the motel a once-over. It wasn't a bad place. Not upscale, but not a run-down joint, either. I wouldn't have felt out of place taking one of their rooms for the night. Apparently Gene's thoughts ran on a parallel.

"Hard to see this motel as a part of the circuit." I understood he meant one of the safe locations for the traffickers. "Too expensive."

I nodded even though I wasn't convinced. "Possibly, but think about this. Anyone coming to meet Jazz Penrod wouldn't go to a run-down dive."

"He's that special, is he?"

"Without a doubt. Anyone controlling Jazz—or another man or woman like him—would charge escort-type prices. They'd never put Jazz on the street for $20 or $50 or even $100. Nope, they'd ask a thousand dollars for a night with Jazz."

"Well, I don't know—"

"Come on, Gene. You've seen his picture. This kid *is* special. And think about this. At eleven thirty this morning, Juan was able to give Paul his room number. That meant he knew the room was available. I doubt he rented the room before he came to lunch. No, this is a traffickers' place."

"You could be right. I'll check into ownership."

"Did you figure out who might have blown the whistle on the raid on the My Other Home?"

"I'm no dummy, BJ. I know human trafficking is big business and generates lots of dollars. Some cops are susceptible to turning a blind eye now and then, but so help me, I looked at the record of every cop who took part in that raid and can't find a one who raises an eyebrow."

"Cops talk. I'll bet the whole department knew the raid was going down."

"True, but they wouldn't know the details. Like *when*, for example."

"They could pin it down to a couple of hours, and that's enough. What do you know about the Citizens' Commission Against Human Trafficking?"

"Like I told you, it's one of those NGOs that's the backbone of fighting trafficking. Across the nation, they probably do more to fight the problem than the police do. The board seems to be all upstanding citizens. Hell, one of our own, Chester Bolton, sits on it alongside Roscoe Haldemain and Bishop Gregory."

"Lieutenant Bolton's on the board?"

"Yep. For about five years now."

"Have you talked to him about the leak?"

"Yeah, I talked to him. And calling it a leak is an assumption, you know."

"Do you doubt it? Those two kids didn't point a finger at that seedy motel by mistake."

"Naw. I don't doubt it. Somebody warned them we were coming."

"Think we'd be welcome at the next board meeting of the Citizens Council Against Human Trafficking?"

"I can find out."

After the crime scene unit gave an unofficial opinion that the only fingerprints they found in Room 110 belonged to the cleaning staff, we all took our various frustrations, stresses, and problems home. All except Henry. He headed for the Blue Spruce and told us not to expect him back tonight.

PAUL AND I took advantage of the privacy to cuddle on the sofa in the den and watch an episode of *The Pacific*, a ten-part series that grew out of *Band of Brothers*. But it was a restless time because Jazz Penrod haunted both our minds. While we lay in the comfort of one another's arms, what was that kid going through?

We were into the news, filled with references to Barack Obama and the antics of Sarah Palin, when my cell phone went off. Henry's outraged voice filled my ear when I answered.

"They hauled me down to the jail, man! No reason. Just invaded my space with guns drawn and threw me in the back of a car."

"Calm down. Are you at the police station or at the detention center?"

"Police station. Been questioning me about weird things. Little girls and little boys on the reservation."

"Were you fighting or driving drunk?"

"Naw. I don't even have a buzz on. Besides, wasn't riding. Came outa the bar with this girl I met. As soon as I threw a leg over the hog, five of them showed up with pistols drawn."

"Okay. Hang on. I'll be down as soon as I can."

"Can that Lieutenant Enriquez do anything?"

"I'll see."

I hung up and called Gene at home. He promised to see what he could find out. Paul and I raced around throwing on decent clothes and were in the front seat of the Impala when my phone rang again.

"Something's not right, BJ," Gene said. "They got a call about a dangerous human trafficker with a gun at the Blue Spruce. Henry's Harley-Davidson was described right down to the license plate. As soon as he showed up to reclaim it, they took him down."

"Did he resist?"

"Not with half a dozen service pistols aimed at his head. I'm on my way downtown now."

"We'll meet you there."

"We?"

"Paul and I."

HENRY WAS a smoldering volcano when Gene and I entered the interview room. Paul remained in the waiting area. A husky detective with a blond buzz-cut I didn't know conducted the interview. He looked startled at the invasion.

"What are you doing here, Lieutenant?"

"Trying to find out what's going on."

"I'm interviewing—"

"I can see that. But why?"

"Sir, this is highly improper. Is this man the perp's attorney?"

"I agree it's improper," Gene said. "This is B. J. Vinson, a private investigator. And a former cop, I might add. My riding partner, as a matter of fact. BJ, meet Detective Charles Zimmerman of our Vice Unit. Detective, will you step outside so we can straighten out a couple of things?"

As soon as we were in the hallway, Gene turned on the officer. "Zim, why did you bust this man at the Blue Spruce tonight?"

"I got a tip this pimp was going to be there. Armed and dangerous."

"Where did this tip come from? Did it name Henry Secatero or merely describe him?"

"Sir, I don't report to you."

"No, you don't. Would you prefer to answer my questions or have me haul your lieutenant out of bed and drag him down here so we can continue a conversation we're going to have anyway?"

Zimmerman, who was about thirty and looked to be bulked up from gym work, backed off. "It was from a confidential source."

"A registered source?"

"No, sir. But I've used him before, and he's always been reliable."

"Who is he?"

"Sorry, but I can't reveal his name.

"What did he say?"

"This guy was supposed to be the local organization's connection to the Navajo Reservation. A lot of—"

"I'm aware the reservation has a problem with traffickers. Did they call this so-called pimp by name?"

"Yes, sir. Henry Secatero. Description too. That guy in there matches it to a tee."

"Was he armed?"

"No firearm, but a knife that borders on illegal."

"Why did Vice make the bust instead of SVU if that was the info?"

"Because I'm the one who got the tip. What's the problem, Lieutenant?"

"The problem is that man in there works in the coal mine on the reservation, and while he might chase all the women on the reservation, he doesn't sell them. You've been given a bum steer, Detective, and I'd like to know where it came from. We'll straighten this out tomorrow when your lieutenant's on duty. Uh, today's Friday, so make that Monday morning. Are you going to hang on to Mr. Secatero or cut him loose?"

"If you vouch for him, I'll cut him loose."

I noticed a slight hesitation before Gene said the words that released Henry. I understood it. After all, I was the one who knew Henry, not Gene.

Once we left the stationhouse, Gene headed home while Paul and I took Henry back to the Blue Spruce to collect his bike. Henry went silent in the back seat of the car as we climbed the long hill eastward up what had once been Route 66 but was now East Central Avenue.

"You gonna pick up your bike and come on home, or are you going back inside?" Paul broke the silence.

"I go back in, I'm gonna end up back at the police station for busting some heads. How come they came for me like that?"

"The detective said he received a tip about an armed and dangerous sex trafficker named Henry Secatero in the club. They set up a stakeout on your bike."

Henry tried to modulate his voice and almost succeeded. "Who'n the hell would claim that?"

"Zimmerman said a confidential informant fingered you by name, rank, and serial number—so to speak."

"Juan knew about Henry. Figured out he was in town, remember?" Paul said.

"I do. And I think we just identified the informant. Which is interesting, because while the detective wouldn't name the informant, he said he'd used him before and found him reliable."

"Go pry the name out of him," Henry said.

"Gene tried, but Zimmerman refused. Gene will contact the man's supervisor Monday and see what he can find out. But if what happened this morning didn't tell us we've been blown, this confirms it."

"Shit," Henry exclaimed. "What does that mean for Jazz?"

"Nothing good."

Chapter 12

JAZZ ALWAYS knew when something was up. Silver Wings—who by now he'd reduced to simply Wings—gave him powder cocaine most of the time. But when the man wanted something special from Jazz, Kim always brought the glass pipe shaped like an erect penis. Jazz snickered the first time he saw it and asked if somebody didn't understand which end got sucked on. The powder lasted longer but the pipe gave him the biggest, fastest jolt. This afternoon Wings promised the pipe when Jazz joined his swimming party.

Jazz stood at the picture window and gazed at the pool across the wide lawn. Although he had no way of knowing for sure, he judged it was the weekend. Five men lounged on chairs or splashed in the water. Fuck 'em. He wouldn't go. He wouldn't "join the party" as Wings insisted. What could they do to him? Beat him? He wished they'd try. He needed to hit someone. He'd considered slugging prim, trim Kim when he refused to give up Wings' real name. He knew Kim had the name. The slender Asian acted as butler, answering the door when callers arrived. Did everyone ask for Mr. Silver Wings? No, they asked for Mr. Smith or Jones or Winterbottom.

He watched Kim's graceful white-coated figure move among the guests, delivering drinks and lighting cigars or cigarettes. Did Kim know jujitsu or karate or any of that other oriental kickass shit? He might just find out one day.

Jazz felt a stirring in his belly. His legs itched as if tiny sugar ants crawled across them. Wings told him the afternoon pipe waiting for him poolside was a bong with cannabis added. The time or two Wings provided a bong, Jazz liked the way he banged on the ceiling and came down mellower.

He glanced at the bed where a skimpy scrap of red-and-blue material lay. That was supposed to be his swimsuit. It didn't even have a butt to it, just a little cord that fit between his cheeks. Might as well just go naked.

Jazz paced, jumped into the shower to wash off bugs that weren't there, tried to sleep but couldn't lie still on the bed. Nothing worked. Finally he gave in, put on the ridiculous bathing suit, and snugged a big beach towel around his waist before leaving the bungalow.

Conversation around the pool ceased as he stepped through the doorway. His flesh crawled beneath the stares of the men as he strolled toward them. No one said a word until Wings indicated the chair beside him.

"Reserved just for you. But shed the towel before you sit."

Fighting an uncomfortable feeling of something—mortification, probably—he dropped the towel and quickly fell into the lounge, feeling the weight of the strangers' stares as he did so. He closed his eyes and tried to relax. He wasn't shy. He'd had lovers and was proud of his body. But this was different. He was on display. No choice in the matter. He opened his eyes when he heard Wings tell Kim to bring Jazz's pipe.

It was the bong. Great. Not only was the hit better, but nobody could crack jokes about the shape of the thing. He lit the pipe, inhaled deeply, and held the smoke in his lungs for as long as possible. Immediately his nausea went away. He came alive. Aware of every pore on his body, the light sprinkling of hair on his arms, his nails on his toes. If he really tried, he could probably caress his soul.

"You've got a winner there, Rex. Where'd you find him?"

Rex? Was that Wing's first name? It was a start. A flush of self-satisfaction warmed his cheeks.

"He found me in a motel room." Jazz was as startled as anyone at the sound of his own baritone. He hadn't intended to say that. Say anything.

"Well, lead me to that motel," said a bulked-up man with a forest of graying hair on his chest and belly.

"Don't bother, Tom," Wings—or Rex—answered. "There aren't any more like him."

"My God, he's incredible. I've never seen anyone as beautiful as he is, not even a woman." This from a slender man just crawling out of the pool introduced as "Doc," a man who carried a professional air even as he was raking Jazz with steel gray eyes.

Jazz felt his cheeks sting. Didn't they know he could hear them? He took another draw on the pipe, and things seemed less personal. Let 'em look. He spread his legs more comfortably and heard muffled gasps. He closed his eyes again to concentrate on the smoke in his lungs.

"What'd you pay for him?" a hard-muscled man lying with a youth on a double lounge asked. Jazz glanced in his direction and saw the kid wore the white brand in his hair. One of his long, thin hands rested on the man's inner thigh.

"Asked twenty-five, but I chiseled them down to twenty-two." Jazz nearly jumped when Rex put a hand on his arm. "Well worth it, let me tell you."

"Big?" Doc asked.

"Fucking A," Jazz said, surprising himself once again.

"From the horse's mouth," Doc contributed.

"Appropriate comparison," Rex said with a self-satisfied smirk in his voice.

A burst of energy propelled Jazz out of his chair and into the pool. He tried swimming, but the uncomfortable cord buried between his buns chafed. He stopped and tore the tiny suit off, casting it over the heads of the startled men at poolside. Ignoring exclamations that sounded like cheers, he swam as if a horde of demons were on his trail.

Just as suddenly, his store of energy evaporated, leaving him tired and weak. He clung to the side of the pool and yelled for Kim to bring him his suit.

"Oh no," Rex said. "You threw it away. You go get it."

Jazz scanned five pairs of eager eyes. Fuck it. He pulled himself out of the pool and strolled to the chair where he'd left his towel, bringing a cascade of dripping water with him. He picked up the terrycloth and buried his face in its softness. As he lowered the towel, he saw to his horror that he'd left his pipe smoking. Jeez! He'd wasted most of it. Still exposed to the men's stares, he picked up the bong and sucked the last of the smoke into his lungs. Then he threw the towel over his shoulder and leisurely strolled back to the bungalow.

As soon as the door closed behind him, Jazz looked around for something to punch. He pummeled the cushions on the sofa until his energy ebbed again. Then he threw himself on the bed and put an arm over his eyes as waves of shame swept over him. His belly fluttered. His heart stuttered… raced. What was the matter with him? Why did he parade around like that? That wasn't like him.

He listened to the door open and close without removing his arm to take a look. Which one would it be? Did it matter?

"That was quite a show you put on out there."

It was Tom, the man with the gray chest and belly hair. Jazz lay with his eyes closed, face half-hidden by his arm.

"The bidding really shot up after that display, I can tell you."

Jazz took a breath and exhaled.

"You haven't finished drying off. Here, let me do it for you."

The man brushed his body with the soft towel. The swipes soon became caresses, and before long, Tom cast the towel aside and substituted his lips. Jazz lay without making a sound as the man took what he wanted. He willed his flesh to fail but felt himself grow firm. Jazz concentrated on listening to the blood sing in his veins while Tom brought him to climax.

Chapter 13

SATURDAY MORNING I was in the den reading a follow-up story about the January 12 Haitian earthquake that killed 230,000 people and made 1,000,000 citizens homeless when Gene surprised me with a phone call to inform me the Citizens' Council Against Human Trafficking would hold a board meeting at eleven Monday morning in Roscoe Haldemain's corporate offices boardroom. We were invited to attend around eleven thirty after the routine stuff—like the reading of the minutes and such—would be out of the way. Paul and Henry both fumed in frustrated silence because they couldn't go to the meeting with us.

Gene chose to walk to my building on Monday, and after he collected me, we hoofed it a block and a half to the Plaza Tower adjacent to the Hyatt Regency at 3rd and Copper NW. Del Dahlman's law firm, Stone, Hedges, Martinez, etc., also known as the Blahs—as in blah, blah, blah—took the entire top floor of the tower. Del was my first long-term lover, who fell away when he couldn't deal with my getting shot on the job with APD. After some rough times, we managed to salvage a friendship, for which I was grateful. In fact, he was my best client. He threw a lot of business my way.

Haldemain and Haldemain, Attorneys-at-Law, LLC were anything but ambulance chasers, but they must have been slightly lower on the lawyer scale because their offices were on the floor below the Blahs. That was still a better address than most of the horde of attorneys in Albuquerque could manage.

"Two Haldemains?" Gene asked as we exited the elevator and headed for the suite.

"Yeah, his older brother, William P., started the firm. Roscoe joined him soon after. I get the feeling William does the work and Ross—as he likes to be called—is the public or PR face of the team. It's a successful firm. I've done some work for them from time to time."

We pushed through the heavy double doors and walked into a sumptuous waiting room to confront a spectacular brunette receptionist.

She apparently expected us because she immediately ushered us into a large conference room occupied by four men and one woman. The windows of the Haldemain conference room framed the same Sandia Peak and Manzano mountain chain as did the Blah meeting room... minus ten feet of elevation.

Ross performed the introductions, although Gene and I already knew everyone, at least by sight. The woman was a bouncy, five-foot-two dynamo named Betsy Brockmire. The story was that her Chicago commercial builder husband died a few years back and left her enough money to come west to pursue her passion as an activist for women's rights.

I'd met Bishop Justin Gregory socially a few times but could not claim to really know the man. He showed up in Albuquerque from somewhere in Georgia about five years ago and founded the Temple of Our Lord on High, which was actually on Lomas, although it was appropriately located in the Northeast Heights. The church was originally a black congregation, but I'd heard that Anglos and Hispanics had begun to attend. I knew nothing of ecclesiastical affairs but wondered how the pastor of a single church could be a bishop, but it was all right by me if no one else objected. At around 190, he was a bit rotund, but his white-streaked coiffure gave him a dignified, grandfatherly air even though he couldn't have been more than fifty.

William Haldemain could have been his brother's doppelgänger so far as size and way of carrying themselves were concerned. Ross probably stood my height—six feet—and closer examination showed William to be an inch shorter. The most striking thing about the two men was their hair. Ross's was brown with silver at his temples, drawn back in what my father once called a duck's tail. William's black locks were similarly adorned with silver and styled in an identical manner. The two men looked to be wearing perpetual crowns.

The fourth man in the room, Lt. Chester Bolton—better known as either Lieutenant or Bolt, depending upon your status—headed the Homicide Department at APD, under which the Special Victims Unit fell. Barrel-chested and no-nonsense, he was a police officer of some twenty-five years' service. He'd taught a class or two at the academy when I went through it, and I was convinced he had it out for me—possibly because I was gay—until the day I graduated. Then he told me how proud of me he was.

"And what brings you to us?" Ross said after everyone settled down.

Gene and I had argued earlier over how to answer that question. I wanted to remain vague and simply nose around to learn what we could. My ex-partner said Bolton was too smart for that. He wanted to lay it all out on the table.

Gene answered the question. "A few days ago, BJ contacted me regarding a young man by the name of Jasper Penrod who'd gone missing from his Farmington home. He goes by Jazz. Since there was some evidence the missing man came to Albuquerque, his half brother went to BJ for assistance because he and his brother once helped BJ on a case up in the Bisti area. By reviewing Jazz's laptop, we've determined he contacted someone through nm.lonelyguys.com and started an online relationship. Jazz is gay, by the way. Shortly after they started communicating by Skype, Jazz disappeared. No one's heard from him since. We think he's been snagged by human traffickers, specifically sex traffickers.

"How old is the child?" Betsy asked.

"He's not a child. He's a half-Navajo man twenty-one-years of age."

"Impossible," she said. "Victims are usually female and between the ages of thirteen to fifteen. He doesn't fit the pattern."

"Not the usual pattern," I said. "But I read his emails, and Jazz was definitely being lured into the scene by a fellow who called himself Juan. This Juan took his time and was quite skillful in his approach. As soon as he saw Jazz's photo, he knew he had gold on the other end of his internet."

I slid the close-up photo Jazz provided Juan across the table. William Haldemain snatched it up.

"There must be some mistake. This kid can't be that old. Eighteen at the most." He slid the photo to his brother.

"Mother Nature was kind to Jazz," I said. "Good genes, I expect." I slid over another photograph. "And this is the photo the pimp sent Jazz, claiming it was of himself. Notice the white streak in his hair. We believe that's the brand of this particular 'family.'"

After that photo followed the first around the table, Betsy was less assertive in her denial the situation fit the usual picture. Gene laid it all out for the five individuals. He told them of contact with both Gaspard and Juan, of picking up the two "branded" kids, and the abortive raid on the west-side motel… everything. The fact that Juan also had a white spot on his crown immediately painted him as a victim in Betsy's eyes. I wasn't so sure.

"You think that's a brand?" Ross ran a hand over his graying temples. "Hell, then I guess I'm a vic too."

"And me," William joined in, mimicking his brother's hand brushing.

The bishop merely pointed at this gray-speckled head. "Me too."

The lieutenant laughed. "What I have left up there probably qualifies me, as well."

"As a matter of fact," Gene said. "We've come across the name 'Silver Wings' as one of the pimps." He reconsidered. "Or maybe one of the johns."

"Any description?" Lieutenant Bolton asked.

"Sorry, nothing more than that name."

Once they asked all their questions, each member of the board pledged assistance. Betsy agreed to put out the alarm to her sources immediately. They'd spare no effort in trying to find Jazz. Once that was out of the way, I spoke up.

"I know this missing man. He's very independent, very self-sufficient. He was openly gay but not promiscuous. Bristled at the thought of prostituting himself. I'm having trouble understanding why he doesn't simply walk out of the situation. Go home. Call me. Flag down a police officer. It doesn't make sense."

"It doesn't make sense to you or me," Betsy said, "but it does make a crazy kind of sense to the victims. And if you've described this Jazz accurately, you may have answered your own question."

"How so?"

"He was a proud young man, clearly attractive, making it on his own. But something must have been lacking in his life if he went on the internet looking for companionship. I suspect he was seeking something deeper, more meaningful. He gets roped into coming to meet this Juan character. Juan gives him what he wants and establishes a relationship.

"Then Juan introduces something new. A drug of some kind. Probably crack cocaine. It's powerful and very quickly addictive. Juan claims it will make things infinitely better between them. And it does, temporarily. Then the victim finds he needs the drug more than he needs the relationship. Juan suggests he can earn his way by taking care of a few friends. The first thing Jazz knows, his lover is pimping him out to people who can pay. Not street contacts. More like Jazz is now a high-priced escort.

"One day Jazz might wake up to what's happening to him and decide to get out of it. But what does he do? They've kept him broke. He needs his fix regularly. But worse, he's ashamed of what he's become. The thought his family and friends will learn what he did is a powerful psychological benefit to his pimps. They probably locked him up at first, but I doubt that's necessary now."

I left the meeting with a cold shiver running down my back. What if my friend couldn't face the consequences? What then?

Chapter 14

AFTER LUNCH Henry took off on his Harley, on the lookout for street kids with white spots in their hair. I did not try to discourage him. After all, our search for Jazz was blown by the abortive meeting at Flying Star last Friday. I just hoped he didn't get busted by a cop thinking he was trying to buy some underage kid's services.

I spent my time calling other law jurisdictions—such as the Rio Rancho Police Department and the Sandoval County Sheriff's Office— to put out the word we were on the hunt for a victim named Jazz Penrod. I even called Sergeant Dix Lee at the Farmington PD. We'd worked together on the Bisti murder case in which Henry and his brother were involved. She knew Jazz.

"Well, well, if it isn't that handsome hunk from down Albuquerque way gracing the other end of this line," she said as she answered her page.

"How's my favorite cop?" I came back at her.

"Don't give me that. Your favorite cop has short hair and never wore a skirt. You calling about Jazz? Hope you found him."

"No, but think we found his trail."

"Does it lead right back up here?"

"Wish it did," I said.

"Maybe it does. We found his Jeep Wrangler the other day. Or at least the Navajo Tribal Police found it parked at tribal headquarters in Window Rock."

"In Arizona?"

"Yep. They called Lonzo Joe when they saw a BOLO he put out on the vehicle. You remember Lonzo?"

Lonzo was a Navajo detective with the San Juan County Sheriff's Office who interfaced with Farmington PD a lot since he worked out of the shared lab on their premises.

"Sure do. How's he doing?"

"Right as a rain dance. Anyway, he processed the Jeep. Nothing. Whoever drove it last wiped it clean. Even the places they sometimes

forget, like the rearview mirror. Lonzo stirred up everybody on both sides
of the reservation border, but nobody's found hide nor hair of Jazz."

"That's because he's not there. He's down here, and so was his
vehicle."

"Then what's it doing back up in our neck of the woods? Misdirection,
maybe."

"Exactly. It's probably been there for a while. The pimps want us
to think he's still in the Four Corners area."

"Pimps?"

I walked her through the entire situation. When I finished, she was
silent for a moment. I could mentally see her sitting there twisting a long
strand of blonde hair between two fingers. A sign she was thinking.

"BJ, can you hold on? I think Lonzo's in the building. I want you
to talk to him."

I twiddled my thumbs for five minutes before she and the San Juan
County detective picked up receivers simultaneously.

"Hey, man," I said at the sound of his voice. "You ever get that
dog-fighting ring rolled up?"

"Yeah, including a couple of family members of the sheriff's. Made
me real popular, I can tell you."

Dix broke in. "BJ, the reason I wanted to catch Lonzo is because of
this sex trafficking thing."

"Yeah, it's a problem over on the rez," Lonzo said. "There's so much
poverty and alcohol the pimps think they can steal our kids and nobody'll
care. Well, I care. We care. But Jazz doesn't fit the profile. He's—"

"Yeah, I know. He's older than usual, and he's male, not female."

"Oh, they take boys too. But you're right, it's mostly girls. And they
occasionally take men and women, but generally to indenture them for labor,
not for the sex trade. Although sometimes they find themselves exploited
that way after they're sold to someone. An added benefit for the buyer."

"You've both seen Jazz and know what a package of raw sex he is.
I'll fax you a copy of our file so far, but there's no question in my mind
he's been sold to someone in the sex trade. Question is, is it someone
local or someone somewhere else, possibly out of the country."

"They move them sometimes," Lonzo said. "But not so much out
of the country nowadays. But then, I gotta admit, Jazz is special. What
does the FBI say?"

"Haven't called them in yet."

"Why not?"

"My ex APD partner is lending me a hand, but if something doesn't break soon, we'll call on them. Anything you can do at that end?" I asked.

"Maybe. Do you have any idea what brand the particular family who took Jazz uses?"

"A spot of white-dyed hair."

"I've seen it. And you're right, that's a brand for some bad dudes we labeled the White Streak family up here."

"Cartel guys?"

"Probably. But maybe not the kind you think. We keep hearing whispers up here that it's a Bulgarian criminal gang who hires local muscle for assistance."

"Do you know their circuit?"

"Here in New Mexico, it's from all parts of the state to Albuquerque, and from Albuquerque to Juárez. From Juárez to Santa Cruz. From there... wherever."

"So if they're moving him, it's probably through the El Paso-Juárez area?"

"Most likely. BJ, there's a guy on the rez I think is a local contractor for them. He fingers kids and isolates them so they can be taken."

"That's not the way they got Jazz."

"I realize that. They used the internet to snare him. But I'm thinking this guy might know some of the stops on the circuit. Specific motels, truck stops, things like that. It might help get a line on some of their safe houses."

"It might. Why haven't you already picked him up?"

"In the first place, I don't have jurisdiction over there. In the second, not enough evidence."

"Turn me loose on him. I don't have the same constraints you cops do. Who is he, anyway?"

"Fellow by the name of Nesposito. Julian Nesposito. He used to be a holy man. Performed healing rituals, but things went wrong in his life. He lost the Harmony Way. Son killed to a car wreck caused by alcohol. Wife gave up and died. Nesposito was one of the first miners on the rez but got so messed up he lost that job. They still call him Hard Hat up here."

"What makes you suspect him?"

"No visible means of support, but he's driving a new Dodge pickup. Spends his time roaming the back roads... visiting relatives, he claims. He got caught with one girl, younger'n usual, around eleven. Claimed he thought she was his cousin's girl and was taking her home. I think the family knew better, but they were either bought off or too scared to rat on him."

"Should I come up?" I asked.

"Not yet. Let me have a crack at him."

"Gotta be soon. If I'm right, our attempts to find Jazz have been blown. They might move him soon. If they haven't already."

"Or worse," Lonzo said, sending a chill down my back.

GENE CALLED me on my cell around four thirty.

"Get over here. Right away. My Other Home Motel." I heard someone call his name before he closed the call. It sounded like Carson.

Paul and Henry had been at the conference table in my office listening to a newscast on a portable TV about a pastor down in Florida named Terry Jones who announced on Twitter—whatever that was— he planned on a public burning of the Koran, kicking off riots all over the Muslim world. As soon as they heard I'd been summoned, they abandoned the TV and insisted on going with me. We piled into the car and pulled out of the parking lot, heading west on Central. All I could do was fend off their questions with "I don't know." But I was alarmed. There had been a strain in Gene's voice that didn't show up often.

Police cars blocked us from approaching closer than a block from the motel. Gene had paved the way for me, and we were escorted on foot to the parking lot, where I spotted my old partner consulting with some other cops. One was Lieutenant Bolton. Bolton spotted us first.

"BJ, what are you doing here?"

"I called him," Gene said.

"Why? Oh, because of the Penrod kid?"

Gene viewed my companions with a jaundiced eye. "I called you, not these two."

"Couldn't leave them behind. What's going on, Gene?"

"A slaughter. That's what it is. Three adults and I don't know how many children. At least half a dozen."

"Oh God!" I heard Henry mutter. He started for the door to the office, but two policemen intercepted him.

"We have to be patient, Henry. Gene will get us in as soon as he can."

"Wrong. I'll get you in as soon as the crime scene boys give us the go-ahead."

"Any IDs?"

"One of our guys recognized the motel manager, a man named Willie Slutter. No ID on any of the others as yet."

"Lieutenant," Henry said. "I gotta get in there and see if one of them's my brother."

"Dial it back, guy. I can't even get in there until the forensics people are finished. Their lieutenant's promised to clear a way for BJ and me to take a look as soon as he can, but he's not going to stand for all of us tromping over the place."

"Let me go instead of BJ. I know my own brother."

"You ever seen a dozen bodies with their brains shot out laying all over the place? How do I know you won't throw up all over the crime scene from what you see and what you smell? It's the abattoir smell that gets to you the worst. No, I'll take BJ when they give me the okay. He's been through things like this before and can identify your brother—if it's necessary."

I must have checked my watch a dozen times, but I still had no idea how much time passed before the unit admitted the medical examiner. He beckoned to us, and we walked inside right behind OMI personnel. The front lobby was not particularly clean but not disordered either. The sight just beyond the lobby brought me to an abrupt halt.

Bodies cluttered the wide hallway clear to the far end. Hours had passed, but I could still discern cordite mixed with the heavy, clogging odor of blood and urine and feces. And the sickening smell of exposed brainpans. As the crime scene lieutenant directed our steps toward the far end, we passed small, crumpled figures. Others stretched out in the act of fleeing. A few sat against the walls, as if they had merely waited for death.

The lieutenant, a man named Toledo, halted before entering the hallway. "There are seven children and three adults. This one we've identified as Willie Slutter, the motel manager. I suspect he was hit first. Then the other two adults."

He stepped into the hallway and paused. I recognized the man at his feet. It was the Dominican, Florio Gaspard. From the fright frozen on his features, he'd faced his executioner. The third man wasn't a surprise. Juan Jose Flores-Gurule, who'd called himself Juan Gonzales when he contacted Jazz, had made it to the end of the hall but not through the doorway. He'd been shot, as had the other two men, through the torso, and then through the back of the head. The killer wanted to make sure they were dead.

I shook my head involuntarily. The stench was about to overcome me. "No more adults?" I asked.

Lieutenant Toledo shook his head. "Just kids. Some as old as seventeen or eighteen, but no adults."

"Could we see the older ones?" Gene asked. "The man we're looking for looks like a kid."

With obvious reluctance over further tromping on his crime scene, Toledo showed us two more bodies. Neither was Jazz. But I recognized one. Clancy Truscott, the Oklahoma City runaway we'd snagged on the street and supposedly saved, had returned to the fold to die with the rest of his "family."

Nearly overcome, I staggered out of the motel back into the relatively fresh air of an urban environment.

Chapter 15

HENRY SAGGED against the fender of the nearest patrol car after I told him his brother wasn't among the dead inside the motel. He sat there, as if in a stupor, while tension seemed to flow out of him. I understood the feeling.

Declining coffee, I opted for a bottle of water to rinse out my mouth before dumping the rest over my head to wash away the aura of death clinging to me. I regretted giving up smoking years ago. A lungful of smoke might clear out whatever crawled inside me in that slaughterhouse.

When Gene was finished talking to his people, he and Lieutenant Bolton walked up to us. "You okay?" Gene asked.

"That's a hell of a shock to the system," Bolton said.

"Not my first time," I answered.

"Bet you never saw anything like that, not even when you were with APD," Bolton said. "Marines, maybe."

"Not even there. I've seen multiple murder scenes before, but nothing like what we just walked through. But I'll get over it. Gene, something doesn't make sense to me. Have you ever heard of pimps killing their entire family just because someone was on their trail?"

"Nope. The logical thing to do would be to send Gaspard and Gonzales—or whatever his name was—over the border. A mass killing like this—especially kids—is going to stir up the entire community, not just the cops. Seems counterproductive to me."

"Me too. I've got to think this over. I'm missing something."

Bolton spoke up. "This is probably a cartel thing, and they made the mistake of failing to realize this is not Mexico."

"You think the cartel wiped out the entire White Streak family?"

"Who?" Bolton asked.

"The White Streak family. That's what the San Juan County deputies call the gang that took Jazz Penrod."

"They've run into them before, huh? I'll have to check with them. Anyway, we're doing an after-action debriefing tomorrow. I'd like you to attend and add what you can."

THE *ALBUQUERQUE Journal*'s headline the next morning screamed "Massacre on the West Side." The radio and local TV stations talked about the murders as if no other news happened that day. Bolton ran an efficient meeting at 400 Roma NW—APD headquarters—that started at 10:00 a.m. promptly. The briefing room was full, and while I knew many of the officers from my time in service with the department, I kept my head down and my mouth shut, as was expected of a rare outside guest admitted to such a setting. Until the lieutenant called on me, that is. Then, despite my natural inclination to hold my cards close to my vest, I shared the information Detective Joe gave me, including the name of the suspected gang contact, Julian Nesposito.

I didn't learn much during the debriefing except that there were two weapons involved. The body shots were from a 9 millimeter with extra markings on the slugs, which probably indicated a silencer was used. The head shots were from a .22... cartel style.

Other than that, CSU—the crime scene boys—hadn't turned up much, but there was much more work to do before they were finished. I wondered who would end up running this case. Special Victims' Unit certainly had a claim, but so did Homicide and the Gang Unit. But that was their problem. Mine was to find Jazz Penrod. To Bolton's credit, he passed out copies of the photo of Jazz I'd given him and put his guys on alert for the missing man. Of course, Gene had already done that, but the more people looking, the better.

After the post-op, I returned to the office and huddled with Hazel and Charlie at the small conference table in my private office.

"Nothing makes sense," I said after reporting the results of the meeting at headquarters. "A massacre like this will receive national news. That puts human trafficking and sex trafficking in headlines around the world."

"It's a multimillion-dollar business. Maybe they're so big they just don't give a damn about the bad publicity," Charlie said.

Hazel shook her head. "Publicity like that will make things harder for them. Millions of people who never think about such things will be alerted now. I agree with BJ. It makes no sense."

"Unless...." Charlie drew out the word.

"Unless what?" Henry asked.

"Unless it wasn't the cartel that did the killing."

Paul straightened. "A rival, you mean?"

"Could be. But I was thinking something else." Charlie shifted in his chair. "I'm not up to speed on human trafficking. But if I understand it right, it consists of at least two parts. The gang that does the kidnapping and works the victims."

"Right," I said. "Call that the cartel."

"Okay, the cartel. Then there's the locals they hire to support them."

"Such as the motel manager," Hazel suggested.

"Could be. Maybe the cartel owned the motel, or maybe they just made a deal with the owner for the exclusive use of the place for their vics."

"I see," Paul said. "The same could be true of truck stops and truck drivers. Cafés. Medics."

I told them of my conversation with Detective Lonzo Joe and encouraged Charlie to pursue his train of thought.

"Yeah, like that Nesposito character up on the reservation. A whole pipeline supporting the gang's activities. What if one of the local support groups got worried they would be exposed if the gang got rolled up?"

"Someone well-entrenched here and unwilling to flee to another country if things went bad," I said.

"Wait a minute," Hazel exclaimed. She rushed to her desk and pulled out some files before returning. "There's something in one of these transcriptions of your notes and tapes about someone. I don't remember a name. But something triggered a recollection. Why don't we each take a transcription of interviews and see if we can locate it."

"Whatever *it* is," Charlie said sourly.

An hour elapsed before Hazel let out a little cry. "Here it is! Paul, you ought to remember this." She read aloud from a transcript of Paul's aborted meeting with Juan at the Flying Star on Friday, August 13.

And if you know where Jazz is, well, let's just say that while I'm not usually into threesomes, I'd make an exception for him.

That had been Paul speaking. Juan came right back at him.

Wish I did, dude. Last time I heard, he was all wrapped up in Mr. Silver Wings.

Mr. Silver Wings? Who's that?

Dunno. That's all I ever heard him called. You see him on the scene from time to time.

Scene?

You know, parties.

Parties? How do I get invited to that kind of party?

Hazel rifled through the remainder of the transcript, but that was the only reference to "Silver Wings." I asked her to get the actual recording so we could hear the spoken words. After listening to it, I asked if they'd noticed anything.

"He sounded very respectful when he spoke of this Mr. Silver Wings," Paul said. "I noticed it at the time."

"Yeah, and Juan took a long time to answer Paul's question about who Silver Wings was," Henry said.

"Like he was sorry he'd mentioned the man," Hazel added.

I nodded agreement. "He realized at that moment he'd made a mistake. And after that, he made another one by acknowledging Jazz was a top. Then he brought things to a head and got out of there."

"He never intended to keep that date with Paul at the motel, did he?" Charlie asked.

"I don't even think he reserved the room. He just made up one on the spot and left."

"I think so too," Charlie agreed. "Because Juan wasn't the only one who made a mistake."

"Right. You did too, Paul. By pushing too hard on Jazz. And then, of course, Gaspard—who was roaming the area—spotted Don Carson recording everything on his laptop with the Dragon program."

"Could three simple words—*Mr. Silver Wings*—really have cost Juan his life? And the life of all those others—the children?" Hazel asked.

"It's a stretch, but it's possible. But that raises the issue of how this Silver Wings knew he'd been mentioned."

"Juan could have worn his own bug, and somebody was listening in on us," Charlie said.

"Possibly. Or Gaspard might have seen it on Don's screen."

"I don't think so," Hazel said. "He'd have to have very quick eyes to spot something like that by simply strolling past. The screens fade as you pass them."

Paul nodded. "I agree. Maybe Juan confessed his mistake."

"Or," I said, "maybe it's a leak. Like with the raid on the motel."

"That's easier to believe. Juan wouldn't admit to making a mistake, and Hazel's right. Not much chance Gaspard saw it on the screen. A leak makes sense."

"Who else knew about the meeting?" Henry asked.

"Nobody but APD," Charlie said.

"Don't forget the Citizens Council Against Human Trafficking," I said. "What do you think of when you hear the term 'silver wings'?"

"A plane?"

Hazel sniffed. "I think of a distinguished gentleman with streaks of silver at his hair."

"And if 'silver wings' refers to someone's hair, every man I saw at the CAHT board meeting had silver in his hair."

"I've seen Betsy Brockmire's hairdo," Hazel interjected. "She qualifies as well."

My heart sank down somewhere around my ankles. "My God! Have we screwed around and got a bunch of people killed?"

Henry added to the acid burn in my stomach. "Including my brother!"

Chapter 16

I CALLED Gene and convinced him to meet me at Cocina Azul on Mountain NW. The best way to tear him away from a busy schedule was to invite him to lunch. And Cocina Azul served his kind of plate… heavy on chili and spicy sauces.

He heard me out over a plate of huevos rancheros with refried beans and rice. He finished eating before he responded to my theory that someone other than the cartel was cleaning up behind himself. My cheese enchilada was virtually untouched.

"That does explain a few things. Somebody doesn't want to take a nosedive. I don't care how bloodthirsty a cartel is, it doesn't kill its own without a good reason. Not the whole family anyway. But somebody protecting his butt, that's different."

"Exactly."

"If we accept your theory, you know what that means, don't you?"

"Jazz is either dead or will be soon," I said.

"Not necessarily. My bet is that this White Streak family sold him to somebody. Probably for a lot of money, given the way that kid is built and looks. Might've been here or might have been somewhere else. Mexico, anywhere in the world."

I hauled out my digital recorder. "I don't think so. Listen to this."

Gene listened to the dialogue between Paul and Juan and then asked me to play it a second time. "I see what you mean," he said. "Last time Juan saw him, he was with Mr. Silver Wings. That implies a local man." He stopped and frowned. "But maybe it doesn't mean that Silver Wings is local after all. He coulda flown in to take delivery of the kid. Then flew him out."

"You checked all the flights for someone looking like Jazz."

"True, but those were commercial flights, and there were a lot of them since we don't have a real tight time frame. But it probably wasn't a commercial flight. Private plane would be easier and safer. Slip over the border and land on some remote ranch, and there wouldn't be any record of anything. Could have been by car, but I'm betting on a private plane."

"And I agree with you, if that's what happened. But that meeting with Juan took place last Friday. Today's Wednesday. I think he's still here."

"Then I have one question for you. Why wasn't he among the bodies at the motel yesterday?"

"He's too valuable. The cartel took a hell of a loss when somebody shot up that motel. Maybe they're counting on Jazz to recoup a part of it." Hope clogged my throat as I said the words.

"The cold-blooded mass murder of ten individuals tells me value doesn't enter into this very much."

"I know I'm reaching, Gene. But I think Jazz Penrod is in Albuquerque, and I think he's still alive. For how much longer, I don't know. I'm damned well convinced that we've been tipping our hand to the cartel that runs the White Streak family, and it makes sense that Silver Wings is the conduit."

"That's pure supposition. You don't have a shred of proof of that. Hell, you took two of their people right off the street. That was what tipped them. One of the bodies in the motel was that Truscott kid. He went right back to them. He's a better candidate for your leak than a mystery man... who'd probably be a cop."

"He wasn't the leak on the raid. He had no way of knowing about it. Besides, Silver Wings doesn't have to be a cop. The Citizens' Council Against Human Trafficking has been advised of what's going on at every step. If the words 'silver wings' refers to a head of hair, we met five candidates for the title last Monday."

"Five? You're including Betsy? I just listened to your tape twice, and Juan said *Mr.* Silver Wings. And besides, one of the remaining four candidates is a cop, remember."

"Lieutenant Bolton."

"Who SVU reports to, I remind you," Gene said.

"Are you arguing for me or against me? Who better than that to tip off the pimps?"

"If you're talking literally, Bolton might have some silver in his hair—what there is of it—but you can't call him silver-winged."

"No, but he's a perfect conduit. He sits on that board and probably tells them everything. Why not? You told me yourself NGOs are a big part of the battle against the traffickers."

"Well, if you're right, you've put somebody else in their sights, you know."

I slapped my forehead. "Nesposito!" I calmed my racing heart. "But he's up in the Four Corners area. No reason to believe he knows anything about Silver Wings."

"You willing to bet his life on that?"

I tugged out my cell phone and dialed Lonzo Joe's office at the San Juan County Sheriff's Office. He was out. Yes, they'd notify him I was trying to get in touch with him. No, they couldn't share his cellular phone number with me.

I hung up and dialed Dix Lee at the Farmington PD. She was in and had no trouble giving me the detective's number. By the time I paid our bill and we reached our cars in the parking lot, Lonzo was on the line.

"You must be prescient, BJ," he said.

I put him on speaker and let him know an APD lieutenant was privy to our conversation. "Why's that?"

"I'm out on the rez. Came with a tribal officer to talk to Julian Nesposito. Got there just in time."

"What do you mean?"

"When we turned down the road to the old man's house, there was a Vespa a hundred yards or so ahead of us. Nesposito came out of the house at the sound of the motors, and we saw the driver of the scooter pull a piece. We hit the siren, and that threw the killer's aim off. He got off a shot or two before he took off over the desert hardpan. We stopped to make sure Nesposito wasn't hit, and by that time the Vespa disappeared. I heard about your murders up there yesterday. Sounds to me like somebody's cleaning up the landscape."

"Right you are. The name Silver Wings mean anything to you?"

"Nope. Let me ask Officer Begay." I heard muffled conversation for a moment before Lonzo came back on the phone. "Doesn't mean anything to him either. But we'll ask around and see if we can learn anything."

"What about your guy on the scooter?"

"We called for air cover, but he'll be gone to ground long before that shows up. Couldn't follow him in a patrol vehicle."

"A scooter, you say?"

"Can you believe it? The would-be killer got away on a damned Vespa. A scooter."

"They aren't that fast, are they?"

"Not like a cycle, but it was enough to get the job done. He was out of range before we even got out of the car."

"A local?"

"Must be. Who'd drive up to the rez on a motor scooter, for crying out loud?"

"Maybe not so dumb. You can throw a motor scooter in the back of a truck and cover it with a tarp."

"Right. Begay's on the radio right now arranging for a roadblock in the area. Maybe we can scoop them up."

"Them?"

"Somebody's gotta drive the truck. Or maybe the would-be killer drove both vehicles."

"Okay if I come up and talk to Nesposito?"

"Navajo Police Department's gonna hold on to him for a while, but I'll see if I can get us in. I'll find out what the disposition of his case will be and let you know something later."

Lonzo followed up that afternoon with an email that Julian Nesposito would be kept at the Shiprock district tribal police headquarters, where we could question him tomorrow afternoon.

EARLY THE next morning, Paul, Henry, and I drove to the Double Eagle Airport on the west side of town. Once there, we piled aboard Jim Gray's Cessna and took off for Farmington. Jim was a Vietnam vet charter pilot I had used for years. His silver-and-cherry Cessna SkyCatcher was familiar to me, but to accommodate the three of us, he rolled out his six-seater, a 2005 model Cessna T206H Stationair with clamshell doors. This craft was also silver-and-cherry—Jim's UNM school colors.

Farmington lay northwest of Albuquerque on the Colorado Plateau some 182 car miles, which takes almost three hours to drive. I have no idea of air miles, but Jim put us down at the Four Corners Regional Airport in about half that time. By prior arrangement, Lonzo Joe picked us up in a county van and drove straight to Shiprock.

A heavyset no-nonsense tribal detective with bad skin and a keen mind, by the name of Vernon Tsosie, put us through the wringer about our interest in Nesposito before allowing Detective Joe and me to accompany him to an interview room.

"Hard Hat, some people to see you," Tsosie said as he barged through the door of a small room occupied by a surprisingly dignified-looking man in his late fifties or early sixties, only now thickening around the middle. Joe had told me he was once a holy man, and that wasn't hard to believe.

He had a placid look about him. I'd also learned he worked as a youth as a miner—coal, turquoise, copper—where he picked up the moniker of Hard Hat. His grandfatherly gaze didn't have much in common with the avaricious stare of a heartless trafficker. But I'd learned over the years that eyes were not necessarily windows to the soul.

Lonzo Joe started things off. "Hard Hat, we're looking for Jazz Penrod."

"Know him. Not seen him in a while? He missing?"

"The White Streak family's got him. We need to know where they'd keep him."

He gave an almost invisible shrug. "Don't know nothing about that."

Tsosie took control of his interview. "Hard Hat, your string's run out. We've been onto you for years but couldn't prove nothing. But now your own people's trying to get rid of you. Time you cooperated. Might save your own miserable hide."

The clear-eyed stare grew hooded and exposed the villain in him. It was almost as if the man shifted before our eyes. *Shifted* in the Navajo meaning of the word. A different creature sat before us now.

"Vern, I did a sing for you when you was six years old. You owe me your life."

"That was a holy man I owed my life to, Hard Hat. You're not that man anymore."

"Hear I wasn't the first one the bugger tried to bag." The words were calm and placid.

I spoke for the first time. "Ten, Nesposito. Ten dead. Three men and seven children. Some of them you probably sent to them. Thirteen, fourteen-year-old boys and girls. Shot with a 9 millimeter and finished off with a .22. I saw them all."

"They came for you next," Lonzo said. "Pure chance Officer Begay and I were headed for your place at the same time. Otherwise the count would be eleven."

"You describing a cartel hit down in Albuquerque. You ever seen a cartel hitman come for anybody on a kiddie's scooter?" Nesposito asked.

"They'll come any way they can," I said. "Looks to me as if somebody at the top's cleaning up behind him. You might be the only one left standing. Are you going to help us keep you alive?"

"What 'chu want?"

"You ever hear of a man called Silver Wings?"

Those tired brown eyes with red streaks changed once again. They clouded over as Nesposito made a connection. "Never knowed anyone called that."

"Yes, you do," I pressed. "I saw it in your eyes. You know him, and that told you it wasn't the cartel killing their own people. It was Silver Wings. And if you figured that out, you know he'll kill anyone who can connect him with the family, and that includes you."

Nesposito's arm on the table twitched, but he tried to mask it by sweeping it across the table to point at Lonzo. "You seen the man who tried to kill me. His face and head was covered by a helmet. But he was slim as a girl. Hell, coulda been a girl for all I know." He smiled, and it turned nasty before it died. "Maybe it was. More'n one female on this rez got reason to try to take me down. You know, promising them something and then not delivering."

A sickening sensation burned through my esophagus, leaving a bitter taste in my mouth. "Only a fool would believe that, and I don't think you're a fool. Just do this for me. Tell me who Silver Wings is."

"Not admitting I know any Silver Wings, but use your head, son. I had to guess, I'd say he was a big muckety-muck down there in Albuquerque. Somebody who'd lose everything, it ever got out he was connected to the traffickers. Hell, ask these fellas. By now they figured out that clan's run by some Bulgarian mobsters. They gotta have local connections to make things work."

"If that's true, didn't Silver Wings just sign his own death warrant?" Lonzo asked.

"You mean by killing the Bulgarians' kids? Why? He can give the cartel as many as they want."

"He didn't just kill kids," I said. "He killed three of their men."

"You mean Juan and Florio—" He bit his lip, but the mistake was irretrievable. A bell can't be unrung. His shrug this time was obvious. "That's what I heard, anyway. Two pimps. Dime a dozen. Don't know who the third man was."

"Manager of the My Other Home Motel," I said.

"That part of their circuit was blown anyway. You guys tried to raid it not long ago. Leastways that's what I hear."

"You're well-informed," Tsosie said.

Nesposito's grandfatherly look returned. "I got my ways."

"All right," I said. "Then use those ways to tell us what happened to Jazz Penrod. He was taken in by one of the men killed at the motel."

Nesposito studied me a full thirty seconds before responding. "Jazz, now he's different from the other kids you got killed."

The statement shook me a bit. Was I responsible for getting them killed?

"He's quality goods," Nesposito went on. "People over in Farmington been getting into trouble over Jazz since he was fourteen. Somebody paid good money for him. Maybe he's out of the country, sold off somewhere you won't never find him." He lifted his chin and cocked an eye at me. "Or maybe he was dangerous to Silver Wings, and he's dead too. Either way, he's headed out of these United States or to the morgue. You can count on that."

We went at the old man for another thirty minutes, but he clammed up and sat in stone silence as we nattered on.

I WAS judicious in my description of the Nesposito interview to my two companions on the way back to Albuquerque. Although Henry was well aware of the danger his brother faced, I didn't want to give voice to Nesposito's warning. Halfway home, Lonzo contacted me. Detective Tsosie called him after we left to report the old man had said something about his white friends oughta look into one of those outfits up there in Albuquerque that took care of trafficking victims.

I knew of only one—the Citizens' Council Against Human Trafficking. Haldemain's NGO.

Chapter 17

GENE WANTED to go straight to Bolton; I insisted we talk to Betsy Brockmire first. Despite Hazel's description of her silver-adorned hairdo, I was inclined to take Juan at his word. He'd distinctly said "*Mr.* Silver Wings." Finally, Gene agreed to talk to her before speaking with the lieutenant. He phoned and set up a discreet meeting at my office late afternoon after we returned from Farmington.

I didn't want to overwhelm her but couldn't refuse Henry and Paul a place at the table. By the time Hazel ushered her into our conference room, Gene, Henry, Paul, and I were already seated. Betsy was accustomed to dealing with men, but the presence of another woman might give her a sense of support, so I asked Hazel to join us.

"Whoa, what did I do to deserve such a reception committee?" Betsy asked.

"We need your advice," Gene said after she took a seat at the foot of the table opposite me. "You recall we came to see you about a missing Farmington man. A fellow by the name of Jazz Penrod?"

"I do."

"There have been some disturbing developments on the case," he said.

"Like a massacre of ten souls the other day," she speculated. "Unusual, to say the least. Was Mr. Penrod among the victims?"

"No, but that doesn't reassure me a great deal," I said. "There was an attempt made on another man up in Farmington; however, a local detective foiled the killing."

"Was the killer apprehended?"

"No." I spent a few minutes describing the situation without naming the mark.

"I take it you're speaking of Julian Nesposito."

"How do you know that name?" I asked.

"From you, I gather. At least I understood you were the source when Lieutenant Bolton told the members of our board about him. I'd heard rumors about the man, but according to the Navajo Tribal Police, no one was ever able to prove anything."

"What do you know about him?"

"Not much. But I do have one interesting story. When girls—and boys—disappear from the Navajo Reservation, they seldom return. One girl did. She disappeared when she was thirteen and reappeared when she was fifteen. She was pretty messed up both physically and mentally, but she was clear about one thing. Nesposito took her in his car to a remote area and left her there. Not long after that, a man in a truck came by and offered her a ride. He also offered her a drink. When she woke up, she was in Albuquerque."

"What did the authorities do when they heard her story?"

"Hauled in Nesposito, who told them a glib story. The girl needed to pee, so he dropped her off and drove on up the road to lend a relative twenty dollars. When he came back, she was gone."

"And that was it?" Gene asked.

"Apparently so," Betsy said. "Nesposito appears to have good connections."

"How solid is your board?" Gene asked suddenly.

She started. "What do you mean?"

"What I mean is, we tell the board of directors of the Citizens' Council Against Human Trafficking—"

"We call ourselves CAHT," Betsy interrupted. "It's easier and quicker."

"Okay," Gene continued, "we tell CAHT about an upcoming raid on a motel, and bam! It's blown. We tell that same board about someone named Silver Wings, and ten people die, including our only two connections with the gang, Juan Gonzales and Florio Gaspard. And they all end up killed execution style. We tell you about Nesposito, and someone goes out to the reservation and tries to kill him. Coincidence?"

Betsy squeezed the bridge of her nose between two fingers. "Lieutenant, are you forgetting the entire police department had exactly the same information? Why point at us?"

I interrupted. "Betsy, how many employees does the council have?"

"Employees? Why, just me, a secretary, and two computer and telephone people."

"How old are they?"

"College kids, recent grads. And we have a few volunteers who give us time each week."

"No 'silver wings' among them, I take it. Yet, your board has three who qualify. Four, if you count Lieutenant Bolton. What he has left is gray."

"And I daresay there are plenty in APD who have that qualification, as well. And on the street—"

"People on the street wouldn't have the information," Gene said.

Betsy's chin took on a stubborn set. "Exactly what do you want from me, Lieutenant?"

"An open mind. Did you have any indication something was amiss? Operations that went wrong? Anything like that?"

"Operations? We have no operations. We take distress calls from victims and try to get them help. We interface with the proper jurisdictions and find counselors and temporary sanctuaries. We collect tips and information and pass them on to the authorities. And nothing has gone wrong or changed that I can see."

"We all like to believe our associates' motives are pure," I said. "Can you suspend that belief for a moment and search your memory? Can you think of anything that doesn't seem quite right?"

"Not at all."

"Can you tell us what part each of your board plays in your organization?"

"My assistants and I do the work while the board approves my actions and helps set goals. And raises funds, of course."

"None of them take an active part in the daily operations?"

"The bishop does. He's a large part of our sanctuary program."

"He meets the victims, interacts with them?" Gene asked.

"Oh yes. That's necessary for him to adequately play his part."

"Do you do follow-up contacts with the victims you help?"

"Sometimes when one is having a particularly difficult time readjusting. Some of them are tragically damaged by what they've gone through. They are self-loathing and disgusted at what they've become. Some are suicidal. As I told you about the young man you are looking for, the higher his standards were before he was taken, with the passage of time, who he was before makes it difficult for him to break away. Aided by whatever drug they've hooked him on, of course."

Gene continued his interrogation. "Do you visit the bishop's church? See the victims turned over to his care? Check for yourself how he's doing?"

She nodded. "As time allows, yes."

"And you've never seen anything to make you question how he's handling his end of the project?"

"Never. He seems to have an affinity for the victims, particularly the children. Just being in his presence sometimes brings a few of them out of their shell."

"Once they leave his care, where do they go?"

"Various places. Some are able to return home. Some go to state facilities. Those who are addicted to drugs are referred to rehab treatment."

"Are the Haldemains active in any way?" I asked.

"When legal help is required, they step in and do their part. Other than that, they do not ordinarily interface with the people we help."

"Ordinarily?"

She flushed. "I'm not comfortable discussing my associates like this. Aren't accusations being made here?"

"Not at all," I replied. "We're trying to get the lay of the land to see if we can spot a likely place for a leak." I placed a digital recorder on the desk. "I'd like you to hear something. The voices on the tape you're about to hear are those of my associate Paul Barton and one of the pimps who was killed in the motel the other day. We have evidence that man, who called himself Juan Gonzales, lured Jazz Penrod to Albuquerque and then somehow snared him into the White Streak family. In the tape, Paul's acting as a shill, trying to draw the man out. He was successful to the extent that they met at the Flying Star."

Betsy listened carefully to the portion of the tape I played, the part where Juan mentioned Mr. Silver Wings. She leaned back when I turned it off.

"That's the name you asked about at our board meeting."

"Right, and it brought a lot of jokes about all the silver hair in that room. What's your impression of Juan's voice when he mentioned the name on the tape?"

"Respectful. Almost like this young man—Jazz, was it?—should have been honored to receive attention from such a man."

"My impression as well. What does that tell you?"

"A couple of things, actually," she said. "This Mr. Silver Wings is probably rich and quite well-connected and obviously gay. And a player. By that I mean he's well known to the pimps."

"The kind of man who might very well buy a handsome, athletic youth."

"Yes. Sounds reasonable. If we're right in our assessment, he's not the kind of man who would share his prize. Let me restate that. He might share the victim with a close circle of friends, but not with just anyone."

A shiver ran down my back. I hadn't considered that possibility. "Does this remind you of anyone?"

"Heavens knows we all have our peccadillos, BJ, but I don't recognize the man we're speaking of. Not personally, that is."

Gene asked the question I was dancing around. "Does this remind you of any of your associates on the board?"

"The bishop is happily married to a wonderful woman who shares his work within the congregation and without. Ross—that's Roscoe Haldemain—is divorced—"

"Second time, I believe," I said.

"Actually, third. He's prominently mentioned in the society pages escorting this lady or that to various occasions. He asked me out once, and I would have accepted, except that I draw the line at dating business associates. William lost his wife a few years ago to a car accident. He was very devoted to her and is taking a long time to recover. They are all fine, upstanding men of the community. I should add that the Haldemain brothers are quite wealthy and have no need for additional money. The bishop would be, as well, but he continually pours his personal funds into his church."

"And I imagine his church has an endless need for funds," Gene said.

"Is there anything else I can help you gentlemen with?" Betsy asked as she stood.

Henry grunted in frustration.

Chapter 18

STARTLED, JAZZ sat up on the couch where he'd been lying when Kim entered the bungalow. He hadn't seen the Asian for a few days. He noticed the absence because Kim normally delivered his pipes or lines of coke. The last couple of days, food and the cocaine had been left poolside in covered trays. He'd watched from the bungalow window as a short, stout woman in what he assumed was a maid's uniform placed one of the trays on a table and returned inside the house. He knew from testing the doorknob that the heavy mesh screen door was kept locked.

Kim stepped to where Jazz lay on a sofa dressed only in denim cutoffs. "You put on clothes. You come with Kim to get groceries. Help carry."

Jazz's heart raced. Kim was going to take him out of this prison? He swallowed. "Bring me my pipe first. I'll get dressed while you get it."

"Get pipe when we get back."

"I want it now."

"Not until we get back. Mr. Silver Wings say you help Kim. You come."

Half-inclined to refuse until he got his pipe, Jazz gave in to the excitement of getting out of the house. He deliberately slipped off his cutoffs and pulled on underwear and a pair of walking shorts before donning a polo shirt and sandals, smirking inwardly as Kim watched every move through expressionless black eyes. Jazz recognized hooded desire when he saw it.

JAZZ THOUGHT his heart would burst from joy as they drove down a street called Coors Boulevard NW. For the first mile, he was so engrossed in watching people and cars and scenes of everyday life that he forgot to plot his escape. Should he bolt from the car when it stopped for a traffic light or simply wait until they reached the store? Maybe there would be a cop around. Or a security guard. What would he say? *Help, I'm being held prisoner!* How would that go over? He wasn't shackled, and there was just one skinny Chinaman to guard him.

No, better to just give Kim the slip and make more careful plans. His legs started to itch. He resisted the urge to scratch until he could stand it no longer. Then he felt the familiar onset of nausea in his belly, accompanied by mild cramping. His mouth went dry; the hair on his arms stood up. Christ! Just get the groceries loaded and get back home.

There *was* a cop just inside Albertsons supermarket as they entered, and he seemed to take some interest in them, but Jazz kept on Kim's heels as the man went about his shopping. When they paid at the cashier, he hoped to get a glimpse of a credit card and learn the rest of Kim's name. But his companion paid with cash.

The cop wasn't at the exit when they left the store, laden down by party supplies, but Jazz saw him standing nearby talking into a mike through the window of his patrol car. The cop's back was to them. He turned without spotting them just as they passed.

Jazz was sweating, and the cramps were taking hold by the time they left the nearby liquor store and headed for home. It was only when Kim parked in a three-car garage that Jazz thought to look at the make of the car. A Mercedes four-door. Green. He caught a snatch of the license plate before Kim opened the trunk: 825-something or the other.

The shakes really hit Jazz by the time their purchases were put away; about all he could manage was to collapse in a poolside chair until Kim brought him his pipe. A slight gasp of pleasure escaped his lips when he saw it was the bong fortified with a little marijuana.

His nerves settled but hadn't yet started to soar when Wings appeared and took a seat on an adjoining lounge. "I heard you took a little trip today."

Jazz tried to be brusque, but a smile escaped him. "Felt good."

"If you continue to behave yourself, we can have some more trips. Maybe overnight trips to some nice places. I've been thinking of a jaunt to Mexico. How would you like that?"

An alarm bell tried to go off, but the drug silenced it. "Be okay, I guess. Don't speak any Spanish."

Wings laughed. "You don't have to. Just wave dollar bills at them, and they all magically speak English. And if mamacita can't, then the granddaughter can. Good pipe?"

"Yeah. Good."

"As you probably surmised from the supplies you and Kim bought, I'm having a party tonight. Usual bunch. Nothing special, but I want you to be nice to my guests."

"Anybody complain yet?"

"You're *surly* nice. Be *nice* nice. You give them what they want, but you could be a little more… *social* about it."

Anger boiled up inside Jazz, almost ruining a good smoke. "None of them complain to me."

"Oh, you satisfy them just fine. Very well, in fact. But be a little more amiable about it, all right? I'd like them to see what I see when I look at you."

Jazz took a hit and held the smoke in his lungs until he felt nicer. Then he asked, "What's that?"

"A nice, engaging, handsome boy."

"Man," Jazz shot back at him. "A boy couldn't handle the gang you run with."

Wings gave him a peculiar look.

Somehow Jazz felt he'd said something wrong. "Okay, boy," he backed off.

Wings broke out in a big smile.

JAZZ WAS churlish by the time Wings' guests gathered at the pool. Kim never gave him his afternoon pipe when Jazz was expected to attend a party. Jazz went through his usual internal routine. He told himself he wasn't going to parade around before those men. He'd stay in the bungalow. Then the cramps and uneasy stomach arrived in spades. His nerves jangled. He brushed off bugs that weren't there. Sometimes it seemed like Kokopelli, the Hopi prankster and storyteller, was picking on him. When his physical discomfort drove him out the door, Jazz no longer wore the ridiculous bathing suit. Denim cutoffs were easy to slip out of when he felt the need to swim.

Did he really *need* to swim, or was he coming to enjoy the public display of nakedness when he rolled the cutoffs down and stood for a moment before striding to the pool? A hush always fell on the small crowd as he exposed himself. Was it pride or shame he felt? Didn't matter. He wasn't going to do it tonight. He'd just stay in his lounge and enjoy his pipe. Then maybe he'd fall asleep. That would drive Wings batty. The thought brought a smile to his lips. He frowned. He wasn't sleeping much these days.

A brief silence ensued as he strode out of the bungalow until the beefy Tom called out a greeting. It was the same bunch, Doc and Sam and the skinny kid who never left Sam's side. But there was a new one too. A good-looking guy so aggressively masculine he didn't fit in with this group. Probably around thirty, with a body that looked like the man lived in the local gym. He was introduced as Chip. Still irritable from lack of his pipe, Jazz stared at the man. If Wings sent this guy to the cottage later, there might be trouble. This guy probably wanted what Jazz wasn't about to give. Wings oughta know that by now.

He wasted no time heading for the lounge chair reserved for him... the one with the pipe on the table beside it. The bong again. Good. He lit the pipe and drew in the magical smoke. He held his breath, well aware that inflated lungs made his pecs look larger. He frowned. How did a thought like that sneak in? Was he becoming what Wings wanted him to be? He attended his pipe in silence and let the conversation wash around him.

After a while he began to pick up pieces of information sprinkled among otherwise meaningless words of male bonding. Doc, he decided *was* a doc, but a doctor of what? Sam, he was willing to bet, was a builder of some kind. Successful too. His watch looked like one of those with a crown on the face that cost more than most people make in a year.

As his attention moved to Jamie, the kid with Sam, Jazz's thoughts turned sour. Skinny—though with some body definition—with long blond hair, the guy never moved more than two feet from Sam's side, all the while watching the hard-muscled man with adoring eyes. He constantly kept a hand on his idol's bare leg or naked belly. Jazz shivered. Was that *his* future?

Tom, the hairy-chested man, carried an air of authority even while wearing nothing but a bathing suit. Tom had come to the bungalow several times, always permitting Jazz to take a passive role while lying on his back with eyes closed.

Wings—or Rex, as these people called him—was the leader, or was that just because he was the host? As he sucked on the pipe and allowed the smoke to take deeper control of him, Jazz realized that wasn't it at all. Wings dispensed. Wings controlled what they all seemed to want. *Him!* He controlled who came to the parties. Who came to the bungalow later.

Jazz's guts roiled at the thought of what would come next. Had he figured out enough about these people to give him an edge? He'd have to think on that, find some way to test his advantage. But first, he needed to survive the night.

LATER THAT evening, his fear proved right. The brawny Chip entered the bungalow and came into the bedroom where Jazz lay waiting. His excitement was evident. The man was undoubtedly attractive and carried authority in the same way Tom did, but he wasn't Jazz's type. Chip stripped and fell on him, his mouth seeking his lips. Jazz managed to lift his head and took the kiss on his neck. Chip's hands roved him swiftly, roughly. And he wanted what Jazz feared. He tried to flip Jazz over on his stomach. Jazz resisted.

"So you want to watch me do it, huh? Okay with me."

"I don't do that," Jazz said in a steady voice.

"You'll do whatever I want, kid."

Without warning, the aroused man clipped him hard on the chin. Jazz saw stars, and the bed swayed drunkenly. Then Chip pursued his goal. As the man lifted his legs, Jazz managed to bring his feet together on Chip's chest. Still woozy from the blow, Jazz straightened his legs. He sensed rather than saw the husky man fly off the bed and strike the wall. He lay semihelpless, struggling to prepare himself for the vicious attack that would surely follow. But it didn't come. The next thing he knew, Kim was helping Chip get dressed while Wings stood bedside, touching the growing bruise on Jazz's chin.

"You okay?" the man asked.

"Yeah. He wanted what he couldn't have."

Wings nodded. "I warned him."

"You keep him away from me. I see him again, we gonna lock horns."

Wings eyed him speculatively for a long moment before speaking. "He won't be invited back."

Jazz met the man's eyes and saw the hard glint disappear, replaced by hunger. Now Wings would pursue what he wanted, and Jazz hoped he had the strength to give it to him.

He gripped the soft hand caressing his bare belly and looked Wings in the eyes. "I'm a top. Won't ever be a bottom."

"It's an acquired taste, Jazz."

"Uh-uh. Not for me. That's one thing I won't do, but there's another thing too."

"What is that?"

"I don't want to go to Mexico. I just want to stay here—" He swallowed and forced the words. "—with you."

The wary, dangerous look on Wings' smooth features mellowed. "We'll see."

Chapter 19

I WAS in the office alone on Saturday morning when the phone rang. It was Gene.

"BJ, we've had a sighting of Jazz."

I came up out of my chair. "When? Where?"

"Patrol cop was at Albertsons on Coors when he spotted Jazz. He went back to his unit to take another look at Jazz's photo and call it in. After that, he went inside the store and searched, but he couldn't find them."

"Them?"

"Yeah, looked like Jazz was with another man."

"Silver Wings?"

"Not unless Silver Wings is an Asian."

"Was he restrained in any way? Seem coerced?"

"Not according to the patrolman, whose name is Small. They walked through the door side by side and disappeared inside."

"Does the store have cameras?"

"Yep. We've got a shot of them as they paid the tab. Seemed to be party supplies."

"Anyone recognize the man with Jazz?"

"Nope. But I've got a copy of the tape. You can take a look if you want."

FIVE MINUTES later Gene waved an officer out of his office and beckoned me inside. He punched a button on the tape machine as soon as I was seated. My heart took a leap when I saw a handsome face flash before me. It was Jazz, all right. No question about it. He looked to be in good shape. He was thinner, but they weren't starving him—which was sometimes a problem—and he acted normal. He was dressed casually in shorts and a polo shirt that clung to his trim body.

"That's him. He's okay."

"Almost," Gene said. In answer to my lifted eyebrows, he backed the tape up to where they arrived at the Albertsons cashier's station.

We could see glimpses of the two as the clerk finished ringing up the customer before them. The Asian was stolid, placid, economic in his movements. Jazz seemed jumpy by comparison.

"See right there," Gene said. "He's picking at his skin. That's a sign he's hooked on something. And watch him put the items from the basket onto the counter."

Now that Gene called my attention to it, Jazz's movements weren't as graceful or coordinated as the man I knew. "They've got him hooked on something," I said. "But what?"

"No way of telling from this. Methamphetamines. Heroin. Crack cocaine. The pimps use them all as a means of control."

"They didn't take Jazz to be a streetwalker. He's worth more to them than that. Meth would burn him out too fast. And he wouldn't voluntarily use the needle."

"You mean the Jazz you knew wouldn't. You don't know what all he's been through. They might have restrained him and shot him up until he was hooked. Besides, you can smoke heroin too."

"True. If I had to guess, that's how Juan netted him. They developed a decent relationship after Jazz came to meet him, but Juan told him the crack or heroin or whatever it was would make things even better. After Jazz got hooked, Juan turned him over to Silver Wings."

"Probably something like that. But the cartel didn't just give Jazz away. They sold him to Silver Wings."

"Unless Silver Wings *is* the cartel," I said.

Gene pulled a scowl. "Don't think so. If he was, everyone in the family would have known it. He'd have to kill a lot more than ten people to give himself protection. No, this is somebody who works with the higher-ups. A facilitator. A protector."

"At least this tells us Jazz isn't dead or shipped out of the country."

"Not yet, anyway," Gene said.

"Silver Wings doesn't seem to be worried if he lets him out in public."

"That's a puzzler. If he's as connected as we think he is, he'd know there's a stop-and-question order out on Jazz with a photo attached. Why would he let him out now?"

I didn't like the answer I came up with. "Maybe Jazz hasn't been kidnapped. Maybe he's with them willingly."

"Or he's staying with them willingly because they furnish him the drug."

"If this happened yesterday, why are you just getting the info?"

"SVU says they waited until they had a copy of the camera surveillance to give me. Then they put it on my desk."

"Where you wouldn't have seen it until Monday."

"If I hadn't come in today."

"Deliberate?"

"Come on, BJ. These are cops. Ones we've grown up in the department with. Hell, you know most of them."

"Let me remind you, there's a leak."

"Yeah, I looked into that. You know the department's always stretched for resources, and we don't have the funds to handle half of what we need to. So the NGOs, the citizens' councils, and the churches have stepped in with money and help. They're carrying the big end of the load in combating human trafficking. Especially the churches. As a result they're privy to everything. They even sit in on perp and vic interviews. Nobody likes it, but we can't afford to turn them away. They're resources."

"What you're saying is that Betsy's council and Bishop Gregory's church know everything that's going on."

Gene punched the desktop with his right forefinger. "Right down to the last detail."

"That means that if our suspicions are correct, then they know—"

"That Jazz Penrod's been spotted by the police," Gene finished for me. "And depending upon his circumstances...."

"That might not be good for his health."

"At a minimum, he's shipped out of the country."

"And at a maximum," I said, "he's destined for a 9 millimeter in the chest and a .22 in the back of the head."

"Damn! I hope our first break's not our last," Gene said.

"Can I borrow that video over the weekend?"

"Don't see why not. There's also some scans of the parking lot from a couple of outside cameras. You want those too?"

As SOON as I got home and showed Henry the store's camera scan, he brightened before he frowned. "Looks good. Man, he looks good."

"Does he?" I asked.

"See what you mean," he said as we watched his brother unload the shopping cart at the cashier's station. "That's not Jazz's usual moves. He flows like water. That was almost stop and go. He's hooked, ain't he?"

I nodded. "The question is, what on?"

"Can't answer that," Henry said, "but we know someone who can."

"Nesposito," I said, grabbing for the phone. Lonzo Joe didn't seem to mind me interrupting his Saturday. I put him on speakerphone and filled him in on the latest.

"Glad Jazz is alive and kicking. Wasn't sure he would be after that massacre down there last Tuesday. So you wanna know what the White Streak family feeds its vics?"

"And Julian Nesposito just might have the answer. Is he still in custody?" I asked.

"So I understand. Tribal cops found somebody willing to file a complaint about their missing girl."

"You think he'll give us the answer?"

"Might. He's not going to give up Silver Wings but might not see much harm in telling us their drug of choice."

Henry put in his two cents. "You tell him if he doesn't, Louie Secatero's going to come knocking on his door. And whatever my dad leaves of him, I'll take care of when I get back."

Once that call was completed, Henry fired up his Harley and headed for the Albertsons on Coors. Didn't make any sense. Jazz was long gone, but Henry wanted to cruise the area looking for something. Jazz. Or a slender Asian male. I didn't put up any fuss. That was better than my friend drowning his fears in the Blue Spruce, where Detective Zimmerman might pop him again.

Paul was at the country club discharging his duties as aquatic director and wouldn't be home until later that afternoon, so I sat down at my desktop in my home office and started a long, boring review of the parking lot tapes. They were time and date stamped, but I covered a much broader swath of time for fear of missing something.

I was on the verge of giving up when I spotted it. Two men, one pushing a shopping cart of bagged groceries, walked down an aisle and headed for a car. Jazz and his minder. They stopped at a Mercedes. The sun was at the wrong angle. Couldn't make out the color before the camera continued panning to the left, losing the view of the two men. By the time it returned to the area, there was nothing but a vacant parking spot. I thought of calling Gene and asking him to locate the shopping cart for possible fingerprints, but that took place yesterday. How do you pick out the right cart from a hundred others and then take fingerprints of everyone who's touched it since? You don't.

Nonetheless, I phoned Henry but got no answer. He probably couldn't hear the thing ring or feel his cell phone vibrate while he was aboard the bike. He called me back ten minutes later, and I told him to keep an eye out for a Mercedes, probably a four-door and probably dark. He sighed in exasperation and counted four in the parking lot where he'd stopped to return my call.

"All right, I'll watch for a Mercedes with my brother or a Chinaman in it. Okay?"

Detective Lonzo Joe phoned back shortly after noon. He'd driven to the tribal police's Shiprock district office to interview Nesposito again.

"The old bastard said they use a whole range of drugs. Meth, because it's cheaper and available."

"That would burn Jazz up too fast," I said.

"Yeah. That's what he said too. They also use heroin, both injected and smoked. That's a possibility, but he thinks they'd use crack cocaine on Jazz. Quick to addict. Pleasant high, even if the comedown's hard. Simple to fix a pipe."

"As I understand it, crack takes its toll on the body too."

"They all do, BJ. Every last one of them's poison to the system. But coke probably takes more time to do the damage if his pimps control the rate of usage. It accelerates, all right, but if they slow the rate of acceleration, they'll get more use out of Jazz."

Lonzo turned aside from the phone for a moment, and I heard another voice. Then he was back on the line. "Hard Hat says they sometimes use a bong with some cannabis added to bring the user down slower."

"Didn't know you needed vaporization for crack."

"You don't, but the bong with cannabis eases the stress on the body. You understand that's not a scientific fact, just what the pimps believe. Look, they're about to question Nesposito again, and I want to sit in. Talk to you later."

AROUND TWO, the phone rang again. When I answered, all I heard at first was wind and road noise.

"BJ! You ain't gonna believe it. I found him," Henry blurted.

"You found Jazz?"

"Naw. I found the Mercedes. I'm on his tail now."

"Give me his license plate."

"New Mexico. Let's see, 825-RLZ."

"Great. Color? Model?"

"Older model, can't tell you anything more'n it's green."

"Good. Now back off, and let the cops handle it."

"No way. This guy's gonna lead me to my brother."

"Henry—"

"Uh-oh. Think he made me. He took off like he was goosed."

"Let him go. Where are you?"

"Coming outa that same Albertsons parking lot."

"How many in the car?"

It was hard to hear. The roar of Henry's motor grew louder. Wind noise increased. "One. The Chinese fellow. I got a good look at him as he got in the car."

"Can you ID him again?"

"You bet your ass!"

Henry went silent then as he pursued his quarry. Then, "Uh-oh. Jumped a red light. Hold on, I'm going for it."

"Henry, don't!"

The motor raced for a moment. "Shit! I picked up a cop. He's hauling me over."

"Stop for him, Henry, but don't break the connection. Give him the phone."

I managed to dial Gene on my landline by the time I heard a strange voice in my ear. Gene came on, so I held both receivers to my mouth.

"This is Officer Gillis. Who'm I talking to?"

"Officer Gillis, this is B. J. Vinson. I'm an Albuquerque licensed investigator, and the man you stopped is my operative. He was in pursuit of a vehicle holding a man involved in a kidnapping case."

With my frustration building, I sought to make the patrolman understand what was happening. Gene, who could hear me speaking but not Gillis's responses, finally interrupted and asked me to get the officer's station and badge numbers. After telling Gillis I would be responsible for any fine Henry was assessed, I hung up. Henry called back ten minutes later. Gillis let him go with a warning after the officer held a protracted conversation with Gene.

I sat and took turns cursing and praying. Praying that the net Gene would have immediately thrown out snared the Mercedes and its driver. Cursing when I realized that if they failed, Silver Wings would have one more indication we were closing in.

To keep from going crazy, I used one of the databases available to licensed private investigators to run down ownership on the Mercedes, using the tag number Henry gave me. Within a minute the name Desert Enterprises, Inc. popped up on my screen. The information available was the bare legal minimum. An address in the 10000 block of Montgomery Street NE. Not Montgomery Boulevard, a major east-west artery that bisects the city as Montgomery on the east side and Montaño on the west, but Montgomery *Street*, which I knew to be an address just south of Eldorado High School in the far northeast heights area of Albuquerque. The sole contact for the corporation was a name familiar to me: Brookings Ingles, attorney for the local underworld.

THE FACT that Ingles agreed to meet Gene and me at my office on a Saturday afternoon put me on my guard. I didn't think Brookie, as his intimates called him, would bestir himself on a weekend for anyone short of a cartel boss, yet Gene ran him to ground and prevailed upon him to grant us an audience. He would likely have commanded we come to him, but he probably didn't want a lowly lieutenant and a private gumshoe infecting his home. Or his office, for that matter.

The first thing that caught my eye when Ingles walked into my office was something I'd forgotten about the man—the tufts of silver at each temple in his sleek brown hair. They looked like silver wings. Could this be *the* Silver Wings? He was connected and able to provide cover as well as defense. He performed those tasks daily in his role as a noted defense attorney.

Ingles fit the mold in just about every way. But did he have a pipeline inside APD to feed him details such as a pending raid on a west-side motel? He probably knew as many cops as Gene and I did. Had this man ordered the murder of seven children and three adults simply to protect his identity?

"Gene. BJ. What's so urgent that I have to leave my family picnic to meet you two?"

"Possibly the life of a young man," Gene said.

"Sounds ominous."

In the barest terms possible, Gene sketched our predicament and turned to the matter of Desert Enterprises, Inc. at 10002 Montgomery Street NE.

"Who?" Ingles asked. "I never heard of them."

"You incorporated them and are the contact of record."

He waved a hand in the air. "Incorporated hundreds of companies I don't have anything to do with except act as their lawyer."

"You don't know James Hillion or Matthew Friedrichs or Apollo Nava?"

"Ah, now it's coming back. They're the incorporators. But we did business by phone. Don't know them."

I spoke up. "What can you tell us about 10002 Montgomery Street NE?"

"Just that it's a rent-an-office place in the northeast heights."

"How do you know that?"

"Because I signed the office lease for Desert Enterprises."

"Does anyone live on the premises?" I asked.

"I dunno. You'll have to ask the manager of the building. And before you ask, I don't know who that is."

Chapter 20

Jazz woke to find Kim poking his chest with a slender finger.

"You get up now. Mr. Silver Wings say we go on trip today."

Irked to be awakened from his first good sleep in days, he snapped, "Trip? Where? I don't want to go to Mexico."

"Not Mexico." Kim fluttered a graceful hand. "West somewhere."

Jazz sat up, taking note of Kim's eyes on his naked chest. "What time is it? Hell, what day is it?"

"Sunday. The day is Sunday. Time is six thirty. You pack small bag. Mr. Silver Wings say we stay overnight. One night. Then we come back here."

"I'll just stay here."

Kim's voice hardened. "You stay, you stay without your pipes. How you like that?"

Jazz kicked back the covers, allowing Kim to see that he slept naked. The manservant did not leave until Jazz closed the door to the bathroom behind him.

After a shower, Jazz joined Silver Wings on the patio near the pool for a breakfast of eggs over easy, hash browns, link sausage, and rye toast. After only one egg and one link, he grew nauseated. He swallowed hard, struggling to keep everything down.

Wings chatted amiably about how much he would enjoy the upcoming trip while Jazz sought to control his breathing and his rebellious gut. Before excusing himself to go get ready to leave, Wings told Kim to bring Jazz a pipe.

Left alone on the patio with his crack, Jazz fretted over where they were heading. For all he knew, Wings might load him in a car and drive straight to Mexico. The smoke calmed his fears. He'd raise a ruckus at the border, and that would put an end to that.

He was dozing when Kim appeared at his side and told him to get his bag. Within five minutes, the three of them piled into a Mercedes—not the green one Kim drove—and headed west on Interstate 40 until Wings instructed Kim to exit the freeway and head north on a bumpy dirt road. Five minutes later, a house appeared on the road before them. Beyond that was a bigger building that looked to be a hanger. A white twin-engine aircraft sat in front of it. His stomach clinched. They were *flying* somewhere. His fear of Mexico rose again, but he did as instructed and climbed into the back seat of the plane. He didn't know what kind it was, but it had what looked to be cargo space between the pilot's and copilot's seats in front and two side by side seats in back. Bolt-holes made him think some seats had been removed.

Wings walked around the plane with a man Jazz never saw before, checking things out. Then he climbed into the plane through the back door and made certain Jazz was buckled in before making his way to the front and claiming the left seat. Apparently his jailer was also his pilot. Moments later, the left engine cranked, and when it was running smoothly, the second coughed to life. Once they were airborne, Kim came back and handed Jazz a second pipe. It was the cock-shaped glass pipe he'd first used with Juan in what seemed a lifetime ago. Where was Juan? He hadn't seen his former lover in days… or was it weeks? He'd lost count of time. Once they achieved altitude and talk became possible, Jazz shouted to ask where they were going.

Wings spoke over his shoulder. "Got business in Gallup tomorrow. Going over today to see some sights, have a good dinner, and rest up for my meeting."

Jazz considered the answer. Was it true? The hollow feeling in his belly made him wonder. He glanced at Kim. All he could see of the small man was his head. He seemed relaxed. Calm. Jazz snorted to himself. That meant nothing. Kim was always calm.

Occasionally the two men spoke, raising their voices rather than using earphones. Finally a question the houseboy asked snagged his attention.

"Same place we dumped the Vespa?"

As Jazz struggled to understand those words, Wings shook his head.

"That's up in the wilderness area. We're over the malpais. The lavalands. What's he doing?"

Jazz quickly closed his eyes as Kim's head moved. Breathing through his mouth, he willed his taut muscles to behave.

"Seems asleep."

"This is as good a place as any. Nobody'll find him here."

Jazz peeked through half-open lids as Kim climbed out of his seat and headed his way. There was a long pause as Kim struggled with something. Jazz looked again and was horrified to see the houseboy open the aircraft's cargo door. The atmospherics changed as the seal was broken, and the plane wobbled for a second.

Then Kim's hands were on him, unfastening his seat belt and tugging at his torso. "You come. Kim show you something. Come."

Jazz got to his feet. If Kim tried to shove him out of the aircraft, he'd take the fucker with him. He blinked, wondering why he wasn't scared out of his wits. That pipe hadn't tasted right. They'd put something in it. Shit!

He quit cooperating and felt the strength in Kim's slender, muscled arms as the man backed toward the gaping doorway. He needed to be ready when the Chinaman tried to turn and put him in the doorway. Still without a plan, Jazz felt panic rise in him. He began cooperating and felt Kim's grip loosen.

"Show me what?" he mumbled, gathering the mental and physical strength he was going to need.

"Something pretty. Beautiful. You see. Come with Kim."

Jazz took a step and felt as if he and Kim were dancing slowly toward the open hatch… toward eternity. He felt Kim's arms tighten and knew this was when the man would swing him into position before the door.

At that moment the plane's right wing dipped alarmingly, hurtling both of them toward the gaping hole. The maneuver was so sudden and abrupt that they had no opportunity to prepare. Just as they reached the doorway, Jazz threw his arms wide and spread his legs. His action broke Kim's hold on him. Jazz saw the horror in the man's eyes as he dropped out of the hatch and was snatched away by the wind and the prop wash.

Jazz desperately spread-eagled against the fuselage as gravity and the rush of air sought to pull him outside. His back bowed. His spine creaked painfully. He hung on for as long as he could, but his strength was fading. He thought of his mother and his brother and all those who would never know what happened to him. A little moan escaped him as one arm partially gave way, pushing him farther out of the craft.

Then the plane righted itself, and the terrible pressure eased. He had almost recovered his balance when he heard Wings call out.

"Is it done, Kim? Is he gone?"

Shocked back into his senses, Jazz willed his paralyzed muscles to respond. He crawled on all fours back to his seat and hid in the narrow space behind it.

"Jazz, you okay?"

Wings' voice almost shocked him into replying, but he covered his mouth and nose with a hand as the terrible awfulness of what happened penetrated his sluggish mind. Wings had deliberately killed his manservant. His right-hand man. And the bastard thought he'd gotten rid of him at the same time. What would Wings do when he discovered that wasn't true?

He froze as he heard the click of a seat belt. Wings was coming back to check for himself. See if he'd been successful.

"Too bad, Kim," he heard a hollow voice say. "You were a good man, but you knew too much."

Jazz started at Wings' next words but controlled the urge to rush the man and shove him out the gaping door. "Sorry, Jazz. You were the greatest fuck I've ever had, but people are closing in on me. Need to clean things up. If you'd agreed to go to Mexico without causing trouble, you'd still be alive."

The door thumped, and the atmospherics changed again. He heard Wings return to the pilot's seat. Almost immediately the plane banked again. Jazz guessed they were now heading back to the airfield they'd departed from.

His head ached, and his limbs lost all strength. Fright? Or was it something they put in his pipe? Jazz fought to stave off unconsciousness, but his world grew smaller and smaller until he was oblivious to everything.

HE WOKE with a grunt as the plane hit the airstrip. He glanced beneath the seats to see Wings manipulating the instruments, but the engines were so noisy, the man couldn't have heard him. Should he rush Wings while he was occupied or wait until they came to a halt? Wait. Was that a decision or inertia?

But once the engines shut down, things grew quiet. Wings fooled him again. He exited by the door at his shoulder. Jazz lay as he was, hardly able to believe he'd not been detected. Then he heard Wings and the man who'd attended them at the takeoff talking.

"Short flight. Got a call to come back for a meeting."

"Too bad. Everyone deserves a Sunday off. Where are your passengers?"

"Dropped them in Gallup. One of them has relatives there."

"Oh, the Indian guy, huh? Quick for a trip to Gallup."

"I didn't even shut down the engines, just dumped them out the door and got clearance to take off again."

"You want me to put the bird to bed, Mr. Haldemain?"

Haldemain! Was that Wings' real name? Jazz strained to hear more, but the two moved away.

As he waited to make sure Wings was gone, Jazz was surprised to feel movement. It took a minute to figure out the stranger was pushing the craft into the hanger. He heard another voice, a woman's, calling instructions. Eventually the big building cast a shadow over the plane. Heat in the stuffy interior eased a bit.

Now? Should he reveal himself now and ask for help? They might have a phone, so he could call someone. Who? The police? He heard the two speaking again, right beside the plane.

"I don't like that man." The woman's voice.

"Don't much like him either. But I ain't about to cross him. His money's good, but I got a feeling he's a man you don't cross."

"I hear you on that."

Mindful of the unseen man's caution, Jazz remained where he was until discomfort and his bladder forced him to move. He was unable to stand straight in the confines of the cabin, but movement felt good. He took sadistic pleasure in pissing all over the pilot's seat and the control panel. He hoped it shorted out every wire in the whole damned airplane. But the truth was that without any liquid since breakfast, he probably wouldn't do more than stink up the place.

After that he climbed out of the stuffy craft into the heat of the tin-roofed hanger. He had no intention of leaving until dark, but he satisfied himself the side door to the building could be opened from the inside before he settled in a corner to wait.

The nausea and cramps didn't show up until almost sundown, but his nerves prickled, and he scratched at unseen insects an hour before that. He managed to remain where he was until dark by pacing the building and railing in whispers about Wings and Kim and Juan and all the rest of the fuckers he'd ever seen or heard of.

After the deep darkness of the hanger, when he finally wandered outside the world seemed as luminous as a sun-drenched day. He spotted a water spigot at the side of the shed and spent a long time slaking his thirst. Then he looked around, wondering for the first time if there was a dog on the premises. But he heard nothing.

A single light burned in the house, which looked to be adobe or stucco. Living room, probably. A flicker now and then told him the couple watched TV. Rage flooded him. They were inside, fed and comfortable and watching the tube, while he was cramping and itching and God knew what else. He grasped a rock in his hand to toss through the window before reason returned.

Orienting himself, he walked toward what he believed to be I-40 to the south of the house. As he neared the edge of the building, he noticed something shiny catching the moonlight. A bicycle.

Mentally saying thanks to the couple or Coyote or maybe God, he tossed a leg over the contraption and started off down the road. The cycle's light was so dim he took more than one spill as a wheel dropped into an unseen washout, but the exercise helped keep his other problems at bay. Despite the cool high desert air, he was sweating heavily by the time he reached the overpass to the highway. He stood blankly watching a few cars occasionally pass beneath him before shaking off his lethargy.

To the left was Albuquerque and Haldemain and his pipes… and BJ, if he could find him. To the right lay Indian country. Another bout of cramps left him weak and exhausted. Semirecovered, he wheeled the bike down the ramp and set off to the east… toward Albuquerque.

Traffic was light. Even so, he tried to keep to the shoulder but still got a couple of honks. Before long he was leaking sweat like his essence was flowing out of him. His thirst built even as his strength ebbed. It became harder and harder to push the pedals and keep the front wheel pointed where he wanted to go.

He was on his last legs when he spotted a single pair of headlamps—weaker than most of the others—crest the hill on the opposite side of the freeway. Entranced, he watched the tiny lights grow bigger as they neared. They seemed important for some reason. His heart stuttered in his chest. Silver Wings? Had the man figured out he was alive and was coming for him? Maybe it was a mistake to piss all over his airplane and steal the bicycle. As Jazz stared at the steadily approaching lights, he knew one thing. They were important to him.

Suddenly aware he strayed to the left, he jerked the wheel and tried to return to the shoulder of the road. The headlamps had almost reached a spot opposite him when a deep-throated air horn blast from behind shook him so badly he lost the pedals. A huge eighteen-wheeler roared by, the wash of its passing first drawing him back to the center line and then shoving him toward the shoulder so violently he lost his balance and pitched off the bicycle and crashed headlong into the ditch. Everything went black.

"HE DEAD?"

The voice coming out of the darkness partially revived him.

"Help me get him up."

"Maybe something's broke. Maybe we oughta leave him where he is."

"Can't do that. He's all bummed up. He's bleeding from the head pretty good. Gimme your shirt."

"Use his. He won't know the difference."

He wanted to open his eyes and see who was hassling him, but he just couldn't manage it, no matter how he tried. He hurt. His belly clawed at him and his throat went dry and his head thundered. Cold air puckered his chest as his shirt was ripped away. Why didn't they leave him alone?

"Come on, Klah, I ain't gonna be able to handle him by myself."

"I swear, Uncle Gad. Aunt Dibe's right. You'd be rich if you quit taking in strays."

"Shut up and help me."

"You take him home, she's gonna give you the rough edge of her tongue."

"Had it a time or two in my day. Come on, boy."

Jazz felt himself lifted in the arms of angels... if angels swore in two different languages. Strange. Two languages. And he understood both. Maybe he was an angel too. He wished they'd speak another tongue to see if he understood that one as well.

When they tossed him into something... probably the bed of a truck... he knew he was no angel. He hurt too much.

"Ride in the back with him," the older, deeper voice said.

"No way. He's not gonna bounce out. I'm riding up front."

Jazz drifted off as soon as the truck pulled onto the highway but came awake again as the vehicle veered and climbed a ramp. They stopped before turning right. Shortly thereafter, the road grew so rough he came awake amid a shower of aches and pains. But he still didn't manage to open his eyes.

He had no idea how long they traveled, but eventually the truck slowed, turned, and came to a halt. Doors banged. Then a woman's voice.

"Thought you'd be back earlier'n this."

"Woulda," the younger male said. "But we stopped at an accident."

Silence, and then the woman spoke sharply. From right beside the truck bed.

"Lordy, Gad, what you done now? Looks like this fella needs to be in a hospital, not at our place."

"Our place was closer."

"You oughta seen it, Aunt Dibe. We saw this feeble little light way down the other side of the highway and wondered what it was."

"Klah thought it was Coyote with his tail on fire."

"Did not. Just said it looked like a prank he might pull. Anyway, when we got close enough, we saw this guy on a bicycle."

"On the freeway?" the woman asked. "Lucky the state patrol didn't pick him up. You can't ride a bicycle on a interstate."

"Mighta been luckier for him if they had. A big semi came up behind this jasper, and the wash tumbled him down in a ditch. He was zonked and bleeding by the time we got to him."

"Bet that trucker didn't even stop."

"Probably didn't even know what happened," the older man said. "This one's been out of it ever since."

"Who is he?"

"Dunno. Didn't have no ID on him. Didn't have nothing on him."

"Jazz!" He couldn't believe he spoke until he heard the group gathered around him give a collective gasp.

"Jazz?" the younger voice asked. "That's not a name, that's a beat."

"Jazz," he repeated, sounding like a croaking frog.

"Jazz what?" the woman asked.

His eyes flew open. He didn't know. His mind groped for an answer. "What you said earlier."

"What did I say earlier?"

"Jasper. You said Jasper. That's my other name."

"Jazz Jasper?"

He frowned into a nut-brown face creased with a few well-earned wrinkles. Her gray hair still held touches of black in it. Jazz Jasper. That didn't sound quite right. But it would do for now.

Suddenly he retched and his legs jerked up to his chest. He rolled over on his side and shook, biting his tongue to keep from screaming aloud.

"He's on something," the woman said. "Them's withdrawal pains if I ever seen them. What you got us into now, Gad Hatahle?"

Chapter 21

PAUL ROUSED me from a restless sleep by pulling me to him. I sighed in the comfort of his warm embrace.

"You were moaning and tossing," he said.

"Sorry, I'll go to the couch."

"I like it this way. It's nice having the house to ourselves again."

Henry had reluctantly returned home yesterday, saying he had to report for work Monday morning—this morning—or else lose his job at the coal mine.

"You're worried about Jazz?" Paul asked, apparently referring to my thrashing about in my sleep. "I have to admit I get jealous about you obsessing over such a handsome hunk. You're tempted by him, aren't you?"

"Wouldn't be honest if I denied it," I admitted. "But don't worry. I belong to you."

"I know that. Just like I belong to you. Still, that green-eyed monster shows up now and then."

"Yet you went out of your way to help find him. Put yourself at risk, even. Why?"

Paul sighed and settled his long body against me before answering. "Three reasons. Jazz is a good guy and doesn't deserve what's happening to him. He deserves my help. And second, I did it for you. To help you."

"And third?"

"It's my job as an investigative journalist." He clutched me to him involuntarily. "Hey, that sounds pretty good, doesn't it? Investigative journalist."

"And you are one. How many freelance articles have you sold so far?"

"Half a dozen. Thinking about doing a write-up on that underwear bomber that tried to blow up an airplane last Christmas. You know, about radical fundamentalists and all." He squirmed to get comfortable against me. "Not exactly making expenses yet, but it's a start. Someday I'll be able to quit my job at the country club."

"Disappointing all the girls and half the guys at the pool," I said.

But he wasn't willing to turn frolicsome. "He's in real danger, isn't he? Jazz, I mean."

"To be honest, I'm afraid he's already out of the country or dead."

His involuntary shiver shook my body. "I hope not."

I fought a catch in my throat. "Paul, make love to me."

As dawn's blossoming light filtered through the drapes, I watched Pedro the Dragon dance and prowl as our passions built. Gradually my world shrank to the beautiful man above me.

I WAITED until nine that morning before parking in the lot of 10002 Montgomery Street NE in front of a one-story white slump block edifice proclaiming itself to be the Northeast Heights Office Building. The sign outside held half a dozen names, presumably of those renting offices. Desert Enterprises, Inc. was listed as Suite 103.

A plump fellow about my age sat at a desk behind a counter to the left as I entered. I automatically scanned his brown hair for a bleached spot, but this guy—Wayne according to his name tag—didn't wear the brand. According to him, no one from Desert Enterprises was in. He offered to take a message.

"Perhaps you can tell me a little about them," I suggested. "What exactly do they do?"

"Have no idea, sir. I just take their phone messages and let them know when someone is at the front desk asking for them."

"And what is their phone number? I wasn't able to find it in the yellow pages."

He handled that one easily enough, and I entered the number into my phone. "Thank you, and who generally staffs the office?"

"They don't show up very often, but then they do, it's usually Mr. Nava."

Wayne gave me a description of a small, dark man with wavy black hair, but he was beginning to grow wary at my line of inquiry. He clammed up completely after learning I was a confidential investigator.

Lt. Gene Enriquez can be an intimidating fellow when he wants to be, and Wayne wasn't built to withstand the likes of him. After I called my former riding partner to the premises, he talked his way into the Desert Enterprises office without a search warrant or any legal right to do so. But the cake wasn't worth the candle. The office was one big room with two empty desks. There was no sign of occupancy since the furniture likely belonged to the building, not the company.

As Gene and I stood in the middle of the empty room, he threw me a glance. "It's nothing but a mailing address. You think there's any chance this Mr. Nava's gonna show up again?"

"Not after Brookings Ingles warns him off," I said.

"You think this has anything to do with the White Streak family?"

I shrugged. "Who knows? It might be some shady deal Brookie had going that just showed up on our radar. At any rate, it's shut down. You think it's worth getting the crime scene boys out to take a look?"

"Naw. It's wiped clean. Besides, I got no probable cause for anything like that. But let's see if we can get a telephone log out of the guy up front."

Wayne readily produced a log and a lease when prompted. There were few calls on the log, and they appeared to be from only three numbers. One I recognized as Brookings Ingles' office. The other two were probably the other two incorporators' numbers. Gene would run them to ground.

We learned little from the lease that we did not already know. Brookings Ingles had executed on behalf of the corporation as its attorney. The corporation was described as providing professional business services, which explained nothing. Interestingly enough, the company prepaid a year's lease up front. A photocopy of the cashier's check was stapled to the lease.

"Drawn on a local bank," Gene noted. "But I'll bet you a beer it's paid by funds wired to Ingles' account. But I'll follow up anyway."

As we walked out into the parking lot, my cell phone rang. It was Det. Lonzo Joe.

"BJ, you've got a lead on Jazz?"

I tapped Gene on the arm and halted beside my Impala. "We had a confirmed sighting last Friday but nothing since then. Frankly, I'm worried that the pimps have been alerted about that. Why do you ask?"

"Somebody from APD pulled his prints from our system."

"Why would they come to you instead of going to AFIS?" I asked, referring to the FBI's Integrated Automated Fingerprint Identification System.

"We don't register our juvie prints there. Neither does Farmington PD. And Jazz was a juvenile the last time we took his prints."

"So who asked for the prints from here?"

"A Vice detective by the name of Charles Zimmerman, but you didn't hear it from me. If you check with him, cover my ass, okay?"

I closed the call and leaned against the fender of Gene's nondescript brown Ford sedan and pursed my lips.

"What?" he asked.

"That was Lonzo Joe."

"The San Juan County detective who tipped us on Nesposito?"

I nodded. "That Vice detective who picked up Henry just checked San Juan County for Jazz's fingerprints." I headed off his obvious question. "They don't register juvies with AFIS."

"Charles Zimmerman?"

I nodded. "Let's call him. He had a reason for asking. Maybe Jazz showed up again."

Gene hesitated, raising my antenna. "Naw. Rather talk to him in person. Vice is… well, sort of another world. It's like they don't know the rest of us even exist. Probably have to go to his supervisor."

"Who's that?"

"Vice reports to Bolton."

"The Lieutenant Bolton who's a director of CAHT?" I asked.

"The same."

"Maybe the council asked them to check."

"Then why would Zimmerman do it?" Gene asked.

"Delegation," I suggested.

"Okay, but why would the council be checking?"

"Maybe Betsy found something after our talk with her."

"We don't need a face-to-face meeting with her," he said, reaching for his phone.

Betsy had no news of Jazz and had not asked that his fingerprints be pulled. She volunteered to ask around to see if someone else in the organization did so, but Gene hastily asked her to simply drop the matter and closed the call.

That left Zimmerman… and his boss, Bolton. I agreed with Gene's careful approach but likely for different reasons. His had to do with APD politics and procedures; mine were motivated by the fact Bolton was a board member of CAHT, which was rapidly moving up on my list of possible leakers to Silver Wings.

"Bolton can be an ass sometimes, but he's still a cop," Gene said after I voiced my feelings."

"Isn't he married?"

Gene hesitated. "Why would you ask me that? Oh, I see. Jazz is gay. Yeah, he's married, but the word is Bolton's eyes wander."

"To the other side of the aisle?" I asked.

"Surprise the hell out of me if he did, but who knows?"

"What about Zimmerman?"

"Don't know much about him but don't like what I do. He's been in Vice for a few years. Used to be undercover, but not now." Gene shook his head. "In my opinion, you don't leave a guy in Vice for long. Zimmerman's as macho as they come but don't think he's married. If I recall correctly, he has a sexual harassment complaint or two. By women," he supplied before I asked.

I ran a hand over my face. "In my experience, sex is sex for some guys. Doesn't matter much who with. Especially the aggressive types."

"Maybe so, but I wouldn't want to call Zimmerman gay to his face."

"You're making my case. A riverboat shall be my horse."

"What the hell does that mean?"

"It's something my mother used to say when she meant there were alternative explanations for something. Or as I like to say, those who harbor self-doubts rale loudest against what they fear in themselves."

"When did you get to be a philosopher? Come on, let's get moving."

"Zimmerman or Bolton?"

"Zimmerman first… if we can find him."

We did. He was getting in his car, another anonymous Ford like Gene's, except it was blue. He rolled down the window as Gene hailed him.

"Zim, I understand you pulled prints from San Juan County on a fellow named Jazz Penrod."

"*Jasper* Penrod, yeah. But he goes by Jazz, I guess. Why?"

"What was your interest?"

"His name came up in something I'm working on. Can't say much about it, but he's a brother to the guy I picked up at the Blue Spruce. The one you got sprung."

"Half brother. What was the info on Penrod?"

"Just a whisper. Enough to make me want to know more about him. That's all I can say."

"You know we're looking for him, right?"

"Yeah. All points. Bet I find him before you do."

"If so, you better deliver him in one piece."

"Do my best. But if he resists…?"

Zimmerman backed out of his parking space and pulled away. As we watched him go, I asked a question.

"Do you believe him?"

Gene's shrug was almost invisible. "No reason not to. But let's see what Bolton has to say."

Bolton was in his office but made us wait ten minutes while he finished talking with one of his officers. He was friendly enough after he waved us in. "BJ, you rejoined the force?"

"No. Don't think they'd have me if I tried."

Gene was tired of fooling around. "Bolt, Zimmerman called San Juan County for a set of Jazz Penrod's fingerprints. You know why?"

"How do you know that?"

I appreciated the way Gene handled that question. "Because I did the same thing, and they told me to see a Vice detective named Zimmerman who'd just called on the same matter."

"And why did you want them?"

"You know we've been looking for this guy ever since he got pulled in by the White Streak family."

"As we all know, that gang doesn't exist any longer. And we have the gristly remains to prove it."

"Any progress on those killings?" Gene asked.

"Something must have prompted you to pull those prints."

"Something must have prompted Zimmerman to pull them as well. What was it?"

Bolton pursed his lips for a moment as he ran a big hand through what was left of his hair. Like many men who are follicle impaired on the scalp, his arms were hairy. "Don't have all the details of what he's working on, but he believes he's found a Navajo connection to the gang that got wiped out the other day."

"A fellow by the name of Nesposito's the Navajo connection. And he's in custody for a child molestation case on the rez."

"Zim's found another one. That same fellow you got released the other day. He didn't appreciate you interfering in his case, by the way."

"Henry Secatero?" I asked. "You can't be serious."

"Apparently Zim is. Says he can connect him. He figures the brother's mixed up in it too, and that's why you can't find the kid. He disappeared voluntarily."

"Preposterous!" I said. "I know that family. Henry may play the field, but he does it with grown-up women. He holds down a good job. He's a solid citizen."

"But his brother's gay, right? And he disappeared right before those ten people, including kids, I remind you, got slaughtered. And one of them who bought it was the guy you identified as this Jazz character's contact with the gang. That's worth a look, wouldn't you say?"

I opened my mouth to respond, but Gene beat me to it. "What about this Mr. Silver Wings? Have you had any hits on that alias?"

For some reason I felt relieved when Bolton transferred his attention to Gene. "Not in the system anywhere. None of our CIs have come through, and we've picked at them hard."

I imagined that was true. Vice... hell, the police department... lived and died by their confidential informants.

"What about you?" Bolton asked him.

"It's not my case."

That earned Gene a horse laugh. "When's that ever stopped you? Why did you contact San Juan County? You could have got the kid's prints from MVD."

"So could Zim. But I wanted the same thing he wanted. Any details on the kid's card that might help us find him."

"Do you know where he is?" Bolton asked.

"No, I don't. Do you?"

"No idea. But I'm looking. Wouldn't be hard to imagine him holding the gun that killed those kids and his lover."

Gene got me out of there before I did lasting damage to my APD contacts.

Chapter 22

HENRY DIDN'T answer his cell, so I dictated a callback request on his phone and as an extra precaution, I left a message for him at his chapter house. Navajo chapter houses functioned as sort of local government and social gathering places for various clans on the reservation. After I finished delivering my message for Henry to contact me right away, I casually asked the girl on the other end of the phone if she'd seen Jazz lately.

"No, sir. Not in a long time. You know, you're the second person to ask about Jazz today."

"I am? Who was the other?"

"Hosteen Nesposito."

Surprised she still accorded the man with the honorific of Hosteen, I asked if he'd phoned or asked in person.

"He was right here. Came by on some business and then stopped to chat and ask about Jazz. Strange that we haven't seen him. Jazz usually shows up every few weeks. It's been over two months since he was here."

I thanked her and hung up, anxious to run down Lonzo. When I finally reached him, he confirmed that his contact on the Navajo police told him the tribal court allowed Nesposito to bond out of jail. In fact, Lonzo said the case was beginning to unravel. The complaining girl's father started equivocating. In Lonzo's opinion the man had been both intimidated and bought off.

"Aren't the Navajo authorities afraid Nesposito will run?" I asked.

"Why? The rez is the safest place for him. Somebody, presumably from the big bad world out there, has already tried to kill him. Why would he leave?" Lonzo thought a minute and answered his own question. "Course, he has some family down at To'hajiilee. He might go there."

"You mean on the reservation west of me?"

"Yeah."

The Navajo Reservation in the Four Corners area was the largest Indian reservation in the United States, consisting of some 17,000,000 acres spread over 27,400 square miles in three states: Arizona, Utah, and New Mexico. Established by treaty in 1868 following the release of some 9,000 Navajos from imprisonment at Bosque Redondo, it was now the home of the descendants of the Long Walk.

However, there were other, smaller, noncontiguous reservations of Navajos strewn across the landscape. One of them was the To'hajiilee Indian Reservation, some thirty miles west of Albuquerque, lying north of I-40. It was home to what were once called the Cañoncito Navajos.

"Why would Nesposito be asking about Jazz?" I mused. "He's been taken by the traffickers."

"Maybe Nesposito knows something we don't know."

"Maybe I know somebody who can get it out of him. And I've already left a call for him."

"Be careful, BJ. Don't screw up the case against the old bastard."

I hung up puzzled over why Julian Nesposito was asking about Jazz. Why would someone who *worked* for the cartel be looking for a man already *taken* by the cartel? Although I didn't know exactly why, my heart took a little leap in my chest.

HENRY PHONED that evening while Paul and I were supping on some of my companion's green chili chicken stew. Nobody made it like Paul, but as soon as Caller ID identified Henry, I forgot about the hot bowl in front of me.

"Thanks for calling me back. Wanted to give you a heads-up. You remember that Detective Zimmerman who busted you at the Blue Spruce."

"A bunch of them busted me, but I assume you're talking about the guy in charge. The one who questioned me later. Yeah, I remember the bastard. Why?"

"He's telling his superiors that he's investigating you and Jazz as being a part of the human trafficking ring on the rez. Claims Jazz disappeared on purpose before he could be brought to justice."

"Lying son of a bitch. Didn't know the Albuquerque Police Department could reach that far. Up here, I mean."

"There's a task force working on trafficking, includes feds and locals. They can reach anywhere."

"Whadda I need to do?"

"Keep your head down and your nose clean. And most of all, don't lose your cool if they come question you."

"Maybe I should just go on a vacation."

"Last thing you want to do, man. They'll take that as a sign of guilt. Just keep living your life, but I thought you ought to know. Gene and I are working on this end to see what else we can find out."

"Thanks."

"One other thing. Nesposito's out on bail."

"I heard."

"And he's asking around about Jazz."

"You're kidding me."

"Afraid not. At least, he asked at your chapter house. When I left a message for you, the girl on the phone told me Nesposito asked about Jazz earlier today. Might not hurt to go see why he's asking. But, Henry...."

"Yeah?"

"Don't beat his head in. In fact, don't touch him. Bruises and cracked bones might get Nesposito out of the trouble he's in right now."

There was silence on the phone for a long second. "I'll get Louie to tackle him. If you think I've got a reputation, you oughta meet my old man sometime. I think he'd rather beat an answer out of a guy than get it voluntarily."

"Okay, if you can control him."

"Fifty-fifty chance."

"Let me know what you find out."

I closed the call and filled Paul in on the conversation. I ended the explanation with a question. "Have you checked Juan's email recently?"

"Few days ago."

"It's still up?"

"Yeah. The carrier will close it out if it remains inactive for ninety days or so. I've left a couple of messages, but no one responds."

We finished our meal, cleaned up the kitchen, and retired to the den, where television got short shrift. Our carnal activities were much more interesting than *The Good Wife*'s legal problems.

SEVERAL ANXIOUS days passed without any word from Henry. I was tempted to call but stayed off the phone. He would contact me as soon as he had something to report.

In the meantime Hazel put me to work on other cases, claiming we needed to pay the bills somehow. Of course, she knew my schoolteacher parents invested in Microsoft when it was a little business conducted from a garage here in Albuquerque. As a result of that, they'd left me an estate of $12,000,000, which I hadn't touched in a meaningful way. Still, she was determined that the investigative business made it on its own, and that meant paying cases instead of pro bono work for friends.

Even though I was the boss, Hazel ruled the administrative end of the business, and I found myself hotfooting it around town with a camera trying to establish a connection between a local banker and a known con man. The connection wasn't difficult to establish. They lunched together, golfed together, and hit bars together, but there was nothing to indicate they weren't simply social friends. Until I backtracked and started checking receipts, that is. The con man paid for everything: golf fees, caddy fees, drinks, dinners… everything. Didn't exactly establish criminality, but it was enough for the bank to rein in their vice president. I turned in my final report and bill on Thursday morning and got back to what was really on my mind: who was Silver Wings, and where was he holding Jazz.

Pretty well convinced CAHT was the source of the leak to Silver Wings, I cajoled Betsy into meeting me for drinks after work. As I drank beer, she sipped a Tom Collins and assured me none of the board members had done anything out of the ordinary since we last spoke. She again denied her organization was the culprit. I went home discouraged and anxious over my friend's state of health.

MY CELL went off at ten that evening, just as the Channel 13 news program started. Henry's low voice rumbled through the ether. I told him to hold it while I killed the TV and put him on speaker so Paul could hear.

"Sorry to be so long getting back to you," Henry said after I gave him the go-ahead. "But Nesposito disappeared for a couple of days. Louie caught him as he was leaving the chapter house this afternoon and invited him for a beer. A couple of six-packs, as a matter of fact. Dad said the old coot seemed interested in talking to him too."

As Henry told the story, the two loaded up beer and a fifth of rotgut before driving out into the countryside. When they found a place isolated enough, they sat on the tailgate of Louie's truck while they guzzled Budweiser. Both were hard drinkers, so they were likely both drunk before Nesposito surprised Louie by asking if he'd heard from Jazz. That started things off, and when Louie demanded to know why Nesposito was asking around about his son, things got physical.

"Did your father manhandle him?" I asked.

"Roughed him up some, but he said the old man threw the first punch. At any rate, we know why Nesposito was asking about Jazz. They found his fingerprints on a stolen bike abandoned on I-40."

"Who found the bike?"

"Dunno. Maybe that Albuquerque cop who's been nosing around. All I can tell you is that the traffickers know about it."

"Where on I-40?" I asked.

"Little west of Albuquerque. Maybe twenty miles."

"What's out there?" Paul wanted to know.

"Not much at that particular distance," I said. "It's mostly checkerboard land. You know, Indian, government, and a little private."

"And To'hajiilee," Henry said.

"That's a little farther. More like thirty miles," I said. "But you know what this means, don't you?"

"Yeah. My brother's loose and was trying to get to town. And if they're still looking for him, he's still free."

"Then why hasn't he called someone? You, your father, his uncle… mother. Someone."

"If he was that close to Albuquerque, he'd have called you," Henry said.

I disagreed. "He knows your phone numbers. He probably doesn't remember mine from three years ago."

"You remember when we were looking for Lando Alfano up here on that case?" Henry said. "We asked the same thing. Why didn't he call the family for help?"

"And the answer was that he'd been hurt. Maybe that's what's happened here. What shape was the bike in?"

"Dunno. Nesposito just said it was in a ditch beside the freeway."

"Did the old goat give up Silver Wings?" Paul asked.

"Uh-uh. Earned him a couple of extra pops, but Louie said he wouldn't budge. My guess is he knew my dad would just beat on him some, but this Silver Wings would do lots worse."

"He's already tried," I reminded them. "Henry, did we screw up the feds' chances of nailing Nesposito?"

"Don't see why. The old man got drunk and picked a fight."

"That's the story?" I asked.

"That's the story."

"Stick with it."

Once again, Henry hesitated. "This means the traffickers are on the hunt for Jazz too, doesn't it?"

"Yeah, and Nesposito is just the tip of the arrow," I said.

Chapter 23

JAZZ CAME out of a restless sleep fighting a pair of strong arms encircling him in the abject darkness.

"Easy, dude. Having a bad dream or something."

It took a moment to realize Klah clutched him to his chest as they lay on the mattress on the dirt floor of the little shack beside the Hatahle hogan. In the two days since the Hatahles rescued him from I-40, the younger Navajo had been standoffish at best and hostile at worst. Jazz started to rise, but it felt good to be held, and Klah didn't seem uncomfortable. He relaxed.

"I know you're having trouble remembering things," Klah said at last. "But you called out a coupla things. Silver Wings. Juan. Kim. That mean anything to you?"

Jazz's mind spun, leaving him momentarily dizzy. "Bad dudes," he mumbled, shaking his head. "Sometimes I feel like I got rats in the attic."

"Sometimes you act like the lights is on but nobody's home, but you get okay after a while. Those dudes… you remember them now?"

Jazz shivered. "Yeah. Sorta. Silver Wings, he's the worst. Juan was…." He swallowed hard. "Juan was okay until he betrayed me to Silver Wings."

"Silver Wings? What kinda name is that. He a blood?"

Jazz shook his head against Klah's hard-muscled chest. "White. Bad. Real bad." His head ached as he tried to remember. "He's why I was pedaling down the highway on a bicycle in the middle of the night."

"Getting away from him, huh?"

"Yeah."

"And this Kim. Who's she?"

"Him." Jazz experienced a sudden image of the room tilting and Kim blown out through a hole in the wall. No. No, it was an airplane. Kim fell out of an airplane. Because Silver Wings tried to kill them both. "He was a him."

He groaned, and Klah pulled him closer. Jazz looked up and in the dim ambient light made out the shape of the other's head. He clasped the arms holding him. "Didn't know you wanted anything to do with me. Figured you wanted me gone. Outa here."

"I thought so too," came the reply. "Guess I was jealous."

"Jealous? Of me? Why?"

"You're so fucking good-looking. Pretty, really. Beautiful. Never seen a guy like you before. First thing I thought was that my girl'd go nuts over you and forget all about me."

Not quite understanding why, Jazz touched Klah's cheek and mumbled, "Believe me, I'm no threat to you and your girl."

Slowly, hesitantly, Klah lowered his head until their lips touched. The moment became intense. Klah's tongue intruded; Jazz accepted it. Finally Klah drew away.

"Man!" he said in a breathy tone. Then after a moment, "That's not the first time I've kissed you."

Jazz kept quiet.

"Last night—the first night we slept here—I watched you sleep. Don't know why I wanted to, but I did. I kissed you. It was... nice."

Jazz lay still, comfortable in Klah's arms.

"And I touched you too." His hand covered Jazz's groin. "Here." There was an audible gulp. "Wow. It moved."

Without understanding anything other than a growing need, Jazz pulled free of Klah's embrace and pushed him flat on his back. They both slept in their shorts, so a lot of muscled bare flesh pressed together. He rubbed his torso against Klah's and then kissed him fiercely. Heated groin to heated groin, they lay for a moment before Jazz asked in a hoarse voice, "Are you ready?"

"I-I think so."

Slowly, skillfully, Jazz drove them up the mountain of ecstasy and brought them over the top. Although he knew better, he felt as if this were his first ejaculation.

They lay beside one another basking in the afterglow of sexual satisfaction, Jazz on his back with Klah's hand resting on his chest. Although he sensed his lover was asleep, rising doubts and fears tormented Jazz. He turned away from Klah and hugged his knees to his chest as recollections of exciting couplings floated into his consciousness. Trysts with Juan, beautiful, satisfying love spoiled by drugs and betrayal. The looming image of a man called Silver Wings brought a gasp and anger... and dredged up another name.

Haldemain.

DIBE PERFORMED a hand trembling and decided Jazz's spirit was out of harmony because of the action of outsiders. He needed an Enemy Way ceremony. Neither Jazz nor the Hatahles possessed enough money for a nine-day ceremony like that. So far as Jazz could see, the Hatahles lived a hand-to-mouth existence. But Dibe made a pair of earrings for a local shaman and promised three hand-trembling treatments to induce Hosteen Pintaro to sing a few songs over him. It wasn't a proper ceremony, but the old man sized things up.

"You bad outa harmony. What they say your name is? Jazz. That ain't no name. You come to us because of a bicycle, *tsi'izi*. So that's your name to me. Bicycle."

Jazz nodded.

"You ain't got no people here to sing for you. What I done is all I can do without no proper ceremony. Costs money. Time. You understand?"

With nausea building in the back of his throat, Jazz swallowed hard and nodded. "Yes, sir."

"*Ni'ii'niti* got a hold a you. Cocaine. That stuff makes a man live his life too fast." He pounded his chest. "Heart beats like a drum. Nerves burn up. Belly dry up because you ain't hungry no more. You keep it up, you look old as me in a few moons. How long you been on it?"

Jazz blinked and shook his head. "I don't know. Not long. What day is this?"

"Day the whites call Tuesday. August 24."

A little groan escaped Jazz. He'd come down to meet Juan in early August. "Maybe a month."

"Uh," the old man grunted. "Ain't long, but that stuff grabs hold fast."

Hosteen Pintaro asked how he took the drug and how often. Then they sat in silence for a long time before the old shaman got up and busied himself at a table. After what seemed like an ungodly amount of time, he shuffled back with a couple of mason jars full of something that looked like tea and a small pouch. He handed it all to Jazz.

"You hear me now, Bicycle. You drink that tea like it was your mama's milk. When that's gone, you get some more. You gotta pee out the cocaine. It's gonna hide in your bladder and your liver and in all kinda places. You drink the tea."

Pintaro motioned to the pouch. "Got some vitamin C and D there. Take 'em, and when they gone, take some more. You need zinc, so eat pumpkins seeds, garlic, sesame seeds, mushrooms. You need beans and nuts and brown rice and whole wheat bread and green leafy stuff. Red meat, fish, chicken, milk, cheese. You gotta eat that stuff so it'll crowd out the cocaine. It's stubborn stuff. It hangs on. And you gotta exercise and sweat it out. Run. Don't walk nowhere, run. And when you get stronger, you gotta take a sweat bath. Lotsa sweat baths. I can't do no more for you. But you do what I say, hear me?"

"Yes, sir." The words were automatic. His stomach was turning over from the list of things the old man wanted him to eat. He didn't want to eat. He didn't get hungry.

He found Klah waiting outside the hogan as he left. He paused to take a swig of the strong tea and was surprised that it seemed to help his stomach cramps. They didn't go away, but they weren't as severe.

Dibe sat him down and peppered him with questions about his session with Pintaro. She nodded. "Them things he told you to eat, they got minerals and things in them. And you need eggs and beef liver and onions too." She nodded emphatically. "The old man told you right. And you gonna run ever' morning when the sun rises. You get up to ten miles a day and we'll figure you're a Diné warrior. Up until then, you just a kiddie playing at being a warrior."

"Dibe, how are we going to afford all those things?" Jazz asked. "I don't have any money or any way to get any. Unless I go steal it."

Gad looked at him sharply. "That what you wanna do?"

He thought for a moment before shaking his head. "No. Never stole nothing... except that bicycle, and that was to save my life."

"Damned near snatched away your life. That bump on the head was worse'n we thought. You're away with the fairies more'n you oughta be." Dibe patted his hand. "Don't you worry. We'll figure a way to get what you need."

The first thing they did was sell Klah's three championship bull-riding cups to buy some of the food items. Jazz objected, but Klah said they were his to do with as he wanted.

The next morning, Jazz started to run. Klah ran with him, and even though his leg didn't seem quite right, he outran Jazz, who had no strength, no stamina... no will. As soon as he recovered from the run, he and Klah stripped and crawled into the sweat lodge Gad prepared for them. Sweat popped out on Jazz's exhausted body, enervating him further. After they'd had enough, Klah helped him out of the little hut. Jazz regained some energy fast when Gad threw a bucket of cold water over him to rinse off the sweat.

KLAH SEEMED perfectly fine with their new relationship, and Jazz came to understand that in Klah's understated way, his new lover looked forward to their bouts in bed as much as he did. They acted normally around others, but they must have thrown too many looks at one another. It was hard to put anything over Dibe, and two days later she asked a question out of the blue.

"So it's that way with you two, huh?"

"What way?" they both asked at once.

"You both happier'n a hound with two tails. Who you think you fooling? Is this the life you lived before we found you?" she asked Jazz.

"I-I don't know. I guess so. At least, it feels that way."

She threw a thumb at him. "This one's trying to get back in harmony." She cast her other thumb at her nephew. "And this one's trying to throw harmony away."

"One man's harmony isn't the same as the next man's." Jazz wondered where that came from even as he uttered the words.

"That's true enough. And I'll not judge." She held a hand before each of their faces. "I feel plentya crap coming outa both of you but can't rightly say if it's this thing you found betwixt the two of you."

Gad never mentioned the subject, although Jazz was certain the man knew what he and Klah did in the privacy of the little shack.

When he stopped being so totally absorbed by his own problems, Jazz learned that Klah would have been out on the rodeo circuit earning money—competing and working as a stable hand—but he was recovering from a broken leg he suffered when a bull he was riding went down. Klah got red in the face when Gad said he was a fellow who "rode 'em right into the ground," but Jazz figured that beneath the tickling, Klah was proud of the proclamation.

Dibe earned a little from her hand trembling, but To'hajiilee wasn't big enough to require her services that much. The place sounded big— 78,000 acres—but there were fewer than 2,000 people living there.

Gad was a handyman, repairing all kinds of things for anybody who could pay him a dollar or two. Jazz surprised them both by pitching in and carrying more than his weight in the fixing-up trade.

"This musta been what you was," Gad said. "Before your troubles, I mean. You handy with your hands, boy."

Jazz shrugged. "Seems sorta natural, so maybe it was."

In addition to running every day and helping out when he could, Jazz and Klah went small-game hunting with an old .30-30 single-shot Gad owned. Not much to bag other than rabbits, but they brought home plenty of those. His morning run built up his strength and his wind, so the hunting jaunts were pleasing to him.

One day as they walked back toward the hogan, Klah stopped dead in his tracks. Jazz turned and walked back to him.

"We ever gonna talk about it?" Klah asked.

"Wasn't sure if you wanted to."

"Bustin' a gut to hold it in, and I don't even know how you feel about it... about me."

"Keep coming back for more, so I must feel okay?" Jazz said.

Klah flushed and stomped away. Jazz caught up and stopped him with a hand on his arm. "Sorry, man. But it wasn't more'n a week ago that some white bastard owned me, and I *had* to give it to him."

Klah's eyebrows climbed. "Had to?"

"Had to if I wanted to eat. Or have a roof over my head." Jazz stopped short, realizing how hollow that sounded. "If I wanted the crack pipe they brought me...."

Everything hit him at that moment. The enormity of what he'd allowed them to do to him. His complicity. His degradation. His shame. Jazz's voice caught in his throat, and his shoulders shook.

Klah led him to the deep shadow of a juniper and held him in his lap, hidden from the world. "Don't get heebie-jeebies, man. You be all right. *We'll* be all right."

Jazz clung tight and wept soundlessly, tears blinding him. Klah cradled him as he would a child, rocking back and forth with Jazz in his arms.

Jazz's bout of self-pity passed, leaving him angry. "That fucking Juan. Turned on me like a snake!"

"Who's Juan?"

There in his lover's arms, Jazz told Klah about Juan and how great it had been until it wasn't anymore. Until Juan hooked him on pipes and betrayed him to Silver Wings. At least he told the parts he remembered, but there were big holes in his memory. Klah listened until he ran out of words, then pulled him tighter.

"You don't have to worry. I won't do to you what that Juan did. Not ever. I-I got feelings for you, Jazz." Klah pushed him up and held him by his arms, forcing Jazz to look at him. "You gave it to me honestly, so I owe you that back. I love you, man. Never said that to nobody before. Not even my girl. Guess I sound like a fool, but—"

Jazz smothered his words with a kiss. When they parted, he studied Klah's inkblot eyes. "Don't... don't know if I can say it back. Not right now. I'm too crippled up. Too scared. But, man, I feel something."

Just as abruptly, his mood changed. He scrambled away from Klah. "Don't touch me, man. I'm dirty."

"Dirty? How?" Klah reached for him, but Jazz shrank away.

"All those men. I did it with all those men. I paraded around and let them look at me in a swimsuit that didn't even have a butt in it." He shivered. "I musta liked it if I did that, huh?"

"Jazz, you did what you had to. When you say dirty, do you mean a disease or something?"

Jazz's body shuddered like a witch gave him a good shaking. "Silver Wings made me wear protection." He shivered again. "With everybody but him."

"And was he... you know?"

"He was healthy... except in the head, maybe."

Klah reached out and pulled Jazz to him again. "Then you ain't dirty. Nothing those men did to you made you dirty. I can see right through you, Jazz. And you're all clean. Squeaky clean."

Just as Jazz began to accept Klah's words, the stomach cramps struck... hard. He hadn't brought any green tea with him, and the sickness and brain fog made him want to die. Perhaps he would have... if not for the comfort of his lover's strong arms.

THE SUN lay low on the horizon before Jazz's torment eased enough for them to move. With Klah's help, he made it back to the Hatahle camp. He walked the last few yards on his own. Dibe wasn't fooled.

"Look a little blue around the gills, boy. Bad 'un, huh?" She picked up a jug and ladled out a splash. "Take some of old Pintaro's green tea. Seems to help."

Jazz drank it greedily. "Thanks. It eases my guts some."

"Gad and me been talking. Can't decide if you're one a them urban Indians or come from the big rez. I know you got some white blood in you, but your true blood's strong."

Jazz flopped down on the floor of the hogan beside the two and frowned. "Seems like my dad's a blood. Mom's... Mom's...." His voiced died away as the image of a small woman with blonde hair that wasn't quite blonde and pale blue eyes wavered before him. "I guess she's a white lady."

"And your real name's Jazz Jasper?" Gad asked.

"Yeah. Well, Jazz and Jasper seem right, but not together." His head started to ache.

"You don't run into a man calling himself Jazz much. Me'n Gad's heading up to Window Rock for a ceremony in a coupla days. You wanna go with us?"

Jazz glanced at Klah before shaking his head. "Don't think so."

Dibe pursed her lips but refrained from asking why. He felt obligated to explain anyway.

"I-I gotta figure out what's going on first. There's somebody out there hunting me. I gotta figure out what to do next. Best just to hide out here until then."

"Son," Gad said. "You ain't hiding out. Ever soul at To'hajiilee knows there's a Jazz amongst us. Likely some kinfolk up on the big rez does too... by now."

Jazz seemed to shrink inside himself. Maybe it'd be better just to let them catch him. At least he wouldn't hunger for a pipe every minute of the day and crumple over into stomach cramps and feel like throwing up. Shit. It was only sex, anyway.

He drew a shaky breath and squared his shoulders. It was a hell of a lot more than that. Crap, it wasn't even sex. Not real sex. Not an urge created by love and desire. It was just animal grunting and satisfying someone else's lust. Muscular contractions. Surely he was worth more than that.

WHEN JAZZ got to feeling better, Klah wanted to go to the little community of To'hajiilee. He didn't say so, but Jazz suspected he wanted to visit his girl, someone named Mai Jinosa. The walk wasn't more than five miles, but Klah planned on riding his rodeo pony, a pinto named Shin Bones, or sometimes just Bones. Came from when they were both younger, the pony kicked him on the shins whenever he got a chance.

Gad owned a plow horse he hired out to do planting in the fall and agreed Jazz could ride Tankerous. Jazz figured the real name was Cantankerous but that slipped into the shortened form over the years.

As Jazz stood staring at the sturdy horse, it became crystal clear that he was a town Indian. He knew he was supposed to sit astride the big black's back, but he had no idea how to get there or what to do after that. After Klah showed him how to mount and handle the placid animal, they rode northeast toward town.

Jazz figured Klah wanted to continue his talk about what was building between the two of them, but his lover didn't open his mouth. They rode in silence. It was an easy, comfortable silence until Jazz figured out Klah was puzzling over what he'd say to Mai. He almost snickered when he imagined his bashful friend introducing them by saying "This is Jazz. He's fucking me while I'm fucking you." Then it didn't seem funny anymore. Seemed like a problem.

The little community of To'hajiilee looked like a dozen others he'd seen. Some parts old; some new. Some very old. The people were familiar, making Jazz understand he'd spent some time on a reservation after all.

Klah pulled up in front of a double-wide mobile home with a little ramshackle stand facing the street in front of it. The place seemed deserted.

"Mai's probably in the house. They only man the stall when there are tourists in town." He was about to throw his leg over Bones's back when he paused. "Wonder what an Albuquerque cop's doing here?"

Jazzed glanced at a blue Ford parked a little way down the dusty road. "How you know that's an Albuquerque police car?"

"Looks like one to me. License plate's official."

"Maybe it's feds."

"Uh-uh. State plate. Besides, I know a cop car when I see one."

Jazz opened his mouth to argue when he observed a man standing near the car talking to a woman. He thrust a piece of paper at her, but she backed off and walked around him. Jazz's heart stammered. He slid off Tankerous's back with the animal between him and the car. He snatched at Klah's arm.

"That man, you think he's a cop?"

Klah took a good look before sliding to the ground beside Jazz. "Yeah, I'd say so. Why? You know him?"

"Think so." Jazz shook his head as the familiar ache started again. "Will you walk by him and see if he gives you one of those things he's holding. If he does, just accept it, but don't say anything. See if you can notice his name tag."

"He doesn't have one. He's wearing civvies, man. You know him, go talk to him. Maybe he can straighten this all out for you."

Jazz shook his head. "Think... think he's one of the men chasing me."

"The *cops* are after you?"

"I don't know if they are, but he's one of the men... you know, one of the men Wings gave me to. Chip, they called him. But I think they used phony names. Do it for me, please."

Klah handed him Bones's reins and walked down the street. Jazz watched from beneath Tankerous's long neck as his companion halted when hailed by the man. Klah accepted what appeared to be a poster, scanned it, and shook his head. Then he sauntered on down the street, still holding the piece of paper while Chip moved closer, hailing passersby and giving them a copy of his poster.

Jazz's breath caught in his throat. No doubt about it. This was the husky guy he'd tussled with when the man wanted to screw him. The one Wings had had to settle down. Jazz's hands balled into fists. He fought to keep from stepping out and slugging the bastard, but Chip moved away across the street to accost a couple more people. After that, he got in his car. As the cop drove away, Klah appeared at Jazz's side.

"Good picture, man. Sexy."

"What are you talking about?" He grabbed the poster and stared at his own face looking back at him. Below the photo he read: *Jasper Penrod, AKA Jazz Penrod, wanted for questioning.* Below that was information on how to contact Detective Charles Zimmerman of the Albuquerque Police Department.

"I've got to get outa here, man," Jazz said. "Somebody's bound to tell him I'm here."

"Nobody gonna tell a white cop nothing. Don't worry about it. At least we know what your real name is." Klah looked at the picture critically. "Man, you are one pretty dude."

"Shut up. You think it's safe to go back to camp now?"

"Yeah. The cop headed off down the road back toward I-40. He's halfway to Albuquerque now. Let's go."

"I can find my way. You go look up Mai."

"She'd have come out by now if she was home. They mighta gone to Albuquerque."

They were silent on the ride back to the hogan, but for a different reason this time. Jazz was wrapped up in his thoughts. They were looking for him. How did Wings even know he was alive? The bastard thought he'd gone out the plane door with Kim. What happened? How had he given himself away? He let out a grunt. Crap, he'd peed all over the man's plane. And he'd stolen the bicycle.

Then another thought struck. They were killers... or at least Wings was. If they found him here, would they kill Klah too? And Gad? And Dibe? He didn't share this last thought with the Hatahles when he and Klah arrived back in camp, even though they told the others all about the incident. Despite his fears, he allowed Klah to convince him nobody on the reservation would tell a white cop nothing.

ALMOST A week later, a stocky, burr-headed man drove up to the camp and waited in his vehicle until Gad went out and invited him in. The stranger's gaze went straight to Jazz when he came through the hogan entrance, but he went through the usual routine, greeting Gad and Dibe respectively and then shaking hands with Klah and uttering the name Jazz learned everyone on the reservation used for Klah except for his family. "Howdy, Left-Hand. You got your leg back yet?"

Klah bent his left knee and flexed his foot. "Damned near. Be back riding them toros before you know it. Like you to meet a friend of ours. Jazz, this is Milton Atcitty."

Milton took his hand and said, "Jazz, huh?"

Jazz thought it odd that there was no exchanging of clans, something that always took place when Navajos met other bloods they didn't know. Of course a man traced his lineage from his mother's clan, and Jazz's mother wasn't even a Navajo. Children were *born to* their mother's clan and *born for* their father's. To marry within one's own clan was forbidden, as it was considered incest. Jazz smiled inwardly. Whatever else he and Klah were doing, they weren't committing that crime.

Dibe interrupted to offer coffee. Soon they all sat on blankets on the floor of the hogan chatting about life at To'hajiilee. But there seemed to be an undercurrent. After a few minutes of this, Gad asked their guest what brought him to the camp.

Milton stuck out his thick lips a moment before answering. He seemed to stare off into the distance midway between Left-Hand and Jazz.

"I got a uncle up on the big rez. You might know him. He goes by the name of Julian Nesposito but everybody calls him Hard Hat." Milton squirmed on his blanket, making it clear he wasn't comfortable. "Uncle Hard Hat got himself in some trouble over some pimps—you know, some traffickers—in the outside world. Not saying there's anything to it, but then he shows up asking about a fellow that went missing up there. Me'n my dad figured you oughta know." He scrambled to his feet. "Anyway, that's what I come to say." With that, he left so fast he was hardly polite.

Dibe spoke from the doorway where she'd gone to watch their guest leave. "Now we know why you run into that Albuquerque policeman last week."

"Why?" Jazz asked, halfway afraid to hear the answer.

"Here's the way I figure it," Gad said. "Word got around a stranger showed up down at To'hajiilee, so the cop comes nosing around. Don't take him long to figure out nobody's gonna tell him spit. So they get ahold of old Hard Hat and have him ask the questions. Been rumors for donkey years the old goat's been shilling for the sex traffickers. Surprised nobody's shot the bastard between the eyes 'fore this."

"He got powers, that's why!" Dibe said, rejoining the rest of them on a blanket. "He used to be a holy man."

"Gone over to the other side," Gad snapped. "Anyways, while nobody's gonna talk to the white cop, there'll be somebody who'll talk to Hard Hat, either because they're afraid of him or maybe just because he's one of the People."

"I need to get out of here, right now." Jazz started to rise, but Klah caught his arm.

"Not so fast. We gotta figure out what we're gonna do."

"Gad and me can take you to the big rez when we go up for my ceremony later today. Can drop you anywhere you want along the way."

"No," Klah said. "That won't work. We gotta think of something else. Albuquerque, maybe."

"That's where Silver Wings is," Jazz said. "But maybe I need to face him down and settle this."

"No!" Klah said again, emphatically this time. "We need something else."

Gad stared in his nephew's direction a minute. "My brother was a good man, but he decided to live down at Alamo with the Enemy Navajo.

We brung you up here when him and your mother got taken in that car wreck six years back. You still know anyone down there?"

"That's it," Klah said. "I'll take him to Alamo."

Dibe snorted. "That place is littler than To'hajiilee. How long you think it's gonna take for word to get back to the big rez?"

"It'll give Jazz time to figure out what to do," he said. "He knows his real name now. Maybe the rest of it will come back to him."

"How'll you get down to Alamo?"

"Horseback. We'll do a moonlight flit while everybody's sleeping."

"Bones can't carry you both all the way to Socorro County," Gad said.

Klah rubbed his nose. "I'll see if I can talk Mai outa her horse. She might lend him to me."

"And then tell everybody about it," Dibe said. "Hosteen Abbo covets my grandma's squash blossom necklace. He's about to get it."

"I can't let you do that," Jazz protested.

"Don't see how you can stop me, boy. We need some money anyway for our trip up to the big reservation. Was gonna pawn it, but I'll get more from Abbo. That gewgaw will bring lots more'n it takes to buy a horse. You boys get ready to leave while I go dicker with that old thief."

Jazz could not believe how difficult it was to leave what most of the world would consider a primitive dwelling but which to him was the most comfortable place he could remember. Nonetheless, after Gad and Dibe returned with a roan tied to the back of the truck and some worn tack gear in the bed, he and his companion waited until dark before setting off to the southeast. In fewer than ten miles, he knew one thing for certain. He was going to be one sore son of a bitch by the time the sun came up.

Chapter 24

HAZEL BUZZED me on my office phone. "BJ, Henry Secatero is on the line."

I hadn't heard from him since he called to say Nesposito claimed Jazz's fingerprints were found on a stolen bike. That was a week ago. Nothing since then. I punched a button and called a greeting.

"That old man the Navajo cops arrested is dead," he blurted. "The news is all over the rez."

"Nesposito? How? When?"

"Dunno exactly when, probably sometime Wednesday or Thursday. But the how's clear enough. Shot in the head."

"Where?"

"You remember Big Hole Canyon?"

"Where we found that murdered California PI?"

"Right. You remember there's a landing strip up on the mesa?"

"Remember it well."

"Right there. They found his pickup with him laid out in the bed, covered by a tarp."

"Anybody know who he went to meet out there?"

"No such luck. He was a tight-lipped old bastard."

Henry said a friend in the tribal police told him persistent winds in the area pretty well erased any physical evidence of a plane landing or taking off, and while people in a couple of distant hogans heard a low-flying craft, no one admitted to seeing it. Since that strip was used to bring in contraband, most folks didn't *want* to know about the comings and goings of mysterious aircraft.

When we had first found the makeshift landing spot, I assumed it was someone shipping in drugs. Given what I now knew, I suspected it was contraband coming in and human victims going out. My blood surged at the thought. "Any reason for me to come up?"

"Don't see why. Don't think you'll learn anything."

"Okay, I'll let Lonzo Joe know."

"He already knows. I saw him at the chapter house. The locals called him in because of his interest in Jazz's case. I did learn one thing. That old man took a run down to To'hajiilee Wednesday, maybe the day he died. Matter of fact, he probably stopped at Black Hole on his way home and met his maker."

"Why To'hajiilee?" I asked.

"Remember I told you he had relatives down there. Guess he went to see them."

"He wasn't supposed to leave the reservation, was he? A requirement of his bond."

"To'hajiilee's part of the rez." Henry paused. "Well, part of the Navajo Nation, anyway. Maybe he just wanted to say goodbye before they hauled his ass off to prison for the rest of his life."

"You know the man, I don't. Was he that sentimental about family?"

"All the Diné got strong family ties. But I see what you mean. No, I wouldn't peg him as caring about anybody but himself."

"Tell me about that stolen bicycle with Jazz's fingerprints on it again."

"Not much to tell. My dad said Nesposito told him they found a bicycle in a ditch beside I-40."

"Where on I-40?" I asked.

"Vague. Maybe twenty miles or so west of Albuquerque."

That confirmed my recollection of things. "And To'hajiilee is about thirty miles, right. Think I'm gonna take a run out to To'hajiilee."

"Nobody's gonna tell you nothing," Henry said with certainty. "Maybe I oughta take a run down to Albuquerque and go with you. Today's Friday, and this is Labor Day weekend. I've got three days off. Maybe I'll have time to sneak in a visit to the state fair. With any luck, Jazz can go with me. You gonna wait for me to get there before you head out?"

I didn't respond to his optimism. "Makes more sense than going alone."

"Gotta finish my shift, so it'll be late. You got a pad for me?"

Paul and I took in a movie called *Green Zone* but were home when Henry rang the doorbell at 10:00 p.m. We talked the case over for half an hour before he went to bed, pleading exhaustion. He'd worked a full day before driving down to Albuquerque.

A few minutes after that, Paul flopped over in the bed beside me. "I'll swear, every time Henry's around or Jazz is even mentioned, you get horny as hell. I'm gonna get jealous again."

"But you're going to cooperate, aren't you?"

He snapped on the table lamp and gave me a wicked grin. He left the light on so I could watch Pedro prowl while his master performed.

SATURDAY MORNING was a big day at the country club pool, so Paul worked while Henry and I headed for the reservation to the west. He directed me to drive to the Laguna exit. I'd always associated the name with the Laguna Indians and was surprised to learn the To'hajiilee chapter house was located not far outside that community. I waited in the car while he went inside.

A quarter of an hour later, he came out clutching a poster and looking sour. He thrust it at me. "Took this down off the bulletin board."

"Damn, Jazz takes a good picture."

"The girl inside said this white cop was passing around the poster and asking questions. My guess is nobody told him nothing. But she told me there was a stranger on the rez staying with a family named Hatahle somewhere southwest of the village. Shit, it'll take us the rest of the day to run them down. So close. So damned close."

"You know what this tells us, don't you?" I asked.

"Why that old man came down earlier this week. They might not talk to a white cop, but they'll talk to another Navajo. Especially one they're afraid of." He thought that one over. "I dunno. What he was accused of doing might put him on the far side of the arroyo from most folks. Come on, let's find the Hatahle camp."

When we started asking questions, Henry mostly talked to young women. Almost without fail, they all but fawned over the handsome man. Why hadn't I had a magnetic personality like that when I was a buck?

Eventually we found ourselves traveling down a faint dusty road with Henry at the wheel. He claimed people considered the driver as the one in control of the situation. Before long, we got directions to the camp.

We drove for four miles before a hogan off to our right caught our attention. He turned into the clearing before the log dwelling and waited. Eventually a weathered man came out and waved to us. Henry, motioning for me to stay where I was, got out to exchange a few words with the man. The old fellow first motioned down the road and then, after a few more questions, pointed to a black stock horse in a pen beside the hogan.

Henry got back in the car and let out a sigh. "We're a mile short of the Hatahle camp. But the fellow says nobody's there. That's their plow horse he's taking care of while they're gone."

"Gone where?"

"Window Rock or maybe Crownpoint. Some ceremony. Apparently the Hatahle woman's a hand trembler."

Somewhere in the back of my head, I knew a trembler was a sort of diagnostician in Navajo medicine. "Did he know anything about Jazz?"

"Little cagy about that. Said somebody was staying with them but claimed not to know a name. I told him we'd drive on down anyway to see if anybody stayed behind. He knows they didn't because of the horse, but he didn't make any objections."

A mile down a kidney-jarring road, we came to a hogan with a small shack beside it. After hollering and honking to no avail, we got out and checked the buildings. Vacant, although somebody obviously lived at the camp. We found nothing that gave us a clue Jazz had been here.

"What do you think?" I asked.

"I think he's back on the big rez with the Hatahles. Maybe he'll get ahold of Louie or his mom."

I took out my phone. "You got any bars?"

"Nope."

He drove two miles back up the road before we got phone service. He called his father while I dialed the Penrod home. A minute later we both hung up and shook our heads. No one had heard from Jazz.

Henry smashed a fist into his palm. The noise was startling. "Crap. He was here. I feel it. Seems like we're always coming up with more heat than light."

"Hold your horses, guy. Believe it or not, we're closing in on him. A couple of weeks ago we had no idea he was even in the country."

"Yeah. I guess."

"I hate to think bad thoughts," I said, "but what if Nesposito collected him and delivered him to the cartel—or more likely Silver Wings—at Black Hole Canyon? It makes a crazy kind of sense. If Silver Wings has Jazz back, he wouldn't need Nesposito any longer. In fact, the old man would present a threat instead of an opportunity. After all, they tried to kill him once. He was probably still alive because he promised to deliver Jazz."

"Shit!" he said. Then he straightened and looked me in the eye. "Let's go find Nesposito's kin. His brother lives here."

"Why would he tell us anything?"

"Might have to lean on him some."

"How about taking some of the tribal authorities with us?" I suggested.

"Naw. You'n me'll do the job."

Finding the Atcitty camp—apparently Nesposito and his brother were from different fathers—wasn't an easy chore either. After two false starts, we ended up at the right place. The brother—Fred—wasn't home, but one of the sons, Milton, was. Once again I remained in the car, but this time Henry and Milton walked over beside me to make conversation. After the clan greeting, they switched to English.

Milton looked at the poster of Jazz Henry handed him and turned pensive. "You know my uncle?"

"Met him," Henry answered, preserving the reluctance to mention the recently dead—especially one said to have powers. "Didn't know him real good. He was spooky. Sorry, man, didn't mean to—"

"That's all right," Milton said. "I thought he was spooky too. Especially the last few years. You ain't here 'cause he sent you before...?" He let it dangle to avoid mentioning the murder.

Jazz poked his finger at the flyer. "I'm here because that man is my brother. My little brother. Somebody took him, and I aim to get him back."

Milton nodded and turned to look in my direction. He was one of the Navajos who wouldn't look directly at you. An eye avoidance thing. "Okay. But who's he?"

"He's a friend me'n Jazz helped out once. Now he's paying back. He's an ex-cop who's a private investigator. We're just looking for my brother, that's all."

Milton held up the poster and nodded again. "Yeah, that's him. He's staying with Gad and Dibe. Said his name was Jazz."

"You know where they are? Nobody's at the camp. Neighbor's taking care of their plow horse."

"The plow horse? What about Klah's pinto?"

"Who's Klah?" I asked.

"Klah Hatahle. He's Gad's nephew. They raised him ever since his folks got killed in a car wreck down in Socorro."

Henry scratched his chin. "The man didn't say nothing about a pinto."

"I heard Dibe sold a squash blossom she'd been hanging on to forever. Maybe bought another horse."

"You know where Gad and Dibe went?"

Milton looked uncomfortable for a minute and then apparently decided to come clean. He told of going to the Hatahle hogan and warning them his uncle was asking questions about somebody named Jazz. "I got the feeling that put a burr under their saddle," he finished.

"Now everybody's gone," Henry said. "Any idea where?"

"Dibe said she had a ceremony up at Window Rock. They were heading up there to get ready for it. Guess Klah and Jazz went along."

"Do they have a stock trailer? I asked.

"No, but when Left-Hand's rodeoing, he rents one."

"Left-Hand?" I asked.

"'Klah' means left-handed," Henry said.

WE DROVE back to Albuquerque in relative silence, each nursing his own thoughts. Paul was home from his job at the country club and hard at work on his second vocation, writing an article on the local Greek Orthodox church's approach to Christmas that he hoped to freelance to a regional magazine.

After a bite to eat, I phoned Gene at home and talked things over with him before phoning Charlie, also at home, and asking him to start locating cow pasture landing fields west of town. Then we assembled in the den to discuss what Henry and I learned today. Paul heard both of us out before commenting.

"It's obvious, isn't it?" he asked. "Jazz went with the Hatahles back to the big rez. He's trying to get home without getting caught by the cartel or Silver Wings or whoever's after him."

"That don't hold water," Henry said. "He'd call me. All he's gotta do is ring me and yell help." He got up and paced. "Maybe I better head home. If he's up there, he needs to be able to reach me."

"That might be exactly what you need to do, but let's think this through first," I said. "He can call Louie or his uncle Riley if he reaches the rez. If he can, that is. I keep remembering that in the Bisti case, our missing man got hit in the head and lost his memory, at least some of it. What if Jazz had an accident on that bicycle? After all, it was abandoned at the side of I-40. What if he's having trouble remembering things?"

"Amnesia?" Paul asked.

"Possibly. Or else he knows he's in danger and doesn't want to endanger anyone else. You know, I'm intrigued by this fellow Klah's pinto pony. If they all went to the reservation, why isn't the neighbor taking care of it too?"

"You said he's a rodeo hand," Paul noted. "Maybe he's off rodeoing."

"According to their neighbor, he's recovering from a broken leg," Henry said.

"There's more than one way to make money at a rodeo besides competing," Paul said. "They use stable hands, vendors, clean-up guys, clowns."

"That's true. And maybe that's the way it is." Henry punched the air. "Dammit! We oughta be able to find him!"

I cleared my throat. Both of them looked at me. "I'll call Hazel and have her check hospitals for a man with amnesia. But there's something bothering me more than the fact Jazz is still missing," I said. "I faxed Gene a copy of that poster Henry took from the chapter house. He confirmed what I was thinking. That's not an official APD poster. It's something Zimmerman printed up on his own."

"Which means…?" Henry asked.

"It doesn't mean anything, but it sure makes it *seem* like Zimmerman's looking for Jazz, not the police department."

"I thought Gene put out an APB on Jazz."

"He did. But this poster is above and beyond. Zimmerman's got something going that has nothing to do with Gene."

"You said he claims Jazz and me are in the trafficking business," Henry reminded us.

"And that doesn't sound right either. Even though Lieutenant Bolton confirmed that's Zimmerman's opinion… in a backhanded way."

"What are you saying?" Paul asked.

"I don't know. I'm just thinking out loud. But if we're just conjecturing, it wouldn't be hard to make a case that Zimmerman is searching for Jazz just a little too hard." I felt compelled to add, "Of course, he's Vice and that's a whole other kettle of fish. It's possible that someone told him you and your brother are involved in trafficking, and he's just trying to do his job."

"Then why the unofficial wanted poster?" Paul asked.

"Exactly. And who found the bicycle they got the prints from? Gene can't find any report of it. Lonzo Joe nosed around on the rez, and they didn't find it. And another thing, normally Zimmerman would ask the fingerprint boys to get him a set. But he called personally."

"Are you thinking what I think you're thinking?" Paul asked.

"The traffickers need protection, don't they? Who better than a cop? And that explains the leaks we've experienced," I said. "When I called Gene earlier, I asked him some of the same questions. He didn't have answers, but he's beginning to have questions, just like we do."

"Hell, tell Lieutenant Enriquez... uh, Gene to call in Zimmerman and get some questions answered," Henry said.

"I suggested that. But Gene's balking. I think it's because of Zimmerman's boss, a lieutenant named Bolton. Who is, by the way, on CAHT's board."

"Who's CAHT, and what does that matter?" Henry asked.

"I see." Paul ignored him. "CAHT leaks. Bolton's on the board, and Zimmerman—who seems to be going off the reservation, if you'll pardon my pun—reports to Bolton, squaring the circle.

"So what do we do?" Henry asked.

"You have a decision to make. Go back home or not? I'm going to try to find where that pinto went. And Milton Atcitty mentioned another horse too. Something about a squash blossom necklace buying a horse."

"You'll need me to get answers. I'll call Louie and let him know what's going on," Henry decided.

"Another thing, I called Charlie and asked him to start looking for a wind-sock airfield west of town."

"Why?" Paul asked.

"Think about it. Nesposito met a plane at Black Hole and died. Jazz was riding a bicycle twenty miles west of town. How far could he have gone on a bicycle?"

"That doesn't necessarily tie those two things together," Paul said.

"Nope, but *west* does. He was spotted on the west side before he escaped, remember? And Henry saw the Asian driver on the west side."

"West it is," Paul said. "You guys don't think you're going to leave me behind tomorrow, do you?"

"What about work?" I asked. "Sunday's another big day at the pool. Especially Labor Day weekend."

"I'll call in. My *other* job takes priority this time."

I smiled inwardly. Paul was going to make a good investigative journalist.

Chapter 25

JAZZ SUFFERED in silence. He was sick to his stomach and needed green tea, but that wasn't the real problem. He could hardly walk. And when he did, he moved stiff-legged like a kid who'd soiled his pants. The first night on One Sock, the roan Dibe purchased for him, left his inner thighs stinging and burning. After two days horseback, Jazz couldn't bear anything on his legs. Eventually they arrived at Alamo, and Klah received permission to move into his parents' abandoned mobile home. Most of the windows were broken, but it provided some shelter from the tail end of New Mexico's monsoon season, which had struck with a vengeance again yesterday.

At the moment he lay on his back with his naked legs in the air while Klah painted his bare flesh with liniment, something that added to his pain. Klah assured him that when the stinging went away, his flesh would heal faster. He bit down on a twig to keep from shouting aloud.

"Damn, man! You're killing me," he gasped at length. "I need some more of Hosteen Pintaro's witch's brew."

"Almost out of the tea, man. You need to make it last."

Nonetheless, Klah handed over a nearly empty canteen. Jazz took a slug, resisting the urge to guzzle all of it.

Almost immediately his innards settled, although the sensitive flesh on the inside of his legs continued to burn. He lowered his legs, resting them across Klah's thighs. The moment grew intimate, sensuous... but he felt nothing but gratitude for his companion's attention.

Was this what it was like? Love? Having someone care for him at difficult moments. As his rebellious guts settled down, he reached for Klah and pulled him atop him. Despite agitating his legs again, the warm body pressed against him felt good and comfortable, even with the rough denim of Klah's trousers and shirt between them.

"L-Left-Hand," he started. No, this called for true names, not nicknames. "Klah, up until a couple of months ago, I was a happy-go-lucky guy having a good time living my life. I don't remember it all, but I remember that much. I had people who cared for me... you know, family.

But I didn't have one thing I really craved. I didn't have a lover. That's not quite right. I didn't have anyone who loved me."

He drew a breath that almost turned into a sob. "That's what got me into all this mess. I started looking for someone who'd be mine. Mine alone."

Holding Klah close, he told it all, starting with meeting this hunky Albuquerque private detective who turned down his advances because he was already committed to someone else, and thinking how great that was. He told of looking for such a lover on the reservation and in Farmington without success. As the words tumbled out of him, more and more of his past opened up to him, and names danced at the edge of his mind, still elusive but close.

"You already told me this. None of that stuff cuts no ice."

"Not all of it, and I need you to hear it all. It's important to me." Jazz waited for Klah to nod. "So I went on the internet and met this guy named Juan Gonzales. We danced around, sending emails and talking on Skype. I got comfortable enough to come to Albuquerque and meet the dude."

Jazz's sigh came right from his soul. "It was wonderful, Klah. He liked what I liked. He was interested in what interested me. And he was a great lover. That was my first mistake. My second was believing him when he said taking a hit on a pipe would make things even greater. It did, all right. But before long I needed that pipe more and more… and more."

"My cousin got into crack. Bad stuff. He's dead now," Klah said.

"That's when he gave me to this guy called Silver Wings."

Jazz recounted his time in the bungalow at the back of the big house and the pool parties and doing things with men he didn't even know or particularly like. He told of almost escaping but backing out because of the pipes. He told Klah everything, including Silver Wings' attempt to kill him by trying to dump him out the open door of the airplane with Kim. His memory of his time with the traffickers now revealed to him, he told of hiding behind the seat in the plane to make Wings think he was dead and of his escape that night on a stolen bicycle. That was when Klah and Gad picked him up, still half-unconscious from his fall.

When he finished, they both fell silent. Jazz tightened his hold on Klah. "Are you disgusted by me. By what I did?"

Klah raised his torso so he could look into Jazz's eyes. "Man, I thought you was gonna talk the hind leg off a donkey. I already knew what I needed to know. You're the miracle I've been waiting for."

"Nobody's ever called me a miracle before."

"I'll bet they have. You just didn't listen."

Jazz's heart swelled, crowding his chest and making it hard to speak. "I-I love you, man."

"Why?"

"Because you're a good man. Because you're a good friend. Because you're a great lover. Because my heart tells me so."

"Don't worry," Klah said with a smile. "I'm already wearing your brand and earmark."

"What about your girlfriend? Mai?"

"That was sorta casual... for both of us," Klah said. "I've found what I didn't even know I was looking for. Something that makes me happier than I've ever been. Mai? Well, we were having some problems. It wasn't really a solid thing for her. I have the feeling she won't go to pieces over losing Klah Hatahle." He sobered. "How do you know I'm not like that Juan fellow?"

"You're not. You've got real feelings for me. You not only tell me that, but you show it every day. Every minute."

Klah kissed him then. And as they parted, Jazz spoke in a near whisper. "But I'm afraid." He put his fingers to Klah's mouth to stop him from speaking. "Afraid you'll get tired of me being sick and getting the shakes and going cranky. Afraid that someday somebody'll show me another crack pipe, and I'll leave you and Dibe and Gad and follow the cocaine. Afraid I'm not as good as you are."

"Jazz, you the best man I ever knew. And when we get you free of that shit, you'll be even better. We gotta get you that Enemy Way. I'll go back to rodeoing and make enough money for one. If I string together a couple of winning purses, that'll be enough. I—"

Jazz pulled him down and cut his words off with a soulful kiss. "You're not going back to rodeoing until that leg's completely healed. You hear me? I'll either figure out how to paddle my own canoe or we'll both put up with it until it goes away on its own. The shakes aren't coming so much anymore."

"No, but you get down low, man. Real low. Sad. Sometimes I'm afraid you'll hurt yourself. You shiver and shake in your sleep. It still has its grip on you. Tell me something. You know your name now. Why don't you go find your people?"

Jazz went quiet before trying to explain himself. "I do remember some of it, Klah. I know I have a mother. And an uncle, I think. But she's not a blood. That's why I got a honky name. Don't think she and my dad were married. Maybe he ran off and left her, for all I know. I know I've met him, but I don't remember much about that. But he's where I got the blood."

"Okay, so go see them in Farmington or wherever. Find out the rest of it."

"How can I do that with somebody looking to kill me? If I go home, don't you think they'll be watching for me there? Crap! I don't know what to do. And…and how can I tell them what I've done?"

Klah touched his arm. "Just like you told me. They not gonna hang you out to dry." He brushed Jazz's cheek with a forefinger. "Anyway, we'll be safe enough here till you figure it out. Right now I gotta clean up and get you some more tea up at the minimart. We need some more of those vitamins too. Dunno what we're gonna do about the other stuff. I can cook but not all that stuff Dibe fixed."

"We'll figure it out. You got enough left in that poke she gave us for the tea and vitamins?"

"The wolf ain't at the door yet, but I gotta find some work to keep us going."

"I can help, just like I did with Gad." Jazz frowned. "Unless you think I've gotta hide out in this trailer."

"Everybody already knows you're here."

"Then save me some wash water. I'm going with you. I don't care how funny I walk."

"Okay, but first I gotta show you something." Klah walked to the front of the battered trailer and tossed aside a scruffy rug, revealing a trapdoor. "My mom…." His voice caught for a moment, but he cleared his throat and continued. "My mom stored a few things under the trailer, so my dad made her this trapdoor. If anybody comes nosing around, you've got a place to hide."

"Won't someone see me under the trailer?"

"Naw, there's skirts… you know, siding around the whole thing. But it's flimsy, so don't go brushing against it."

JAZZ REFUSED to ride One Sock into the settlement until Klah said they'd need to buy a couple of jerry cans to fill with water. Jazz managed to mount, but halfway there he bailed and went shank's pony the rest of the way. Klah laughed aloud before joining him afoot. Jazz felt like he walked almost normally as they entered the small community of *T'iis Tsho*, which was the Navajo name for Alamo. As best he could remember, it meant Big Cottonwood Tree. As they went, Klah pointed out things he remembered from his childhood. Jazz found it odd that this breakaway community, even smaller than To'hajiilee, had been governed by a school board for most of its existence. Even though there was now a chapter house, the school board was still responsible for the K-12 school, early childhood care, adult education, roads, and the wellness center among other things, according to Klah.

The reservation of more than 60,000 acres existed much for the same reason To'hajiilee did: people undertaking the long trek back from Bosque Redondo stopped at a spring and declared they would go no farther. Of course, many of their brethren considered Alamo ancestors to be Enemy Navajo, those who collaborated with the Spanish. "*Doodaa,*" responded most of those asked today. "It isn't so."

Klah encountered a few people who knew and recognized him along the way, but they were all older folks. Until they reached the mart, that is. Four men about their age sat in the shade of the building, laughing and talking.

"Klah? Klah Hatahle, that you?" The speaker was a short man with heavy shoulders and chest and spindly legs. To Jazz, it looked like everything the man ate went straight to his torso and never made it to his extremities.

"Cheese! Good to see you, man. Thought you'd be gone from here by now."

"Someday. What you doing back?"

When Klah introduced Jazz to the group, the only name he caught was "Cheese." Probably because it was an unusual nickname. Or perhaps it was because he was disconcerted by the fact Klah gave Jazz's name as *Tsi'izi*... Bicycle.

"What kinda name's that?"

"I call him *Tsi'izi* on account of the first time Gad and me set eyes on him, he was riding down I-40 at night on a bicycle."

"Jeez, man. Was you sitting on your brains?" one of the others asked.

"Till a semi blasted by and shoved him off in a ditch."

"Okay, Bicycle it is."

Klah poked a finger at Cheese. "This one's real name's Dalton Apachito. He still thinks everybody calls him Cheese 'cause he's a honcho. But it's really 'cause his last name means Apache. So he's that Cheesy Apache."

Everyone laughed, although Jazz figured that was a story told every time the group met someone new.

Cheese screwed up one eye and gave Jazz a look. "My dad got a call from the big rez about a fellow called Jazz. Don't guess that's your real name, is it?"

"It ain't," Klah said. "Who was doing the asking?"

"Just some guy who knows my family."

"Well, this ain't him," Klah said. "Don't want my friend to get mixed up with that Jazz they're hunting."

"How you know he ain't?"

"Because they asked about a guy called Jazz up at Dipping Water too. And he was supposed to be in his forties."

Jazz knew "Dipping Water" was the approximate meaning of *To'hajiilee*.

"How come they're looking for him?"

Klah shrugged. "Something about white cops wanting him for spitting on the sidewalk or something."

"Okay, bro."

Jazz felt like the minimart was doing highway robbery when they went inside for supplies. He didn't know how he knew, but he was pretty sure the prices were a lot higher than they would have been in Farmington. *Farmington.* That name fit well on his lips. That *had to be* where he was from, where his mother and uncle lived.

After they loaded their purchases aboard the horses and hoofed it back down the road, Jazz asked, "How does it feel to be back home?"

"Cuts two ways. Some good memories, but it makes me remember why I didn't mind leaving."

"What do you mean?"

"My mom and dad are all around me. I see a place here where we picnicked. The school where my mom worked. The place where they...." His voice trailed away.

"That's bad, man. Sorry I dragged you back to all this. But at least you got to see some of your old friends."

Klah snorted. "Yeah. Friends. Cheese was bigger'n me in school and used to beat up on me all the time. I'm the one gave him that name."

"Oh crap. Can you trust him?"

"About as far as I can heave that big can of water Bones is carrying."

Chapter 26

PAUL DIDN'T manage to completely elude work at the country club but finagled a short shift. He left once he was satisfied everything was covered. He returned home just as Henry and I finished breakfast on Saturday morning. We piled into the Impala and set off for To'hajiilee with Paul in the back seat, so conversation with Henry was easier. I knew he'd talked to his father, Louie, early that morning.

"No sign of Jazz on the reservation yet?" I asked.

"None."

"Did he find the Hatahles?"

"Didn't have time. There was three ceremonies going on spread all over the place. Found out the Hatahle woman's a hand trembler with a pretty good rep, so she's probably at one of them. But if Jazz is with them, he hasn't surfaced yet."

I swerved to dodge a squirrel and took the off ramp at Jefferson onto I-40 heading west. "I don't think he's in the Four Corners area. It's possible this Klah fellow left his pinto with someone else, but my guess is he and Jazz took off for parts unknown as soon as Nesposito's nephew let them know Hard Hat was asking questions."

"An Albuquerque cop on the rez probably shook them a little too," Paul said.

"Henry, I think you said Klah is the Hatahles' nephew. Do you know his background?"

He shook his head. "Don't know nothing about him."

"Guess that's part of our mission. How about I drop you on the street while we go to the chapter house and try to convince someone there we're the good guys. By the way, this is a Sunday before a national holiday. Is the chapter house going to be open?"

"Probably be lots of people there. This is still tourist season, you know." Henry took off his hat and ran fingers through his hair. "Good luck with learning anything, but it's worth a shot anyway."

When we dropped Henry on the dusty streets of the little settlement, he immediately approached a girl at the side of the road. He tipped his big black Stetson and was engaged in earnest conversation before we were out of sight.

As soon as a young woman in a traditional velveteen skirt and blouse stepped out to greet us at the chapter house, I elbowed Paul and told him to take the lead.

"Good morning, gentlemen, welcome to the To'hajiilee Chapter House. My name is Irene, and I have a brochure right over here." She indicated the way with a clank of silver bracelets heavily adorned with blue-green turquoise nuggets.

Paul flashed his best smile. "Thank you, ma'am, but we're men on a mission. Maybe you can help us."

Her welcoming attitude faded a bit as Paul set off on a discourse to convince her we had nothing but the welfare of our friend in mind when he started asking questions about Jazz Penrod. Her natural reluctance to share information with outsiders partially crumbled beneath Paul's charm offensive.

"There was a man named Jazz—at least, that the name he went by—here for a while. But I understand he's gone now."

"Yes, he was staying with the Hatahles. Gad and Dibe have gone to the big rez, but we don't believe Klah and Jazz went with them. Do you know where they are?"

She shook her head, apparently shaken that Paul knew so much.

"Jazz's brother, Henry, is with us. He's in town trying to find out what he can." Then Paul took a gamble. "You see, Jazz was stolen by the traffickers, and we're trying to get him back to his people."

Something happened to Irene's face. Her eyes flickered. Her lips froze. I thought I understood.

"Yes, ma'am," I said. "That's why Hard Hat Nesposito was asking around about Jazz."

Mistake. She went round-eyed, and I belatedly recalled some Navajos weren't comfortable talking about the recently dead.

"That's... that's terrible. I never met this Jazz person, but I understand he was a nice man."

"That he is, Irene." Paul took over again. "Klah's pony is gone, so we assume they went somewhere on horseback."

"I believe Mrs. Hatahle sold a family heirloom to Hosteen Abbo. She might have bought another horse," the young woman said.

"Do you know who from?"

Confusion and uncertainty twisted her features. "My little niece was stole by the traffickers. Hope you find your friend." With that, she turned and walked away.

HENRY DID a little better than we had. He located a couple of people over at the To'hajiilee rodeo grounds who knew Klah. They confirmed Dibe Hatahle bought a roan horse and some tack gear. That argued the Hatahle nephew and Jazz had set off somewhere on their own. One of the men Henry talked to knew that Klah had a place he liked to visit whenever he felt life was pressing on him hard, a little lean-to he'd built on a tiny, unreliable spring on the eastern slope of Plate Mesa.

"So where would he run?" I asked. "Solitude or to a big town where Nesposito doesn't have relatives?"

"I'd go to my hideaway place," Henry said.

Paul frowned. "I'd go to Albuquerque and hide out among people."

"People talk," Henry said.

"Okay," I said. "We have two possible places they would go. But Henry's right. We need to check out the one that's closest at hand. You think you can find it?"

"I have general directions, but they're mighty damned vague."

"Let's have at it."

Henry's directions led us north on Trail 56 past the chapter house, even beyond the school board's building. Eventually Paul piped up. "I thought I'd seen the back of beyond before, but this is desolate."

"This is home," Henry muttered, "to a lot of us."

That afternoon, after a couple of false trails, we located Klah Hatahle's lean-to. Judging from the fact it leaned drunkenly lee of the wind, no one had been there in a long time. Henry cursed and punched his left palm with a fist, an increasingly familiar gesture of frustration for him.

Defeated for the moment, we agreed to go home and get some rest in order to start off fresh in the morning. Looking for Jazz in Albuquerque was going to be an arduous task.

UPON ARRIVAL at home, I found a series of messages from Hazel. Apparently she hadn't been able to reach us by cell. I'd failed to watch the bars on my phone. We were probably off the grid while searching for Klah's hideout.

Most of the items had to do with office business, but she also relayed a message from Gene. He'd attempted to question Detective Zimmerman about his unauthorized poster on Jazz but hadn't been able to locate him. According to his boss, Lieutenant Bolton, Zimmerman was on an undercover assignment and could not be contacted. Bolton merely looked at the poster and said that Vice did things their own way.

Chapter 27

Jazz leaned on the handle of his Bully Tools weed cutter, taking pleasure in watching Klah's wiry, graceful figure swing his scythe-like implement. Jazz's chest swelled with an emotion that defied definition. Nonetheless, he kept edging toward calling it what it was. But recollections of Juan's betrayal got in the way every time. He smiled to himself and started swinging his weedwacker along the barrow ditch on his side of the road. The sharp smell of the cut weeds and the dust his weedwacker raised was somehow pleasing to him.

Klah had managed to get them work with the Alamo School Board clearing ditches alongside the busier roads on the reservation. Jazz mentally shook his head. The school board, for crying out loud. It not only ran the school, it was also responsible for roads. Klah told him the school board was the biggest employer on the reservation. They even hired the only policeman on the place.

Despite the heat of a late summer sun, Jazz enjoyed the work. That is, he enjoyed the activity. He'd stopped running daily and now relearned that exercise, along with the diet Dibe and Hosteen Pintaro laid out for him, kept his cramps… and usually his nausea at bay. He still craved the crack, but he'd come to understand it was a mental thing that sometimes utilized his guts to make itself known. Still, there was no question in his mind he was getting better, and swinging a weedwacker daily helped.

It didn't take long for Jazz and Klah to learn that walking to the far end of their assigned section and working back toward the settlement eliminated a long walk home at the end of the day. Now judging the work shift to be over, they hoisted tools to their shoulders and headed for the school board building. After putting their equipment away, they wordlessly walked to the wellness center, where they showered and changed into clean clothes they'd packed with them.

Afterward they resisted the urge to grab a prepackaged sandwich at the minimart, instead returning to the trailer so Klah could fix a stew with the ingredients Jazz needed for his damaged system. Jazz came to hate green tea, but then perversely decided he liked it. The vitamins and minerals he required were expensive. Even so, they found it more convenient to get most of them in tablet form. Klah's cooking skills weren't sufficient to utilize all the natural sources of everything Jazz's recovery required.

Tired but restless, along about sundown they wandered to the minimart. They didn't need anything, but it was something to do. They gave the little store the once-over to make certain Cheese and his buddies weren't around before entering. Because they were working men now, they splurged on a couple of strawberry soft drinks and went back outside to lean against the side of the building to sip at them.

"Good pop," Klah said.

"I always liked Cokes, but you got me hung up on strawberry now. What have you done to me?"

Klah grinned, something Jazz enjoyed watching. "Improved your lifestyle. Uh-oh." He pursed his lips, blushed red by the strawberry, and nodded.

"What?"

"Girl I used to know. And she's got her sister with her."

Jazz turned to watch two women in tight slacks walking toward the entrance. One of them did a double take and headed straight for them.

"Klah! I heard you come back. Why didn't you look me up?"

"Hello, Thunder Thighs," he responded.

She turned sideways and posed with one hand behind her head. "You can't call me that no more. I lost my baby fat."

"So I noticed. But you'll always be Thunder Thighs to me."

"All right, but only you. Nobody else can call me that. Who's that with you?"

"Bicycle, this here's Clarise Mockingbird, but I call her Thunder Thighs." Klah looked over her shoulder. "Is that little Maudie I see?"

"Except my sister ain't so little no more. Come on over here and meet Bicycle."

Jazz caught Klah's quick frown but didn't quite understand it. Was his lover going to hold on so tight there would be no room for anyone else in their lives?

Maudie offered a soft hand, prompting Jazz to accept it. She held on a moment as he confirmed his pseudonym. He felt compelled to explain.

"He named me that because he found me right after I had a bicycle wreck on I-40 and can't remember who I am."

She batted big black eyes. "You don't know who you are?"

"Well, sorta. It's a weird story."

"I like weird. Tell me all about it."

"But you gotta buy us sodas first," her sister said.

After Klah returned with two bottles—a Coke for Thunder Thighs and a grape for Maudie—they settled in the dirt at the side of the building. After staring at the ground for a minute, Jazz came up with a story.

"This old ram got away. I couldn't catch it on foot, so I grabbed a bicycle and started after it."

"Got away from where?" Thunder Thighs asked.

He ignored her. "He got out on the highway, you know, I-40, so I chased him right up the blacktop. Then this big semi roared up behind me and knocked me in the ditch. Don't remember much after that."

"Aw, that's a big tale," Maudie said.

"All right, it was a Bigfoot. You know, one of those sasquatch things."

Maudie slapped his arm playfully. "Either you're trying to make fools of us or else Coyote's making a fool of you."

"We really did find him riding a bicycle on I-40 after dark," Klah said. "And a semi did roar by. The wash from passing threw him right off the road. Knocked him silly."

"That's your version," Jazz said. "I like mine better." He noticed Maudie's little hand still rested on his forearm.

"What the hell's going on here!"

The booming voice startled all of them. Jazz glanced around to see Cheese Apachito advancing on him. Without another word, the man clapped him up beside the head. He saw stars but managed to roll over and come to his feet.

"What was that for?" he demanded as he set his stance.

"Nobody fucks with my woman." Cheese's flushed face turned dark with blood.

"Didn't know she was your woman," he said.

"I'm not. He's just being a big bully. Like he always does," Maudie said with a pout in her voice.

Cheese lunged at him. Jazz sidestepped, missing a good chance to ring the man's bells with a chop to the ear.

"No need for this, man," he said. "I'm not—"

Cheese came for him again. Jazz didn't know where it came from, but he dropped into a squatting stance and deflected the other's blows with his forearms. When he saw an opportunity, he lashed out with this left and caught Cheese on the nose. The man grunted and came back with a solid blow to Jazz's left shoulder. It rocked him. But he let go with a right, catching his opponent's injured nose again. Cheese instinctively put his hands to his face, and Jazz doubled him over with a jab to the stomach. That ended things. Maudie and Thunder Thighs went to help the bully while Klah urged Jazz toward home.

"Man, you decked old Cheese. Where'd you learn to fight like that?" Klah asked after a few minutes of silence.

"Dunno. Think maybe my brother taught me." He frowned. "Or maybe it was my uncle."

"You have a brother and an uncle?"

"Yeah. Seems like I do. Sounds right in my head, anyway."

"Bloods?"

"My brother is. Uncle's not. Leastways that's the way it seems."

"That trouble back there, you know what it means, don't you?"

"Yeah. I'll have to face him down again."

"Uh-uh," Klah said. "Can't wait for the cat to jump. He'll call the big rez and tell them you're down here. He didn't buy that Bicycle name for a minute."

"Crap. I'll have to leave."

"*We'll* have to leave."

"Man, I've screwed up your life enough. I'll go by myself."

"Uh-uh. You ain't going nowhere without me."

Jazz's heart soared, and the oppression of his desperate situation washed away on a tide of love. Temporarily.

Despite Jazz's worry, Klah insisted they had a day or so to prepare. The school board paid casual laborers after work every Friday, which was tomorrow. They decided to collect their pay before heading out. After discussing it for the better part of a day, they elected to go back to the Hatahle camp at To'hajiilee to see if Gad and Dibe heard any news from the trip to the big rez. Neither of them owned a cell phone—Jazz had long since lost his—and even if he hadn't, the Hatahles didn't own one.

Jazz was a bit leery about another long trip on One Sock. The roan gelding and Klah's pinto rodeo pony had been living easy off the land in a nearby communal pasture. But Jazz had avoided the horse since they got to Alamo, so maybe his thighs weren't so sensitive now.

THEY FINISHED work on Friday, collected their pay, and after a shower at the wellness center, decided to splurge on a prewrapped hamburger from the minimart. As they left the little store, burgers, chips, and sodas in hand, they ran into Cheese Apachito. The bigger youth just glared and entered without speaking.

"I don't like that," Klah said.

"What? He left us alone."

"Yeah. That's what I don't like. He usually snarls and growls like a dog. Part of his bluff. This time he didn't say nothing."

Jazz slowed his pace. "Maybe I oughta wait and talk to him. You know, work things out."

"You might as well try to nail shit to the outhouse wall. You ain't gonna make a friend outa Cheese. Forget him. We're leaving at first light tomorrow."

After they finished their meal—lavish by their standards—Jazz drank green tea and forced down some dried beets. Hosteen Pintaro had insisted that beets were rich in something Jazz needed to combat the cocaine. He hated beets.

He used some of their precious water to brush his teeth and wash away the odious taste the vegetable left in his mouth and prepared to go to bed. A few moments later, Klah lay down beside him on their pallet on the floor of the trailer.

"Where's our tack gear?" Jazz asked. He knew, but needed reassurance.

"On the fence of the pasture. And we hobbled the horses so they'll be easy to find in the morning." Klah lay quietly beside him for a moment. "Jazz, are you over it?"

"Over what?"

"Whatever that Juan guy put under your skin. I-I need to know. Seems like I'm tearing up my life for you." Klah rolled over and rose on one elbow, his hand on Jazz's chest. "Not that I ain't willing to, but I gotta know you won't take off with him if we run across the guy one day."

Jazz drew a deep breath, feeling Klah's hand rise as his chest expanded. It was a good feeling. "Why would I do that? He betrayed me. Got me into this mess. I wouldn't be drinking tea I don't like and eating icky beets and taking pills up the gazoo if it wasn't for him. Well, I kinda like the tea now, but you know what I mean."

Klah laid his head where his hand had been. "I know, but sometimes you still mumble his name when you sleep. So I wonder if you still love him."

"I never loved him. I liked what we did and how he made me feel until…. Well, until he handed me over to the traffickers." Jazz clutched his lover to his breast tightly. "I can tell you one thing for sure, Klah Hatahle. I never felt about him the way I feel about you."

"Say it?"

Was there fear in Klah's whisper?

"I love you. More than anyone on Earth. We're joined, man. Spiritually. Physically. And mentally too. I know what you're gonna say before you say it, and you know how I feel before I do." He ran his hand through Klah's thick black hair. "I don't want anybody but you. To do it with anyone but you. You're part of me now."

Klah whispered his love words before attaching his lips to Jazz's left nipple. Then they surrendered to their need, making love more passionately than ever before. To Jazz, it seemed like their first time, but with the infinite advantage of familiarity.

JAZZ WOKE when Klah shook his shoulder. "Is it time already?"

Klah laid his hand over Jazz's lips and whispered. "Someone's outside."

As Jazz sat up to listen better, there was a thud against the side of the trailer. Moments later, he smelled smoke. "Fire!" he yelped.

"Grab your things and follow me. Stay clear of the door!"

They had slept in their clothes and packed their belongings in anticipation of an early departure. Jazz grabbed his boots and the cheap plastic valise he'd bought at the thrift shop and followed Klah to the front of the trailer. The rear, where they were only moments before, was already being eaten away by flames.

He understood when Klah opened the trapdoor and disappeared below the trailer. He followed immediately and crawled out the hole his lover punched in the siding. Klah was already on his feet, racing through the darkness to their hobbled horses. Jazz followed on his heels. Neither of them looked back until they reached their horses. When Jazz glanced at the distant mobile home, his breath caught. The entire trailer was enveloped in bright orange flames.

Hoofbeats brought him out of his reverie. He vaulted aboard One Sock as if he'd been doing it all his life and followed the white rump of the pinto, barely visible in the night. They rode hard until reaching high ground a mile or so in the distance. Then they wheeled and looked back the way they came. Flames from the burning trailer were still visible. And now there were signs of other activity. Someone had come to fight the fire.

Jazz's blood boiled. His fingernails bit into his palms as he held his pony's reins. "Silver Wings! Haldemain!" he snarled.

"No. That was Cheese Apachito. Payback for showing him up in front of the girls. I knew he wouldn't let it go but didn't think he would try to kill us."

Jazz allowed Klah to select the route and set the pace. The sun was up, and they were riding side by side down a dusty road with the smell of sunflowers and sage in the air, when Jazz spotted a plume of dust in the distance.

"Car," he said.

"Yeah. Coming fast. Better move over."

They reined their horses into the ditch beside the road and kept riding. The racing car took shape as it approached. There was something familiar about it. As it roared past, enveloping them in a thick cloud of dust, Jazz gasped.

"It's the cop!" they said in unison.

No doubt about it. The driver was the husky man who called himself Chip when he tried to rape Jazz at one of the pool parties. The same man who drove an Albuquerque undercover police vehicle and handed out posters claiming Jazz was a fugitive. Zimmerman was his name, if he remembered correctly.

Chapter 28

FRIDAY NIGHT, Henry called and said he'd learned that Klah Hatahle didn't originally come from To'hajiilee like his aunt and uncle. He'd lived with his folks on another little crumb of the Navajo Reservation called Alamo, located down in Socorro County, until his parents were killed in a car wreck. That gave us another place to search.

Henry agreed to meet Paul and me at Alamo the next day at 11:00 a.m. Our trip was an easy one, west on I-40 and south on Highway 169 for something like a total of eighty-five miles. I wasn't certain where Henry would start from. He worked at the Peabody Coal mine near Kayenta, but I had no idea where he lived on the reservation. At a minimum, I estimated he faced a five-hour drive.

Even so, we saw his gunmetal pearl Harley-Davidson Sportster parked outside the chapter house when we arrived exactly on time. Henry was inside, talking to a girl at the receptionist's desk who was obviously thrilled to be speaking to such a fetching package of machismo. As he spotted Paul and me, he excused himself and walked to meet us. The grin he used on her faded away, replaced by a frown of worry.

"He was here," he said as he reached to grip my hand. "As late as last night. Him and Klah were living in Klah's folks' abandoned trailer." He turned to greet Paul before continuing. "And then somebody torched the trailer in the middle of the night."

"Was—" I started.

"No bodies. And their horses are missing from the pasture. Folks around here figure they burnt it down."

"Why?" Paul asked.

Henry shrugged. "No idea. To hide something, maybe. Fingerprints or something like that."

"That makes no sense," I objected. "All anyone has to do is show a photo to get an ID."

"And that's what happened even before the fire died out. Early this morning, some Albuquerque cop showed up with that wanted poster on Jazz."

"Zimmerman?" I asked.

"She described him as a body-builder type. Short blond hair, hazel eyes."

"Damn," I exclaimed. "That bastard could have set the fire."

"That's what I figure, but there's another possibility. The girl told me a kid nicknamed Cheese got into a fistfight with Jazz last Wednesday outside the minimart. Jazz put him down. She said Cheese ain't somebody to let that go by. So coulda been him."

"What were they doing here?" I asked.

"Got a day labor job with the school board weeding road shoulders."

"School board?" Paul asked.

"Long story. Worked something short of a week. Collected their pay yesterday after work."

"What would they have done then?" I wondered aloud.

Paul spoke up. "Been me, I'd have headed for the first store for some treats."

"That'd probably be the minimart," Henry said.

"Let's check it out. See if anything happened," I suggested.

The girl minding the cash register at the minimart acknowledged seeing Klah and his friend Bicycle yesterday along about sundown. She heard about—but didn't witness—the fight. It was apparent from her voice that she would have appreciated watching the altercation.

"But when they left yesterday, they ran right into Cheese as he was coming in. Thought maybe I'd get to see a dustup. But they didn't even say nothing to one another. Just walked past like the other'n wasn't even there."

By way of thanks, I bought three drinks from the cooler, and we huddled outside. Henry opened our conversation.

"Sounds to me like Cheese got smoked some more by seeing them. Probably went off and sulked until he worked himself into firebombing the trailer."

"Was it firebombed?" I asked.

"Don't really know. Girl at the chapter house just said it was arson. Didn't know no more'n that."

I leaned against the south wall of the minimart. "Okay, let's accept your view of things. This guy Cheese sets the trailer on fire. Zimmerman, probably following the same trail we did, learns Klah originally came from Alamo. So early Saturday morning, he drives down here looking for Jazz. And he finds him. At least, he learns Jazz was here. The fire would have called attention to Klah and his friend, Bicycle."

"Why Bicycle?" Paul asked.

"Somebody was looking for a guy named Jazz, so couldn't call him that," Henry replied. "Probably tagged him with something from the first time he set eyes on Jazz. Bicycle."

Paul nodded. "Makes sense."

"If their mounts are missing, they're horseback. Any clue to where they might be heading?" I asked.

"Maybe back to the Hatahles at To'hajiilee," Henry said. "Be hard to ride a horse around Albuquerque."

"What makes you think they'd head for Albuquerque?" Paul asked.

"Everybody I know's got kin or friends in Albuquerque. A town with lots of people is a good place to hide."

I dry-washed my face. "Albuquerque's where the people who took him are. Of course, he'd stay clear of the west side where he was held, but that's still taking a risk. That said, Jazz is bound to realize the pimps have contacts on the reservation."

"Sure he does," Paul said. "They already chased him away from To'hajiilee."

"Him and Klah are on horses," Henry said. "They'd stand out like a gold brick on a coal pile in Albuquerque."

"Don't forget the state fair," Paul came back at him. "It has a rodeo. Be lots of people on horseback. Maybe not riding on the streets so much, but there'll be some."

"They say the pony Klah is riding is his rodeo horse, so it could be," Henry said.

I sought to introduce some reality. "They could have ridden anywhere, even headed to Mexico. Henry, why don't you call your dad and have him start looking for the Hatahles on the big rez. Then head for Albuquerque and check the state fair. Even if you don't find them, maybe you can find someone who knows if Klah has relatives of friends there. Nobody'll talk to us, but maybe they will to you."

"And you're going to…?"

"Head for the Hatahle camp. If they're back, we'll see what we can learn. If they won't talk to us, we'll call you on the cell—if we can get bars—so you can speak some Navajo to them."

"What if Zimmerman caught up with Jazz and Klah?" Paul asked.

"Don't even want to think about that possibility. I'll call Gene and have him ask around the department. If we need to communicate with one another but can't reach the other party, call Hazel and give her the message."

WE WATCHED the ditches and kept our eyes out for vultures all the way to To'hajiilee in case Zimmerman caught up with Jazz and Klah. We bumped down the washboard track—it didn't qualify as a real road—to the Hatahle camp to find it occupied. I learned my Navajo courtesy from New Mexico's most famous author, Tony Hillerman, and remained in the car until a squat man with gray-black hair clasped behind his head in a man bun came out of the hogan and waved to us.

We got out of the Impala and introduced ourselves. The man, who answered to Gad Hatahle, did a double take at Paul's name but turned to me as the elder. "How can I help you?"

"I'm trying to locate your nephew Klah and the man with him, Jazz Penrod. Are they here?"

Gad's face gave nothing away, but something happened to his eyes, making me aware he had just gone on alert.

"Mr. Hatahle, let me explain."

"Maybe you better come in and do it." He led us to a small firepit before the hogan and settled in the dust. A middle-aged woman with an independent look about her came through the opening and sat down beside Gad.

"My wife," he said simply. "Dibe."

"I'm—" I started.

"I know who you are." She turned to my companion. "And you're Paul. You the one looking for him when you got in touch with that Juan fellow, ain't you?"

"Yes, ma'am."

"It's all right, Gad." She touched her husband's arm as she switched her look to me. "And you're that private investigator fellow from Albuquerque."

"That's right, ma'am."

"Cut out that 'ma'am' stuff. I'm Dibe, and he's Gad. We done some nosing around up on the big rez and found out a little about our dogie. And that's what Jazz was like, a poor orphaned calf, when we first seen him." She looked at her husband. "Ain't that right?" Without waiting for confirmation, she continued. "Well, he ain't here. Him and Klah both took off after we got the warning that old warlock had his claws out for him." Apparently she didn't want to call Nesposito by name.

"We know. They went to Alamo."

Dibe nodded. "That's right. Guess you are a detective, after all. But not like that other one that come nosing around this morning."

"Detective Zimmerman was here?"

"That he was," Gad said. "And he acted like he had power here. Went through our whole camp." He nodded to himself and smiled. "And we let him. Wanted him to see there wasn't nobody else here." He motioned over his shoulder to the wooden shack. "Thought he was gonna tear it down before he got it in his head the place was empty and didn't have no hidey-holes." Both he and Dibe cackled.

She took up the tale. "He'd been down at Alamo and said there was a fire, so he come up here to look. Truth to tell, we're a little worried. You know about a fire?"

"We and Jazz's brother, Henry, were just there. Klah's trailer was torched, probably by a local that Jazz got into a fight with, and burned right down to the wheels. But they didn't find any bodies in the trailer. And their horses were missing. They managed to get out and take off. Jazz's brother headed to Albuquerque to see if they went there. We came here to talk to you."

"How come he went to Albuquerque?"

"State fair's opening," Paul said. "Where there's a fair, there's a rodeo. Thought Klah might be trying to make some money working there."

"Fair assumption," Gad said. "Klah's got a cousin up there name of Pete Toadlena. Don't know where he lives, but he hangs out in a place called the Blue Spruce."

"Then Henry can find him. That's his hangout when he's in Albuquerque."

"He oughta know that Pete's a rodeo hand too."

I walked out from under the canopy of trees sheltering the camp and managed to raise Henry. He was still on the way, but I conveyed Gad's information just as the signal faded.

Before returning to the others, I opened the trunk of my car and retrieved one of the cheap throwaway cell phones I keep for informants and other contacts and plugged a charger into the vehicle's lighter. While the instrument charged up, I returned to the fire. "Got him. He doesn't know a Pete Toadlena, but no doubt he'll find him. Mr. Hatahle... Gad, if your nephew and Jazz are horseback, how long will it take them to get here? Provided they're returning, that is."

"Two, three days. Lotsa cloud cover lately. If it keeps up, they can push the horses a little harder. Two days."

"If they left sometime last night, they wouldn't have had time to get here. I'm charging up a cell phone I want to give you. I'll have my office manager activate it. It's preprogrammed with my phone numbers... home, office, and cell. Cell's the best. If they show up, will you please have Jazz contact me?"

Gad studied the flames a moment before answering. "Jazz is all messed up in his head. He remembers some things, but he don't others. Things he oughta know."

"There was a cut on his head the night Gad brought him home," Dibe explained. "Didn't even know his own name right then. He finally managed to come up with Jazz, but he hooked it up with Jasper. Didn't know it was really Penrod till that Albuquerque cop showed up asking about him."

"Jasper's his actual first name," I said. "But he started answering to Jazz when he was a kid. But you recognized Paul's name, so obviously Jazz remembers him. If he won't call me, have him call Paul."

My companion handed over a card he'd printed to let the world know he was a freelance investigative journalist.

"Dibe, I understand you sold a family heirloom to buy Jazz a horse. Can I help you get it back?"

"Hosteen Abbo ain't gonna part with it. And if he does, he'll hold you up same as a masked man with a gun. 'Sides, it done more for us than just buy a horse."

"Point me at him, and let me have at it."

"That'll wait until our two strays are safe and sound."

Gad stirred the dying coals with a stick. "What's that Albuquerque policeman all about? Jazz a criminal?"

"No, he's not a wanted criminal. That poster Zimmerman showed you is a phony. Has Jazz told you anything about what's happened to him?" I asked.

Gad answered. "Shared what he could remember. Talked about a Silver Wings. His blood tends to rise when he thinks about that one. We kinda put together that he'd got mixed up with them slave traffickers. You know, sex traffickers."

I nodded. "He did. And I believe he was escaping from them the night you saw him have that bicycle wreck. Sort of a mystery how they hung on to him as long as they did."

"Wasn't no mystery about it," Dibe said. "That boy was hung up on crack cocaine when he come to us. Bad shape. Laid right here on the ground and shook and shimmied so hard I thought he was gonna die."

"How is he now?" Paul asked.

"Some better. I'm a hand trembler, you know. I figured he needed a ceremony, but nobody had money for the proper kind. But Hosteen Pintaro set him down and told us the kinds of vegetables and drinks and herbs he needed. He got some better after that."

"Lots better," Gad said. "Still has the longing but not the hurting. At least not so bad."

Dibe pointed a long finger at Paul. "You... Paul. You got a connection with Jazz?"

My companion looked blank for a moment before he caught her meaning. "No. I met him once three years ago. I only contacted Juan Gonzales on the internet trying to find out where Jazz disappeared to."

"You oughta know that Klah and Jazz, they found one another."

"Good," I said. "If Klah's kin of yours, then he's good people. And that's what got Jazz into this mess in the first place. He was looking for a good man."

She nodded emphatically. "Well, he mighta taken the hard way, but he found one."

PAUL WAS silent as we pulled away from the Hatahle camp, but as soon as we swung onto I-40, he turned in his seat to face me. "Now we know why Jazz hasn't reached out for help. He didn't know where to search."

I grimaced. "That's part of the answer. But I also expect that he's deeply ashamed of what he's gone through and wasn't ready to talk about it. That's why his memory seems to come back in snatches."

"What if he's so ashamed he heads to Texas or California or somewhere?"

"Then there's nothing we can do about it. But at least he has one thing he didn't before."

"What? Oh, you mean Klah. Yeah, he sounds like a solid citizen. Glad they found one another."

Five miles passed before he spoke again. "I hope he shows up so we can catch that Silver Wings guy and put him where he belongs. Have you figured out the Zimmerman contact yet?"

"I suspect it's a Bolton contact, and Zimmerman's just his hammer."

"You think the lieutenant's Silver Wings?"

"Don't know about that. But I think he's involved some way."

"Maybe Henry will have better luck than we did."

After we arrived back at Post Oak Drive, I phoned Hazel at home and learned she'd received no message from Henry. Paul wanted me to call him, but I knew he'd contact us when he had something to report. Besides, I wanted to phone Gene and let him know Zimmerman was on the prowl again… or still.

Henry didn't call, but he showed up around eleven looking for a place to stay for the night. He'd located Pete Toadlena, and together they'd made the rounds of Indian hangout places looking for Klah and Jazz. They'd struck out, but that was no surprise. The two hadn't had time to reach Albuquerque by horseback. But at least Henry alerted Pete and his friends to watch for the men.

Then Henry delivered the real shocker for the day. Louie had called to let him know the Navajo Tribal Police wanted Jazz for questioning in the death of Julian Nesposito.

Chapter 29

SATURDAY MORNING I tried to run down Lonzo Joe at the San Juan County Sheriff's Office. No luck. The dispatcher said he was off duty for the weekend and intended to visit his family on the big rez. Repeated calls to his cell went straight to voicemail, which led me to believe he was out of range of a tower.

After Paul and Henry left in Paul's Charger, heading for the state fair to check out the rodeo hands to see if anyone had seen or heard from Klah, I lost patience and dialed the flip phone I'd left with Gad. He hadn't seen "a hair of his nephew's head," as he put it. I couldn't simply sit there and molt, so I drove downtown to my office, where I pulled out all the transcriptions Hazel had done of my notes and sat down to figure out a time line. *Could Jazz have killed old Nesposito?*

After half an hour of orienting myself and marking down dates and events on a calendar, I came up with the following:

Sunday, August 22, Gad and Klah rescue Jazz after his bicycle wreck on I-40 and take him to To'hajiilee.

Wednesday, August 25, Jazz and Klah see Detective Zimmerman at the village and learn Jazz's name is Jasper (Jazz) Penrod.

Thursday, August 26, Louie Secatero confronts Nesposito and learns Jazz's fingerprints were found on a stolen bicycle.

Tuesday, August 31, Milton Atcitty warns the Hatahles that Nesposito is searching for Jazz.

Wednesday, September 1, Dibe sells her grandmother's squash blossom necklace and buys a pony for Jazz. The boys depart that day for Alamo.

Wednesday, September 1, Nesposito is killed on the lip of Black Hole Canyon on the big rez, *some 200 miles away!*

Most likely before Jazz and Klah ever left To'hajiilee.

I leaned back in my chair and relaxed. There was a good chance we could satisfy the Navajo police of Jazz's innocence and get the bulletin canceled. At least that would prevent Zimmerman using it as cover in his search for Jazz.

I no sooner completed that thought than the phone rang. Gene was on the other end.

"Bad news. I stopped by the station for a minute and learned the Navajo cops are looking for your buddy Jazz."

"Yeah, I already know. I'm at the office finishing a time line. I know where Jazz was the day Nesposito was killed. To'hajiilee. That's couple of hundred miles away. Believe I can prove it."

"It won't mean much, but I'll put out the word I hear the kid has an alibi. Afraid that won't slow Zimmerman down."

"Have you talked to him?"

"Yeah. And got nothing out of him. He's on a job he can't talk about. That's the line I get."

"Bolton—"

"Bolton's no help. Says he can't interfere with an ongoing investigation."

"Since when?"

"Yeah, well…."

"You got time for lunch?"

"Nah. Glenda and three-fifths of the kids are outside in the car. 'Fraid I'm eating Navajo fry bread and mutton stew for lunch at the fair."

"Why three-fifths of the kids?"

"The oldest two are in wheels of their own. Can't tell you how secure that makes me feel."

POURING OVER my file on Jazz's case yielded no more epiphanies for me, although I considered nailing down Jazz's whereabouts at the time of the Nesposito murder to be a good day's work.

I grabbed a barbecue sandwich at a Blake's Lotaburger on Carlisle and took it home. Paul and Henry would be full of carnival food, meaning I was responsible for filling my own stomach today. They returned to the house midafternoon so Henry could collect his things and head back home. He intended to go by way of To'hajiilee to see if his brother and Klah surfaced. An hour after he left, he phoned to confirm what Gad told me that morning… no sign of either of the two men.

That evening while Paul was at the desk we'd set up for him in my home office, I realized how much he was affected by Jazz's situation, because he'd said little about the fair. Normally he would have told me about the celebration in fine detail.

When we went to bed later to do a little reading before turning out the light—I was working on *Skippy Dies* by Paul Murray; he was perusing Dan Clowes's *Wilson*—he turned to me and laid a hand on my arm. I realized anew how lucky I was to have that hand and the man attached to it.

"Vince…."

"Yeah?"

"Will you tell me something? And be honest about it?"

"Sure. And just to set the record straight, I only lie to my clients. Never to you." That didn't earn me a chuckle. This was serious.

"How do you really feel about Jazz?"

The question shook me a little. Paul was very secure… both in himself and in our domestic situation. "Judging from that query, I think the question should be how do *you* feel about Jazz?"

He went very still. "I only met the guy once. And that was three years ago. But I still remember him… vividly."

I clasped the hand resting on my arm. "He's that kind of guy. Once you see him, you never forget him. To answer your question, if I didn't have you, I'd go after Jazz."

He twitched. "I-I guess that's the way I feel too. And that's what scares me."

"I know. But what you need to understand is that I'm content. I have who I want. How many people can honestly make that statement? Not as many as we think, I imagine."

"But we're still going to look for him, aren't we? I mean, we gotta do that, right?"

"Absolutely. And we'll find him. But neither of us can expect to find the old Jazz. He's gone through a lot since we saw him last."

"I hope it hasn't turned him bitter."

Paul made love to me then, incredibly gently at first, and then with an unexpected fierceness as our time drew near.

EARLY MONDAY morning, I managed to reach Lonzo Joe after I got to my downtown office. The San Juan County sheriff's detective had already heard about Jazz's situation with the Navajo cops. I told him about the timeline I'd worked up and asked him his opinion.

"You get it documented, and that oughta be enough to get the kid off the hot plate. At least as far as Nesposito's death is concerned. You had any news about him?"

"Yeah. Found where he was, but he got chased away by that Albuquerque detective searching for him. Not sure where he's headed. And if I knew, I wouldn't tell you. Don't want to get you crossways with the tribal police until I get that time line nailed down and attested to."

"Understand. I learn anything, I'll pass it on."

As we terminated the call, I heard the warning gong at the front door alerting me someone had entered the office. I heard Hazel greet whoever it was. A moment later, she stood in my doorway and announced Lieutenant Chester Bolton.

"BJ," he boomed as he walked into my office. "I was in the building and thought I'd drop in to see how you're doing."

Yeah, right. The first time that ever happened. I tamped down the thought and told my paranoia to go back to its cubbyhole. "Lieutenant, good to see you. Have a seat."

"Can't stay," he said, plopping his short, barrel-chested form into a chair. He was a man who fit a uniform well. His bars and badge seemed at home on his collar and left breast. The mat of graying hair at the open neck of his uniform shirt lent credence that a man's man occupied my visitor's chair. "Since I was already on your doorstep, just wanted to stop by and see if there was any news on that fellow you and Enriquez were looking for. Been some developments on our end, you know."

I arched an eyebrow. "Know the Navajo police were looking for him to ask about a trafficker's death. Don't know of any other developments."

"Detective Zimmerman's looking for him in connection with some trafficking information he's turned up."

"What information?"

"Don't know the details. But it's possibly connected to those murders in that west-side motel."

My stomach dropped through the floor, but I quelled the instinct to leap to Jazz's defense. "Haven't heard much about that case since all the publicity died away." I kept my voice steady. "Any solid leads?"

"Just the Penrod kid."

He closed his mouth and seemed to wait expectantly. The guy was baiting me. Why?

"Thought you should know APD's getting serious about finding the man. Just in case he contacts you," Bolton finally added.

I tumbled to the message he was delivering. "You don't seriously think that kid had anything to do with murdering ten people at the My Other Home Motel, do you?"

He lifted one shoulder. "Why not? You say he was kidnapped. Word on the street is he escaped and went looking for revenge." He eyed me steadily. "Course, he'd probably need help killing ten individuals at one sitting. You know, someone to hold them in place while he did the killing."

A cloak of dread settled over my shoulders. "Are you saying his brother helped him out?"

"Henry Secatero's got a rap sheet in Farmington and on the reservation."

"Yeah, drinking and fighting. But not murder."

"But that shows a propensity to violence, and you never know what a man'll do when someone bangs his brother. Hear the Penrod kid's queer, but not Secatero."

Once convinced he would not get a rise out of me, he leaned back in his chair and brushed thinning gray hair. "Why are you looking for Penrod?"

"Because his family reached out and asked for help when Jazz disappeared. That's what I do, help people out."

"Yeah. If they can pay the tab." He thumbed his nose. "Having trouble figuring out which side of this thing you're on, Vinson."

My back prickled. "What do you mean?"

"You know as well as I do that a trafficking operation like that needs protection. Who better than a private detective with connections to the police department? A lot of cops know you from your time on the force, including your last riding partner. That gives you insight. Knowledge. I remember you out at that sleazy motel going through the place looking at bodies. And you're trying awfully hard to find the guy who we believe executed them."

I spoke through clinched teeth. "Get your story straight, *Lieutenant* Bolton. The man helping me find him is the brother you claim was the other shooter."

"Oh, my story's straight. Let's just suppose things were getting out of hand and you needed to shut the door behind you. You get a couple of Navajos to do it for you, but one goes off the reservation—so to speak—and you have to find him."

"And do what?" I asked.

"Shut another door. Does Secatero know you intend to kill him too?"

"And just what makes you think I'm the man providing protection to a bunch of human traffickers?"

"Word around town is that you're loaded. Didn't come from being a cop. Probably not from a rinky-dink PI operation either."

"The word on the street is right."

"Around twelve mil is what I hear."

"Right ballpark. But there are a number of solid citizens who know I inherited that from my parents. Have the documents to prove it. Years' worth of documents."

"And where did two schoolteachers come up with that kinda money?"

"Invested in Microsoft before it was Microsoft," I said. "And there are plenty of documents to support that as well."

"I'll just bet there are." Bolton heaved his solid bulk out of the chair and clapped his billed uniform hat on his head. "Nice talking to you."

My fingers shook with rage as I reached for the small digital recorder sitting on my desk. I'd thumbed it on the moment Hazel told me Bolton was here to see me. Now I spoke a few words attesting to the speakers and the circumstances of the recording. That done, I called Gene and arranged to meet him somewhere neutral, cautioning him to watch for a tail as he left the headquarters building.

GENE FLUSHED in varying shades of anger as he listened to Bolton's taped voice. At the end, he flicked off the machine and looked at me. "What's this guy trying to do?"

"In my opinion, he's doing two things. Covering his own butt and doing the bidding of Silver Wings."

Gene snorted. "Hell, he could *be* Silver Wings."

"The hair he's got left is gray, all right, but you can hardly claim he's got silver wings. Or at least what I think of as silver wings."

"But we do know somebody who does. Somebody close to Bolton."

I fingered an itchy earlobe. "Two somebodies that I can think of right off the bat. The Haldemain brothers. But I can add a couple of others to the list, including the chief of police. In the meantime, what do we do about his accusations?"

"Insinuations," he corrected.

"Sounded like an accusation to me."

"That's because you're taking it personally."

I choked first and then burst out laughing. "Guess I was, at that."

"Think it's time I go to my rabbi and see what's going on."

Gene's rabbi was the current police chief. Going to him was akin to taking a parking ticket to the Chief Justice of the New Mexico Supreme Court, but it was his call.

"I'll need your recording," he added as he slipped the recorder into his pocket.

"Make sure I get it back."

Gene left, but I paused to pay the bill and wonder what the hell was coming down the pike next.

Chapter 30

GENE DIDN'T call me Tuesday morning, so I was left to wonder if he'd been able to talk to the chief. Charlie had a good head on his shoulders, so I called him into my office and shared Bolton's insinuations. I finished the telling with "For God's sake, don't tell Hazel."

"She'll find out sooner or later," he said.

"Yes, but by later, maybe we'll have headed this off at the pass."

He just grunted. "What do you intend to do about the situation?"

"I'll take my cues from Gene after he talks to the chief."

"That might put pressure on, not take it off. Talking to the chief, I mean."

"Possibly, but for the moment, we'll go on like usual."

"Yeah, right. Nothing on Jazz yet?"

"No, but I'm heading out to the Hatahle camp in a few minutes. I want to start documenting his presence at To'hajiilee during the murder of Nesposito."

"Don't suppose you can document it during the massacre on the west side, do you?"

I sighed. "Not much chance of that. Best I can figure out, Juan had turned Jazz over to Silver Wings by that time."

"Lot of good that will do us."

"If I can run Silver Wings to ground, it might. He'd use Jazz to exonerate himself from the murders."

"Ten to one he's behind the killings but didn't do them himself."

"No bet."

"Has there been any sighting of that man Jazz was seen with over on Coors?"

I shook my head. "And I can't think of any way to run him to ground."

"You checked with immigration?"

"On the off chance, yes. But I need more information before they can help."

Charlie rubbed his nose. "Well, I checked some more on Desert Enterprises, the outfit that owned the green Mercedes. Their attorney, Brookings Ingles, is the only local connected with the organization. So far as I can tell, they do absolutely no business out of that rent-an-office building on Montgomery Street. I only located one of the incorporators, an Apollo Nava, in Juárez, Mexico. So far as I can tell, he's a sports promoter with an iffy reputation."

"Could we be wrong?" I asked. "Could we have been looking at a Mexican national instead of an Asian on those store tapes?"

"They were fuzzy, but Henry caught a glimpse of him in the car and thought he was Asian."

"Can you get a picture of Nava?"

"Shouldn't be hard," Charlie said.

"Has the Mercedes resurfaced?"

"Nope. And I got one of my friends at APD to put a BOLO out on it. Found one thing interesting, though. Desert Enterprises rented the motel on the west side where the killings took place."

"The My Other Home Motel?"

"Yep. Leased it for a year."

"Well, that ties them into the White Streak family. Makes them traffickers. And as I recall, the guy at the front desk of the rent-an-office building said Nava was the only one he ever saw connected with Desert Enterprises. What was the name of that office building?" I asked.

"The Northeast Heights Office Building, if I remember right."

"Who owns it?"

"A group of medical doctors bought it as an investment. They're all reputable guys. The fellow at the front desk's name was Wayne Hooker. He's the nephew of one of the doctors. No record."

"They're probably not involved. Damned if I can figure out Desert Enterprises' role in all this."

"Probably no more than a nail to hang their hat on whenever it comes to something that has to be legally documented."

"Like the lease on the motel and the title to the Mercedes."

"Exactly," Charlie said.

At that moment Hazel stuck her head in the door. "BJ, there's someone on the phone who claims he's Jazz Penrod."

I dashed across the room to my desk, picked up the phone, and punched the blinking red light. "Jazz! Is that you?"

A husky baritone came over the wire. "BJ? Damn, it's good to hear your voice."

I nodded to Charlie, who broke out in a broad smile. "Where are you?"

There was a noticeable pause before he answered. "The place where you left a phone for me."

He was being cautious. Understandable after what he'd gone through. "Great, you stay right where you are, and I'll be there shortly. Have you called anyone else?"

"Just you."

"Keep it that way for the moment. Hang on, guy, I'm on the way."

I hung up and dialed Gene. Fortunately I got right through. "Tell me something. Is there a legitimate wanted bulletin out on Jazz Penrod?"

"Not that I know of."

"Can you check for me?"

I waited on hold for five minutes before he came back. "Nothing from APD. Still have the request from the Navajo police. Why, you know something?"

"You talk to the chief yet?"

"Got an appointment in thirty minutes. You hang tight, he may want to talk to you."

"I'll be out of pocket. Got a lead on Jazz. Not a strong one, but at least it's something I have to check out." I hung up before Gene could protest. I didn't think our phones were bugged, but a man can't be too careful.

IT TOOK me longer to reach the Hatahles' camp than usual because I drove all over the place for a quarter of an hour to see if I could spot a tail. Of course, if Vice—as opposed to one of their detectives—wanted Jazz, they'd devote enough manpower to make a tail hard to spot. But my gut told me this was something just between Zimmerman and Bolton. Once I got on I-40 at the east end of town by way of the Tramway Boulevard ramp, I carefully obeyed the speed limit all the way to the reservation. I wished Paul were with me, but he'd gone to interview some of the coaching staff at UNM in pursuit of something having to do with the athletic department's funding.

About halfway down the washboard road to the Hatahle camp, I pulled off to the side of the road to see if any vehicle showed up behind me. None appeared, but stopping gave me time to set up my laptop and a portable printer I'd brought with me. Finally satisfied I hadn't been followed, I drove the rest of the way and parked on the road near the hogan. For a minute no one showed, but then Gad came out and waved me inside.

Jazz Penrod emerged from the hogan as I approached, looking as handsome and sexy as ever. Even so, I saw signs of his recent life's journey. A deeper laugh line framing the broad mouth, a tightness around the big, expressive eyes. If I recalled correctly, he'd contacted Juan through nm.lonelyguys.com on June 15, a Tuesday, I believe. Today was Tuesday, September 15. Three months of hell.

He extended a hand, which I grasped before pulling him into an embrace. "Good to see you, guy. You've led us on a merry chase." I held him at arm's length. "Well, maybe not a merry one, but a chase nonetheless."

"Hasn't been merry for me, I can tell you."

"The important thing is you're safe now."

"Am I? That Albuquerque detective shows up everywhere I go."

"We'll take care of that Albuquerque detective," I said a little more confidently than was probably wise.

A young man stepped out of the hogan and moved into the light. He stood around Jazz's height, five ten, and carried about ten pounds or so more than Jazz's one sixty. Analytically, he was probably as handsome as Jazz, but his sexuality was more guarded, nuanced. Jazz's hair was black, but this guy's hair was a type of ebony that made me think I was looking into a void. Jazz introduced him as Klah. I liked him immediately.

"You must be a hell of a guy to babysit this one." Klah blushed at my words. "Let's talk, guys. You've got a lot to fill me in on."

We settled around the firepit in front of the hogan. The low orange flames added little to the warmth of a beautiful day bordering on autumn. I took out my recorder, identified the participants, noted time and date, and laid the little instrument on one of the rocks of the pit. At my prodding, Jazz—hesitantly and with obvious reluctance—told his tale. As far as I could tell, he related it faithfully and in full. I saved my questions until he finished.

"Do you know that Juan and nine others, some of them children, were murdered at a west-side motel sometime on August 17?"

Jazz gasped aloud. "Juan's dead?"

"Shot to death with two more adults and seven children. Execution style."

"Where?"

"A motel called My Other Home."

Jazz's shudder was apparent even across the width of the firepit. "I was there once. When Juan and I first met." He shook his head. "Terrible place to die."

"Do you have any idea who could have done it?"

His eyes went wide. "No. How could I?"

"By seeing or hearing something that ties in to it."

"All I ever saw was Silver Wings and Kim." He flushed and ducked his head. "And the guys who showed up for his pool parties."

"Do you know Silver Wings' real name?"

"Haldemain," Jazz shot right back at me. "I think his name is Haldemain. At least, that's the name the fellow at the airstrip called him."

"That's the time he took you up and tried to kill you and this Kim fellow?" I asked, recalling some of his narrative.

He nodded. "Did kill Kim. He thought I was dead too."

"Then why did they start looking for you?"

Jazz flushed deeper, but it was different this time. "I was mad because he tried to kill me. I-I pissed all over his airplane's seats and instrument panel. And then I stole a bicycle at the house where they kept the airplane."

"Just think, if you hadn't lost your temper," Klah said, "they'd still think you were dead and wouldn't be chasing you all over the countryside."

"Yeah, but it felt good... at the time."

"Do you have any idea where you were when Kim went out the door?"

Jazz shrugged. "Heard them say we were over the malpais. You know, the black lava country."

"What do you know about Kim?" I asked.

"Not much. He was a houseboy, but he was more. I got the feeling he did things for Silver Wings. He reminded me of a cobra. Compact and deadly."

"Could he have killed the people at the motel?"

"Coulda, but why would he?"

"Because when Henry came to me to report you missing, we started nosing around, and the noose got tighter around Silver Wings...

Haldemain. He needed to get rid of anyone who knew he was connected to the slave trade."

Klah spoke up. His voice was a lighter baritone than Jazz's. "Maybe he wanted to get rid of the man who did his killing for him."

"Exactly," I said. "Jazz, I know two men named Haldemain. Brothers. Both lawyers. Did you ever hear a first name? Ross or William?"

"The people at the pool parties called him Rex, but they used phony names around me."

"Describe Haldemain," I said.

"Middle-aged. About your height. Your weight too. Good-looking guy."

"Hair, eyes?"

"Black hair. Maybe dark brown. Black eyes."

"Effeminate?"

Jazz glanced into the fire. "Not... not until we were alone. Then...." He left the rest unsaid.

"Any distinguishing marks. You know, scars or moles?"

"Brown mole right below the left nipple. He... he used to say it was a third one when he had me...." Again his voice died away.

"How about his equipment, anything distinctive there?"

"BJ," Jazz said in a strangled voice, "can we talk about this... you know."

Dibe spoke up for the first time. "Forget I'm here, boy. You need to help nail this snake before he strikes again."

"That's okay, we can talk about it on the way home," I said. "Right now, there are a few other things I need to get straight in my head."

I thumbed on my recorder and had Jazz listen to what we had just discussed. As we listened, I caught something I'd missed during the telling. On the recorder he spoke slowly, as if the memories were either painful or difficult to call up... or both. When the little machine stopped speaking, he filled in a few blanks under prompting. Unfortunately nothing he told us provided a reliable alibi for the murders that took place at the motel on August 17. But it alibied him for Nesposito's killing.

Jazz confirmed my belief he had been deliberately hooked on crack cocaine and then sold to Silver Wings—who was likely one of the Haldemain brothers—for his own sexual gratification and to provide services to friends, probably in exchange for payment. When he finished his tale, I zeroed in on Haldemain's pool parties. When I asked if he could identify any of the participants, he delivered a shocker.

"Yeah. The guy they called Chip was that Albuquerque detective who's been putting up flyers saying I'm wanted by the police."

"Zimmerman?" I asked.

"If that's his real name, yeah."

"Are you certain, Jazz?"

"Oughta be. He tried to rape me, and I put him on his ass. Silver Wings stepped in to keep us from killing one another."

"Son of a bitch!" I swore. "Tell me more about the others. Describe them."

My heart sank when he described the man he called Tom. I switched off the recorder. "Hold on a minute."

It took me no more than five minutes of searching the internet to come up with a photo of Lt. Chester Bolton. He was a well-known and high-profile police officer with plenty of photos available. Jazz studied two of them from different angles before he nodded. "That's Tom. He wasn't so... aggressive as that other one." Then he blinked and shook his head. "He's a cop too?"

I confirmed that for him and tried to find photos of Zimmerman, but he was a Vice cop who moved clandestinely. I found none. Both the Haldemains were public figures, and I soon put a photo of Roscoe on the screen.

"That's him!" Jazz said. "That's Silver Wings."

I pulled up another photo. "What about this one?"

"Yeah. Like I said. That's him. Silver Wings."

"It's not the same man." I flipped back and forth between the two pictures a couple of times before I saw a frown of uncertainty on Jazz's face. "They're brothers," I said. "Which one is Silver Wings?"

The resemblance between the two brothers was so strong that in the end, Jazz was unable to say with certainty which was his captor. "Are they twins?" he asked.

"No, but William's only a year or so older than Roscoe. And they strongly resemble one another. Think a little harder. What color were Silver Wings' eyes?" I asked.

"I dunno. Black, I think. Yeah. Black."

"That would be William Haldemain, if I remember right."

"You know, I never thought about it before, but sometimes his eyes would be brownish, but with some gold and green in them."

"Hazel?" I asked.

"Yeah, hazel eyes."

"That's the color of Roscoe's eyes."

Damnation, could *both* the brothers be Silver Wings?

Chapter 31

WHILE JAZZ phoned his brother, I hauled out my laptop computer and portable printer and used the little house beside the hogan to conduct interviews with each of the others to document Jazz's whereabouts on the days centering around September 1, when Nesposito was killed. I allowed each to read his or her affidavit but permitted no one to sign a document. We needed a notary public for that.

I took Jazz's statement last because it took the longest amount of time. I detailed the facts of his captivity as exactingly as possible. He showed signs of restlessness and some physical discomfort during the long process, but after Dibe brought him some green tea and a platter of fruits and vegetables, he seemed better. While the lengthy document printed, I asked if he'd reached Henry.

"Man, it was good to hear his voice. He was at work, so we didn't have much time, but he knows I'm okay. He thinks I should come straight to the rez. Says he can protect me better there than you can in Albuquerque."

"He may be right, but one thing at a time. Right now we need to inoculate you from Nesposito's killing."

Jazz indicated the documents I'd created. "Doesn't this do it?"

"We've got one more to go. These are good, but an affidavit from Nesposito's nephew will go a long way toward convincing the cops."

"You mean that guy who warned us Nesposito was hunting me for the cops?"

"Hunting you for some reason. Anyway, that's our next move."

"Then what?"

"Probably Albuquerque. For the short run, anyway. I want to get you checked out."

"Checked out? How?"

"You're not yourself, Jazz. You got irritable during my questioning. Uncomfortable. I got the feeling you were hurting once or twice."

"Sick to my stomach is more like it. The tea helps with that. Then Dibe's got a whole host of things I'm supposed to eat. And a few pills… you know, vitamins and minerals." He shrugged. "It helps."

"Maybe so, but you need professional attention."

"Hey, I called my mom after I talked to Henry. Hope that was okay."

From the way he changed the subject, I suspected he wasn't very receptive to medical help. "Sure. I imagine she was glad to hear from you."

"Yeah, but…." His face clouded. "Wasn't any way I could really explain things. You know, without getting into all that… that shit."

He shut down right in front of my eyes. I read embarrassment and mortification in every look and movement. What he did to survive was coming home to him now… hard. He needed a type of comfort and reassurance I couldn't provide.

"Look. I'm going to take Dibe and Gad to see this Milton Atcitty, Nesposito's nephew, and get his statement. Klah will stay here with you, okay?"

He nodded mutely.

MILTON ATCITTY made no objection to signing a statement confirming he had seen Jazz at the Hatahles' camp on Tuesday, August 31. He remembered the date because it was the day before his uncle was killed. The boys left for Alamo the next day, but it was impossible for them to ride to Black Hole Canyon on the big rez in time to murder Nesposito. Of course, some prosecutor could claim Jazz found other transportation and met Nesposito on the rez. It wasn't perfect but better than nothing.

I phoned Charlie at the office and asked him to head down to Alamo to tie down when Jazz and Klah arrived there. As Klah told it, they went to the chapter house for permission to stay in his family's old trailer. Once Charlie agreed to that, we all went to the To'hajiilee chapter house in search of a notary for signatures. I'd take Jazz and Klah later. Right at the moment, I hoped Klah was ministering to Jazz and settling him down.

When we arrived back at camp, Jazz carried around a mug of the green tea and munched on a raw beet. Maybe this voodoo treatment worked. He definitely seemed better. At least he was well enough for the two of them to go have their signatures notarized. After a short debate, we agreed Jazz would go with me back to Albuquerque until Charlie got the statement from the Alamo chapter house, or as Klah said, more likely the Alamo School Board. I scratched my head over that one but didn't ask questions. Once that was done, I'd fax the documents to Det. Lonzo Joe and have him deliver them to the tribal police district station in Shiprock. Not until after that was accomplished did I want Jazz heading in that direction.

Although I told Klah he was welcome in my home, Jazz wouldn't hear of it. This obviously hurt the young man, even though Jazz explained he wasn't willing to put his lover in any more danger than he already had.

"When?" Klah asked.

"When this load of crap's off my back."

"That might be never."

"BJ here works miracles. And he's gonna work one for me too. Right?"

I scratched my chin and gave him the answer he wanted. Needed. "We are. It might take a few days, but we're going to get to the bottom of this."

"How?" Klah asked. "If I heard right, you got the Albuquerque Police Department mixed up in it."

"That's all right," I said. "I've got my own contacts within the police."

A few minutes later, I drove up the rough track toward the chapter house while Klah and Jazz followed in Gad's black, rusted Ford F-150 pickup. I couldn't ascertain the age of the thing but estimated it dated back to at least 1989. Hell, neither the driver nor the passenger in that rattletrap was even a gleam in his father's eye when that vehicle rolled off the production line.

Once the documents were notarized, I allowed the two a few minutes to say goodbye. Even from a distance, I could see the fear in Klah's eyes. Worried that Jazz would get caught up in his past life and never come back again, most likely.

Taking advantage of the interlude, I phoned Gene at headquarters and told him I thought both Lieutenant Bolton and Detective Zimmerman were a part of Silver Wings' sex trafficking group. Gene expressed disbelief, but the tone of his voice said otherwise.

"You learned who Silver Wings is?"

"One of the Haldemains, but I don't know which. Jazz has looked at pictures of both and can't quite decide."

"They look a lot alike, but they've got different colored eyes. Roscoe's are green."

"Hazel."

"Okay, hazel. And William's are brown or black."

"Black. But Jazz says sometimes the eyes were black and sometimes brown."

"Shit! *Both* of them?"

"Possible, or maybe one of them wears contacts to confuse the issue."

"Yeah. Reasonable doubt," he said.

"Of course, Jazz can provide more intimate details, but that doesn't help us much unless we can catch them naked in the showers at the club."

"Not likely."

"What are you going to do about Bolton and Zimmerman?" I asked.

"Nothing until I talk to Jazz. Where you taking the kid?"

"To my house where I can give him some protection."

"Don't kid yourself. If what you say is true, he might be safer in jail on the reservation."

"May end up there, but the first stop is my place. After you talk to him, we'll see. You're sure there's no APD want on him?"

"Not unless it came down five minutes ago. But Bolton could make that happen."

"Can you sneak off and meet us?" I asked.

"Probably not till tomorrow morning without raising eyebrows."

"How did it go with the chief?"

"Rough." With that, he hung up.

A moment later Jazz crawled into the Impala, his tail dragging. "Man, wish Klah could come with me."

"Soon enough. But you made the right decision. You don't want to endanger him."

"No, but what if Chip... uh, that Zimmerman guy comes back and tries to force them to tell him where I am? That'll put him in danger."

"That's true, but he's safer here among people he knows and who'll keep an eye out for him."

He didn't buy my reasoning, but he accepted it for the moment. To distract him, I asked about his time with Silver Wings, drawing every detail I could out of him for my digital recorder. In the middle of this, Paul called on my cell.

"Where are you, BJ?" he asked, not able to mask the strain in his voice. He always called me Vince, not BJ. "Let me put that another way. When do you expect to be home?"

"About an hour, I'd say."

"Did you manage to pick up the brand of peanut butter I asked for?"

Speaking in code yet. "Don't worry. I found it."

"Good. By the way, do you remember Niv's grandmother? The lady you did some work for last year?"

Niven Pence was my across-the-street neighbor's great-grandson. More code talk. "Yes, why?"

"She wants you to stop by. More work, I guess. Anyway, she wants you to come in the back way. Easier for her."

"I see. And I'm supposed to do this before I get your peanut butter to you?"

"Yeah. She sounded anxious."

"Okay."

"You be careful now. Promise?"

"I promise."

I closed the call and thought things over. Something was going on at or near our house. Something that worried him and caused him to enlist Mrs. Wardlow's help. The houses in my neighborhood were old enough to have alleyways behind them. He wanted me to park in Mrs. W.'s alley and enter her house from the back. Presumably with Jazz. Was Paul in any danger?

I kept my fingers off the phone and reined in my imagination only by continuing to question Jazz about his time in confinement. That worked... barely.

I TOOK a back way into my neighborhood, avoiding my usual route, to slip into the alley behind Mrs. Wardlow's home. Leaving the car to block the narrow lane, Jazz and I scooted through the back gate and knocked on the kitchen door. Mrs. W. opened it almost instantly and shooed us inside. Paul stood behind her.

"Zimmerman rang our doorbell this afternoon and demanded to know where you were."

"What did you tell him?"

Paul snorted. "Out detecting, what else? And there have been strange cars passing the house occasionally."

"Undercover police units, no question about it," Mrs. W. said. She flashed a sweet smile. "Is this the young man you've been hunting?"

"Mrs. Wardlow, may I present Jazz Penrod. Jazz, don't let her diminutive size fool you. She's tough as nails. Retired DEA."

Jazz gave a slight start at that last bit of information. "Pleased to meet you, ma'am," he said, a smile dimpling his left cheek as he took her offered hand.

"I understand you've had a rough go if it. Are you all right? I mean, are you hurting?"

"Some. You wouldn't happen to have some tea, would you?"

She nodded. "Some green tea, as a matter of fact. I brewed it as soon as Paul told me you were on the way. How about your other minerals and vitamins? Do you have them?"

"Some."

"Your eyes don't look dilated. Is your mouth dry?"

"A little. But the tea—"

She nodded. "Yes, that will take care of that problem. How about bugs?"

"No, ma'am, they've mostly gone away, but they come back sometimes."

"But you still crave a smoke, don't you?"

"Sometimes it's real strong."

"Tell me what you're taking to fight it."

We stood in the widow's kitchen while the two of them tuned us out. They were in direct communication with one another. Another of the small woman's talents.

Jazz lifted the mug. "The green tea. Red meat, garlic, broccoli, onions, beans, green vegetables. And pumpkins seeds, cashews, spinach. Tomatoes. Beets."

"Any Omega-3 fatty acids?"

"Fish oil and vitamin C tablets when we could afford them."

She turned to me, breaking the spell between them. "He's gotten good advice. Cocaine is addictive, easily addictive, but withdrawal is probably less severe than many other narcotics. Even so, the urge to take it is sometimes nearly overpowering, even though the victim isn't rolling on the floor with stomach cramps."

She invited us to sit at the neat kitchen table with its white cloth and a bowl of shiny plastic fruit centered in the precise middle of it. The room still smelled faintly of the casserole she'd likely served for dinner—probably tuna—as she plunked a huge cup of green tea in front of Jazz.

After offering something to the rest of us, she settled on a chair opposite Jazz and continued her dissertation. "Crack cocaine, which I understand is what you were on, is a strong stimulant that energizes the central nervous system. It places a great deal of stress on the heart, lungs, and brain. A user will have dilated pupils and a dry mouth. He sweats and has little appetite. He becomes restless and talkative. Too much energy to sleep, but when he does, he sleeps like a log. Wild mood swings. Sometimes with hallucinations and confusion. Sometimes he swears bugs are crawling all over him, so he picks and scratches at his skin."

"That explains the bugs you asked about," Paul said. "What was the sorta strange diet he went through?"

"I wanted to know what he was doing to flush the cocaine out of fatty substances in the body. That will help ease the cravings. The Omega acids are important. The red meat provides Acetyl-L-Carnitine, the garlic and broccoli and onions provide another amino acid. Cheese and egg yolks provide vitamin D, beans and green leafy vegetables give him magnesium. Pumpkin seeds and cashews are rich in zinc. It's all a part of an anti-inflammatory diet."

"Is he cured?"

"Oh heavens, no. I'm not sure anyone is ever cured. But he's on the right track. He'll probably require some counseling once he's free of all this mess."

She reached out and covered Jazz's hands with hers. "Sweetheart, I'm afraid you're going to have to stay with me for a few days until BJ gets things squared away. But don't worry, BJ's good at straightening things out."

"Okay, ma'am," he replied low in his throat. "But I gotta warn you, I get nervous—edgy, I guess you'd say—once in a while." He let out a long breath. "Nasty, sometimes, if you want the truth."

"Don't worry, sonny. I've got a bat beside my bed and a Colt revolver under my pillow. And I'm not afraid to use either one of them." She paused and added with a twinkle in her eye, "On you or anyone else."

Chapter 32

A FEW minutes later, Paul walked back across the street carrying a toolbox he'd lugged over as if he were helping Mrs. W. with repairs, while I drove out of the neighborhood using back roads before reversing course and taking my usual route home. I pulled in close behind his black Charger and got out, stretching to mimic a man returning from a long trip or sloughing off a hard day, after which I entered the house by the back door, my usual habit.

These were probably unnecessary precautions. Ours was a settled, geriatric neighborhood built in the fifties. Paul and I were anomalies on Post Oak Drive NW. We hadn't reached retirement age. Not a blade of grass stirred on the street without someone taking notice. Of course, that didn't necessarily mean they'd pick up the phone and notify that detective fellow down the street who provided occasional stimulation for their faltering heart rates of any strange goings-on.

Paul ambushed me as soon as I closed the door behind me. He wrapped me in his long arms and planted a passionate kiss on my lips, reminding me that I would get to watch Pedro prowl on his left pec this evening. We parted all too soon to return to current concerns.

He brushed a brown forelock off his forehead and speared me with his chocolate eyes. "What do we do now that we've found Jazz?"

"First, I need to bring Gene up to date tomorrow morning and see if he's learned anything about Bolton and Zimmerman in light of what Jazz told us."

"And what was that?" he asked, reminding me I needed to bring him up to date too.

Paul heated some of his excellent green chili chicken stew as I sat at the table and related everything that happened. Once I finished, he put on his journalist's hat and peppered me with who-what-when-where-and-why questions.

I leaned back from the table after scooping the last of the stew from my bowl. "Once I get things straight with Gene, I have to take Jazz to the reservation and straighten out any question about him being involved in Nesposito's murder. And I can't do that until I get the statement from whoever gave permission for Klah and Jazz to use the old Hatahle mobile home. I should have it tomorrow."

"Won't the drive to Farmington be dangerous? Lots of places for an ambush on the road."

"True. But I'm not driving. I'll call Jim Gray and charter his Cessna. Detective Lonzo Joe will meet my flight and escort us to the Shiprock tribal police station. Or at least, I hope to arrange that."

"Will they arrest Jazz?"

"Depends on how good a spin job Zimmerman's done on the Navajo police. I believe we can clear him of Nesposito's killing, but they might want to hold him to turn over to APD. That's why I've got to talk Gene into going with me. That way Jazz will appear to be in APD custody."

"Well, charter the big plane. Because I'm coming with you."

CHARLIE HADN'T returned from Alamo by the time I arrived at the office, but Hazel said he called to let her know he contacted the secretary at the Alamo School Board and got a signature this morning. He'd faxed her a copy of the statement, and while it said what it needed to say, I wanted the original document to take with me to Shiprock. Alamo was only an hour—two at the worst—from Albuquerque, so I called Jim's office and chartered a plane for noon. Then I called Lonzo Joe at the San Juan County Sheriff's Office and lined him up. Finally I tackled the hardest nut. I called Lt. Eugene Enriquez.

"No way," he responded to my request. "I got a meeting with the deputy chief that'll take a good part of the day. Won't even be able to meet you like I promised. I'll send Carson to Farmington with you." His former partner was a competent cop, but I wanted some brass with me when I delivered Jazz to the tender mercies of the tribal police.

The trip was delayed for a day, which meant I needed to undo everything I'd set up. Jim was still available, but Lonzo had to juggle his schedule. Worse, he was required to call his contact at Shiprock and say the "suspect" wouldn't show up on Wednesday, as reported, but a day later. I was still enough of a cop to understand delays like that raise suspicions, but it was my fault for not starting with Gene.

When Charlie failed to arrive in the office by midafternoon, both Hazel and I started to fret. She tried raising him on his cell, but it kept going to voicemail. I was heading out the door to start backtracking him when Hazel called me back inside. Charlie was on the line.

"Sorry to be out of touch for so long. My cell was out of reach of a tower. But it was worth it. See you in about an hour." With that, he hung up.

I spent that hour going over cases with Hazel and agreeing to call in our temp help, Mendoza and Fuller, the two ex-cops who were rapidly becoming key to our operation. That was because—Hazel fumed—I was spending my time on cases that didn't pay.

When Charlie arrived, the big grin stretching a newly cultivated gray mustache told me he exceeded expectations. "Got it nailed down, BJ. Tight."

Aware of my fear some prosecutor might claim Jazz had levitated himself to the lip of Black Hole Canyon, killed Nesposito, and transported himself back to Alamo, he'd performed a miracle.

"The secretary who got Klah and Jazz their permission to live in the Hatahles' old trailer house has a crush on Klah, I figure. Anyway, she told me about a family they'd made contact with up the road apiece. I ran down a Jonas Hartz and his wife, Frances. The boys stopped and asked if they could have some water from the well for the horses. The wife ended up asking them to stay for dinner. Loaned them the use of their barn to sleep and gave them some hay for the mounts."

"Great! And what day was that?"

"Wednesday, September 1st."

"The day Nesposito was murdered!" Hazel exclaimed.

"You're right, Charlie. You nailed it down. As tight as it can get."

LATER THAT afternoon when I parked behind Paul's Charger in our driveway, Mrs. Wardlow stood on her front porch and "yoohooed" for my attention. I stepped to the end of our drive.

"You and Paul come over after you get settled," she called from across the street. "I baked some chocolate chip cookies. And you know how Paul loves them."

"Yes'm. About an hour?"

"That would be fine. They'll still be warm by then."

Paul was at the computer in our home office when I entered. When he worked on a story, he became a mouse potato. Right now he was finishing an assignment, a piece on hacking and how to best protect yourself and your computer from it. My opinion was that although his advice might be good today, it wouldn't be work a cup of warm spit a week after it was published. The hackers would simply start looking for weaknesses in his suggested defense, eventually finding one, thereby generating another round robin of attack, defense, and assault from a different direction. We'd managed to move some of our warfare from the countryside to the internet where—as has been true from time immemorial—the largest army does not always win.

I was banging around in the kitchen, frying eggs and scorching bacon, when Paul walked in and hugged me from behind. The warmth of his body felt good... reassuring. All was right with the world. Our world, at least.

"Unfortunately we've got to eat and go over to Mrs. W.'s," I said.

"She having trouble with Jazz?"

"More likely Jazz is having trouble with her. No, this is for chocolate chip cookies, or so she says."

"Oh... yum!"

Mrs. W. and her guest both seemed to be getting along fine. He complained—albeit mildly—about all the vitamins and minerals she'd stuffed down him, but he was more relaxed than yesterday.

"I talked to Klah," he volunteered after we took places around the kitchen table with some of the promised cookies on small plates before us. She'd decided that cold milk went better with her rich cookies than coffee and provided tumblers of cow juice. After a taste of each, I couldn't argue with her logic.

"Everything okay with the Hatahles?" I asked.

"Yeah. No strangers knocking on the door. Can Klah go with us to the rez?"

"I know you're anxious to see him again, but this thing isn't over. Do you want to put him in danger?"

Jazz sighed, and I could see a bout of depression approaching despite being loaded up on vitamins. "No. Can't do that."

"We're leaving for the Double Eagle Airport early. I want to be in the air by eight o'clock. Lieutenant Enriquez is going to pick us up at seven. He'll accompany us."

"Will I be under arrest?"

"No, but if the tribal police have been asked to hold you for APD, then APD will be right there with us." The room fell silent as I eyed Jazz across the table. "Why didn't you tell us about Jonas Hartz and his wife?"

"Who?"

"The couple who fed you and allowed you to sleep in their barn."

He sat straight as if hit by a cattle prod. "Jeez, BJ, I didn't remember them. Didn't even know their names. I'd… I'd been off the green tea and some of the vitamins for a couple of days by then. Sorry."

"That's okay. Charlie found them and showed them your photo. They alibied you for the day Nesposito was murdered."

"Thank the Lord," Mrs. W. murmured as she patted Jazz's hand. "The rest of you need some more cookies, but it's time for this fellow's special snack." She left the table and returned with a tin of chocolate chips for us and a saucer loaded with slices of beets, broccoli florets, chick peas, almonds, and some unidentified items for Jazz. He sighed but didn't argue, merely picked through the plate, trying to act as if he enjoyed the things.

Then she told us in no uncertain terms that Jazz needed to be in a recovery program where they could deal with some of the psychological problems she'd observed.

THE NEXT morning, Gene picked Paul and me up before driving around to the alley behind Mrs. W.'s house. Jazz, looking a thousand percent better than yesterday, hopped into the front seat of the APD Ford with Gene. Mrs. W. pressed a thermos and small knapsack on him, which undoubtedly contained things needed for his anti-inflammatory diet. I put him in the front seat because I knew my old APD partner was anxious to grill Jazz and wasn't about to wait until we were airborne to start asking questions. In fact, he asked the first before we were out of the alley.

"You sure Silver Wings is one of the Haldemains?"

"Not sure of anything, sir, except that one of the photos BJ showed me is Silver Wings. You'll have to ask him about the name."

"We don't have time to dance around the barn, son. Just answer my questions."

"Yes, sir. But I want to answer them exactly. If I said I knew his name was—"

"Okay, okay. We got the ground rules down. Do you think you could identify which brother he is if you saw him in person?"

"If I saw him and heard him speak, yes, sir."

Gene spoke over his shoulder. "BJ, Roscoe's in district court this morning. We could swing by and let Jazz have a gander."

"Tempting, but we've already delayed the Navajo Tribal Police once. Don't want to do it again."

"Okay, Double Eagle Airport it is."

On the twenty-minute ride, Gene peppered Jazz with questions. I knew why he zeroed in on the August 17 time period, but Jazz did not. That was the day the massacre at My Other Home Motel took place. Jazz wasn't much help, because he'd been turned over to Silver Wings by then and was confined to a small house at the back of a big backyard fronted by a mansion surrounded by a big adobe wall. Originally he'd been locked in, although later the door was left unsecured. He confirmed that the man called Tom who attended Wings' pool parties was Bolton four different times when Gene asked the question four different ways.

Then he popped the same question over his shoulder at me. "No question in your mind it was Bolton?"

Jazz answered for me. "The uniform in the picture changed things some, but the man in the picture was the one called Tom."

"There you go," I said.

"Was Bolton... uh, Tom, present at the same time Zimmerman was there?" Gene asked.

"The cop I saw at To'hajiilee?" Jazz asked. "He was only there once. At the last pool party, as a matter of fact. That's when Chip... uh, Zimmerman tried to rape me, but I put him on his ass. And yeah, Tom was there. Uh... Bolton, that is."

Gene snorted. "No wonder Zim's got a hard—uh, is looking for you so hard. He can't put up with that kind of shit."

Jim was waiting for us when we arrived. He hustled us aboard his Cessna 206 Stationair and fired up the engine. In minutes we were airborne and headed northwest toward Farmington. Gene kept questioning Jazz until we set down at the Four Corners Regional Airport, where Detective

Lonzo Joe loaded us aboard a San Juan County SUV and plied questions of his own as he raced toward the Navajo Reservation. Christ! By the time Jazz was finished with today, he'd be picked to the bone.

DETECTIVE ELMORE Peshlakai—stocky, jowly, and swarthy—didn't look very impressive, unless you were on the other side of a wrestling match with him, but it wasn't long before I understood the apparent esteem Lonzo Joe accorded him. The man peered out of the most unreadable eyes I'd ever seen on a human being as he picked apart and put back together the affidavits I'd brought. And when he learned Charlie obtained one of them, he got my partner on the line and put him through the paces. Once satisfied with those, he relegated my party to the waiting room while he disappeared with Jazz for an interview. I belatedly wondered if I should have brought Del Dahlman with me. He always claimed he wasn't a criminal lawyer, but he'd pulled my legal butt out of the fire more than once.

After a few minutes, Peshlakai returned and invited Lonzo and Gene to join him. I sat and watched Paul stew and fume and pace restlessly. I nursed some angst as well, but I'd learned to hold mine inside until the crisis was past. Then I could blow.

After two hours, Henry and an older version of Henry came through the station's double doors. In minutes I shook hands with the legendary Louie Secatero, Jazz's and Henry's father. He was as devastatingly handsome as his sons but with a more mature air. They sure made them good in the Secatero clan.

"How'd you know we were here?" Paul asked after things settled down.

"Hell, the whole reservation knows you're here. As soon as we heard, I called Dad and we started out."

"Don't tell me, Louie has a motorcycle too," I said.

"Damned right. Best way to get around before the snow falls," the older Secatero said. "Then I drive my truck." Louie's voice was more gravelly than Henry's, which was heavier than Jazz's. "Can't tell you how much we appreciate you finding Jazz for us. Bound to have run up a bill. You let me know how much, and I'll collect some funds from around the family."

"Mr. Secatero—Louie—Jazz and Henry did me a hell of a favor a few years back when I was searching for a fellow who was lost and hurt. Put themselves on the line for me with the law when we located him. Jazz doesn't owe me anything."

"They got paid for what they done. You ought to be too."

I thought for a minute. "Tell you what, Louie. There is something you can do. There's a couple down in To'hajiilee who took Jazz in and gave him shelter. The woman started him on the road to recovery from the drugs the kidnappers hooked him on. She sold a family heirloom, an old squash blossom necklace, to help him. Can you check and see if we can get it back to her?"

"Who is she?"

"Dibe Hatahle."

"The hand trembler? Who'd she sell it to?"

"If I remember right, a man named Abbo. Hosteen Abbo."

Louie scowled briefly. "It's done. I'll take care of it."

The blunt way he said it gave me a quick chill down my spine. "Uh...."

"He'll sell it to us," Henry said. "We know the family."

"If you need any help from me, let me know," I said.

"Won't need any. But thanks."

Peshlakai walked into the room at that moment, followed by Jazz, Gene, and Lonzo. Jazz looked worse for the wear. A smile played at the corners of Jazz's broad mouth when he spotted his father and brother, but the Navajos kept their "Indian face." Gene gave me an almost imperceptible nod of the head.

Apparently the Secateros and the Shiprock detective knew one another, and I didn't want to inquire how. They were reasonably civil to one another, but Louie's "What about my boy?" held a little aggression.

"He's free to go. He didn't have anything to do with old Hard Hat's murder. But the murder might have something to do with him."

Louie let out a grunt. "Huh?"

"That warlock was trying to run down Jazz for somebody in the outside world. Somehow that got him killed. They'd tried it once before"—he threw a thumb at Lonzo—"but Detective Joe here chased the killer off before he could do more than throw a couple of rounds at the old man. Apparently the bozo finished the job out on Black Hole Canyon later."

Peshlakai half turned and glanced at Henry. "Course, that don't mean this one didn't do the deed for his brother." He favored Louie with a blank-eyed stare. "Or you, for that matter."

"Pesh, we been all over this before. We didn't do it, and you ain't got nothing that says we did."

"You're right. Not yet. But Jazz is clear of it. You can all go."

WE TOOK Jazz by his house in Farmington to briefly reunite him with his mother and uncle. The situation was too dangerous to let him stay permanently, and the jury was still out as to whether he would go deeper into the reservation with his brother or return to Albuquerque with Paul and me.

Eunice Penrod was still the small, shy woman I saw three years ago, but she had aged. More lines in her pleasant face, nervous starts of the hands now and then... doubtless due to her son's disappearance. She folded her tall, handsome son in her arms and cried softly on his shoulder as he murmured reassurances.

Riley, her brother and Jazz's uncle, hadn't pumped up his six-foot stature, but he'd added twenty pounds. Still, he looked like someone you didn't want to mess around with. His eyes lit up a little as he watched mother and son engage.

"Glad you found him. He looks good." Riley addressed the words in my general direction.

"He's recovered some," I said. "But he's not free of the cocaine yet."

"Don't know if he'll ever be," Paul put in.

"Damned bastards!" Riley fumed. "Don't see how they got him hooked. That boy never even tried marijuana, much less the harder stuff."

"They're good at manipulating people," Gene said.

"Hope you got the whole damned bunch of them in jail."

"Not yet," Gene came back at him.

While the Penrods reconnected, the five of us stood in the small front yard of the neat cigar-box house that looked like every other residence on the street... except for the trellis roses Eunice nurtured on either side of the front door. Henry got us started.

"I think he oughta come with Louie and me. We can put him so deep on the rez nobody'll ever find him."

"Except another Navajo," Lonzo Joe said. "And you'll be surrounded by them."

"And not a one of them will lay a hand on him," Louie said.

"Don't kid yourself," the county detective responded. "The traffickers have already replaced Nesposito. Probably with more than one. I'm sure Hard Hat wasn't in this all alone. And we won't know who they'll be. Not for a while. In the meantime, they're free to hunt him down for their Albuquerque bosses."

"And don't forget," Gene added. "We need Jazz to identify Silver Wings. He's got it narrowed down to two men, but we've got to be sure we pick up the right one."

"So who's going to protect him in Albuquerque? You?" Henry snorted. "I hear APD's in this thing up to their ears."

Gene flushed. "Yeah. Just like you Navajos have some bad apples, so do we. But we know who they are now. We just have to root them out."

"That's not going to be easy, is it?" Paul asked.

"No, but we'll stop the rot."

"BJ, what do you think?" Henry asked.

"Jazz and I talked this over some. There's nothing he wants more than to snag Silver Wings. He wants him locked up and the key thrown away. He can't help us do that from the reservation."

"What about the danger?" Louie asked. I'd always held the opinion that the man more or less abandoned Jazz and his mother except for some financial help, but I began to understand that as he'd gotten to know his son over the last few years, he was more engaged… more of a father.

"I believe we can protect him. I trust Lieutenant Enriquez, and he knows who to trust inside the department. Jazz doesn't stay with Paul and me, but he's nearby where we can show up in a moment's notice. I believe he'll be safe with us."

A few minutes later, Jazz came outside and put an end to the speculation. "I'm not gonna live my life hiding out. I'm going back to Albuquerque and put those sons a bitches away."

ONCE JIM Gray got us airborne and headed toward Albuquerque, Gene and I did some strategizing. He didn't say much about his talk with the police chief, which I understood and honored. But I got the feeling they'd agreed to delay bringing in Internal Affairs. Gene had a little time, but not much. There was always the possibility Bolton would go to IA on his own to lodge a complaint against Gene.

"I don't think so, BJ. So long as they don't think I'm proceeding against them, I believe Bolton will let sleeping dogs lie. A move like that would assure him I'd lodge a complaint, and he'd be down in the swamp right along with me. If we can proceed quietly, then we've got some time."

"Not sure how to proceed quietly. Once you start asking questions—"

"I'm not. You are."

"Okay, and the place to start might be the CAHT. Betsy Brockmire."

"Are you thinking of taking Jazz into the lion's den?"

"Why not? He can face the two Haldemains and pick out Silver Wings."

"I dunno, BJ. It'll be Jazz's word against that of a prominent attorney. Who do you think's gonna be believed?"

"Jazz can describe the guy right down to the way his testicles hang."

"How the hell do you get a judge to agree to make a man disrobe for a personal inspection of his gonads? And that's not exactly proceeding quietly."

"No, but the best way to keep Jazz safe is to get his testimony on record."

"I know some people who'll argue with you about that."

"Okay, what do you think about us meeting Betsy outside the office and having a private talk with her?"

"Better. But you're assuming the whole bunch isn't tainted. What if she's a part of it? What if the whole council is?'

"I'm open to suggestions. But if there's a reaction, it won't be through the Albuquerque Police Department. It'll be a face-off. Maybe a deadly one."

"Eat your words! Don't talk like that." Gene relented. "But in view of the killings at the west-side motel and Nesposito's death, you may be right. Hard to believe anyone at APD's involved to *that* extent."

"Who was in charge of investigating the My Other Home Motel killings?"

Gene screwed his face into a scowl. "Bolton. All right, I've got an open mind. So who's gonna call Betsy?"

"I will."

Chapter 33

EVEN THOUGH autumn did not officially start for five more days, Betsy already celebrated the season when she walked into Elderberry's Kocina on North Fourth wearing a white blouse with an orange-and-brown leaf pattern. Harvey Elderberry obviously wasn't Spanish, and he'd perverted the Spanish word *cocina* by spelling it with a *K*, but he served good food in an out-of-the-way location. And his place was as rich in delectable odors as any other Mexican food place in Albuquerque. Gene and I stood as Betsy made her way to us. Jazz and Paul sat at a nearby table.

She acknowledged us and then started in on me about insisting on lunch on such short notice. "I hope it's something important," she finished.

I beckoned toward Paul and Jazz. "Gene and I think it is. Betsy, I'd like you to meet my companion, Paul Barton."

She gave him a sweet smile. "Nice to meet you."

"And this is Jazz Penrod."

Her eyes went owlish. "*The* Jazz Penrod?"

"One and the same. The object of our search. Jazz, meet Betsy Brockmire of the Citizens Council Against Human Trafficking."

He smiled, dimpling one cheek. "Pleased to meet you, ma'am."

"Thank goodness you're safe! Tell me what happened."

"Sit down, guys. This is going to take a while, so we'd better eat first." By design, Jazz took a seat at her left.

"Just a bowl of posole for me," Betsy said. "I want to hear his story."

Once we were through the rushed meal, I handled the discovery bit, explaining how we'd managed to run Jazz down and get him to relative safety. After that, Jazz told her what she really wanted to know. How he'd been snared, trapped, and exploited. I was proud of him. He told it all logically and methodically, withholding nothing and carefully choosing words so as not to sound vulgar. He flushed at times, went pale at other times, and grew morose during the telling, but it all came out.

When he ran down, Betsy reached over and covered his hands on the table with her own. "I am so sorry you went through a nightmare like that. But you seem amazingly well recovered from the ordeal. Especially the cocaine."

"Yes, ma'am. I had help from some Navajo healers. They put me on a diet."

"Good. Do you still crave the drug?"

"Something fierce, sometimes. But I just drink some green tea or eat a beet or something until I can handle it."

"Then you are already on the proper diet, but you need counseling. Bishop Gregory can help us there." Her pleasing, powdered countenance creased in a frown. "This Silver Wings. Do you know who he is?"

"Yes, ma'am. His name's Haldemain."

Betsy gasped and clutched Jazz's hands so tightly he looked as if he wanted to wince. "Haldemain? Our Haldemain? I can't believe it. Which one?"

"I don't know. I've seen photos of both, but I can't pick him out. If I saw him in person and heard his voice, I'd know."

"They... they do look a lot alike. But the eyes. What color eyes did he have?"

Jazz looked confused. "Black, mostly."

"Mostly?"

"Sometimes they were greenish brown. Hazel, I guess you'd call them."

She went paler than her powdered cheeks. "*Both* of them?"

He shook his head. "No, ma'am. It was the same man all the time. That much I know for sure."

"How?"

Jazz flushed. "Uh... I've seen.... Uh, I know it was the same man."

Betsy reddened. "Oh, I see."

"No, ma'am, but I did."

Paul stifled a nervous laugh.

I stepped into the awkward moment. "We think he wore contact lenses to confuse the issue. Even though he obviously didn't intend for Jazz to survive."

Her eyebrows rose.

"The plane ride, Betsy. Did either of the brothers have an Asian houseboy named Kim?"

"Sorry, I don't know much about the Haldemains' domestic situation. We're good friends at the office but don't socialize. After they lost their wives, that is."

"Which one of them is a pilot?"

"They both are."

"I believe you told us Roscoe was divorced, but William lost his wife to a car accident. When was that?"

"About five years ago. In 2005, I believe."

Gene took over the questioning, and Betsy grew more guarded. Gene found out little, in fact, nothing that we did not already know. The brothers lived on the west side just off Coors NW in houses about a mile apart. Betsy had been a guest in both places, although not recently, but recalled nothing that helped us. Both homes had large backyards with pools. She did not recall a bungalow at the far end of either lawn.

When Gene finished, I dropped another bombshell in her lap. "Jazz also identified another individual who attended the pool parties Silver Wings held." I slid a photo across the table.

"Lieutenant Bolton?" she exclaimed. "Oh my Lord! Jazz, was there ever a black pastor at these parties?"

Jazz shook his head. "No. No black men."

Her sigh of relief was audible. Then she straightened her back. "I'm finding it difficult to accept what you're saying. The Haldemains are upstanding citizens and decent men. And Lieutenant Bolton? No, I simply cannot accept this. You've provided no proof of any sort. Just this man's word." She clutched Jazz's hands again. "And after the ordeal he's suffered, it's no wonder he's confused."

I raised my hands palm up across the table. "And there, ladies and gentlemen, you have the crux of our problem. Credibility."

LATER THAT afternoon, Jazz and I slipped into a district courtroom where Roscoe Haldemain was defending a case. We both wore shades but otherwise made no attempt to disguise ourselves. Jazz tensed as he gazed at the man addressing the court.

"That's *him*!" he said. "Well, maybe," he whispered in a lower tone. "Something about the voice. Close, but... but...."

I leaned over to him. "We have to be certain, Jazz. We're about to ruin a man's life. Let's sit and watch and listen awhile."

I could feel the tension building in Jazz. He dry-washed his hands and jiggled his right knee. He licked his lips. It was easy to see the need for a crack pipe rising inside him. Betsy and Mrs. W. were right. The detoxing diet was helping, but he needed counseling. Nonetheless, we sat at the back of the spectators watching the trial of two men accused of home invasion, unlawful restraint, and assault. Apparently the prosecution was finished with its case, because Roscoe Haldemain called witnesses and put them through the paces. When the judge announced a recess for the day, we remained where we were until Roscoe finished talking to his clients and walked down the aisle past us. His attention was diverted by his second-chair lawyer, so he passed without taking notice of me.

Jazz followed close on my heels as I trailed after the two men. They halted for a final word before parting. Just as I opened my mouth to call him, Haldemain's brother appeared at his side and detained him with a hand on his arm.

Jazz's arm shot out. "That's him! That's Silver Wings."

I gripped his shoulder as he started forward, but the damage was done. William glanced up at the sound of Jazz's voice. He kept a practiced, passive attorney's look on his face, but the eyes flickered as he took a second look at Jazz. This was Silver Wings.

"BJ," William Haldemain called. "What are you doing here? Testifying on a case?"

"No, not today."

"Who's your friend?" he continued, holding out a hand.

Jazz ignored the offer to shake, but his hands balled into fists.

"This is a friend of mine who's been missing for a few months," I said. "Thankfully, we've found him."

"Excellent." He turned back to his brother.

"You bastard!" Jazz snarled. "You tried to kill me!"

I tried to rein him in. This was neither the time nor place for a confrontation, especially if Jazz became physical. "Take it easy."

He shrugged me off. "You *did* kill Kim. Almost got me too."

"Kim?" Roscoe said. "You're speaking of Kim Liu? Why he returned home to Taipei a month ago. Isn't that right, William?" Nobody called William Haldemain *Bill*, not even his brother.

"Precisely. I don't know what your problem is, but you've obviously confused me with someone else. And if you repeat such nonsense again, you'll find yourself back in this building… this time as a defendant in a slander case."

"I think you should know, Haldemain, that park rangers are searching right now for Kim's body," I bluffed.

"BJ, you're wasting your money. The malpais is a very big area to search for a body. But if you find one, and it proves to be Kim, please let me know. I'll send condolences to his family in Taiwan."

With that, the brothers walked away.

"You're just gonna let him go?" Jazz demanded.

"For the moment. But William Haldemain, Esquire, just made a big mistake, and I've got it recorded right here." I patted the digital recorder on my belt. I'd thumbed it on when we walked over to the Haldemains.

"How's that?" Jazz asked.

"Neither one of us mentioned the El Malpais National Monument, but that's where he assumed we'd be looking because he knows that's where he dumped Kim out of the plane."

"Great! Then we got him."

"Don't get your hopes up. The monument covers something just under 200 square miles. And the drop site might not be in the national monument, just somewhere in the vicinity."

"Crap!"

"But right now we've got other things to worry about. We've tipped our hand. Now we have to make sure you're safe."

"I can handle that punk!" A snarl tinged Jazz's voice.

"Right. But it won't be him coming for you. And if it is, you won't see him until it's too late."

Chapter 34

THE NEXT morning, which happened to be a Saturday, folks all up and down Post Oak Drive NW were atwitter at the police car parked in front of number 5229. Gene insisted on posting a twenty-four-hour guard on my house... even though Jazz was secretly stashed across the street with Mrs. Wardlow. That was okay; the cop was handy to either place, should he be needed. I knew how boring such duty could be, so the officer, a sandy-haired fellow named Pedington, spent a lot of his time inside the house in front of the TV or talking by cell phone with his wife or playing chess with Paul.

Betsy Brockmire phoned me at ten, sounding worried.

"What's wrong?" I asked.

"I-I couldn't believe what you told me yesterday, so I came back to the office and began looking through records. Only my office girl and I were here, so I didn't raise any alarm bells," she hastened to add. "But I found something disturbing."

She was obviously having trouble facing this thing and needed prompting. "Yes?"

"Dozens of young people, mostly children, go through the council. I keep good records, so I can tell you what happened to most of them... until they leave the bishop's program, of course. But... but...."

"Spit it out, Betsy."

"I find that three of them seemed to have disappeared *before* they made it to the church. Mind you, these are unstable people who are not terribly reliable."

"That said, you've found something that bothers you. Tell me about it. What about these three cases caught your attention?"

"They... they were all boys. Sixteen to eighteen years. The overwhelming majority of the victims we deal with are female, so...."

"These stick out like sore thumbs."

"You could say that."

"Were they reported to the police?"

"No. So many of them change their minds after they're rescued and just want to go home. Unless there's a reason, we don't contact the authorities."

"Do you have names and descriptions?"

"I have better than that. I have photographs."

"Fax them over to me. Any files you have, as well."

"I... don't... know."

"Betsy, you've come this far with me. Now it's time to come the rest of the way. You're worried about these boys. So let's find them."

She cleared the line, and a few minutes later, a sheaf of papers began chugging through my fax machine providing information on the missing boys. I re-sent the papers to Charlie's fax at home before calling him and asking him and Hazel to see if they could trace the three. Sometimes my conscience bothered me when I handed out assignments on weekends, but not this time. These youngsters might be in danger, and we needed to locate them. Charlie readily agreed.

After that, I sat in my home office and thought for a minute as an idea slowly built. I picked up the phone and called Mrs. W., asking her to sweep off the sidewalk or something and hail me when I went out to the car. Until we knew more, it was best to continue the charade that Jazz was inside my house under guard. A minute later I slammed a baseball cap on my head, stuffed my copy of the papers in a case, and went out to the car. Today it was parked behind Paul's Charger, so I was at the end of the driveway where Mrs. W.'s thin treble caught my attention. We met in the middle of the street.

We exchanged greetings, and she tittered when I mentioned the effect on our neighbors of a cop car staking out my house. "That'll give the busybodies something to talk about until Christmas," she noted.

"Invite me in for a cup of coffee or something. I want to show Jazz some photos."

Two minutes later we walked into her kitchen where Jazz was repairing a frayed cord on her toaster. He brightened when he saw me.

"Anything new?"

"Maybe. I want you to look at some pictures and tell me if you've ever seen any of these boys before."

I spread photos of three good-looking but haggard youths on the table. Jazz looked at each in turn, shaking his head until he reached the third. He did a double take. "Damn, I know this guy, but he sure looks different now."

I took the photo from his hand. It was labeled James Guess of Ardmore, Oklahoma. "Different how?"

"Skinny. He looks buffed in that picture, but last time I saw him, he was lots skinnier."

"The drug," Mrs. W. said. "That's what long-term use does to you, Jazz."

"Damn!" Jazz repeated.

"How do you know him? Where did you see him last?" I asked.

"He was at some of Silver Wings'… uh, Haldemain's pool parties. They called him Jamie, and he came with a guy they called Sam."

"Ever hear a last name?"

"No. They always used phony names around me. But I got a feeling this kid was permanently attached to the guy. And I figured Sam was in construction. The others were always asking him questions about how to build this or repair that. Once he offered to have his construction foreman come around and look at someone's house. That was the doc, I think."

"Doctor? Of what?"

Jazz shrugged. "Dunno. They just called him Doc."

"Was Jamie coerced?"

"Didn't seem to be. He hung all over Sam like he was a lap dog or something." Jazz flushed suddenly. Likely wondering if he appeared the same way to Jamie. Not if I knew Jazz.

I departed, leaving Mrs. W. to pull Jazz out of the funk I'd dumped him into. Before I was halfway to the office where I had better databases to conduct searches, Mrs. W. phoned to say Jazz remembered some talk about Sam being the guy who built the bungalow at the end of the backyard where Jazz stayed. By the time I walked through the door to my office—discovering Hazel and Charlie already there and hard at work—the task I'd given myself had changed.

There were literally hundreds of small construction and repair shops in Albuquerque, but I decided to start big. An hour later I was ready to call Paul and ask him to have Officer Pedington bring him and Jazz to the office, cautioning him to go through back alleys to pick up Jazz without being seen.

Thirty minutes later the patrol cop ushered Paul and Jazz into the office. I called them all into the conference room to an array of photos on the table.

"Jazz, see if you can identify this Sam fellow. Haldemain is a powerhouse lawyer, and it stands to reason his associates will be, as well. I've identified the city's most prominent commercial, apartment, and residential homebuilders and found pictures of most of them. Some are fuzzy newspaper shots, but others are advertising brochures and program advertisements. Take your time and go through them. See if you can identify Sam."

Jazz lifted his ever-present thermos and took a quick gulp of green tea before nodding. I left Jazz and Paul and the officer shuffling through the information while I returned to the computer to start looking for James Guess of Ardmore, Oklahoma.

I'd located what I believed to be his parent's house and telephone number by the time Hazel and Charlie reported they'd contacted the other two missing boys' relatives. No sign of either of them. But we managed to find one of the missing youngsters before Jazz was finished with his search. Charlie faxed photos of the missing youths to a friend in the medical examiner's office on the off-chance one or both met a bad end. His hunch paid off. Brian Jones, a drug overdose case, lay in the morgue labeled John Doe. Charlie's friend didn't have the details at home but promised to check the record Monday morning to see if there was anything suspicious about the death.

I'd just digested that tragic news when Jazz rushed into my office waving a slick sales brochure. Paul and Pedington were hard on his heels.

"I found him, BJ! I found him."

Sam turned out to be Willard Dean Metz, one of the largest custom-home contractors in the state. His Metz Homes, Inc. built subdivisions in Albuquerque, Belen, Rio Rancho, and Santa Fe, turning Dean into a millionaire many times over. I knew him casually as a married man who gave off sparks letting insiders know he was available for any kind of action. He was one of those macho guys who paraded his wife around on his arm while casting a predatory eye on anything that walked upright.

Charlie and I got on the phone to contacts and soon came back with the identical interesting tidbit. Dean Metz had a nephew living in a small guesthouse on the grounds of his mansion. Someone variously identified as James or Jamie. Bingo!

Charlie called Tim Fuller, one of the retired cops who helped us out now and again, to start sitting on the Metz home to keep an eye out for Jamie Guess. We generally called on Tim for these kinds of stakeouts because he was divorced, whereas Alan Mendoza, our other fallback help, was married.

I WENT to bed satisfied we'd made a little progress today. With any luck Tim would get a line on this "nephew" living at Metz's house. He'd turn out to be Jamie Guess, more than likely. Apparently Paul was gaining some confidence as well, because he and Pedro wanted to prowl. And whenever they were on the prowl, I ended up exhausted… happy but exhausted.

Paul had just snapped off the table lamp after a cat's lick—a quick wash—when I sat up. "What was that?"

"Dunno." He frowned. "A boom!"

I bounded out of bed and grabbed my slacks. "Handgun." Stuffing my feet into slippers, I grabbed my Ruger from the lamp table and raced outside as another explosion sounded from across the street. The police unit was empty with the door half open, as if Pedington left in a hurry.

When Paul and I reached the front of Mrs. W.'s white brick, we heard noises from behind. Taking our cue from that, I slipped through the gate and motioned Paul to remain behind me. As I arrived the back-porch light came on, giving me a clear view of the large backyard. I saw nothing other than Pedington flashing a torch in the far corner with his weapon clenched in his right hand. I hailed him softly to keep from startling him.

"Somebody tried to break in," he said as he walked toward us. "The widow met him with a forty-five. She's a spunky old gal."

"Ex-DEA," I explained. "And the second shot?"

"Her too. She shot at the guy as he went over the fence. Missed, apparently. Probably shot low to keep from doing damage to the neighbors."

Lights on either side of the house came on, and gray-haired residents appeared in various types of night attire. Pedington shooed them back inside.

Mrs. Wardlow was sitting at her kitchen table with a big wicked-looking handgun lying in front of her. I could tell by the way she was rubbing one blue-veined hand with the other that the recoil had hurt. She sat up straighter when Paul and I came through the door.

"That bastard tried to come in right through the back door. Can you imagine?"

"Did you see who it was?"

"No, just a dark figure working like hell to jimmy my locks. But I showed him a thing or two."

Jazz stood tousle-headed beside her chair. "You see anything?" I asked him.

"No. I was asleep before things went boom."

I turned back to the widow. "Surprised you missed him."

"Oh, I wasn't trying to hit him. Just send him packing."

I glanced at Pedington. He nodded. "Somebody was working on the locks, all right. Scratched the hell out of them. And I found a place he tripped and fell before he got his ass across the rear wall."

"Hit?" Paul asked.

"No sign of blood. Think he was just spooked."

"Not a professional?" I asked.

"Mighty bad one, if it was."

"Better call the station. Some of the neighbors probably already have."

"I called it in on my shoulder unit," Pedington said.

Within minutes the neighborhood was awash in police cars. But whoever tried to get inside Mrs. W.'s house was long gone.

ON SUNDAY Gene came over to the house with Pedington's relief, a dark-headed fellow named Young who didn't like chess but played a mean game of checkers. Uncertain over whether the intruder last night was sent specifically or it was some hood looking for a score, I was all for ending the facade that Jazz was at our house. But Mrs. W. wouldn't hear of it. She scoffed at the danger to herself and declared if the bozo came again, she'd not miss.

Gene already knew of last night's events and our confrontation with the Haldemains at the courthouse the prior Friday. He wasn't happy about any of it. Nonetheless, the events were sufficient for him to maintain our stakeout.

The Metz development was new to Gene. After listening to what we'd learned, he decided this was something we might be able to exploit. There wasn't enough evidence to obtain a search warrant for the builder's home, so Tim was probably our best chance of determining if the Guess kid was inside. Gene called the stationhouse and discovered there was a poster on a James A. Guess from Ardmore, Oklahoma, but it was two years old. The kid was sixteen at the time of the issue.

Gene sighed after he shared the information with Paul and me. "He's eighteen now. Emancipated." After a moment's hesitation, he added, "That's all right, we can at least stop him and question him. Maybe spook Metz." Then, Gene being Gene, he got Jazz on the telephone and put a series of hard questions to him. He hung up and expressed satisfaction that Jazz was telling the truth.

As Gene was about to leave the house and return home, Tim Fuller called. Metz had just pulled out of the gate to his property and driven north on Coors. A youth who appeared to be Jamie Guess was in the front seat with him. I asked Tim to stay on their tail without being discovered, if possible. We waited an anxious twenty minutes before Tim called back to say he was in the Cottonwood Mall parking lot outside Dillard's department store. Metz and Guess had gone inside, but Tim was parked on their vehicle, so they wouldn't be leaving without his knowing it. I told him to remain where he was, and we got in gear.

Gene sent Officer Young scurrying across the street for Jazz without bothering to indulge in subterfuge. Gene and Jazz took off in Gene's brown Ford, closely trailed by Young in his APD unit. Paul and I followed in the Impala.

Ten minutes later we located Tim in his car, parked near a black vintage Caddy that shone and sparkled like a classic car with all new parts.

"They're still inside," Tim said as he crawled out of his own vintage vehicle, an Oldsmobile that did not have the look of a carefully restored classic. "You want me to go root them out?"

"No, for all we know they might be enjoying a movie. Tim Fuller, this is Officer Ken Young." The two men shook hands. "And this is Jazz Penrod."

"The guy we been trying to run to ground?" Tim acknowledged Gene before swallowing Jazz's hand in his big mitt. "You okay, guy?"

Jazz nodded. "Yep. Holding my own."

"Tim, there's no question Metz is with the kid in the picture you were given? This James Guess?" Gene asked.

"Caught a good look at him when they came out of the gates to the Metz estate, Lieutenant. They passed right by me on foot when they went inside after I parked. It's him, but lots skinnier." He nodded over my shoulder. "And here they come."

Two men emerged from the Dillard's door loaded down with packages. Even half a parking lot away, Metz's broad muscular build was recognizable.

"Jazz, you and Officer Young get in his patrol car and wait for a signal," Gene said. "Tim, probably be better if he doesn't get a good look at you."

Metz slowed as he spotted Gene, Paul, and me standing by his car. I saw from his look he recognized me, and probably Gene, but Paul was strange to him. He walked up confidently.

"What can I do for you gentlemen?"

"Mr. Metz, I'm Lt. Eugene Enriquez of—"

"I know who you are, Lieutenant. Hello, BJ. What do you need?"

Gene turned to the young man at his side. "Need to talk to this man. Son, are you James Guess?"

"Y-yes, sir."

"Are you aware there's a bulletin out on you?"

"M-me? Why?"

"Your parents had the Ardmore police put one out when you disappeared from home."

"He was a minor then," Metz said. "He's eighteen now. If you'll move aside, we'll be on our way."

Gene held up a hand. "Just a minute. Mr. Guess, are you being held against your will or under any duress?"

"No! I mean, no."

"Very well, I accept that statement, but there are a few things I want to clear up for the Ardmore police. Step over here to my car for a moment." Gene put a palm on the builder's chest. "Not you, Mr. Metz, just Mr. Guess."

The contractor looked apprehensive as Gene led the young man away. I smiled inwardly. "That means you're left with me. Oh, this is my companion, Paul Barton. And I'd like to introduce you to someone else, although I believe you've already met." I beckoned toward the police unit. Jazz and Young got out. For one brief moment, I saw fear in Willard Dean Metz's black eyes, but he held himself together.

"No, don't believe I've had the pleasure," he said as Jazz walked up to him.

"Hello, *Sam*. Bet you didn't expect to see me again, did you? How did Silver Wings… excuse me, Haldemain… explain my absence? Come to think of it, how did he explain Kim's disappearance?"

"Sorry, but I don't have any idea what you're talking about."

"Sure you do, Metz," I said. "But let's have Jazz go say hello to Jamie and see his reaction."

"Wait a minute!" Metz exclaimed. "Sure, why not. You guys be sure to see that James gets home safely. My wife is waiting on some of these things we picked up."

"I think it would be better to come downtown with your friend. He probably needs the support. He doesn't look very stable to me."

"I'm going home."

Young stepped up. His black uniform, equipment belt with holstered pistol, and a bright shiny badge pinned to his uniform shirt made him look formidable, even though he was a smaller man than Metz.

"Sir, we're just asking you to come downtown to fill in some information on the kid who's been missing for the last two years. Might help get him back to his folks." Young had a cool head on him.

Metz grew uneasy when Jazz walked away and leaned into the open passenger-side door of Gene's Ford. He threw his packages, and those abandoned by Guess, into the Caddy and stood watching the car a couple of rows away where three individuals talked about something that might impact his life in a serious way. Eventually, he had enough. He faced Young.

"Am I under arrest, Officer?"

Young hesitated but knew the limits of his authority. "No, sir. But I think it would help us to—"

"Then I'm out of here. You know where to find me, BJ." He crawled into his vehicle and roared out of the parking lot.

I watched him go. William Haldemain and Lt. Chester Bolton, and anyone else involved in the ring, would know about our confrontation within minutes. Maybe Young should follow him and arrest him for talking on a cell while driving.

Chapter 35

PAUL, YOUNG, and I walked over to Gene's car in time to hear James Guess go ballistic. Panic clearly etched on his face, his head swiveled to follow Metz's Caddy out of the parking lot.

"Why is he leaving?" His voice came out in a squeak. The kid had undoubtedly been attractive, probably even sensual, at some time in the past, but he was now rail thin, and the weight loss made him gaunt in appearance. Hollow cheeks and hollow eyes do not a good picture make. "He can't just leave me here!"

"He just did," Gene said. "That ought to let you know how things stand. You're on your own, my friend."

"H-he won't do that. He paid $5,000 for me. Cash money. He told me so."

Jazz spoke from the back seat. "Silver Wings claims he paid twenty grand for me—you heard him say so. But he still tried to dump me out of an airplane. It's called protecting your butt, Jamie. They all do it. We're nothing to them."

"Protecting their butt from what?"

"You don't get it, do you?" Jazz said. "What those guys did to us is illegal. You say Sam... uh, Metz bought you? That means you're a slave. A slave's property. And they'll get rid of property when it isn't carrying its weight."

"Listen to him, Mr. Guess," Gene said. "Every one of those guys who attended Haldemain's pool parties is going down. And they'll do everything possible to avoid that."

Jamie sobered momentarily but turned skeptical again. "You can't do that," he said. "Those other policemen won't let you."

Gene glanced out the window at me before giving the kid his full attention again. "What policemen?"

"Dean said we'd always be safe because one of us was a bigwig in the Albuquerque Police Department. I always figured that was Tom." He twisted to look at Jazz. "And that guy you put on his ass. You know, Chip. He had cop written all over him."

"Could you identify Chip if you saw him?" Gene asked.

"Sure." The kid's eyes went wide. "Oh no! You're not gonna get me mixed up in all that."

"You are mixed up in it," I said. "Let's consider a few things. You've been cut loose. Do you have any money?" He shook his head. "I didn't think so. You can probably find a cardboard box to sleep in tonight and a meal out of a restaurant dumpster. But where are you going to get the coke or whatever Metz has you hooked on?"

A bead of sweat ran down Jamie's forehead. "D-Dean's not abandoned me. I'm important to him. He loves me."

"Does Mrs. Metz love you?" Gene asked. "I imagine she'll take this opportunity to get rid of you. You said Metz claimed you were his nephew, but I'm sure she didn't fall for that. She's just been waiting for an opportunity to get rid of you, and this is it. She'll be in his face the minute she finds out you're trouble. And remember, if she walks on Metz, she takes half of everything with her. You think you're more important to him that that? Let's see if you are. Let's drive to the house and push the bell on the front gate and see if he lets you in."

"There's a way I can get in. Just let me off—"

"Oh, no. You're going in the front door or not at all. Do you want me to drive to the Metz home?"

"Yes! Please."

We drove to Willard Dean Metz's house in a three-car convoy. Gene wasn't about to let Young go back to the stationhouse until he knew Jazz was safe, but we released Tim Fuller to go home for some much-needed rest.

Gene halted before the stately stone gates—securely locked, by the way—and poked a button on a speaker. I got out of my car and walked up so I could hear what was going on. Nothing. No answer from the house. He even held down the call button so Jamie could make his own impassioned plea. "Dean, honey. It's Jamie. Please let me in."

GENE DROVE the devastated young man downtown to police headquarters, once again with a two-car convoy following along behind. Jazz rode with Young in the police unit. The two police vehicles were able to park inside the gates to the side entrance. Paul and I found a parking spot on the street in front of the downtown Bank of America. We climbed the steps to the white police building and walked into a situation. Just past the cop guarding the entryway, we came upon a confrontation. An actual showdown of sorts. Lieutenant Bolton and Detective Zimmerman blocked the way, flanked by two uniformed officers. One of the embarrassed officers was in the awkward process of informing Gene that he was under arrest.

"On whose orders and for what?" my friend bellowed.

"For being a part of a sex trafficking ring and possibly for murder," Bolton said. "On my orders. And cuff the kid as well. He's likely the shooter in the motel massacre case."

The chief of police, an impressive man named Lamar Huddleston, walked up behind Bolton. "Belay that order," he said in a subdued roar. The chief was an ex-Navy man. "Nobody's arresting anybody. Now let's go to my office and straighten this all out." He turned to Jazz. "You and this other young man stay here with Officer Young until we finish. Hello, BJ. You hang around too. We shouldn't be long."

As we found seats in a waiting area, I reviewed what I would have done in Gene's place. He was bringing two witnesses against Bolton and Zimmerman to the police station after Metz undoubtedly alerted them to what was happening. I'd have called my rabbi and let him know what was up. That explained why the chief happened to be in the stationhouse on a Saturday afternoon.

About thirty minutes later, one of the officers reappeared and took Jazz with him. An hour later, he came back and traded Jazz for James Guess. I didn't particularly want to query Jazz there in the station, but Paul's newspaper instincts got the better of him, and he started in on the who, what, when, where, and why.

After a few abortive questions, Jazz shrugged. "They just asked me to repeat my story. So I did."

"Were you in an interview room?"

Jazz shook his head. "Nope, in this big office. There was an extra man there, somebody Lieutenant Enriquez called Deputy."

"One of the deputy chiefs," Paul guessed. "Did they ask you about the pool parties?"

"Oh yeah. And I told them right out loud that *Tom* was at every one of them. Not only that, but he came back to the bungalow with me once or twice. He denied it, but when I described the mark on his left hip, he kinda toned it down."

"Mark?" I asked.

"Yeah. A pinkish thing on his left hip below the waistline. Birthmark, they called it. And I told them about dumping that detective, what was his name?"

"Zimmerman," Paul said.

"Yeah, Zimmerman on his ass."

"Maybe James Guess will corroborate everything for you," Paul said.

Jazz frowned. "I dunno. He's beginning to look pretty strung out to me. My guess is he's missed his afternoon feeding."

"Feeding?" Paul asked. "Oh, you mean the drug. You know what he's on?"

Jazz shook his head. "No idea. But he's gonna need some help pretty soon." He turned to me. "Will they help him?"

"They'll get him medical help."

Another hour passed before Gene entered the room. "Come on, guys. Let's go home. BJ, I'll take you and Paul to your car. Young, you're returned to regular duty. Officer Pedington will take Jazz back."

With a slight nod of his head, Jazz acknowledged the officer who'd watched over him yesterday.

Since our car was just across the street to the east, I assumed Gene wanted to talk to me. As soon as we pulled out of the police lot, he headed west, presumably to give us some time for discussion.

"Everything's on hold right now," he started. "The chief ordered everyone to step back and take a deep breath."

"Do you have a problem?" I asked.

"Not as big a problem as Bolton does after Jazz got through verbally stripping him naked. We've all showered in the exercise room, so everybody in that room was aware that Jazz knew what he was talking about. Then he did the same for Zimmerman. The Guess kid wasn't as forthright or forceful as Jazz, but he backed up everything your boy said. The Doc at the pool parties turns out to be a dentist named David Cole."

"Bolton gave him up?"

"Naw. Guess described him, and the deputy chief in the room piped up and said that was his dentist. And the chief recognized the description of William Haldemain's house. He's been to a few parties there, although of a different sort. Remembers the bungalow at the back. Commented to Haldemain about it after it was built."

"What happens now?" Paul asked.

"Bolton and Zimmerman are on paid suspension while Internal Affairs takes a look."

"Why aren't they under arrest?"

"Don't get ants in your pants. This will take some time."

"Does that mean the danger to Jazz is past?" Paul again.

"Not at all. Haldemain's out there, and if we're right, he's killed before. Won't hesitate to do it again if it'll save his skin. And Jazz's and Guess's testimony is the only difference between Bolton being suspended and me surrendering my badge. If they aren't around, a big part of Bolton's problem goes away."

"Where is Guess?" I asked.

"He damned near had a fit by the end of the interview, so he's turned over to the drug unit at UNM Hospital. Under guard."

"And Bolton and Zimmerman are free?" Paul asked.

"Free as birds. And they'll stay that way unless IA turns up more than we have now."

"Did Jazz tell them about Kim?" I asked.

"Yep. Park service at El Malpais has been alerted, so they'll keep an extra sharp eye out for a body."

"How about Haldemain's plane?" Paul asked.

"They'll take a look at it, but don't expect to find anything."

"What about this Kim fellow's fingers scratching at the door frame as he slid out?"

"The way I recall it, Jazz said Kim was holding on to him. Jazz was the one holding on for dear life at the door frame. One more thing," Gene said.

"What's that?"

"I've been given the west-side motel murder case."

"That means you've been given Homicide," I said.

"Temporarily. Until Bolton's situation is clarified."

MY PROBLEM for the rest of the weekend was keeping Jazz convinced he still needed to be careful. He kissed Gertrude Wardlow on her powdered cheek and moved across the street to our house. Perhaps it was the invincibility of the young, but he believed the worst was past. He wanted to get out of the house, go somewhere, do things.

Fortunately Klah and the Hatahles showed up on our doorstep Sunday afternoon. The family was there to attend the New Mexico State Fair, although it was clear to me that all Klah really wanted was to spend time with Jazz. Whatever his motives, Klah supported me in the belief the danger was not yet passed. After Gad and Dibe left to go look up relatives, Jazz and his guest spent just enough time with us in the den to be polite before disappearing into Jazz's bedroom. We didn't see much of them for the rest of the day or night. Officer Pedington caught on, but he refrained from saying anything.

Chapter 36

MONDAY MORNING I drove to the office, leaving the rest of the household at home. Officer Pedington was still Jazz's minder. Charlie and Hazel already knew most of the news thanks to Charlie's police connections. The stationhouse fairly rattled with talk and speculation. Gene was genuinely liked, but Bolton was also well-respected, so the force was divided in its loyalties. Zimmerman's plight didn't seem to raise much sympathy for him, so he might prove to be the weaker link.

William Haldemain wasn't arrested, but he did agree to come to the station voluntarily for questioning, accompanied by his attorney— Brother Roscoe, of course. I would have liked to be a fly on the wall for that interrogation, but this was just sparring time. Normally Gene would have bided his time and collected his facts before netting the big fish for an interview, but his hand was forced. Haldemain and Bolton had likely already talked. Giving them more time would just allow them to harden their respective stories. Gene needed to get Haldemain on the record.

"I thought the chief finally called in Internal Affairs to handle anything to do with APD involvement," Hazel said.

"He did," I replied. "But Gene's got the motel murders, and he's casting a wide net."

"Good heavens! You don't think Bolton and Haldemain are involved in that, do you?"

Charlie speared his wife with a blue eye. "Who benefits?"

"Remember," I said. "The killings took place when Haldemain started cleaning up behind himself."

Once their questions were answered, we settled down to regular cases bringing in regular money. That is, they did. I tackled a mountain of phone calls from people I'd ignored lately. A couple were from local news or TV reporters. Those I avoided. As if I needed a reminder, Paul called to say a couple of newshounds showed up on our doorstep demanding to talk to Mr. Penrod. Mr. Penrod, I took it, was still shacked up with Mr. Hatahle.

Midafternoon, I received an invitation to an interview of my own at the police station. I walked to headquarters and was admitted inside, where I lost two hours of my life to some intense questioning by Don Carson. Don was a competent cop and drew out of me what he needed. Then he allowed me to volunteer more information for the record. Only after he concluded the interview and I was taking my leave did I realize how key my investigation into Jazz's disappearance was to the case. And this case was rife with police politics.

I made it through the rest of the day. In fact, it was after eight when enough seemed to be enough. I was preparing to go home for a peaceful evening with Paul when a tired-sounding Gene called me on my cell. "I can't say much, BJ," he started, "but we have Haldemain spooked. Both Haldemains."

"I imagine so. They counted on Bolton to protect them—"

"William might have. But I don't believe Roscoe had anything to do with all this. He was caught flat-footed."

"Hard to believe. Those two walk hand in glove. Doesn't make much sense that one brother led such a life without the other brother knowing about it."

"That may be," he said. "But if I had to guess, I'd say William was a pretty straight shooter until his wife died five years ago. He defended a big trafficker in court back in '04, and that's probably when he made contact with the Bulgarians or Albanians or whoever they are. He probably didn't start sampling their wares until after the wife's accident, but I think he was throwing them shade for about a year before he lost her."

"Why, for crying out loud?"

"Money. What else?"

"His law firm makes him a fortune every year. What would he need with more money?"

Gene snorted. "Asks the man with twelve million bucks."

He knew better than that.

"With some people, it's the making, not the spending," Gene went on.

While my old partner and I fell into the comfortable habit of tossing suggestions for solving problems back and forth, Charlie stuck his head in the door to say he and Hazel were on their way home. I waved an acknowledgment and continued the conversation with Gene. With half an ear, I listened for and heard the reassuring click of the lock as Charlie keyed it from the outside.

In Gene's opinion, the best way to get William Haldemain was to bring the feds in on the act. Human trafficking was against federal law, and they were more experienced in cases like these. They could dig into the finances better than local authorities. That was a new wrinkle. So far he'd handled the situation in-house. Maybe he figured he needed the feds to roll the whole cartel up. However, Gene wasn't about to let go of the west-side motel murders to the FBI or anyone else.

The next time I glanced at the clock on my desk, an hour had run and it was dark outside my window. Time to bring this to a halt and address it tomorrow with a fresh brain. As I was about to express the idea, my office phone rang.

"Hold on, Gene. Somebody's calling on my office line." I laid the cell phone down on the desk and grabbed the landline receiver. There was no ID on the caller, so I punched the button activating the line without knowing who was on the other end.

"BJ, this is Chester Bolton," the distinctive voice said clearly.

"Lieutenant Bolton," I said loud enough for Gene to hear. "This is a surprise. Can I put you on the speaker? I'm trying to add a key to my key ring and am having trouble. I can work as we talk."

"Anybody else with you?" Suspicion clouded his voice.

"No, everyone's gone home. But if it makes you uncomfortable, I can forget it."

Bolton sighed. "No. That's all right. You're fortunate you can accomplish two tasks at once. Wait until you get my age. It becomes more difficult."

I punched the speaker button. If Gene was still on the phone, he could listen in on our conversation. "Okay, go ahead, and I'll see if I can multitask." I pulled out my key ring and threw it on the desk with an audible thump. Might as well have sound effects for the charade. "How did you know to call me at the office?"

"Called your home. Whoever answered said you were still at work."

"Okay. What can I do for you?"

"I think we may have gone about this mess all wrong. We need to sit down and discuss things rationally."

"You need to do that with Lieutenant Enriquez."

"That would be too formal. And let's be frank. You kicked all this off when you started looking for that Navajo kid."

"That Navajo kid has a name." I glanced toward the door as I heard a slight noise. Someone rattling the outside door?

"Of course. I believe it is Penrod. Jasper Penrod. Although I understand he prefers to be called Jazz."

I frowned. That sounded like a stall. "What do you propose?"

"I'm in the heights and can be at your office within twenty minutes, if you'll wait for me."

"I can meet you somewhere in between. In a public place. A restaurant, perhaps?" Another noise. The snick of metal on metal. The hair on my neck rose. The long-healed wound in my right thigh burned.

"This should be a private meeting. Twenty minutes. That is all. Will you be there?"

A stealthy noise in the entry. I silently opened my top right drawer. Damn! The only weapon in there was the Colt .25 semi. A peashooter. My Smith & Wesson 9mm was in the Impala's trunk, and my Ruger 57 Magnum was at home.

"BJ, are you there?" Bolton's voice pulled me back to the conversation.

"Yeah. Still here. Got distracted by the key ring but got the job done."

"Will you wait?"

"Sure."

Someone was in the office with me. I couldn't be certain, but every fiber in my body cried out for caution. I could vaguely hear the lieutenant's voice rattling in the phone, but my attention was centered elsewhere. The lights were off in the outer office except for a small lamp on Hazel's desk she left on overnight. My scar zoomed past burning directly to aching… and that was all the confirmation I needed. Someone was out there.

Quelling an urge to demand to know who was there, I spoke in as near normal voice as I could manage into the phone receiver. "Okay, Lieutenant. I'll hang on here." After that, I grabbed the Colt and eased my chair over to get away from the window that faced the street in order to avoid being silhouetted.

When a dark form filled the doorway, I rolled out of my chair to the floor to the right of the desk. Something spit fire as the smothered roar of a handgun filled the office. My chair rolled backward from the force of the bullets. I pulled off three quick shots at the flame, firing blindly at the door. The pop of my little peashooter sounded ridiculous. Nonetheless, I caught a grunt and heard the bang of metal against a wooden desk. He'd dropped his weapon… I hoped. Was he down? I heard no one grubbing for a lost handgun.

I crept to my desk and fumbled for the remote. Because I sometimes worked late at the office, some years ago I'd installed a device where I could remotely turn lights on and off in various offices. When my hand found the little plastic rectangle, I punched the top button. The lights in the hallway—which was effectively Hazel's office—went on. I'd moved around the desk and started for the door when a form barreled through and caught me with a shoulder. I crashed backward into the desk, sending papers and the lamp and the telephone crashing to the floor. My little semiautomatic flew out of my hand. I reeled backward and rolled off the desk onto the floor, smashing my lamp beneath me.

There was a pause as Charles Zimmerman regarded me through cold, hard eyes. In the semigloom, I saw what appeared to be blood on his chest. He labored to catch his breath.

"Couldn't leave it alone, could you? Had to have that half-breed son of a bitch! Well, it ends now."

When he reached for me. I grabbed for the first thing available, which turned out to be my banker's lamp. The fall from the desk had broken off the green shade, leaving the two hollow metal tubes that supported it standing straight up from the base. I thrust it upward, hoping to block a blow. But he was too close. The two metal tubes caught him in the belly and the side.

His eyes flew open in shock. He staggered but did not fall. With an effort he retreated, pulling the metal prongs from his body. He refused to give up and came for me again. But he was no longer quick and precise. I grabbed a glass paperweight from the floor beside me and swung blindly. It made contact. He dropped to the floor without a sound.

I scrabbled across the floor, grasped the butt of my little pistol, and whirled around. He lay unmoving on the flat of his back. The paperweight had caught him directly on the right temple. Zimmerman would never move again. Not of his own volition, that is.

I rummaged around in the wreckage of my office and found the telephone. Panting heavily, I lifted the instrument to my ear.

"Z-Zimmy?" Bolton asked.

"Bolton, you bastard!" I yelled. The phone clicked as he hung up.

I righted my overturned chair with two holes in the back dribbling white stuffing and dropped into it, exhausted. My thigh banged as if it were a bass drum. I took a shaky breath and considered what to do. Paul. I needed Paul. But first I needed to reach Gene.

Gene! He'd been on the cell phone, I dropped to my knees and rooted around in the detritus for the little instrument. Tinny shouts emanating from it helped me locate the thing quickly.

"BJ, what's going on!" he yelled again as I picked it up.

"I-I've got a situation."

"I know. I heard it all. Are you all right? Are you in danger?"

"All right. Danger's past. As a matter of fact, he's lying dead on my floor right now. It's Zimmerman. He came through the door blasting away."

"Sounded like a silencer. That's premeditation. And I'm a witness. I heard the whole thing."

"I should have Bolton on record. I activated my recorder as soon as I knew who was calling. This oughta take them down, Gene."

"Maybe so, but right now we gotta worry about you. Hold on, buddy. Somebody oughta be at your door right now. Go let them in downstairs. I'm on my way."

I could hardly muster the strength to get up and sidle around the body on the floor. The stairs were beyond my capacity at the moment— shock, I figured. I rode the elevator down, thinking that over the years I'd killed two men in this building. Was management going to get fed up with my escapades, or did they spice up life a bit?

By the time I reached the glass front door to the building, I saw the worried visage of Sgt. Don Carson.

Chapter 37

THE COPS confiscated my Colt for testing—standard procedure—but the picture was clear. The stuffing oozing from the back of my office chair and Zimmerman's silenced, nonissue .38 supported my version of the story, as did the recording my phone made of the event. Then, too, I had the testimony of Lt. Gene Enriquez, who'd listened to the entire thing on my cell phone. The recording of Lieutenant Bolton's call, which remained open until after the shootout, was of particular interest.

Nonetheless, I was hauled down to headquarters to give a formal statement, get swabbed for gunpowder residue, have pieces of my shirt cut out to test the bloodstains. Fortunately it was all Zimmerman's blood.

Captain Patrick O'Bannon handled my case since Gene was a witness of sorts, and the incident seemed to involve members of the APD, two of them being lieutenants. O'Bannon conducted my interview himself, and as I studied his florid face on the opposite side of the table, I mused that even Albuquerque had some of the fabled Irish cops. He put me through the ringer, taking almost two hours to extract every detail of the evening. As his questions commenced to range wider, I understood he was also looking to resolve the claim and counterclaim Gene and Bolton had lodged against one another. It appeared to me that Bolton's recorded phone call and his failure to report the incident went a long way toward resolving that issue.

By the time O'Bannon released me from the stuffy interview room and said I was free to go, a reception committee awaited me even though it was deep into the night. Paul was there, and alerted by Gene, he'd brought a fresh shirt. Jazz was with him, as was his minder, Officer Pedington. Charlie and Hazel also waited, with Hazel once again in the role of my surrogate mother. Gad and Dibe had picked up Klah tonight to visit the state fair and hadn't yet returned. Exhausted, I put them all off and agreed to meet at nine the next morning at the North Valley Flying Star, since my office was a crime scene.

Even Paul didn't get much in the way of details that night. I was exhausted and reacting to overdoses of adrenaline. I went home and zonked.

PRECISELY AT nine, Paul and I walked into the Flying Star to confront a gathering of my closest and dearest friends and coworkers, all anxious to learn the situation. Pedington didn't want to possibly become a witness in a trial, so he took his coffee at a table far away from ours. That was likely the reason Gene did not join us. I was very careful to tell them nothing that contradicted what I'd told O'Bannon.

"Where do you think Bolton is?" Charlie asked when I finished.

"Either at headquarters fighting for his life or halfway to Mexico doing the same thing."

"Why?" Paul asked.

"Think about it. Someone—presumably William Haldemain—slaughtered ten individuals in a west-side motel when we started closing in on him. That's why he killed his houseboy, Kim, as well as Nesposito. Why he tried to kill Jazz. And likely why Zimmerman tried to kill me last night. Isolating himself."

"You had no direct knowledge of his involvement," Charlie said.

"No, but he knew I was the one trying to put the pieces back together again."

"Wonder how Metz is feeling right now?" Jazz asked.

"Cautious, I'd say. And the same for that dentist fellow. And they'd better keep a close eye on that Guess kid in lockup."

"You think there are more of them in APD than Bolton and Zimmerman?" Hazel asked.

"Bolton ran an entire division. He picked out Zimmerman as a bad apple. Why should we assume there are no more of them?"

Jazz dry-washed his face. He looked as though Klah had worn him out. "What about Silver Wings... uh, Haldemain. Have they picked him up yet?"

"I don't imagine so," Charlie said. "They're a couple of steps away from him yet."

"He'll just get in his airplane and fly off somewhere. He'll get away."

"Possible," I said. "But he has a lot at stake. He may decide to stay and fight until he sees his situation is hopeless. *Then* he'll fly away."

Charlie scratched his bald scalp. "Besides, Lieutenant Enriquez probably has the plane staked out. But something doesn't make sense. Bolton's an old-time cop. Experienced. Why would he pull a bonehead move like trying to kill you in your own office?"

"That's been nagging at me too. I believe Haldemain's the answer. Haldemain pulls all the strings. He wanted me out of the way and pushed the lieutenant into doing something he didn't want to do."

"Hell, if he hadn't called you and stayed on the phone, everything would have fallen on Zimmerman's back."

"If he'd simply called the department and reported what he heard, he'd be clear as well. Why didn't he?" Hazel asked.

"Maybe he was afraid Zimmerman wasn't dead, just wounded and able to spill the beans."

I nodded. "Possibly, but even so, reporting it would have bought him some time. More than likely, he thinks Haldemain knows everything has fallen apart and will come for him. Possibly send the Bulgarians for him."

Charlie shook his head. "We'll get it figured out in time."

Hazel turned practical. "When do you think we'll get possession of our office?"

"Maybe sometime tomorrow," I said. "Why don't you work from home until I can get us an answer."

Shortly after that, Charlie and Hazel headed home while the rest of us took off for 5229 Post Oak Drive NW. To Jazz's great joy, Klah was asleep under his black hat while stretched out on a chair on the front porch. State fairs have a way of wearing out people, be they young or be they old.

After we arrived home, the only thing I wanted more than Paul was another shower, even though it was only noon. Halfway through it, he made the thing perfect by joining me beneath the running water, letting me stand with my hands against the wall while he washed my aching carcass. Later, as he joined me in bed, I wondered what Pedington was doing, since Klah and Jazz were likely engaged in similar activities.

I quit wondering about such things when Paul pulled me to him and whispered in my ear. "I was scared to death when Gene called me and said there'd been a shooting. I ought to get you to promise to drop this private detective thing and take up gardening." He reared up above me, and Pedro stared at me from his left pec, looking expectant. "And I'm going to start it off by plowing a furrow."

He did it. Quite adequately and thoroughly, I might add.

WEDNESDAY, I relented and decided to go to the state fair, although I took Jazz's police minder, this time Officer Young, along with us. Now

I'm not hung up on livestock, so I generally visit the fine art exhibit, the commercial stalls in the Manual Lujan Building, the Spanish Village, Indian Village, the African American exhibition, call it a day, and avoid crowds for the next week or so. With Jazz and Klah along, we spent most of our time *with* the livestock and a couple of hours watching a rodeo. I have to admit, watching a rodeo was far more interesting when you have a real rodeo hand in the stands explaining the nuances. When we returned home, I was beat. After eating a bowl of soup and taking a shower, I hit the sheets so exhausted that not even Pedro could rouse me.

The next morning, a team of detectives went to question Dr. David Cole and found a flustered nurse struggling to cope with patients arriving for appointments their dentist hadn't bothered to keep. To make matters worse, the good doctor wasn't answering either his home phone or his smartphone. The detectives then went to his bachelor pad and found no Dr. Cole nor any evidence of a struggle.

All of this Gene told me when I talked to him midmorning. I immediately asked if anyone had an eye on William Haldemain.

I could almost hear him shaking his head over the telephone. "No. IA believed I put someone on him, and I thought they did. So there's no accounting for his time yesterday or today. I've got someone trying to locate him now."

"How about his plane?" I asked.

"It's parked at the makeshift strip west of town. I've got a man in the house keeping an eye on it."

"What about Metz?"

Gene snorted in disgust. "He's at work in his corporate headquarters on Menaul. He doesn't seem bothered by the absence of his boy Jamie."

"Where is the kid?"

"UNM hospital. They'll stabilize him and send him to a recovery center. He's hooked bad. Heroin, apparently. Eventually, that'll probably be enough to snare Metz, but the kid's got to be able to testify."

"How long will it take Metz to figure that out?" I wondered aloud. "How about Bolton?"

"On the run. Not at home, at any rate. But the whole department's on the lookout for him. We'll get him."

"If he doesn't make the border first."

"Well, yeah. There's that."

"What's the status on the west-side motel massacre?"

"I've reviewed Homicide's case. Not much there. Bolton decided it was tied in with drugs and human trafficking and assigned it to Vice."

"To Zimmerman, you mean," I said.

"You got it. And Zimmerman's records don't show a damned thing. Make-work, not hard work. Does that tell you something?"

"Yeah, that he probably had a hand in it."

"What about the feds? They should have been all over it because of the human trafficking."

"Bolton convinced them it was a homicide, so it was his case," Gene said. "They went along with it. You want my opinion, Zimmerman did the killing himself."

"Maybe," I said. "But I'll bet Haldemain's man Kim was part of it too."

"Could be. You'll recall there were two different shooters."

"We've gotta find Bolton."

"I've alerted all the border crossings, but if he's connected with the traffickers, they've got a hundred ways to get him across the border without going through a legal POE."

FIFTEEN MINUTES later the mystery of Lt. Chester Bolton's whereabouts solved itself. Hazel stepped into my office, newly reclaimed from the crime scene boys.

"There's a guy on line one who claims he knows something about Lieutenant Bolton, but I think it's Bolton himself."

I picked up the phone and punched a button. "Yes, Lieutenant, what can I do for you?"

"I want a meet."

"You know where my office is. It's shot up a bit, but I'm here."

"I'll meet you somewhere neutral. Like the west mesa."

"Do you think I'm crazy?" I asked.

"Do you think I am? You get hit now, and I'm nailed for it. I wanna make a deal. Surrender myself. I don't trust Enriquez not to shoot first and ask questions later."

"Why me? You've got lots of friends on the force. Surrender to one of the captains or deputies. Or the chief himself," I said.

"You're the guy Zimmerman almost waxed. I want you speaking for me."

"Why would I do that?"

Bolton made a noise through his nose. "You want Haldemain, don't you? You want your boy, Penrod, off the hook for the motel murders. Meet me on the rim of the escarpment a mile or so north of the Montaño entry. I'll get out of my car and stand in plain sight."

I made a quick decision. "Be there in forty minutes."

"Alone."

"My partner Charlie Weeks will be with me."

Bolton hesitated. "Okay, but I talk to you alone."

"No problem."

HAZEL PUT up a storm of protest, but Charlie and I headed over to Coors, turned north, and took the Montaño exit past Petroglyph Park up onto the west mesa, a flat stretch of land west of Albuquerque atop the escarpment of lava laid down by volcanoes called the Five Sisters 10,000 years ago.

In something just over twenty-five minutes after Bolton's call to me, we spotted his car at the very edge of the escarpment overlooking the city of Albuquerque, not more than five hundred yards from where I'd dropped out of the sky on a murderous gang leader and rescued Paul in what I called the Zozobra case. I tapped the brake pedal as Bolton got out of his Mercedes with a large pistol in his hand. When we were close enough to recognize, he held the weapon in the air and tossed it back into his vehicle through an open window.

"Don't mean he doesn't have a backup," Charlie muttered.

"No, but at least he doesn't have that cannon in his fist."

"He was afraid it was someone else, wasn't he?"

I nodded. "That would be my guess."

"Then why did he put the nose of his car at the edge of the escarpment? That's a fifty-foot drop-off. He foreclosed his options. Bolton's too savvy a cop for that."

Without answering, I halted twenty feet behind the parked Mercedes sedan. Bolton stood as he was while we got out of the car. A small, awkward silence built. He broke it.

"Thanks for coming, BJ. Don't know if I'd trust you if the situation was reversed."

"Charlie gives me a lot of confidence."

"Agreed rules? I talk to you alone?"

"Charlie will wait here. We'll walk a few yards away from the cars for privacy. You armed?"

"Peashooter in an ankle holster. You?"

"S&W 9mm in back belt."

He nodded and turned to walk away from the cars. I stopped him.

"First, Charlie and I want to know why you called me. After all, your buddy, Zimmerman, tried to kill me two days ago… with your help, I might add. Aren't you worried about payback?"

"Zimmerman worked for Haldemain more than he worked for me. As for payback, that's why I called you. I wanna turn myself in, but I want to survive the event."

"Gene Enriquez will welcome you with open arms. He's looking for you, as a matter of fact."

"Yeah, I can imagine."

I shook my head. "I don't get it. The safest place for you is APD headquarters."

"Come on, BJ, you were a cop. Those guys know I've betrayed them after spending years holding their feet to the fire."

"Go to the feds. Human trafficking is a federal offense."

"Enriquez is going to hold on to those west-side murders."

"I see. You want to trade info on the motel massacre for a deal."

"Seems like a good place to start."

"You need Enriquez, not me."

"Enriquez *through you*. You're close. Buddies. You can motivate him to see nothing happens to me in the system."

"You give him the killers, and that's more motivation than I can provide."

That short exchange, held in Charlie's presence, laid out what Bolton wanted. He was afraid for his life on the outside but wasn't sure there was a safe place on the inside. Not without special protection. Prison's not the safest place for a police officer. Fleeing to Mexico? The Bulgarians had better connections there than he did. Again, a federal prison seemed safer to me, but he saw it differently. He was afraid of his brothers in blue, but at the same time he was more inclined to trust them than anyone else. In the end he permitted me to call Gene, who agreed to come attended only by Carson.

Gene's a thoroughly professional police officer, but I could see the rage boiling inside him as he accepted Bolton's surrender. Gene placed Bolton's two weapons in evidence bags before locking the Mercedes and calling for a truck to come pick up the vehicle. Then Charlie and I trailed Gene's brown

Ford back downtown. Once Bolton disappeared inside APD, there wasn't much we could do—Gene wasn't about to let me sit in on the interview—so I dictated my statement to an officer, and we returned to the office.

Midafternoon, Gene met me for coffee at Garcia's on North Fourth. The place was small but nearly deserted at this time of day, so he felt free to talk.

"Bolton confirmed William Haldemain is Silver Wings," Gene opened. "He used contact lenses now and then to confuse the issue, but Bolton claims Roscoe Haldemain knew nothing about his brother's involvement with the Bulgarians."

"How about the motel killings?" I asked.

"The two shooters have already got their reward. The Chinese houseboy, Kim, who was a cold-blooded killer, by the way, and Zimmerman. They're both dead, but maybe we can lay this at Haldemain's feet. That's where it belongs."

"Did Bolton have a hand in it?"

"Claims he didn't know anything about it until afterward. Even then, he says he investigated it according to protocol. Of course, he put Zimmerman on it. Not clear if he knew at that point Zimmerman was one of the killers. He did the initial shooting, by the way. Kim came along behind and shot them in the head."

"You believe him?"

Gene shrugged. "You know what's hard to wrap my head around? That Haldemain would go to such lengths to isolate himself. Bolton said William played around with most of those kiddies, and the motel manager knew him. So he just ordered them all killed. You'd think he'd know that would cause a big stink."

"Yeah, but he counted on Bolton and Zimmerman to keep things under control. Then he started getting rid of those closest to him. Like Kim and Jazz."

Gene laughed. "Bolton said Haldemain went apoplectic when he found Jazz was still alive. He was more upset over Jazz pissing all over his cockpit than he was that the kid survived."

"I assume Haldemain was responsible for Nesposito's death too."

"Bolton believes so but can't prove it."

"What does he say about Dr. Cole's disappearance?"

"Doesn't know anything about it. He says the doc was so paranoid about someone finding out he liked boys, the man might just have pulled up stakes and run for the hills."

"Maybe Cole figured Haldemain would try to clean house again."

"And Metz?" I asked.

"We'd like to charge him with involuntary servitude, but that Guess kid is so unreliable, not sure we can get him for that. Feds might try, but we probably won't."

"And that leaves Mr. Haldemain himself. Where is he?"

"Dunno. Not at his house. Not coming to the office anymore, and his plane's still out west of town. We have a watch on his credit cards, so he'll show sooner or later."

"He's probably got more than one bolt-hole prepared. What does Roscoe say?" I asked.

"Just that he's his brother's attorney, and not much more."

"Need to run something by you, Gene. Now that things have broken, I'm guessing there's not much danger to Jazz any longer. I'm having trouble holding him close to the house. He's in love and wants to get out and share the world with Klah."

"Klah. That young Navajo, huh. Presentable-looking enough, I guess."

"Presentable? He's downright handsome. But what about my question?"

"I think Haldemain's a selfish, vindictive son of a bitch, and if I'd just thrown him over for a kid my own age, I'd be looking over my shoulder."

I screwed up my face in thought. "Yeah, normally that's the way I'd read it too. But Haldemain's got bigger problems than being spurned."

"True," Gene said. "And you're right at the bottom of those problems. And by extension, so is Jazz Penrod. Haldemain's going to trace those problems right back to the kid. And like we agreed… he's vindictive."

"Shit! At least you've got a minder on him."

"Until the end of the day. My captain's convinced this thing is all but wrapped up."

"Well, double shit."

JAZZ HAD enough. He told his minder of the moment—Pedington this time—he wanted to go to the fair one more time before it closed for the season. The cop could come along or not, but he couldn't come in uniform. The young officer declined but hung around long enough to haul Jazz and Klah to the fairgrounds on East Central Avenue, which was on his way back to the stationhouse.

Chapter 38

AFTER THEY left, I poured a glass of red wine and sat on the sofa in the den. I chose the sofa hoping Paul would join me for a little cuddling. Instead he called me into the little office I maintained at the house. Actually it wasn't so little since it comfortably held both our desks.

"Look at this." He motioned to the landline telephone on his desk. He held the receiver in his hand.

"What am I looking at?"

"Recent calls. Do you recognize that 385 number?"

A feature on my telephone systems—both at home and downtown at the office—recorded calls dialed as well as calls received. It's a function I use to bill my clients for expenses.

"No. It's not yours?"

He shook his head. "I looked back. BJ, there are several short calls over the last few days."

"Maybe Jazz or Klah called it."

"It started before Klah came. Back when Jazz was over at Mrs. W.'s."

"Then it would have to be Pedington or Young."

"Right, and Young wasn't here today." He pointed to the two most recent numbers. They were the identical 385 phone number. "It had to be Pedington. The most recent call is mine. I dialed it out of curiosity."

"Maybe he called home."

"Maybe so, but nobody answered when I called. His call lasted two minutes."

"You're suggesting something nefarious? If so, why would he use our telephone system? Why not use his own? He carries a cell phone. We've both seen him use it."

"That's what got me to thinking. Everybody checks the most recent calls received. Nobody checks calls out. Maybe they're calls he didn't want tied directly to him."

"That would mean—"

"That would mean he was up to no good or he was calling a girlfriend."

I took the receiver from Paul's hand and dialed Gene at home. He answered sounding harassed. Normal for a homestead with five kids ranging from one preteen to four already afflicted by that condition.

"Just headed out the door. Got roped into going to the fair," he said. "Again. Be glad when the damned thing's over."

"This weekend, my friend." I told him of Paul's discovery. We examined the "girlfriend" thing, but it didn't hang together for a series of one and two-minute calls.

"Gimme the number. I'll have somebody check it out. Pedington still on duty?"

"Nope. Jazz invited him to the fair or to go home. He's dropping Jazz and Klah off at the fairgrounds and heading to the station. What do you know about him?"

"Borrowed him from Bolton's division, but Bolton didn't give him up if he was part of his network."

"Maybe he was on the perimeter, and Bolton didn't want to contaminate him."

"Doesn't sound like perimeter to me. Look, where will Jazz and Klah go? Indian Village. Where else?"

"They were headed to the rodeo. Klah's a bull rider recovering from an accident."

"Okay, so looks like I'm going to the rodeo," he said with a sigh hiding in his voice.

"Paul and I will leave now. We'll wait for you at gate three."

GENE, GLENDA, and the youngest, a cute eleven-year-old named Heddy, met us at the gate. The rest of the kids had already scattered, probably to the carnival rides. Glenda planned on shepherding Heddy there as well. Then she would look at a few exhibits and try to corral everyone back home in Gene Jr.'s Camaro. That likely didn't fit with Gene Jr.'s plans, but so be it. If she got stranded, she'd give Gene a call on the cell. That settled, Gene, Paul, and I headed for Tingley Coliseum on the east end of the fairgrounds.

The rodeo had not yet started, but fans already streamed into the arena. Gene flashed his badge to gain the three of us entry to the back area where the working part of the show took place. As we stalked around in the guts of the rodeo, dodging contestants, animal handlers, clowns, officials, and a host of unknowns, Gene's phone rang. The 385 number proved to be an unregistered cell phone... in other words, a throwaway.

My blood pressure was rising by the time we found Jazz in what appeared to be a blind alley created by arena panels. He and Klah talked to a young man in chaps, introduced to us as Pete Toadlena, Gad and Dibe's nephew who lived here in Albuquerque. From his cautious reaction, Pete made Gene as a cop and probably nursed suspicions about me as well.

"Any sign of trouble?" Gene asked.

"Nah," Jazz said. "These are rodeo people. Good people. Not interested in trafficking."

"What did Pedington say on the way down? He put up any fuss at being dismissed?"

Jazz shook his head. "Glad to be off the hook, I think."

"He make any phone calls on the landline while you were in BJ's house?" Gene asked.

Klah and Jazz exchanged puzzled looks. "Nah," they both said, almost simultaneously. "What's up?" Jazz added.

Gene backed off. "Not sure. Someone mighta been trailing you. Just wondered if Pedington tumbled to it."

Jazz glanced at Klah but spoke to me. "That stuff's all over now, isn't it? Nobody's gonna traffic me again... ever."

"I think you're missing the point, Jazz," I said. "Silver Wings isn't interested in you for sex any longer. He's looking to shut you up."

Jazz shook his head. He was having none of it. "Why? You've got that other lieutenant... Bolton. And the cop, uh, Zimmerman's dead. And we're in the middle of a crowd." Even as he spoke, I could see the need for cocaine rise in him, just as it did whenever tension made an appearance. He probably wished for a pipe right about now... a mug of green tea, at the very least.

My right thigh began to twinge. But that old scar was a worrywart; it broke out in a case of nerves whenever something threatened, real or imagined. A glance around showed people rushing this way or that, going about their business. Except for the roustabout, leaning on a chute gate fifteen yards away. And a clown talking up a cowgirl ten yards the other direction.

"What you want me to do? Go into hibernation?"

"Wouldn't be a bad idea," Gene said. "Look, guy. Twelve people are already dead because of this Silver Wings fellow. And BJ was damned near one of them." When that brought a frown, Gene bored in and indicated Klah. "And what about this fella here? You willing to put his life in danger?"

"I can take care of myself," Klah said.

"That right? I hear you're banged up from a busted bull ride. You can move when you need to, can you?"

"Maybe he's right, Klah," Jazz said.

"What if we stay right here with friends? Nobody's gonna try anything with this many people around," Klah replied.

The roustabout moved on, but the clown talking to the blonde was still trying to work his magic. Wonder what he looked like beneath all that paint and the twenty-gallon Stetson? She was probably wondering the same thing, because it didn't seem as if she knew him. That was the body language I got, anyway. I vaguely heard Gene explaining that a crowd wasn't always safe; sometimes it was cover.

I turned back to them. "Jazz, this won't go on forever. Haldemain…. uh, Silver Wings is on the run. When we get him, things should be over. There's also something we haven't told you."

"What?"

"Your minder, Pedington, was making one-minute calls to a throwaway number from our house phone. We think it might have been Silver Wings on the other end."

Jazz's eyebrows rose. "My cop babysitter was reporting on me to the guy who wants to kill me? Hell, Pedington was a decent guy for a… uh, cop." Shock suddenly sparked his eyes. "That's why somebody tried to break in to Mrs. W.'s. He was after me!"

"Probably," I said. "But he didn't figure on a tiny, elderly woman being an ex-DEA agent."

Jazz put the rest of it together. "If you're right about Pedington, he let someone know Klah and I were headed to the rodeo."

"Exactly. Gives somebody time to set up an ambush."

"Here?" Apparently he recalled Gene's caution about crowds and turned to Klah's cousin. "Pete, do you know all these people?"

Toadlena shook his head. "Most of them, yeah. But not all. Half a dozen people right around here I don't know. Maybe he's right, Jazz. Maybe you oughta get outa here."

Jazz looked defiant, but he said the right thing to his companion. "Okay. You wanna stay here or go with me?"

Klah almost looked hurt. "Go with you, of course."

Pete gave a shout, and two tall Navajos sauntered over. "Hey, guys. Give us some cover, okay?"

With Pete in the lead, a tall cowboy on either side of him, and Klah guarding his back, Jazz made his way out the back of the building. Gene, Paul, and I were ready to follow along behind when I noticed the clown taking an interest in the procession. Gene nodded at me, and we walked around a corral fence while Paul followed the others. Watching from between the fence slats, I noticed the man take out a cell phone, punch a button, and wait. As soon as he started talking, we walked over in time to hear him say, "...out the back way."

Gene flashed his badge as I snaked my hand back to touch the butt of my pistol in my belt. The clown took note and closed his phone immediately. "Help you?"

"Yeah. You can come down to headquarters with me."

"What for? I got a job to do here."

"It's your second job I'm interested in. Who were you talking to?"

"None of your business. I got a right to make calls to anybody I want."

"Not to warn them your mark is heading out the back door. Hand over your phone."

"What if I refuse?"

"Then we'll go downtown for sure."

The lanky man handed over his small flip phone with obvious reluctance. Gene manipulated it and then held it up before me. "Recognize anything?"

"That's the same 385 number we saw before. Try it."

Gene punched Redial, and a moment later said, "Hello, Haldemain. We need...." He pulled the small instrument away from his ear and shrugged. "Whadda ya know. He didn't want to talk." He addressed the clown. "What's your name? Got any ID?'"

"Lenny Dogwood."

Gene's chin dropped. "Cripes, BJ. This guy's a cop. I recognize his name. His old man's a sergeant downtown."

"That's right, Lieutenant. I'm on the job."

"Who's supervising?"

"Well... uh...."

"That's what I thought. Let's go."

Gene took the young officer by the arm and led him outside. We caught up with the others as they were about to enter the fairgrounds proper.

Gene called Paul over and asked him to go find a policeman on duty at their headquarters tent down by the Fine Arts Building.

We waited five minutes before Paul brought up a beefy corporal. Gene turned Dogwood over to the officer and asked that he be escorted downtown and held until he arrived.

Paul and I hustled Jazz and his retinue to my Impala in the parking lot while Gene went in search of his family to let them know his weekend had been interrupted. I could imagine Glenda's reaction. "So what else is new?"

GENE AND I sat opposite an attractive young officer with only stray streaks of clown paint at his temples and smeared in his brown hair. Paul remained at the house with Jazz and Klah. Officer Young should have joined them by now.

Gene put a touch of menace in his tone. "What were you doing at the rodeo, and don't give me any crap."

"On the job." Dogwood hesitated before trying to enhance his bluff. "Something Bolton put me on."

"Bullshit. Bolton's suspended, and you answer to me now. Whose number did you call to say they were leaving by the back entrance? Look, son, your dad won't be able to help you much if you don't cooperate."

Dogwood kept up his stubborn denials until his father, a burly, grizzled man nearing retirement, burst through the door to the interview room. Then the younger Dogwood's defiance collapsed.

"I'm sorry, Dad. Helen and I needed the extra money with another baby on the way, and—"

"Shut up! Don't say another word. Did you ask for your union rep?"

Lenny Dogwood shook his head.

"Well, do it. Right now."

But the officer didn't need a rep. By the time the official arrived, Sergeant Dogwood had pretty well worked out a deal. If Lenny's involvement in the trafficking was limited to merely carrying messages, as he claimed, he'd be permitted to resign from the force without being referred to the district attorney's office. Since the officer hadn't been carrying a weapon in his clown getup, I was inclined to believe he wasn't put there to ambush Jazz. Perhaps to earn his pass, Lenny squealed on two more cops in Bolton's ring.

Once Gene was satisfied that end was tied up, we settled in his office to talk.

"With what Dogwood's told us, I think we've rolled up Bolton's gang," he said. "None of them are killers, except for Zimmerman. Unfortunately that doesn't ease things up for Jazz."

"Not so long as Haldemain's on the loose. I have the feeling he can call on the Bulgarians or whoever it is running the trafficking ring. Do you know, by the way?"

"Best we can figure it's run out of Sofia, so I guess that mean's it's Bulgarians. And I agree, we need Haldemain in hand before Jazz is safe. Of course, Haldemain's not much use to the traffickers any longer, so I don't know how much they'll go out of their way to help him."

"True, but it's not something I can bet Jazz's life on. After all, Haldemain's got enough money to buy their help." I gave a frustrated sigh. "What about Pedington?"

"He's in the interview room with Don Carson right now. Don will get to the bottom of that situation."

"How sure are you of Officer Young?"

"He's one of mine. I trust him, but I can only justify keeping him parked out in front of your place for so long."

With those words ringing in my ears, I gave up and drove home.

WHEN I arrived in the office Friday morning, Charlie was out interviewing a young woman as part of a background check on a possible hire for a new utilities company executive. Hazel was doing Hazel work… without which Vinson and Weeks would have withered and died. She was billing.

With nothing better to do, I phoned Betsy Brockmire at CAHT to ask if she'd seen, heard, or smelled William Haldemain. She hadn't. But she did have an idea.

"I know he has this cabin up in the Jemez Mountains. Maybe he's hiding out there until the storm passes."

"Betsy, this storm's not going to pass. I'm pretty sure the APD did a property title check. They'd have found it by now."

"Maybe not. I think maybe his law firm owns it. Or maybe he and Roscoe formed a partnership to hold title. We had a CAHT board meeting up there a couple of years back. It's very secluded. A genuine log cabin sitting halfway back in the forest, with the front porch facing a little meadow with a stream running through it. Beautiful."

"You don't happen to know how to get to it, do you?"

"He made each of us a map so we could get to the meeting. I think maybe I have my copy somewhere. I'll look for it and fax it to you if I find it."

Ten minutes later Hazel brought me a piece of paper with a map showing a hand-drawn route to a spot in the mountains about seven miles north and east of the little town of Cuba, New Mexico. Cuba lay about eighty miles north of Albuquerque, a drive of no more than an hour and a half. But I had no idea how long the last leg of the journey would take. Experience taught me that some of those county and logging roads were slow going, dodging fallen trees and families of mule deer and herds of elk, both of which vastly outnumbered humans per square mile.

I went to Google Earth on my computer and managed to find what was probably the cabin nestled in the edge of the forest. I used the program to trace me a route from Cuba to the co-ords of the cabin and found that it followed the same general outline as the one on Betsy's map. This was the right cabin.

The building fronted a modest meadow, transected from west to east by a small creek labeled Ria los Pinos. A state or county road ran north of the cabin, but a smaller road, probably originally a logging road, turned south and ran past the cabin to splash across the creek and then curve to the right. Then it meandered off through the Santa Fe National Forest. Two ways in and two ways out. New Mexico's monsoon season had ended roughly a month earlier, so the roads should be in decent shape. I knew from treks to such places as Teakettle Rock in that same general area that the countryside was heavy with caliche clay, and a man might as well be driving on greased glass when the roads were wet.

I printed copies of everything and headed for Gene's office. I had to cool my heels for ten minutes before being admitted, a sign that the brass was still a little skittish over the claims and counterclaims Gene and Bolton threw at one another… even though Bolton was the one on paid leave and yakking his head off to avoid arrest and trial.

Gene took a look at what I found and then pulled up Google Earth on his own machine. Together, we zeroed in on the cabin from a height of probably no more than a couple of hundred feet. A carport shielded the west side of the cabin, but what appeared to be the rear bumper of a car was just visible. Of course, we had no idea of how long ago the satellite passed over the area, so there was no way of telling if we were viewing the cabin in current time.

"That's in Sandoval County," Gene noted. "Need to involve the sheriff's office."

"You gonna ask them to check out the place first?"

Gene shook his head. "That place is so isolated a plane or a chopper would arouse suspicion. Hell, you can hear a car from a mile off up in those canyons. It's going to be hard to get in there without at least making him nervous. But odds are pretty good that's where he's holed up. I want to take Carson and a couple of Sandoval deputies, and that's all."

"What about the feds?"

He shook his head. "I want this guy for the murder of eleven men and kids. Zimmerman can probably be laid at his door too, but I'll put that one on Bolton. I want *us* to take him, BJ."

"Looks like we're headed to the Jemez Mountains," I said.

"You can come. But not Paul. It's gonna take me the rest of the day to set this up and get the paperwork done. We'll plan on hitting the place tomorrow morning. It's a weekend morning. Haldemain won't be expecting us then."

"Paul will give me heartburn over that. He considers himself a member of the press."

"Okay, but he'll have to stay with you at least half a mile back down the road."

"What time do you wanna start?"

"Early. We'll chopper to Cuba and drive in from there."

Chapter 39

WE DIDN'T actually go in blind. When Gene contacted the Sandoval County Sheriff's Office saying he wanted to play in their sandbox, the undersheriff had a deputy do a drive-by with a man from Cuba who ran cattle in the Santa Fe National Forest and was a familiar face to the area. The deputy reported a gold Caddy Escalade in the carport at the Haldemain cabin, prompting the sheriff to authorize participation in Gene's planned takedown.

Early Saturday morning, Gene, Paul, and I piled into an APD helicopter piloted—to my surprise—by Don Carson. He was a lad with many talents. A little more than half an hour later, we set down, not in Cuba, but in a broad meadow not more than two miles from the cabin. Two Sandoval deputies were waiting for us, each in his own patrol car.

A husky corporal with a name tag of Trueblood was familiar with the area and suggested we split into two teams, one approaching the cabin directly, and the other from the Fenton Lake area to foreclose any possible escape route. Trueblood was not happy we had two civilians among us, but he permitted us to ride along, provided we bail out of the patrol car at least half a mile before arriving at the cabin. In fact, he suggested all of us might want to get out at that point. The sound of a car motor carried a great distance at this altitude.

Carson and the second deputy took off first since their route via the Fenton Lake area was longer than ours. They would let us know when they were in position via radio. Gene cautioned them to talk about missing cattle or some such nonsense, as Haldemain was likely monitoring police calls.

Gene spent the next hour filling Trueblood in on what a bad guy William Haldemain, Esquire was. The deputy kept quiet and listened except for an occasional grunt of "Damned lawyers." Trueblood pulled out a blueprint of the 1,500-square-foot cabin the sheriff located in the courthouse that showed only two entrances. One door opened onto the front porch facing the meadow and stream to the south. The other opened to the carport to the west. However, the carport itself opened to the south, the same direction as the front door.

Finally a report of a "dead cow on the road" came across the ether, and we got underway.

The roads were dry but badly rutted by the last rain, so the going was as slow as I thought it would be. After a couple of short radio messages about the cow being "winched off the road" and "headed back to the station in Cuba," both teams were in place. At the bottom of a hill, Trueblood pulled off the road into some brush, and we all got out of the vehicle. In mutters and hand signals, the deputy let Paul and me know to remain there until we were summoned. Then he and Gene, both bearing shotguns, hiked up the long hill and eventually passed from sight over the crest.

"Wish he'd parked at the top of the hill," Paul said.

"Trueblood parked down here so there's less chance Haldemain hears our motor. But you can hike up and take a look, if you want. Don't go any farther than the crest, though."

"Okay."

A confidential investigator must sprinkle himself with patience dust every morning to put up with the long hours of doing nothing when on a stakeout or shuffling through mountains of data to find one small nugget of meaningful info. I parked myself on the fender of the county cruiser and watched my very sexy friend's unconscious manly grace as he walked up the steep hill.

Once at the apex, he stood in the middle of the road looking east for a long moment. Then he kicked the dirt a couple of times out of boredom before moving over to the three-strand barbed-wire fence running along the south side of the road. Once there, something apparently claimed his attention. He stood on tiptoes, one hand on a fence post for a moment, before turning to me and waving.

After I labored up the hill, he thrust a thumb over his shoulder. "That looks like a camera."

I swore an oath before grabbing for my cell. Gene answered with an irritated whisper. "What?"

"Paul found a camera. Haldemain knows you're coming. You're walking into an ambush."

I heard him call to Trueblood and the sound of men crashing through brush before he closed the call.

"Bet the deputies will be on the radio coordinating things! I want to hear how it goes," Paul yelled before taking off down the hill at a run.

I remained where I was to do some thinking. If I were in that cabin and knew the cops were coming for me, what would I do? A typical hardened criminal might hole up and try to hold off attackers. But if I were a lawyer with lots of money and connections to a foreign criminal cartel, I'd skedaddle before the cops got there. But if I had a camera on one road, I'd have them on the other one too. I'd know both exits were blocked. Then what would I do? I'd likely have some escape route planned and take that. Or....

I glanced down the hill at the Sandoval County Sheriff's unit parked on the side of the road. *Or I'd go for a target of opportunity.* Like a cruiser sitting abandoned at the side of the road... where Paul sat in the front passenger's seat, doubtless listening for exchanges between the deputies' shoulder units. The old wound in my right thigh spasmed as I caught movement at the fence line. I started back down the hill at a limping run. I hadn't taken a dozen steps before a man slipped through the fence. Haldemain? I couldn't tell. But I wasn't willing to take chances. I yelled and fired my Ruger three times into the air.

The man, now clearly William Haldemain, lunged the last few steps as Paul scrambled out of the car. The man grabbed my companion around the neck from behind and held him tightly. As I approached, I heard him demand keys to the cruiser.

Impeded as he was by the arm against his larynx, I could barely make out Paul's strangled response. "Don't have 'em. Cop car, for Chris' sake!"

Haldemain shifted, putting Paul between me and him. By now I was no more than ten feet away. "That's close enough, BJ." He pointed an impressive-looking forty-five at me.

I gained another two feet in the act of halting. "Give it up, Haldemain. A whole assault team will be here in a matter of minutes."

"Minutes are enough. Toss that pistol into the woods, and I'll be on my way. May even turn on the lights and siren."

"And get how far? Cuba?"

"You're right. I need to take your lover boy with me. Quite toothsome, I must say. Maybe we can make some magic before we have to part."

"You'll have to kill me first," Paul muttered.

"That won't be a problem. As a matter of fact, it will be payback. BJ's the one who screwed the pooch in the first place."

"That was you buying Jazz."

"Ah, yes. The beautiful Jazz. How is he, by the way?"

Good! Keep him talking. Gene would be here any time. "Recovering from you."

"I was good to him."

"By hooking him on cocaine?"

"Oh, he was already hooked by the time I got him. But enough of that. Toss the gun or die."

"Can't do that, Silver Wings."

"Too bad—"

Paul let go of the arm around his throat and slammed his fist into Haldemain's groin. The man let out a squawk and hunched over. Paul relaxed and dropped straight to the ground.

"Drop the gun, Halde—"

His forty-five roared, but he was still unsteady from the blow to his gonads, and the bullet went wide. I took careful aim and fired three shots.

Epilogue

SUNDAY MORNING, we gathered in the conference room at my office. I chose the office rather than the den of my house because of the size of the gathering. Hazel and Charlie and Gene joined Paul and me and five others: Jazz and Klah, Gad and Dibe Hatahle, and Jazz's brother, Henry. At the last minute, I'd thought to include Mrs. Wardlow. After all, she played a role in this little drama too. They all waited patiently as Gene and I took turns explaining the raid on Haldemain's cabin yesterday morning. Then the questions started.

"I don't understand," Jazz said. "Why didn't he just surrender? What could the penalty be for what he did to me? It sure would'na been the death penalty."

"Don't fool yourself, fella," Gene said. "He did that and worse to lots of others, some of them practically babies. Besides, I was going to hang at least eleven murders on him one way or the other."

"The west-side motel murders?" Charlie asked.

"And Nesposito's."

"Then there's Kim," Jazz said.

"We'll never find that guy," Gene said. "But yeah, him too, if we ever do."

"Why was he hanging around in the Jemez Mountains?" Klah asked. "Why didn't he take off for Mexico or some place?"

"From what we found in the cabin," I said, "he was within aces of doing just that. The cartel was getting him ID under another name together with credit cards, passport, and the works. As soon as that was ready, they were to pick him up by helicopter and take him someplace he could legally exit the country under another name. It was his bad luck that Betsy Brockmire remembered the cabin in time."

"How does his brother fit into all this?" Hazel asked.

Gene fielded that one. "Roscoe was rocked on his heels when he found out what his brother was up to."

"You really believe that?" Jazz asked.

"Oh yeah. His brother was so good at living a double life, Roscoe had no idea. They both are wealthy, so he didn't notice a change in lifestyle. As a defense lawyer, he was used to seeing scuzzy people around the office. Roscoe's so bummed he's thinking about retiring."

"What about that builder—Metz?" Jazz wanted to know.

"Probably can't touch him. You can testify he was at Silver Wings' pool parties, but there's no law against that. Unless you can testify to rape or false imprisonment. Unfortunately James Guess is the only one who can give us Metz. And he won't do it. Probably can't do it. He's really messed up.

"What about Dr. Cole?" I asked Gene. "Have you found him?"

"Found where he took a plane for Turks and Caicos. He wasn't willing to face the publicity and notoriety, I guess. He just up and abandoned his practice, taking his money with him."

"What's going to happen to Bolton?" Charlie asked.

"He'll lose his pension. Probably get busted for conspiracy but will earn some leniency because of cooperating. Spend some jail time, but probably not much."

"How many cops did you find?" Klah asked. "You know, twisted cops."

"Six, including Bolton and Zimmerman."

I slapped the walnut table with my left palm. "That wraps it up, I guess."

"Except for this," Henry said, sliding a piece of paper across the table to me. A cashier's check. "Probably won't cover everything, but it's all Louie could manage to collect. Think the tribe put in some of it."

I looked at the figure. Quite adequate, actually. "It'll do just fine, Henry. I told you it wasn't necessary. Jazz is a friend."

"I know that, but my dad insisted."

"Thank Louie for me, will you?"

"Sure. And this is for you, Dibe. Thanks for you and Gad putting up with Jazz for as long as you did." He slid a box over to the couple.

Dibe drew out her grandmother's squash blossom necklace and hid a smile behind her hand. "Why, thank you! You didn't need to do that, young man."

"And you didn't have to do what you did either. Anyway, thank you a lot."

Mrs. Wardlow, who was silent throughout the discussion, spoke up. "Jazz, you're going to have to receive some counseling, you know."

"I'm handling it all right. Gets better every day."

"Until some stress comes along," I said. "She's right. And Betsy Brockmire is ready to enroll you in Bishop Gregory's program."

"Aw, do I have to?"

"You have to," Klah said with finality.

Hazel leaned back in her chair and adjusted her glasses. "Well, that clears up everything, I guess. How do you want me to label the file, BJ?"

I gave it a moment's thought. "Call it Abaddon's Locusts." I saw her face screw up in an uncertain frown. "Think about it. The traffickers take kids and turn them into something they're not, and then they turn them loose on the world—"

"Just like Abaddon's locusts," she finished for me.

Exclusive Excerpt

The Voxlightner Scandal

A BJ Vinson Mystery

Coming Soon to
www.dsppublications.com

Prologue

Albuquerque, New Mexico
July 2011

AT EASE in his comfortable home at 4818 Post Oak Drive NW, Pierce brushed his chin with a palm, detecting the rasp of a five-o'clock shadow against his skin. The house was silent, disturbed only by his knocking around in the den and the *ticktock* of the ornate wind-up clock resting on the mantelpiece. Overhead lights off, a reading lamp cast a soft pool of light, rescuing the room from darkness. He longed for the mellow smell of pipe tobacco, but his doctor had convinced him to give up the vice last winter after a suspected TIA, a transient ischemic something or the other.

Ensconced in his favorite recliner, he picked up a book from the coffee table and inspected it closely. His latest novel. His third. Just delivered from his publisher in this morning's mail. In a rare moment of brutal honesty, he admitted the most impressive thing on the cover was his name: John Pierce Belhaven. A good name for an author, it rolled off the tongue and lent gravitas to the banal title, *Macabre Desserts*. Although too egotistical to admit being a hack, in moments such as this, he silently acknowledged he was no James Lee Burke. Whenever he attempted some of the Louisiana writer's soaring, poetic passages, they always ended up as muddied puddles of worthless ink that contributed nothing to the plot. What was Elmore Leonard's rule number ten? Leave out the parts that nobody wanted to read.

His next book would be a game changer. Just as the others, it would be a mystery, but this time he'd solve a *real* puzzle. One that had plagued Albuquerque for half a decade. A scandal involving the theft of millions and the death of a respected attorney. A mystery that only he could solve. He'd stumbled on a crucial clue years ago in his capacity as a utility company executive but hadn't understood its significance until he researched his new book. It was a work that would carry him from humdrum to best seller. And the interview with Wilma Hardesty on

KALB-TV that aired this very afternoon put the world on notice he was reopening the moribund Voxlightner case with a terse, hard-hitting tale leading directly to the killer.

This would set them on their ears down at SouthWest Writers, make them sit up and take notice of him... not as a writer, but as an *author*. He quelled an urge to rush to his office on the other side of the house to rifle through the growing file of research on the case.

A noise from the garage brought him out of his chair. He glanced at the clock on the mantel. *Ten thirty-four.* Who could that be at this time of night? Melanie? He shook his head. His daughter hadn't indicated she was driving in from Grants, where she lived with that odious husband of hers. Harrison wouldn't deign to show up at his door, probably not even to pick up his inheritance, should Pierce decide to leave his estranged son one.

He smiled and then faltered. It wasn't sweet Sarah. She was in Arizona visiting her family. His heartbeat quickened. It must be Spencer, although the lad didn't usually show up on Wednesdays. Before walking to the garage door, he arranged the new book on the coffee table in such a way that Spence could hardly miss it. As he reached for the brass doorknob, he heard the gas-fired lawn mower roar to life.

What the hell? John Pierce Belhaven opened the door and entered the darkened garage.

Chapter 1

IF 2011 was the year of the Arab Spring, this morning's *Albuquerque Journal* neglected to mention it. The international lead story—above the fold—reported the bombing of the government quarter in Oslo and the subsequent murder by gunfire of sixty-eight youth activists of the Labour Party by a native Norwegian terrorist.

The below the fold headline told of the death of a local author in a garage fire mere blocks from my home. What snagged my attention was that the terrorist attack in Norway took place today, July 22. The local tragedy occurred two nights ago. Our paper reported foreign events faster than local ones. I put it down to a time differential. After all, today was practically yesterday over the pond.

Paul came into the kitchen, where I sat at the table munching an english muffin slathered with cream cheese and dusted with ground black pepper. He brought with him the aroma of his shower and shave. He had changed aftershave lotion... Brut, possibly.

He stopped at the sight of me. "Whoa, BJ, I was gonna fix omelets."

"My stomach wouldn't wait. By the way, I know why we heard all those sirens Wednesday night. Garage fire just down the street."

"Where?"

I checked the article. "At 4818."

"The Belhaven place?"

"I'll admit you're more social than I am around the neighborhood, but how do you know the Belhaven house four blocks down the street?"

He plopped a bowl of steel-cut oatmeal on the table, apparently abandoning the idea of an omelet. "I know him from SouthWest Writers."

Paul joined New Mexico's largest professional writing association a year ago, when he got his Master's in Journalism from UNM and decided a membership would provide him some valuable contacts. He was probably right, although I had never considered journalism as *writing* until he pointed out that's exactly what it was.

"Can I see the article when you're finished?" he asked.

I rescued the sports section and handed over the rest. A minute later his voice startled me out of a story about the Lobo baseball team. They were having a pretty good season thus far.

"This can't be right."

"Uh." I refused to be distracted.

"BJ." He shoved the article in front of me again. "I can't claim to know the guy intimately, but I do know one thing. He wouldn't repair his lawn mower at ten thirty at night or any other time of day. He'd have the kid who mowed his lawn do it or else buy a new mower." He paused. "But the outcome I can believe. He'd likely spill gas all over himself and somehow set it alight if he made the attempt. But he wouldn't have."

"A klutz, huh?"

"You could say that," he admitted.

"I'll tell you what *I* can't believe. This happened two days ago, and Mrs. Wardlow hasn't broadcast it all over the neighborhood."

Gertrude Wardlow, the septuagenarian widow who lived across the street from this house my late father built, was a retired DEA agent and the local neighborhood watch. But I had no gripes coming. She'd saved my bacon a couple of times when suspects tried to bring cases home to me. More importantly, she'd warned me Paul was in trouble when a gang kidnapped him a few years back.

"Can I assume you smell a story?" I asked.

He shook his head. "I smell a rat. But you're right, I'm going to look into it. Who do you know in the Fire Department?"

I gave him the name of Lanny Johnson, a lieutenant who ran the Arson Squad at AFD. I'd worked with him a couple of times and found him to be a good man. "Course, you can call Gene if you want to know if there's a police case working."

My old riding partner at APD, Lt. Eugene Enriquez, oversaw Homicide. I needed to touch base with him anyway. The powers that be kept threatening to promote him to captain, but he didn't want to become an administrator. That would put him out of the "action," he claimed. The last time I talked to him, he was seriously considering retirement.

I PARKED my white '98 Impala in my spot in the lot at Fifth and Tijeras NW and took the back stairway to the third floor. As usual, I paused a moment to look down on the open atrium that hollowed out the core of my office building before pushing through the door labeled Vinson and Weeks, Confidential Investigations. I'd taken the time to stop by the North Valley Country Club for pool therapy before driving downtown to the office. In May of '04—while I was still an APD detective—I'd been shot in the right thigh by a suspected murderer. Ever since that momentous event, I needed to hit the water now and then to keep the leg from stiffening up. That was how I met Paul. He'd worked as a lifeguard at the country club to help pay his way through college.

Hazel, my office manager and a key cog in our organization, sat at her desk performing some of her magic on the internet. A whiz at locating people electronically, she had been my late mom's best friend and was now my partner Charlie Weeks's wife. She glanced up as I entered.

"Gene called. Mayor's office and an assistant DA phoned. Slips are on your desk."

"What does the mayor want?"

"Didn't deign to impart that information. DA wants to arrange for you to testify in the embezzlement case."

I sighed and walked into my private office. I could get a lot more done if I didn't have to drop everything and testify in court. That had been my lament from the time I was a Marine MP and an APD detective. Some things never change.

I knew what the mayor wanted. There was a vacancy on the civilian police oversight board, and he was considering appointing me. I wasn't certain how I felt about that. To sit in judgment of people I'd served with for nine years—even though that was six years in the rearview mirror now—didn't seem appropriate to me. On the other hand, as an ex-cop, I understood the life they lived minute-by-minute every day. Something else I needed to check with Gene.

I delayed returning the mayor's call, took care of the scheduling of my testimony on the embezzlement case, and dialed Gene's private number. Our phone conversations, although increasingly rare, followed a pattern. Brusque greetings and catching up on family affairs before getting down to business. Given Gene's family of five children, most afflicted with the dreaded teenage condition, he talked a lot more than I did. Today was no different. After he filled me in on Glenda and the brood, ranging from Gene Jr., nineteen, down to little Heddy, twelve, I brought him up to date with news of Paul. Once everything was covered, I asked if there was a police investigation of the Belhaven death.

"The writer toasted in his garage? Why? Should there be?"

"You know the answer to that better than I do, but Paul's convinced there's something funny. Claims Belhaven wouldn't have attempted to repair a lawn mower or anything else. He wasn't a hands-on type of guy."

"We've had that feedback too."

"So you're looking into the death?"

"Like usual, we're satisfying ourselves everything's on the up and up… unless OMI declares it an accidental death. Which they haven't done yet."

"I think Paul wants to write a story on it."

"Have him touch base with Det. Roy Guerra. He's handling it for us."

I LEFT a message on Paul's voicemail providing him Detective Guerra's name and contact information. After that, Hazel waylaid me with a background check on a Dallas man being considered as an executive by a local bank. That took the rest of the day and would consume half of my tomorrow, but this was the bread and butter of our business. Novels and films romanticizing the lives of PIs—as they called us—were so far off-base as to be laughable. Still, the life pleased me, so I had no inclination to bail on the agency and live off the trust fund my parents had thoughtfully left me.

Midafternoon, I heard a familiar voice in the outer office and Hazel's delighted rejoinder. Hazel is perplexed by the gay lifestyle I lead but loves Paul as much as she does me, so I knew he was getting a hug and a once-over. Moments later he came through the doorway and invaded my private space, and a welcome incursion it was. I never tired of looking on his handsome features.

"Hi. Am I interrupting anything?"

"No, come on in."

"I just met with that Detective Guerra guy. Thanks for getting the contact for me."

"Pleased to do it. What did he say?"

"He has his reservations about Belhaven's death, and I added to them."

"Any theories?"

"Couple. I found out Pierce was interviewed by Wilma Hardesty of KALB-TV the afternoon he died. She quizzed him about his new book. And that interview might have cost him his life."

DON TRAVIS is a man totally captivated by his adopted state of New Mexico. Each of his B. J. Vinson mystery novels features some region of the state as prominently as it does his protagonist, a gay former Marine, ex-cop turned confidential investigator. Don never made it to the Marines (three years in the Army was all he managed) and certainly didn't join the Albuquerque Police Department. He thought he was a paint artist for a while, but ditched that for writing a few years back. A loner, he fulfills his social needs by attending SouthWest Writers meetings and teaching a weekly writing class at an Albuquerque community center.

Facebook: Don Travis
Twitter: @dontravis3
Website: dontravis.com

THE
ZOZOBRA
INCIDENT

A BJ VINSON MYSTERY

DON TRAVIS

A BJ Vinson Mystery

B. J. Vinson is a former Marine and ex-Albuquerque PD detective turned confidential investigator. Against his better judgment, BJ agrees to find the gay gigolo who was responsible for his breakup with prominent Albuquerque lawyer Del Dahlman and recover some racy photographs from the handsome bastard. The assignment should be fast and simple.

But it quickly becomes clear the hustler isn't the one making the anonymous demands, and things turn deadly with a high-profile murder at the burning of Zozobra on the first night of the Santa Fe Fiesta. BJ's search takes him through virtually every stratum of Albuquerque and Santa Fe society, both straight and gay. Before it is over, BJ is uncertain whether Paul Barton, the young man quickly insinuating himself in BJ's life, is friend or foe. But he knows he's stepped into something much more serious than a modest blackmail scheme. With Paul and BJ next on the killer's list, BJ must find a way to put a stop to the death threats once and for all.

www.dsppublications.com

THE
BISTI
BUSINESS

A BJ VINSON MYSTERY

DON TRAVIS

A BJ Vinson Mystery

Although repulsed by his client, an overbearing, homophobic California wine mogul, confidential investigator B. J. Vinson agrees to search for Anthony Alfano's missing son, Lando, and his traveling companion—strictly for the benefit of the young men. As BJ chases an orange Porsche Boxster all over New Mexico, he soon becomes aware he is not the only one looking for the distinctive car. Every time BJ finds a clue, someone has been there before him. He arrives in Taos just in time to see the car plunge into the 650-foot-deep Rio Grande Gorge. Has he failed in his mission?

Lando's brother, Aggie, arrives to help with BJ's investigation, but BJ isn't sure he trusts Aggie's motives. He seems to hold power in his father's business and has a personal stake in his brother's fate that goes beyond familial bonds. Together they follow the clues scattered across the Bisti/De-Na-Zin Wilderness area and learn the bloodshed didn't end with the car crash. As they get closer to solving the mystery, BJ must decide whether finding Lando will rescue the young man or place him directly in the path of those who want to harm him.

www.dsppublications.com

THE
CITY OF
ROCKS

A BJ VINSON MYSTERY

DON TRAVIS

A BJ Vinson Mystery

Confidential investigator B. J. Vinson thinks it's a bad joke when Del Dahlman asks him to look into the theft of a duck… a duck named Quacky Quack the Second and insured for $250,000. It ceases to be funny when the young thief dies in a suspicious truck wreck. The search leads BJ and his lover, Paul Barton, to the sprawling Lazy M Ranch in the Bootheel country of southwestern New Mexico bordering the Mexican state of Chihuahua.

A deadly game unfolds when BJ and Paul are trapped in a weird rock formation known as the City of Rocks, an eerie array of frozen magma that is somehow at the center of the entire scheme. But does the theft of Quacky involve a quarter-million-dollar duck-racing bet between the ranch's owner and a Miami real estate developer, or someone attempting to force the sale of the Lazy M because of its proximity to an unfenced portion of the Mexican border? BJ and Paul go from the City of Rocks to the neon lights of Miami and back again in pursuit of the answer… death and danger tracking their every step.

www.dsppublications.com

THE
LOVELY
PINES

A BJ VINSON MYSTERY

DON TRAVIS

A BJ Vinson Mystery

When Ariel Gonda's winery, the Lovely Pines, suffers a break-in, the police write the incident off as a prank since nothing was taken. But Ariel knows something is wrong—small clues are beginning to add up—and he turns to private investigator BJ Vinson for help.

BJ soon discovers the incident is anything but harmless. When a vineyard worker—who is also more than he seems—is killed, there are plenty of suspects to go around. But are the two crimes even related? As BJ and his significant other, Paul Barton, follow the trail from the central New Mexico wine country south to Las Cruces and Carlsbad, they discover a tangled web involving members of the US military, a mistaken identity, a family fortune in dispute, and even a secret baby. The body count is rising, and a child may be in danger. BJ will need all his skills to survive because, between a deadly sniper and sabotage, someone is determined to make sure this case goes unsolved.

www.dsppublications.com